CARN

BOOK

THE STORY OF US

By Lesley Jones

Carnage

WARNING

This e-book contains sexually explicit scenes and adult language and may be considered offensive to some readers. This e-book is intended for adults ONLY. Please store your files wisely, where they cannot be accessed by under-aged readers.

Table of Contents

For my family,

for your love, support

and words of encouragement,

I love you.

CHAPTER 1

I was swinging upside down by my knees on the monkey bars in our back garden the first time I met him; my best friend Jimmie and I hanging, facing each other, eating pop rocks and singing what we thought was a stellar rendition of 'Liza Radley' by The Jam at the tops of our voices. We had heard my big brother Bailey listening to the B side of the 12 inch version of the single 'Start' the week before and saying that he liked it better than the A, he had been playing it nonstop for the last few days. So we had listened to it and learned the words, because Jimmie was in love with each and every one of my three big brothers and was convinced that if she knew the words to their favourite songs, they would notice her and I can't say I blame her, they're all very good looking, Jimmie just hadn't decided yet which of the three she was going to marry. Lennon probably wasn't really an option as he was already sixteen and we were after all, only eleven. Bailey, my eldest brother was eighteen, so that pretty much ruled him out too, so as far as I was concerned, it had to be Marley, the brother closest in age to me that she had to marry, and it was his legs I was pretty sure I could see approaching us from the back of our house.

"George, I can see your knickers, get the fuck up will ya!"

Yep, that was Marls, I had no idea why he was moaning though, he usually loved seeing Jimmies knickers, in fact, I had heard him beg to see her knickers in the past, and then I saw them, the other pair of legs following Marley up the garden towards us. Monkey Boots? Whoever was approaching us was wearing Monkey Boots. I love Monkey Boots, they were already on my Christmas list, despite the fact it was still only August. My thoughts were interrupted by a very loud wolf whistle. I had heard boys do this before, my Dad and my brothers did to me when they knew I'd put a lot of effort into an outfit and my Dad did it to my Mum every time she came down the stairs, dressed and ready for the day and it always made me so happy that he did that. But this, this whistle did something to me that I didn't quite understand, it sent feelings through me that landed in places I was only just realising had feelings. That sound woke something up in my body that I never even knew had been sleeping there.

Jimmie and I swung up at the same time, grabbed the bars by our hands and dropped to the floor, I was pretty sure we were in complete synchronisation and looking like a pair of Olympic gymnasts. We turn towards Marley and take a bow, then collapse into each other giggling like the pair of eleven year old girls that we are. I looked back towards Marls who wasn't laughing; he was in fact glaring at the pair of us. I tipped my head back and emptied what was left of my packet of pop rocks into my mouth, letting the tiny little orange shards explode over my tongue.

I look back toward my brother, waiting for the popping to stop in my mouth so I could give him some attitude about the shitty look on his face when my world suddenly stopped turning, it stuttered for a few seconds, then restarted, erratically matching the rhythm of the candy exploding inside me but when I swallowed, the explosions didn't stop, they went down into my chest and on into my stomach, settling uncomfortably down low in my belly, for some reason the sensation was causing my brain to cease its connection to my mouth, leaving me devoid of speech. I was eleven years old, but I knew without a shadow of a doubt I was staring into the eyes of the boy I was going to love forever, they were big brown eyes and locked onto mine from over Marley's shoulder, he stared at me for a little too long, his eyes then moved down my body and locked onto my chest. Yeah I was eleven, but two years ago I'd started to develop boobs and was now already wearing a B cup, most of my friends were jealous but I hated it, everything started to change when my boobs grew, the boys treated me differently, they knocked on my bedroom door now instead of just barging in, they never came into the bathroom if I was in there anymore for our long chats we used to have while I soaked in an overly full bubble bath, they never pinned me down and tickle tortured me like they used to.

Then just under a year ago, I got my first period and things got worse, we lived in a nice house, on a nice street in a nice area. I had always been allowed to play out late because my brothers were always around to look out for me; we were a large group of about twenty kids, boys and girls, varying in age from ten to about fifteen. It was harmless, sexless fun, innocent, we hung out at the bench on the corner, at the park across the road or down at the little row of shops a street away, up until I got my period, nobody asked who in particular I was going out with, who else would be there, as long as one of my brothers were around, I was fine to go where I liked, with whom I liked. But getting my periods changed everything. I felt interrogated, where are you going, who's going to be there, will there be boys? That's all they seemed to want to know now, whether there'd be boys involved in anything that I was doing outside of our house and at the time I didn't get it, it never occurred to me that at just aged eleven, I could, potentially, get pregnant! My Dad wasn't at home much so it was my brothers that dished out the discipline, my Mum was around but she left it to the boys, to tell me off if I got home late or couldn't be found in my usual hang outs if one of them came looking for me, usually Bailey or Lennon as I gave Marley too much shit. I didn't see why he should be telling me what to do, he was only thirteen himself, and not an adult, yet funnily enough, Marley was the strictest out of all my brothers.

I stood staring at the boy with my brother, the new love of my life. Forget Adam Ant, he had nothing on the boy standing in front of me now, this boy who was so very obviously looking at my boobs.

"Sean, this is my sister George and her mate Jimmie," Marley introduces us.

Sean laughed before speaking, "I thought I was gonna meet some more brothers when you said let's go and see George and Jimmie not a pair of girls with red and pink knickers on."

"My names Jamie and hers is Georgia, but everyone calls us Jimmie and George."

Jimmie states confidently to the new kid, my future husband.

I fold my arms across my chest, which was entirely the wrong move as it just made my boobs look bigger and drew Sean's eyes straight back to them.

"Show us your tits." He gestured with his chin toward me. It's a wonder I didn't disappear in a puff of smoke, I was so embarrassed, even my hair felt like it was blushing.

"Fuck off Maca, she's my little sister, she's only eleven."

I wanted to punch Marley at that moment. I might only be eleven in years but as far as my brain was concerned I knew it all, I was already a woman, I had boobs and periods, I was a grown up. Oh how little did I know.

"Well you're the best looking Jimmie and George I've ever met." He smiled a lazy lop-sided grin as he spoke, not taking his eyes off my chest the whole time.

It rained that afternoon so we all ended up in the summer house my Dad had his blokes build us at the end of our garden. I was never exactly sure what my Dad did for a living when I was younger, I'm even less sure now. He has a construction firm, it's bigger than your average small building firm, he employs about a hundred people at any one time, on top of this he has three car show rooms, selling high end, second hand cars, Mercs, Beamers, Audis and the like, he also owns some properties in East London and Essex that he rents out. Whenever I used to ask him as a kid he used to tell me he was an entrepreneur, but I had no idea what that meant. What I did know is that we had a nice house, I had nice clothes, my Mum and Dad drove nice cars and so did Bailey now that he'd passed his test. We went on nice holidays, either to our own villas in Marbella in Spain or Albufeira in Portugal or to our caravan in Clacton On Sea on the Essex coast. I didn't think too much about any of this when I was younger but as I got older it began to dawn on me that we had more than most.

My Dad had the summer house built so the boys had somewhere to practice their music. The place was built from bricks and sound proofed, then clad with timber so it looked like a timber summer house. Bailey didn't play so much anymore, Lennon played bass guitar and had a pretty good voice but Marley was the star, he too played bass as well as drums and had a great voice. I could play acoustic guitar but I wasn't great, my voice was okay but very average compared to my brothers. Marley had his own band and told me that afternoon that Sean was to be the new lead guitarist and singer; Ritchie, their old front man had moved to Wales with his family at the beginning of the summer holidays. My Dad was a massive music fan and had paid for Marley and his band to advertise for a new singer, they had held auditions a few weeks back at the local church hall and Sean had been their first choice, the fact that he could play lead guitar and the piano was a bonus.

Later I sat curled into the corner of the big old chesterfield sofa we have in the summer house, I had spent half hour trying to crack the Rubik's cube but I've never really been known for my patience so I soon grew frustrated and tossed that on the floor and instead was flicking through the latest copy of My Guy magazine but even that wasn't holding my interest today; Sean came over and sat on the arm of the sofa and asked about my name.

"So how come after having three boys and giving them really weird names, your Mum and Dad finally get a girl and give her a boy's name?"

I looked up at his brown eyes and noticed the tiny flecks of amber he had floating in them, all framed by the longest of dark brown lashes. Answer George. Stop blushing, stop looking into his eyes and answer the question. I swallow and try to wet my lips before speaking.

"My Dad is a massive fan of music, all music, any music… Bailey is named after some bloke who made guitars back in the sixties, my Dad met him or heard about him and liked his name, which I think was actually his surname, not his first name but anyway, my Dad liked it, remembered it and decided to give it to Bailey as his first name, Lennon, is obviously named after John Lennon, Marley after Bob… And me? Well I'm named after my Dad's favourite song – Georgia on my mind by Ray Charles. So I got the name, Georgia Rae but living in a house full of boys, it got shortened to George."

I've told this story so many times to so many different people that I could repeat it in my sleep. Sean listens to my answer and nods his head slowly.

"Well Georgia Rae. I think you're far too pretty to be called an old blokes name. So I'll call you… " He tilts his head to the side as he thinks about what he's going to call me, beautiful, his girlfriend? I don't mind either. "Gia?" he states.

Gia, he wants to call me Gia? No one has called me Gia, its Georgia by my teachers, G or George by my friends and family but never, no one has ever called me Gia. I love it, and it'll be special, just our thing, special, just between us.

"So… is that all right then, if I call you Gia?"

I nod; it's all I can manage. The pop rock is exploding in my stomach again, and once more it's blocking the signal between my brain and my mouth.

CHAPTER 2

The rest of the summer of 1980 is spent watching Marley and Sean practice with Billy and Tommy who make up the rest of Marley's band Carnage.

In September Jimmie and I start high school. School was easy for me, I was in top sets for everything, without really having to put in much effort, I wasn't stunningly beautiful but I was at an age now where I knew my ranking in the 'prettiness' order and I was up there. My parents were both of Irish descent, but looked totally different to each other, my Dad was tall, over six feet, he was broad and he was dark, dark hair, dark eyes, dark skin. My Mum on the other hand was short, about five feet four and very petit, even after having us four kids she was still only a size eight and was pale, skin like porcelain, she had the most beautiful dark auburn hair and the bluest of eyes. My Dad was handsome, all of my mates told me so and my Mum was stunningly beautiful and I wished so much that I looked like her, but I didn't. Where my brothers all looked exactly like my Dad, I was a weird combination of both my parents. I had always been tall for my age, I was way too skinny for my liking, my hair was a dark chestnut colour, when the sun shone through it you could see the reds I'd inherited from my Mum but mainly it looked brown, my skin was darker than my Mum's but nowhere near as dark as my Dad's and my brothers and my eyes were blue, not pale china blue like my Mum's but a very dark blue. Whenever I got a tan in the summer they'd pop right out of my face, they didn't match my dark skin and dark lashes and always drew comments, so by the age of eleven, I knew I wasn't stunningly beautiful like my Mum but I knew I was pretty. Prettier than most of the other girl's in my class, prettier than most other girl's in my year and quite possibly the school. I don't mean to sound flash or like a show off, it's just how it was, girls just know these things.

Love us or hate us, Jimmie and I were the popular girls but that wasn't always a good thing, especially at secondary school; within days of starting as first years, we were attracting the attention of the older boys as well as a few bitchy comments from the older girls. We'd been Queen Bees at primary school; secondary school though, was a whole new thing and introduced us to a whole new level of bitch. On just the third day there I was stopped in the corridor and asked if I wanted to go to a party that weekend by a boy called Dale who was a fifth year. I said "No", as I knew there was no way that my brothers would allow it. Regardless of this, I had some tall skinny blonde girl screaming at me in the lunch hall later that she was going to be waiting at the school gates that night and was going to kick the shit out of me for flirting with her boyfriend, I'd never been so happy to see Marley appear over her shoulder as he came barrelling toward us.

"Debra – fuck off and leave her alone! She's a first year you fucking bully. I've just spoken to Dale, she blew him out, he asked her to the party, she said no and didn't flirt with him at all, and you can tell him from me, if he comes near her again, me or Len will knock him the fuck out! Tell the rest of the fifth years the same fucking thing, she's eleven, they are all a bunch of fucking pervs."

She folds her arms across her chest and looks him up and down and then turns and looks me up and down. "She's your sister Marl?"

"Yeah, my baby sister."

Sean is with him and comes around and stands next to me. Taking me completely by surprise when he pulls me into his side by my waist and kisses my temple, asking into my hair if I'm okay? I nod, this time it's not so much to do with the affect he has on me, it's more to do with the fact that I'm shitting myself that I'm going to get beat up after school by a grown woman. For doing absolutely nothing wrong.

"What's your name?" The girl, woman, Debra asks me.

"Georgia," I reply.

"You're a pretty girl Georgia, you and your mate there are both very pretty, your ruffling feathers round here, you need to keep your head down and stay away from the older boys and make sure everyone around here knows you're a Layton and that Marley and Lennon are your brothers."

She looks Sean up and down, he's tall and looks older than a third year, which he has joined Marley in. Sean is new too; he's just moved into the area and transferred from a different school.

"And who are you? Not another gorgeous Layton that I didn't know about?"

Sean returns the look up and down, but instead of looking at her lustfully as she had done him, he looks at her with complete contempt and I beam. Shit I almost ignite, inwardly of course, because the last I want to do is piss this bitch off again.

"No love, I'm not a Layton, I'm Sean, Sean McCarthy. I'm Marley's mate and Georgia's boyfriend. So make sure all your pervi fifth year mates know to stay the fuck away from her."

What?

He's my boyfriend?

Well shit!

My mouth hits the floor; well that's how it felt anyway. Sean squeezed my hand as he spoke and as I looked around the dining hall I couldn't help but notice that we had attracted quite a crowd. Events from that lunch time soon spread, everyone assumed I was Sean's girlfriend and in turn thought that Jimmie was with Marley, the fact that they walked with us to and from school most days helped to solidify the story and I was over the moon. All of this quickly instilled us as the most popular girls in the first year and made our journey into secondary school life so much easier.

I spent a lot of time with Sean that year, just hanging out as friends, there was lots of flirting, or what I considered flirting but nothing else. I was still too young for anything else and Sean seemed to respect that, he wasn't a saint, I would often catch him looking at my ever growing boobs and I heard Marls tell him on more than one occasion to stop looking at my arse. We never discussed what he'd told Debra Smith in the dining hall that day, he never asked me to be his girlfriend and I was for the most part completely confused as to what I was to him, he kissed my cheek a couple of times, he held my hand when he thought no one was looking and when we looked at each other we knew Sean and I, that there was something going on between us. He was at our house all the time; after school, weekends, and school holidays, he even started coming with us on our overseas holidays. And because of the amount of time the boys spent practicing with the band or doing homework at our house, they very rarely went elsewhere, meaning, there was little chance of him meeting any other girls. Apart from at school, but of course there, everyone already thought he was my boyfriend and I couldn't be happier about that fact.

In the summer of 1982 everything changed, Jimmie and Sean came with us to Portugal; my body had changed so much lately, although my boobs had now grown to a generous D cup, I'd recently acquired a pair of hips that balanced them out and stopped me from looking so top heavy and combined with the extra two inches in height I had grown, I was feeling a little more confident in myself. The first day around the pool, all Jimmie and I wanted to do was get our bodies out in the sun, the boys didn't make an appearance until after lunch. They had stayed up drinking beer with my Dad and Lennon until late and were probably suffering for it a little, my Dad and Len had been up and out very early that morning to play golf, my Mum had gone shopping with a girlfriend who lived over here permanently and was meeting Dad later for dinner.

Jim and I had drunk a bottle of wine before the boys got up and I was feeling very brave as I lay on the lilo in the pool and watched Sean walking across the patio toward a sun lounger. I had already decided this holiday was going to be it, I was sick of playing games. I was hearing rumours that Sean had kissed girls at parties and him and Marley were always talking about girls that they fancied, even in front of Jimmie and me and it left me hurt, angry and confused; boys could be such arseholes sometimes. All of this had led me to the decision to take matters into my own hands this summer. I was going to be fourteen in September, and about to go in to the third year of secondary school, the boys were going into their fifth. The band was doing well and was being booked to play at the birthday parties of a lot of the kids from school, bringing them a lot of female attention. Some of the parties Jim and I went along to, some, like the eighteenths and twenty-firsts, we weren't allowed to and it was killing me. I was over it and wanted him to either be my boyfriend or for me to be allowed to tell everyone at school that we were over so that I could have a chance at finding a different boyfriend. I actually didn't want that at all, I wanted him and nobody else would do. I decided to climb out of the pool and attempt a Bond girl moment. I push myself up from the side and stand and tilt my head to the sky as I shake my hair, then squeeze the excess water out of it; as I look down, Sean is sitting on the end of a sun lounger watching me. Marley has jumped straight in the water and is now terrorising Jimmie, I put my hands on my hips and stand and stare into Sean's beautiful chocolate eyes.

"Come here." He beckons me with his finger, I walk toward him wearing my favourite teeny tiny red bikini, as sexily as you can when you're not yet fourteen and don't really know what walking sexily entails. I stop and stand between his legs while he looks up at me with the cheekiest of smiles on his lips.

"You do know we're in Europe Gia, everyone here goes topless, and I'm a bit disappointed to see you're not up with the times."

"Well that's what happens when you lay in bed for half the day. You miss the best parts, we were topless all morning, and I didn't want my nipples to burn so I just put my top back on."

I didn't.

I wasn't topless at any time but he doesn't know that.

He smiled up at me.

"Well I will be sure to set my alarm and be up early tomorrow morning so that I don't miss anything."

"Well then you will be shit out of luck, my Dad will be here tomorrow and there is no way that I'll be going topless in front of him."

He lets out a long breath and looks beyond me, out across the pool, I can hear Jimmie and my brother giggling and splashing.

"You Gia are a flirt, but one day, one day it will be our turn. Our time."

My heart drops like a stone into my stomach. What?

"Why… why do we have to wait for it to be our time? I'm fourteen in September; everyone thinks you're my boyfriend anyway?"

I sound needy and whiney like a child and I don't want to be a child, I want to be a woman.

"Gia… you have no idea do you? Your Dad and your brothers would kill me, they'd fucking kill me and I respect them all too much to start something with you before you're ready but don't think for a minute that I don't want you. I know it sounds wrong but right from that very first day when I saw your pink knickers, there's been something."

I want to cry, I'm sick of waiting, all my friends have boyfriends and all I have is a lie, just to keep every other boy away from me. It's so fucking unfair! Sean reaches out and touches my hand. I want to pull away, but I don't, his touch does something to me and it pisses me off no end.

"You told everyone that day in the dining hall that you were my boyfriend and everyone still thinks it's true. Either tell everyone that we've broken up or be my boyfriend Sean. I'm fed up with waiting."

I can't believe I've actually said it, I should drink wine more often, the only thing now is, he looks really pissed off. What if he says no, what if he doesn't want me, I will die, I will simply lie down and die.

"Do you want someone else to be your boyfriend G?"

"No."

"Then why can't you just wait for me?"

"Why, I don't get what I have to wait for, I'm almost fourteen, my Mum and Dad have been together since she was thirteen, why do I have to wait?"

He takes a deep breath in through his teeth, and then puffs his cheeks while he lets it out through his lips, his perfect, perfect lips.

"I was just trying to do the right thing G, by you and your brothers and your Mum and Dad; everyone's been so good to me. I don't want to fuck things up."

He drags his hand through his brown curls with his free hand. "Let me talk to Marley, see how the land lies, perhaps if I talk to your Dad nicely, he might let me be your boyfriend. If you want?"

I sit down on the sun lounger next to him; he still has hold of my hand. I nod my head.

"I do want."

"Jesus you two, get on with it. I've watched the pair of you dance around for the past few years and it's getting boring." Marley calls out from where he has Jimmie wrapped around him in the pool.

"See, he's fine."

Sean's shaking his head again. "All this fucking time I've waited and he don't even care."

"Just remember Maca, she's not fourteen yet and she's my little sister, you do anything more than kiss her and I will kill you, then my brothers and my Dad will kill you again."

Sean shoulder bumps me with an even bigger grin on his face. "Just kissing. Dya think you can manage that Gia?"

I shoulder bump him back. "If you really want me to I will, but I was just about to show you my tits."

"Fuck… really?"

I shrug, I'm embarrassed now. I've never even been kissed and I'm threatening to show him my tits?

"I told ya Gia, you're a flirt."

He looks over my face as he talks to me, "Can I kiss ya G, please?"

I nod, maintaining eye contact with him all the while. We turn and face each other, my knees go between his open legs so we can get closer, his hand comes up and cups the side of my face, his thumb rubs over my lips, like his testing them, trying them out with his thumb before he goes in with his lips, my heart feels like it's about to pound out of my chest and go crashing into his; he leans in until his lips meet mine, they are so much softer than I ever could have imagined, soft and minty, he must of just cleaned his teeth, he smells delicious, minty, clean and fresh, I can feel stubble around the edges of his mouth but his lips are so, so soft. He deepens the kiss and without even thinking about it, my hand goes to his dark brown curls and I grab a handful, he lets a little growling noise escape from the back of his throat, which in turn makes me let out my own little sigh.

"Fuck Gia," he says into my mouth.

Sparks go off behind my now closed eyes, it's like a cartoon, when fireworks go off in an enclosed space and they bounce off every surface. That's exactly what it feels like is going on inside me.

"So long… I've waited so long to do that G, you have no fucking idea."

That year, that holiday, it's still one of my best ever. My lips and the skin around them felt permanently bruised and sore from all the kissing we did; Sean never did speak to my Dad, he didn't have to, the fact that we held each other's hand every second we were together made it perfectly clear what was going on between us. It did though prompt my Mum and Dad to sit the pair of us down and give us the 'We trust you and hope that you will be respectful of each other and your bodies… and aside from all that, it's actually illegal for you to be having sex and you could go to jail' talk. We sat there mortified, Sean squeezing my hand so tight I thought it was going to break. Then he did the most amazingly beautiful thing, he let my Mum finish her speech about me being a good girl, bought up the right way and knowing right from wrong and waiting until I was older before taking things too far. I seriously wanted the ground to open up and swallow me whole. Why did we have to have this conversation now, in front of Sean? Sean took my hand that he was holding and kissed the back of it. He cleared his throat before saying.

"Frank, Bernie… I know we're young but I need you to know, that from the first moment I laid eyes on your daughter, I've been a little bit in love with her, I've wanted to tell her for a while now but I wanted to be respectful of you and the boys. You've all been so good to me, you treat me better than my own parents so I wanted to do this right, I wanted to wait until Gia was old enough and until you were comfortable with us having a relationship but I can't wait anymore, I love her and I want to be able to hold her hand and kiss her."

Shit. Don't say anymore in front of them.

"We are too young to be thinking about anything more than that, but, I... we, we just want to be together and for you all to be happy about it."

Fucking hell, I've never died so many times during one afternoon. Where are my brothers and Jimmie when you need rescuing, I bet my parents told them to stay out the way, does that mean everyone is going to know about this little chat? Fucking hell.

"Well... Sean... as long as you respect my daughter, I don't think that we'll have a problem. Would you like a beer son, you must need one after that little speech?"

My parents treated me differently for the rest of that holiday, almost like a grown up. They allowed Jimmie and I to drink wine at dinner, my Mum asked my opinion on her outfits and told me to try my hair in different styles, she spoke to me like I was her friend, not just her daughter. My Dad took on a more fatherly demeanour around Sean and spoke to him about his plans after he finished his fifth year, legally he could leave school if he wanted but our school went right up to sixth form and Sean and Marley were both staying on. I don't think either of them really wanted to study anymore but if they left the education system they would be expected to get full time jobs and this would leave them no time for their music. They had been lucky so far, the money they made with the band meant that they hadn't even had to get a part time job and as their popularity grew they were getting bookings for Friday and Saturday nights and now had a regular Sunday lunch time spot at a pub not too far from where we lived. So as wages for a group of students went, they were doing okay.

CHAPTER 3

Returning to school that September, I was the happiest I'd ever been in my life, after we'd gotten back from Portugal, Sean and I were inseparable. Luckily he was always at our house anyway, all that was different was that now when the band practised, I got a kiss every ten minutes between rehearsals, when Sean came and sat next to me after practise, he would hold my hand, he never stopped paying me attention and I never stopped enjoying it. We were very rarely alone together though, my parents must have drummed it into my brother's heads that under no circumstances were we to be left by ourselves and it was comical at times, the lengths they'd go to. Even if Marley was going to the toilet, he would send Sean to fetch something, just so we weren't left alone, even if it was only going to be for five minutes. What could we possibly get up to in five minutes? Well lots it turned out, Sean was a typical sixteen year old boy and he had needs and despite only being fourteen, he stirred something in me that I have to admit, at times, terrified me. I wanted sex, I really wanted to have sex with him, I have no idea if it was raging hormones caused by my age or if it was just him, Sean, what he did to me, what he caused me to feel but I was totally convinced that the feelings I had, meant that I must surely be a whore, a slut but I didn't care, I just wanted him.

I spoke to Jimmie about all of this but she wasn't quite getting the passion I felt; she and Marley were turning into more like best friends than boyfriend and girlfriend, there was something going on with her but I couldn't quite put my finger on what, she never spoke about other boys and she was at our house as much as she always was but things just weren't happening between her and Marls and it didn't seem to bother her when he spoke about other girls, or when he kissed other girls like I had seen him do when the band came off stage. My Dad had fixed them up with a transit van so they could get from gig to gig with all their equipment; despite working at one of my Dad's car showrooms in the day, Lennon was now pretty much managing the boys, he took and arranged all the bookings, managed the money and as the only one amongst us with a full license, he also did all the driving.

It was Christmas eve of 1982 when I finally worked out what was going on with Jimmie; the band were booked at a local pub, it was a ticket only event and was a complete sell out, we arrived early as the place would be filling up by seven and the boys wanted to have a sound check as they'd never played at this venue before and this was probably going to be their biggest crowd yet, over two hundred tickets had been sold according to Len, and the boys wanted to impress. Not that they wouldn't, they were great and getting better with every show, growing in confidence so much that almost fifty per cent of their songs were originals, written by Marley and Sean mostly, they still did covers, The Clash, The Jam, The Undertones, The Specials being among their favourites as well as some old classics by The Who, Beatles and Kinks, whatever they played, they sounded great and I loved watching Sean up on the stage, especially when his eyes would lock with mine and everyone else would just melt away, me and him, that's all there was, that's all that mattered.

The boys were having a run through of their set when I realised I was cold, the hall at the back of the pub was big and the heating hadn't been put on yet so I went to go back outside to get my jacket, as I walked down the hallway toward the emergency exit at the back of the building where the van was parked, I saw them, Lennon and my best friend Jamie. Kissing like their lives depended on it. I stood and watched for a few seconds, my best friend and my brother and neither of them thought to tell me about it. What about Marley, did he know, is that why they had kept it quiet? This could cause so much trouble between the boys and I wished that I didn't know about it. I watched as they broke apart but still stared into each other's eyes, I knew that look, it's how Sean and I looked at each other, this was more than just a kiss, this was love and I was thoroughly pissed off with the pair of them. As they turned to walk back inside, I walked toward them looking at the ground as if I had seen nothing. Lennon held the door open for me.

"Porge, where you off to?"

"Don't call me that. I want my jacket out of the van. Is it open?"

He threw me the keys as he and Jimmie walked back inside, she didn't look me in the eye as she passed and it hurt a little that my best friend had kept this secret from me. She knew everything about me, every look, every thought, every feeling, why wouldn't she share this with me? He's my brother. Did she not think I would be interested?

I grab my coat, head back inside and look around for Len, he appears through the swing doors leading from the front of the pub, carrying a tray full of drinks; he put them down on the table next to me and shouted for the boys to come down from the stage. Jim appeared at my side, then Sean, Lennon passed out beers to the boys and gave me and Jimmie a bottle of cider each.

"Here's to Carnage! A great gig, a very merry Christmas and great things for the coming year – 1983 boys, it's gonna be our year, I can just feel it. Cheers."

There were kisses and hugs all round; Jimmie felt stiff and informal when she pulled me into her and I felt awkward. Sean wrapped his arms around me and kissed me like he was never going to let me go.

"Merry Christmas G. Stay close to Lennon tonight, it's gonna get busy in here and don't drink too much."

He kisses my nose and looks over my face. "You okay?"

Tears sting the backs of my eyes for some reason and I feel angry with myself for getting upset so I just nod my head.

"What's wrong? You look upset." I shake my head and smile up at him.

"I'm just so proud of you; you sound so great up there, especially the new stuff. 1983 really could be your year you know? Will you still love me when you're famous and your pictures are all over 'The Face' and 'Smash Hits'?"

He pulls me into him tightly.

"I'll love you forever G, wherever I am in the world, whatever I'm doing, it will always be you, I'm yours, for as long as you want me, for as long as I'm good for you, I'm all yours."

"What does that mean? For as long as you're good for me? What does that mean?"

There's a hysterical edge to my voice and I hate it. Why would he say that? He looks around the room before looking back down at me.

"I just worry sometimes, I think your Mum and Dad and even your brothers would prefer it if you was with someone who wanted a proper job, who had something more solid planned for when they leave school; music is all I want G, music and you and sometimes I worry that that's not enough."

A tear rolls down my cheek, I never knew he felt like this, of course he's enough, he's everything.

"I love you Sean, no matter what, I love you, I don't care about anything or anyone else and you will always be enough, always."

The boys are all back up on stage and the place has filled up around us while we've been talking.

Marley calls out, "Maca put my sister down and get up here!"

He winks down at me and as has become his normal greeting or goodbye, whispers into my ear, "Show us your tits?"

One of these days, I would totally shock him and give him a flash. One of these days very soon.

He leaves with a grin and a kiss to the top of my head. They go down a storm that night, the place is packed and the tunes are tight, Lennon seems to be on cloud nine with their performance and buys Jim and me another drink every time he goes to the bar, by the time the boys take a break, I'm feeling pretty drunk. I watch as Sean steps off the stage and some girl steps in front of him and wraps her arms around his neck, I've seen her before, she's short and blonde with big tits, she's dressed all slutty in a see through lace top with a red bra underneath and a little ra-ra skirt and ballet pumps, she thinks she's Madonna. I think she's a whore who needs to get her hands off my fucking boyfriend. I watch as she leans in and tries to kiss him, Sean has hold of her by the waist and leans away shaking his head, he looks up and gives me a truly breath taking smile. She follows his gaze, looks me up and down and while he's still looking at me, she turns and licks his face. I don't see his reaction to that, everything becomes a blur, I fly across the now almost empty dance floor and grab her by the hair, throwing her to the floor. I don't know where the anger comes from, the drink, Jimmie and Lennon keeping me in the dark, Sean's words from earlier about thinking that he's not enough? I have no idea, but it's there and it's not stopping with the hair pulling, I'm on top of her, screaming and punching, I have handfuls of her hair. Then there are hands and arms all over me, voices screaming my name and telling me to stop but I keep lashing out until my arms are pinned to my side and I can't move. I'm carried to the small room out the back reserved for the band. Lennon and Marley have hold of me, telling me again to calm down, my breathing is ragged and heavy and I feel anger like I've never known before, I slap my brother's hands away from me.

"Fuck off, fuck off! Did you see? Did you? She fucking licked him, I'll fucking kill the slut!" I try to get up off the table they have sat me on but they hold me down.

"Where is he? Sean… Where is he?" I'm screaming now, beyond hysterical. Lennon slaps me, hard across the face and I stop dead in my tracks for a split second, then I really let lose, I kick him, claw him, bite, slap and punch him.

"Don't touch me. Fuck off, I saw you, I fucking saw you. Why didn't you tell me? She's my best friend. Why wouldn't either of you tell me you fuckers?"

The door flies open as the room turns silent. Sean, he's here, he's all I want, the rest can fuck off.

"Georgia… What the fuck do you think you're doing? Why, why did you do that?"

"She licked you."

I feel quite calm now that Sean's here. He looks anything but.

"Lots of girls lick me or kiss me or try to. It doesn't mean anything. There's hair everywhere out there, you can't do that G, there's always gonna be girls, women, fans that do shit like that. You can't just beat them up."

What? I shrug my shoulders, more than a little pissed off now that he seems to be taking her side.

"What if that was me? What if someone did that to me, would you just let them? Would you just do nothing?"

"No… of course I wouldn't but you're not in a band G."

"So because you are, I just have to leave it? I just have to stand there like a complete cunt and let girls do that to you?"

"That's enough George!" Lennon shouts from beside me, him and Marley had been so quiet that I had forgotten they were there.

Sean walks toward me. "It's just part of it babe. It doesn't mean anything, it's just part of what we do, I don't kiss them back, it doesn't mean anything but they're our fans and we have to put on a show. You can't do that, you just can't do that."

He kisses my cheek and my hair and I calm down a little bit, but I'm not sorry, I look up as Jimmie comes flying through the door.

"Fucking hell George, you ripped half the hair out of her head!" I stare at her blankly, it all goes quiet.

"You," Marley says, I look up, not sure who he's talking to. It's Jimmie.

"You and him… " He gestures with his chin to Len. "All this fucking time and you've been with him!"

"Marl," Jim, Lennon and Sean all say at the same time.

Sean, Sean knew and didn't tell me? Marley looks at Sean.

"You knew too? You knew what was going on and didn't tell me?"

"No… I didn't know… Not for sure."

"What does that mean?" Marley and I both ask at the same time.

"I watched them… How, they were with each other. I thought that something was going on, but I didn't know."

"Why didn't you say something?' Marley asks him.

"No… I wouldn't do that. What if I was wrong, think of the trouble it might have caused between you two? You're brothers; I wouldn't do that to ya's"

Sean had had a complicated upbringing, his Mum had left his Dad when he was small, she had packed up their things and ran away in the middle of the day with Sean while his Dad was at work, she had taken Sean and left. With Sean's Dads brother! Sean had never seen his Dad again, he had an idea that his Dad had come looking for them and had gotten pretty close, he had attended three different primary schools and was now at his second secondary school. Part of the reason he spent so much time at our house is because he hated his Step dad come Uncle with a passion, he was seven when his Mum left his Dad and over the years he'd worked out exactly what had gone on and he was angry, angry with his Mum and Uncle, angry with his Dad for not finding him and angry with himself for caring.

Lennon looked around at all of us.

"Look, I'm sorry. We're sorry, we wanted to tell everyone but we were scared. I'm eighteen; she's just turned fourteen. It don't look good, it don't look right."

"That's 'cos it ain't." Marley shouted. "It's fucking wrong, she's a kid, she's a fucking kid."

"I'm not a fucking kid and I love him. You're my two best friends, of course I wanted to tell ya's but we… we were scared. I'm sorry George, I've nearly told ya so many times but I was just scared."

We all stand and look at each other; the boys are due back on stage any minute and haven't even had a drink yet.

"Well you should have told us. That's all I'm saying." I give Jimmie and then Lennon a cuddle. Marley storms out without saying a word.

"Fuck… I need a beer," Sean states.

"Go, get back on stage, I will bring you one." Sean brings his eyes down to meet mine.

"Are you gonna behave now G? Can I trust you not to beat up any more of the audience?"

I shrug. "As long as they keep their hands, lips and tongues to themselves… I'll be fine."

He shakes his head at me, kisses me hard on the mouth, then says against my temple. "Show us your tits G."

Lennon and Jimmie have gone to the bar to get the band a drink, we're in the little back room by ourselves and I don't hesitate. I let him step away from me, then pull up my Rolling Stones t-shirt and favourite pink bra and flash him my tits as I slide off the table and stand and face him.

"Fuck G. Fucking hell."

He stands right in front of me, his knees slightly bent, bringing him down lower and looks rapidly between my eyes and my now completely exposed boobs. I watch a nerve twitch on the left side of his jaw and his Adam's apple moves rapidly as he swallows continuously, he licks his lips. I stand and stare while his hand comes up very slowly. He looks at me, seeking approval, I give the slightest of nods, he cups my boob and brushes his thumb over my nipple.

"O… O Georgia," he breathes heavily when he speaks, we hear a noise outside the door and I pull my top down rapidly and we step apart.

Billy's head appears around the door. "C'mon Maca, we're waiting for ya."

"Fuck off I'm coming."

The door slams behind him and Sean and I lock eyes. "Literally G. I'm literally coming in my pants. That was a weeks' worth of waking material there."

He pulls me in and kisses me. "I love ya Georgia Rae, come and dance by the stage so I can see your tits bounce, but don't hit anyone."

I leave that back room, heading for the stage, with Sean's arm slung over my shoulder, feeling like the happiest girl on the planet.

That Christmas still rates as one of the happiest of my life; Sean buys me a beautiful silver necklace. It's a pair of angels wings, joined in the middle with a letter G, I love it and will treasure it forever.

In the February half term of 1983, Sean and I come back from the shops to find my house and the summer house empty; my parents were away in Tenerife, I was allowed to stay home because Marley and Lennon were here, my eldest brother Bailey has moved into a new house in Romford with his girlfriend Donna and they phone every night to make sure I'm home and that there are no wild parties going on. Sean throws himself down on my bed why I put a tape on my portable boom box that I got for Christmas. When I turn around and look at him, he's leaning back on his elbows, running his tongue along his bottom lip.

"Show us your tits G."

I put my hands on my hips and look at him for a while. I'm wearing a vintage looking Marlon Brando t-shirt. It's Marley's but I love it, because it's too big I've tied it in a knot at my hip and paired it with my jeans and a pair of Dr Martin boots. I like girly clothes but I'm surrounded by boys so I like a lot of what they wear too. I stand facing Sean with my hands at my side and swallow hard, I've left my boots at the door so I unbutton my jeans, slide them off my hips and kick them off. Without pausing for breath, I pull my t-shirt over my head and take off my bra; Sean is sitting upright now, his hands gripping the edge of the mattress, his eyes are as wide as saucers. I take two steps toward him and stand between his legs. His eyes slowly make their way up my body and I watch as they move side to side as he looks at each of my breasts, his tongue darts out and over his lips again. He puts his hands on my hips and very slowly slides them up my body, when they get level with my boobs, he cups them in each hand and rubs his thumbs over each of my nipples, he pulls me further toward him and takes the left one in his mouth and sucks it, his eyes looking up at mine all the while. I am shaking so badly, I just hope he can't feel it as he holds on to me.

"G... What… Are we doing this?" I nod my head, we've talked and talked about this, we've been there with our hands and I know that I'm ready, I know that there'll never be any one for me but Sean and I just want to get this first time over with. He's not a virgin, he was shagging girls those first couple of years we were pretending to be boyfriend and girlfriend. Well he was pretending, I thought it was real, it hurt when he confessed but he swears he hasn't touched another girl since we spoke to my parents in Portugal and I believe him. He pulls his T-shirt off over his head and I look down over his body; he and Marley have set up a home gym in the summer house and they have been working out almost daily since my Dad bought it for them as a joint Christmas present last year. He looks so much broader than he did last summer and has a line of hairs running down the middle of his chest, a few around his nipples, then all the way down to beneath the waistline of his jeans. He stands up in front of me, undoes his jeans and pulls them off with his boxers and socks, I pull down my knickers and step out of them and once again he looks me up and down.

"You're beautiful G, so beautiful. Are you sure you're safe?" I nod my head. Six months ago, Jimmie's older sister had told us that if we went to the family planning clinic and complained about heavy periods they would put us on the pill, they did and I had been taking it regularly now for the last three months.

"Yes… Are you sure? You've never done it… without a condom I mean?" We had been learning about this new disease in our social education classes at school, it was called AIDS and somehow people were catching it from sex, I was fourteen, I didn't want to die from a sex disease. My brothers would kill me.

We laid down on the bed, side by side, he kissed me from my ankles to the top of my head and out to my fingertips, he reassured me constantly, asked if I was okay continuously and worshiped me endlessly, then after using his fingers on me for a few minutes, Sean climbed on top. All the while continuing to ask if I was sure and assuring me he'd be gentle.

"I love you Georgia Rae Layton… I love you so much… I'm gonna push inside you now… I'll go very slowly but it might hurt a bit… If it's too much… If it hurts too much G, tell me and I'll stop. Okay?"

I nod, I'm shaking from head to toe, adrenalin pumping through my veins, my heart, my body, which is naked and pressed as close as two people can be, against his. He uses his hand to line himself up and then laces our fingers together at the side of our heads and looks deep into my eyes as he slowly nudges his way inside me, there's no pain at first. I don't feel anything, other than fear, embarrassment and desire. Then it stings, I wince and he stops.

"You okay babe?" I nod and let out a breath. "Just a little bit more and I'll be in."

"You're not in yet?"

He laughs.

"No G… I'm nowhere near in yet. Are you ready?"

"Yes Sean, will you just shag me please."

He laughs and shakes his head and kisses my mouth, then looks into my eyes as he slides in… And oh fuck… In… Ow… And in!

"I'm… Fuck G that feels so nice… I'm in, is it okay if I move?"

I bite down on my bottom lip as he starts to move, and oh does he move, it's not amazing sex, it's not really long, drawn out sex but it is sweet, beautiful lovemaking between two kids, that are absolutely one hundred per cent sure that they'll love each other for the rest of their lives. Half an hour later, we consider ourselves experts and have another go, this time we're entirely different with each other. By the time we go for round three, I'm brave enough to climb on top and experience my fourth orgasm of the day and all I can think to myself is why did I wait so long?

CHAPTER 4

"I think we shall have a boy first, or maybe two, then we'll have a girl."

"Three kids? I only want two."

Sean turns his head and looks up at me with brown eyes, I continue combing my fingers through is dark brown hair, he's wearing it a bit shorter than he used to but there's still enough for me to grab a handful.

"But I want a little girl and she's going to be beautiful like you so she'll need at least two big brothers to protect her from boys like me."

I stroke my hand over his whiskers as I smile down at him; we are totally naked, lying in Sean's bed, his Mum and Stepdad are away on holiday so we've been spending all of our time here instead of at my house. It's a whole year since we first started having sex and we are so comfortable with each other that we have no issues with wandering around with no clothes on in front of each.

Tonight is extra special, I have lied to my parents, they think I am staying at Jimmie's but instead, I'm here with Sean and we're finally going to spend an entire night together. It's cold outside and we've been in bed for most of the afternoon, making love, smoking weed and playing music. I'm now sitting with my back against the headboard of Sean's bed, while he lies with his head in my naked lap, I'm fifteen years old, he's seventeen and there's nothing we don't know about love and life, we have it all worked out.

Sean is working part time for my Dad while he completes his 'A' levels. The band are doing great and have bookings most weekends, they performed at a couple of festivals last summer and are re-booked for the coming summer, they saved enough money to go into a studio and produce a demo tape. Lennon and my Dad have been sending it out to different music companies the past few weeks and they received a call yesterday from one of the biggest companies around, they have a meeting set up for the following Thursday, this really could be it, the big time for Carnage! Well, bigger than playing pubs and birthday parties.

Sean and I have decided that as soon as I'm done with school, we shall get married, that way my parents won't mind when I go on tour with the band, because once they make it big, which they will, a tour will be on the cards and Sean and I don't want to be apart, ever. Once the band have recorded their first album and completed the tour, we should have enough money to put a deposit on a house, then we can start thinking about babies. We've even picked their names, we will have a boy named Beau and a girl named Lilly but now Sean's throwing another boy in the mix, we'll have to think of another boy's name.

"I have three big brothers, it didn't protect me from you, besides, if we have a little girl that grows up and meets a boy like you, then she'll be very lucky."

"I don't want a boy like me sniffing around my thirteen year old daughter G, I will kill him, I swear, I *will* kill him."

I laugh at the way he's getting so angry at a hypothetical situation and I'm squirming inside at the thought of him being an overprotective Dad to our daughter; I smile down at him some more.

"I will make sure she's clued up and knows how to handle a boy like you, if one should come along, besides, if they love each other like we do, does it matter?"

"No, I suppose not but if he puts his hands on her. Let's just not talk about it G, it pisses me off, I don't know how your brothers haven't killed me yet, especially Lennon."

Lennon and Jimmie were still going strong but it was still a secret from both sets of parents, we had told so many lies over the last year so that we could spend alone time with our boyfriends that it would take someone from the Krypton Factor to work out the truth from the lies. My tummy grumbles loudly and Sean bursts into laughter as his ear is on my belly and he must have heard it.

"Let's eat; we need to get ready for the gig soon."

The boys were playing at the local pub tonight; it was their regular gig if they didn't get another booking. This was the weekend before Valentine's Day, and had been booked in as a ticket only night and had been sold out for a couple of weeks. We eat a bowl of sugar puffs each; take a shower, which leads to our first ever shower sex experience before getting dressed and jumping into Sean's new Ford Escort XR3I that my Dad had got hold of for a really good price when he passed his test a couple of months back. I love it and feel like a princess when we drive about in it. The pub is only a ten minute drive but we arrive late and Lennon's not happy, Marley even less so but then that's nothing new, everything seems to piss Marley off these days, I never realised how much he liked Jimmie and he's had a hard time dealing with her and Lennon being together, we used to be so close but he's so moody and withdrawn lately that we hardly ever speak.

"You're late Maca, there are people here already, we sound checked without you. We need to be tight tonight. We've had a lot of interest from the demo tape and about four labels have asked where we're playing over the next few weeks so any one of them could have a rep in the crowd."

I grin up at Sean with excitement; he squeezes my hand in response.

"You'll be fine babe; you know the set inside out right?" I nod with encouragement as I speak but he looks worried.

"We changed it a bit for tonight, a few ballads because of it being Valentines and a few of our new songs, I'll be alright." He says with a shrug. He's so confident once he's on stage, people would never believe how much he doubts himself before he gets up there.

"He fucking better be," Marley mumbles from beside me. "And you behave your fuckin' self, Haley's out there."

Great, just what I need, why don't that bitch just give up, I wonder? I roll my eyes at Marley and hold three fingers up. "Scouts honour, I'll behave, unless she puts her hands on him."

"G!"

"George!"

"Georgia!"

Sean, Marley and Lennon all say at the same time. "Okay, I'm joking."

I hold my hands up. "I'll wait till the next gig before I knock the bitch out."

The boys are just not getting my humour tonight, Jimmie is, she just laughs and shakes her head at me, she's the only one that actually gets that I'm deadly serious. I've had nearly two years of that slut hanging around my boyfriend, she must be eighteen by now, you'd think she would have grown up a bit and gone and got her own boyfriend. The boys all help themselves to a beer from the tray that Billy has just come in with. My taste has matured of late, I now prefer a Southern Comfort and lemonade to a cider or a beer and Billy doesn't disappoint. Despite only being fifteen, I have no trouble getting into pubs or being served at the bar, clubs are a bit harder but Sean usually wangles it for me. Jimmie never has a problem, she looks at least twenty and I'm so jealous. The boys head out to the stage, except Sean, the rest of the band know we have a little routine, they just don't know what it is, and in all honesty I don't think my brothers want to.

As the little back room empties, Sean takes a swig of his beer, I chew on the inside of my lip as I watch him. "Show us ya tits G," he gestures toward my chest as he speaks.

"You've been looking at them for the best part of the day, are you not bored with them?" I say as I pull my top up.

"Never, ever." He bites each of my nipples, then pulls my bra and my T-shirt back down and it's that gesture that makes my insides turn to mush, I love this boy so much, so, so much.

"Come and dance next to the stage so I can watch you move, don't cause any trouble with Haley and don't drink too much, I love you babe." He pulls me in for a hard kiss on the mouth; I knock back my drink as he grabs my hand and pulls me out to the pub with him.

The place is packed and hands reach out from everywhere as Sean walks through the crowd with one arm loosely slung over my shoulder. He stops continuously and shakes hands, high fives and fist bumps his fans but he never lets go of me and I notice how much tighter he pulls me in to him when any of the hands are female that reach out for him. He smiles and nods but that's all of the attention he gives them and my heart swells with the pride I feel at being his girlfriend but I still hate it and I have to fight my desire to slap each and every one of them around their over made up faces. Some of these women must be at least thirty; shouldn't they be at home with their kids or watching Dynasty or something? By the time we reach the stage, I probably have as much adrenalin running through me as Sean does.

He kisses my temple. "Be good, I love you," he whispers before he turns to jump up on stage leaving me with Jimmie and Lennon.

"Woohoo, looking hot Maca!" Jimmie and I turn and stare at Haley the whore. Sean has his back to her and takes no notice.

"George," I hear Len warn from over my shoulder.

I turn and glare at him, "What? I haven't done anything."

He shakes his head at me. The boys kick off with a version of Queens 'Crazy little thing called love' Sean goes all out rocker Billy, curling his lip and swivelling his hips and the crowd goes wild, especially the women. I've never heard the boys sing this song and as good as the performance is, I'm not thrilled.

"Good evening Brentwood and good evening all you lovers out there, are you ready to rock out with us tonight?"

Sean looks out across the crowd as he shouts out his welcome in that husky voice of his; there are about two hundred people in the crowd and he manages to get some kind of response from all of them. "This is a new one of ours," he says as the boys start playing 'Hopeless' one of the new songs they wrote and recorded for the demo tape. The crowd goes mad. I have no idea how some of them are singing it word for word already, the boys put together a compilation tape when they were in the studio, it contains of all their new stuff and a few covers thrown in, they've been selling them after their shows for the last three weeks. These people must be listening to them continuously to know the words and love the songs like they already do. Over the next hour the boys play a mixture of their new songs and songs from the sixties, seventies and eighties and the crowd are loving every moment, and so are the band. Sean lets them know they're taking a thirty minute break and is about to jump down from the stage when he spots Haley standing waiting for him. I fold my arms across my chest and stand and watch what he's going to do, instead of jumping down from the middle of the stage and talking to the crowd like he normally does, he moves over to the left and jumps down straight into my arms. I wrap them around his neck and give him a sweaty kiss.

"Brilliant babe, you were fuckin' brilliant."

He has the biggest smile on his face as someone passes him a beer, he holds my hand while we head into the back room so that he can change his t-shirt, as we walk in, Lennon is shouting at Marley who is already smoking a joint. Len doesn't have a problem with the joint, it's the fact that Marls is smoking now, in the middle of the set and not at the end of the show.

Jimmie and I grab our drinks as Len says, "Girls, can you wait outside please, I need to chat to the boys."

Sean kisses my hair as I pull away from him. We've never been asked to leave before so I'm figuring Len is really pissed off with Marley and is going to give him a bollocking. I'm more than happy to leave, whatever Len is going to say, I hope it works. Marley seems to be permanently stoned these days and when he's not stoned, he's sleeping, he's been missing practice, work and school and my Mum and Dad aren't happy with him and have threatened to take his car away from him, whatever it takes, I just want my brother back.

Jimmie and I head back out to the pub and join Billy and Tom's girlfriends at their table near the stage. Cheryl and Linda are okay but they are both eighteen and don't really have too much to say to Jimmie and me, I know that people talk about us and wonder what Lennon and Sean are doing with a couple of fifteen year olds but they have no idea how it is with us, they don't know our history or the futures we already have planned out, we stand awkwardly and drink our drinks until the boys come back out and join us; for the last ten minutes of their break, drinks are sent over and hands are shook. Marley eventually cheers up when a pretty little dark haired girl comes over and chats to him; they slow things down a bit with the second half of their set and do a few more love songs, then unexpectedly, the boys set about rearranging the stage and a piano is pushed forward, Marley and Billy sit down on stools with their acoustic guitars either side of Tom at the drums.

Sean sits down at the piano and adjusts the mic, the whole place falls silent. “Okay people, this song, this is a bit different for us but it’s something we’ve been working on and tonight I especially wanted to be able to sing it for my girl. Gia, this is for you, I love ya babe.”

Fucking hell, he’s never dedicated a song to me before, he’s sung songs and stared right at me while he’s been singing and I’ve known that he’s wanted me to hear the words. I have, I do, I know we have a connection that no one else understands, we know that other people think that we’re just a couple of kids and we know how wrong they are. My heart is pounding so hard in my chest that I actually step back from the stage slightly, in case the mic picks up the boom, boom, boom sound that it’s making. Sean hits the first note on the piano and I know in an instant what it is. He proceeds to belt out the most beautiful version of Georgia on my mind that I have ever heard, the whole place is totally silent, I hold on to my sob for as long as I can but it gets to the point where I think I’m actually going to puke so I have to let it go. Jimmie puts her arm around my shoulder and Lennon stands on the other side of me and slides his arm around my waist and kisses my hair, we all know in that moment, that without a shadow of a doubt, the boys are destined for greatness, they *are* so talented and as much as I love Sean, the song and the dedication, I get this really horrible sense that I’m losing him, wash over me. I swipe at my tears, tuck the feeling away and smile up at Sean as he finishes the song and walks over to the edge of the stage and kneels in front of me with a rose in his hand.

“I love you G, I’ll always love you.”

The whole place goes off with whoops and cheers as I wrap my arms around his neck and tell him that I love him too, once again, he’s given me one of those moments that will stay with me until the day I die.

CHAPTER 5

The rest of 1984 is amazing for the boys; they land a recording contract with a small independent label and are in talks to support a big American band on the European leg of their world tour in the summer of 1985. The record label insist that the pub gigs have to stop and they spend the last part of the year in the studio setting down tracks for their first album, which will be released to coincide with the tour.

My Dad got his lawyers involved in contract negations with the label and the boys secured a pretty good deal with an upfront amount, which prompted them all to focus full time on their music, they were either in the studio in West London or at our place writing new songs, none of this really had any effect on mine and Sean's relationship. We spent all of our time together and we were still absolutely in love; the only difference it really made to me was the recognition as Sean McCarthy's girlfriend. I didn't use it as an excuse to be a bitch but it did pretty much make me queen of the school. Perhaps now, on reflection, people did consider me a bitch but I was never deliberately horrible or spiteful to anyone. I was choosey with my friends and perhaps now, with hindsight, I was very shallow about who I hung about with. I was pretty, my boyfriend was the lead singer in a band, and my parents lived in a nice house in the best part of town. I had nice clothes and never wanted for anything and I didn't actively seek out friends like me. It just sort of happened. That's how Ashley ended up hanging around with Jimmie and I when she started at our school at the beginning of our fifth year; Jimmie and I were no angels but Ash was truly wild, we smoked, we drunk, we dabbled in drugs, our boyfriends were older and involved with a band, they tried things, we tried them too. Usually after a gig or at a party and we had never tried anything stronger than weed or whiz; Ashley on the other hand, would happily skin up at school and bragged that she had tried coke and could get hold of it any time we wanted, she had an older brother that served up for a living and was willing to give us a good deal, we didn't take her up on her offer.

The boys finished recording their album in March of 1985 and spent the next few months doing nothing but rehearse; the tour would be kicking off in Italy in May, they would be away for four weeks and then on tour in England for three weeks in July. Jimmie and I couldn't go on the European leg of the tour, we were in our last year of school and up to our necks in exams until the end of May, our parents wouldn't allow us any time off; I was so angry with my Mum and Dad. I would be marrying Sean as soon as I left school, I had turned sixteen the September before and once school was over, nothing would stop us from being together. He was going to be rich and famous, what did it matter whether or not I passed my exams but they wouldn't listen, agreeing only to pay for flights so I could see them play in Spain at the end of the second week they would be away. I begged, pleaded and even threatened to kill myself at one stage but to no avail, thinking back now, I was lucky that they let me fly to Spain with my best friend at the age of just sixteen but they knew Marley and Lennon would be at the airport to collect us and it was only a two and a half hour flight.

Walking through customs and into the arrivals terminal of the airport in Spain was my first realisation that the boys were now well on their way to fame, the reviews had been good from the live shows and there had been a lot of hype in the music magazines about the album release, which would happen the week before the UK leg of the tour. Jimmie and I only had a small suit case each as we were flying out again on Monday morning, after spending just three nights with the boys but three nights was better than nothing. I had gone beyond butterflies in my belly as I looked out for Sean or Lennon as we walked into the terminal building, my heart began to sink as I looked around and couldn't see him.

"Dya see them?" Jimmie asked. I shook my head in reply, biting down hard on my bottom lip. What if he'd forgotten about me, met someone else, a page three girl or someone famous, what if he had realised I was just a school girl and he was on his way to being a famous singer. We had spoken every day and he'd said that he loved and missed me but what if he was lying? My head began to spin, I hadn't been able to eat yesterday and our morning flight had meant that I hadn't had breakfast this morning, the airport was hot and noisy, I suddenly felt sick and could feel myself sway. I stopped walking and held onto the luggage trolley while I took some deep breaths, as I regained my balance and the room came back into focus. I suddenly noticed the noise, I thought there had been an accident at first, there was so much screaming. Police and security guards started running in the direction of the noise and a crowd was forming.

"George!" I turn and look at Jimmie. "Bloody hell, you deaf or what?"

"Sorry, I feel a bit dizzy; it's warm in here. What's wrong?"

"You don't think that could be them do ya?"

She gestures with her chin towards where the commotion was going on, as we both stare, the biggest, blackest man I've ever seen appears from amongst the melee with Sean tucked under his arm, Lennon appears behind them; as soon as he sees me Sean breaks free from the black bloke and jogs toward me with the biggest grin on his face. I can't move, my legs are stuck but I don't need to, Sean grabs me around the waist and swings me around in a circle, he sets me down on my feet, then snogs the face off me.

"Fucking hell G, I've missed you, show us ya tits."

And he's there, my Sean, his arms, his smell, his taste and everything is right with world, I'm back right where I was born to be, at his side, I don't know why I panicked and doubted him, the way he looks at me, the things he says, I know without a shadow of a doubt how much he loves me, his eyes tell me as they look into mine and I instantly dissolve into him.

We end up with Milo the black body guard and four armed Policeman escorting us out to the car waiting outside, well I say car, it's a stretch limo… a stretch fucking limo. Jimmie and I scream like the pair of sixteen year olds we are as Len and Sean high five each other, we jump inside, Milo and the driver put our cases in the boot as they shout at a group of about ten girls and a couple of boys that are banging on the window of the car.

"They are proper mental here G, we were on some TV show last weekend and ever since then we can't go anywhere without being recognised, it's been mad."

He pulls me onto his lap as he talks. "Dya like the car? We borrowed it from Kombat Rock."

Kombat Rock are the American band Carnage are supporting, they're world famous and have already had three number one albums and about twenty singles in the charts, they've been around for about eight years, everyone knows them, they have a reputation for drink, drugs, women and smashing up hotel rooms and they are the main reason for my little freak out in the airport building. I'm much calmer now, with my arms wrapped around Sean's neck, his arms around my waist.

"Wait till you see the hotel," Lennon says. "We've been on a tour bus most of the time but the label booked us into a hotel as we are playing here for two nights."

"I booked us into our own room," Sean whispers into my ear. "I can't wait to get you naked."

"Maca, I really don't want to be hearing that, it's bad enough knowing you're shagging my sister, without hearing you talk about it."

"Well you're shagging her mate," Sean tells Lennon.

"Excuse me boys but can we please just stop talking about who's shagging who. Have we got our own room babe?" Jimmie asks Len.

"Yes babe, there's no way we were gonna be sharing with Marley, not the way he's been behaving."

I look up at Sean, then across to Len. "Why, how's he been behaving?"

"Like a whore," the boys both say at once and laugh.

"What about drugs, has he been stoned all the time?"

The boys look across at each other guiltily, great; they've probably all been stoned all of the time.

Sean shrugs and pulls me in for another kiss. "Let's not talk about Marley, you can talk to him later, we're all going for an early dinner before the show."

We pull up at the hotel and Jim and I just stare with our mouths open.

"We're stayin' at the Ritz? Fuckin' hell, George, we're stayin' at the Ritz." Jimmie can barely contain her excitement as we step out of the limo.

"Our bags," I say to Sean as he grabs my hand and starts to lead me inside.

"Don't worry about them babe, Milo or the bell boys will bring them up." Well Sean seems to have adapted to this lifestyle pretty quickly I think to myself.

I travel up to our room in a complete daze; I have stayed in some nice hotels with my parents but at the time, nothing as swanky as The Ritz. Our rooms are decorated nicely but not over the top; as soon as the door closes behind us, Sean pulls me in for the longest of kisses, then he just holds me for a few moments, kissing my hair, my jaw and my neck, all the while breathing me in.

"I've missed you so much G, I'm so glad you're here."

We spend the next couple of hours reacquainting ourselves with each other, in the five and a half years we've known each other this is the longest we've ever been apart. Despite the fact that we've been having sex for the past couple of years, I wasn't really sexually aware at this stage of my life. I was sixteen and probably having more sex than your average twenty five year old but that's only because I was with Sean, if he hadn't have come along, I'd probably still be a virgin. The boys at school didn't interest me. Actually most of them gave me a wide birth because they knew who my boyfriend was and of course because I had three big brothers.

I knew I was pretty, I knew I had a fairly decent figure but I didn't dress in a sexy way, I wasn't aware back then that I could turn heads just by walking into a room. I didn't lust after men or boys, it was just Sean, only Sean, sex for me at this time was only about Sean, one didn't exist without the other. In saying all of that, I'd bought new clothes and lingerie for this weekend, things that were a little bit different for me. A skirt for one and a leather skirt at that, and a pair of red heels. My Dad told me I looked like a Drury Lane whore in the outfit; my Mum slapped him and told me I looked very sophisticated. I chose to believe my Mum; she had great taste in clothes and had helped me pick the outfit I was going to wear for the show. We had a lovely girlie day shopping and I had confessed to her that Sean and I were having sex; it was a bit of a wicked thing to do to her on reflection. We were sitting in a restaurant in Romford town centre. My Mum wouldn't go to Macas or a café; she had this favourite little Italian place that we always went to when we shopped there.

"So you and Sean, it's obviously still very serious between the two of you, this time apart hasn't changed anything?"

I shook my head and looked down at my food, my Mum had poured me half a glass of wine and I took a big gulp, it was past one in the afternoon and I hadn't eaten breakfast, the wine instantly went to my head. I actually had no appetite since Sean had left ten days ago and my Dad had commented the night before that I was looking skinny. I wasn't skinny, not by a long shot but I knew that I'd lost some weight, hence the rich creamy seafood pasta dish I was now tucking into under my worried Mums orders.

"Why would time apart change anything Mum? I love him."

"I know you do babe but you are still so very young."

"You've been with Dad since you were thirteen," I replied defiantly.

"That was twenty five years ago Georgia, things were different, lots of girls got married straight from school, we didn't have the choices you girls have these days, the whole world is so much more accessible to you, so many more career opportunities available to women nowadays." She took a long sip of her wine and refilled both of our glasses as I watched her, her blues eyes and mine are exactly the same shade nowadays, but where her lashes and skin are fair, mine are dark, she's beautiful my Mum but right at that second she looked worried.

"We've always treated you like a grown up George, being the youngest, we just expected more from you and perhaps that wasn't the right thing to do. You and Sean, you seem to be so serious about each other, you know he's already spoken to your Dad about marriage?"

I didn't but I wasn't going to let her know that. "He loves me, we've spoken about marriage, and as soon as he has a deposit saved we want to buy a house."

"What about a job, for you I mean, would you not like a career?"

"How can I get a job if Sean is going to be travelling with the band, and he will be Mum, they are going to make it big, I just know, this tour and the new album are just the start and I want to be there to support him. I want to be able to travel around the world with him, I don't want to be stuck here in some poxy office, waiting for him to call or come home. These past ten days have been bad enough; imagine how long he'll be away when he's touring the states?"

I take a gulp of my wine.

"Okay, well I understand that you're in love right now but what if things change, people do you know, you'll be a different person by the time your twenty, you *will* want different things."

"I will still want Sean, I *will* always want Sean."

"Are you having sex with him George, are you sleeping together."

My stomach lurched and I thought for a second I was going to bring up my lunch, my cheeks were burning; my Mum reached across the table and took my hand.

"I'm your Mum George but I'm also your friend, talk to me."

I nodded my head. "Yes we're having sex."

"Are you being careful?"

I nod again. "I'm on the pill."

"How'd you get the pill? When? Why didn't you ask me to come with you?"

"About a year." I lied; it had been closer to two.

"Georgia, that's illegal, you should have waited."

"I told the doctor that my periods were really heavy and that I was getting terrible cramps and couldn't leave the house so he put me on the pill. All the girls do it."

"Well it's wrong, is this Doctor Weeks, did he put you on it? I will have something to say when I next see him."

"No Mum, I went to the family planning clinic, they gave me the pill and loads of condoms, they'd rather I was on the pill than pregnant and so would I, we do want babies but not yet, we want to see what happens with the band first, we don't want to be taking a baby on tour with us so we want to wait a bit but I want to be a young Mum like you were, we both want that."

"Got it all worked out haven't you, you're too old for your own good George, nobody knows at sixteen how their life is likely to turn out, we all think we know what we want but the truth is, really we have no idea… But, if you are sure Sean is the one and you are already sleeping together then I will support you with whatever choices you make. You will need me in your corner when it comes to convincing your Dad into letting you do anything until you're at least eighteen, he wants you to stay on at school and do your A levels."

I shake my head no. "If Sean's touring next year, then I'm going with him, he earns enough money to support me. Dad can cut me off, he can do what he likes but I'm leaving school and going with Sean."

My Mum takes a deep breath in. "Well, if Sean's the one, we better go and find you something that will knock his socks off, make him realise exactly what he's got waiting for him at home and stop his eyes from wandering over all those groupies that follow the bands around."

My stomach drops to my feet again, groupies, I hate that word; Jimmie and I have discussed them a few times but we haven't really admitted to our fears, Lennon's only their manager and he's still getting girls throw themselves at him. He's told her on the phone, Sean has told me no such thing, he knows how I'd react, I had already thought about running away from home and getting a flight to whatever country he was in I was jealous, it was the reason I had been unable to eat since he left, I trusted Sean, it was the women that I didn't trust and that's what some of them were, women, grown women, not sixteen year old school girls like me and I hated it. Again, this wasn't something I was going to admit to my

Mum, I wanted her to think that I had every faith in Sean and I did to a degree.

I stand in front of the mirror in the hotel room looking at myself, I've sent Sean down to the bar as I wanted to get dressed on my own, I've tried this outfit on three times before I left England but I still wasn't confident enough to put it on in front of him. I'm wearing a black leather mini skirt, a black and red wide banded striped jumper that hangs off one shoulder, black fishnet stockings and red patent leather heels. My newly permed hair is big and I have a pair of big red hooped earrings in my ears and red and black bangles on my wrists. I spray myself once more with my new perfume 'Coco' which I had bought at the airport, pick up my black bag and throw it across my left shoulder and chest so it rests on my right hip and leave the room.

Sean has seen me naked numerous times, we've bathed and showered together, he's kissed every square inch of my body but I had never felt more nervous than I did walking into that bar; that was the first time that I realised I could turn heads. A group of grown men that looked about thirty were all sitting around a table as I walked in and one by one they all looked up at me, one of them winked, which actually calmed me down a bit as I assumed it meant I looked okay.

"Hermosa," I heard one of them say. I had no idea what it meant; I would ask the waiter later. I saw Sean and Lennon at the bar with their backs to me but it was Marley that spotted me first.

"Fuckin' hell, look at George!" I think is what he says, I feel like everyone in the bar turns around and looks at me at once; Sean's mouth drops wide open, I think me and my Mum have achieved the desired effect, his mouth closes and he swallows. Jimmie nudges him from the barstool she's sitting on and he moves towards me, he stops right in front of me and very gently runs his fingertips over my jaw and up across my lips.

"You look beautiful G, like one of them supermodels they keep on about in the papers, except you're more beautiful."

I can't speak, my mouth is so dry through nerves and now I feel like I'm going to cry so I say nothing and let him lead me by the hand to the bar. Marley pulls me in for a big hug, he looks terrible, skinny and gaunt, and his eyes look sunken into his head. Mum will go mental when she sees him. "Look at my baby sister, all grown up, we can't be calling her Porge any more can we Len, can't even call her George anymore really either, so what do we call you, now your all grown up?"

"Try Georgia that is my name," I say to him.

He sounds like Marley but he doesn't, he's talking too fast and too much and he keeps sniffing and wiping his nose and for some reason I feel frightened and I'm not sure if it's of him or for him. I say hello to Billy and Tom, their girlfriends aren't here tonight, they're flying in next weekend and staying for the last week, my Mum was working on my Dad to let me fly back for the end of the tour but I was keeping that to myself, I hadn't even told Jim as I wanted it to be a surprise for Sean, if I was allowed.

We all piled into the stretch limo that was waiting outside the hotel for us just fifteen minutes later, I'd had a cocktail at the hotel bar and my head was swimming but it didn't stop me enjoying a glass of champagne once Lennon popped the cork and filled our glasses while we rode in the back of the car. Ten minutes later we arrived at the restaurant, our doors were opened for us and we were led through the restaurant to a large table in the centre of the room. Lennon explained that all of this had been arranged by the record label, the tour so far was a huge success and Carnage were receiving fantastic reviews and on the back of that any previously unsold tickets were being snapped up because people wanted to see them play as opposed to Kombat Rock.

We'd only been sat down five minutes when a boy of about sixteen came over and asked for autographs, this was followed ten minutes later by an American girl who was going to the show later. I tried not to let it bother me when she only wanted her photo taken with Sean and not the rest of the band, her Mum finally shifted her fat arse out of my face, after taking a half dozen pictures and Sean reached under the table and grabbed my hand squeezing it tight.

"I'm sorry," he whispered, I shrugged and smiled, he was famous now; it's what they had worked so hard for all these years. What was I supposed to say? The girl had gone back to her table and I was here with Sean, holding hands, he might be her fantasy but he was my reality, my future and it was me that would be wrapped around him in our hotel room tonight. Besides, we needed girls like her to buy the album so we could save the money for a deposit on our house quicker, bet she didn't realise that, I should have been grateful to her but I wasn't, I was jealous and I hated myself for it.

We arrived at the venue for tonight's concert an hour and a half later, it was about seven on a Friday evening, Carnage were due on stage at around eight thirty, Kombat Rock at around nine thirty, so we had some time before the show. I'd never been back stage at such a big event, Lennon had offered to get us tickets for the best seats but I hate sitting down at concerts and Sean had refused to let me go into the mosh pit so we would be watching from the sides of the stage instead. I had butterflies as we pulled around the back of the building and saw the crowds queuing to get in, obviously most of the crowd were there to see K R but there were also a lot of Carnage t-shirts and banners that I spotted on the way.

We were shown through the back doors of the venue and Jimmie and I were issued with back stage passes, the boys were changing out of the clothes they'd worn for dinner and we were shown into a function room as they went off to change. The room was already fairly full of people; competition winners waiting to meet the bands, men in suits who I assume were from the record label, a couple of journalists and photographers and lots and lots of women, it made me feel sick, some of them were beautiful, some of them not so much.

A waiter appeared at my side and asked if Jimmie and I would like a drink, we both requested a vodka and lemonade and it was bought back to us in just a couple of minutes. Sean appeared back at my side, he had taken off his Ben Sherman shirt and changed into a vintage looking James Dean t-shirt but he was still wearing his jeans and Doc Martin boots. He looked gorgeous but then as far as I was concerned he looked gorgeous in anything, obviously I wasn't the only one to think so judging by the stares he was getting from what I could only assume to be groupies and the dirty looks they were giving me. A really tall woman who looked about thirty five who had been giving me daggers even before Sean had arrived back, made her way over to us; Sean had his arm around my waist and lent in to kiss my temple as the waiter bought him and the rest of the band members a beer.

"So Sean, who's your little friend? She's very pretty."

He seemed to stiffen up as she approached; he took a long swig from his bottle before he looked the woman up and down. "This is my girlfriend Gia; she's flown in from England for the weekend, just to see me." He turns and looks at me with such a dreamy smile on his face that I almost melt. "Didn't ya babe."

He kisses me full on the mouth and I squirm with embarrassment; as he pulls away, the peroxide blonde is still standing watching us, I look straight at her. "Yes babe, I did."

She runs her tongue over her top lip as she looks me up and down. "How sweet. Don't forget to get a note from your parents when you go back to school next week, I wouldn't want you getting detention."

I smiled nicely at her. "I won't, make sure you notify the pensioners home that you'll be out late, wouldn't want them sending out a search party for a missing resident."

She didn't reply, she just looked at me with her ice blue eyes, like she was trying to think of a reply, Marley appeared at my side. "Fuck off Anna and leave my sister alone, go and find someone's cock to suck. Rocco will be here soon with all the pretty young groupies and you won't get a look in then."

She gave a sneer and a little laugh in Marley's direction. "Fuck you Layton."

"No thanks love." Marley replied. "Been there, done that and got the fuckin' crabs to prove it you dirty whore, fuck off out of my sight before I get security to throw you out."

She glared at all of us, then just turned and walked away, I swear, her legs were nearly as tall as me, she must have been over six feet, she reminded me of Bridget whatsherface, Rocky's wife or girlfriend or whatever.

"Who the fuck was that?" I ask, looking between both the boys.

"The oldest groupie in town," Marley replied.

"She used to be Rocco's girlfriend," Sean said. "But he's traded her in for something younger but she still follows the band around, she seems to think sucking and fucking every other bloke surrounding Rocco will make him jealous and he'll go back to her but he's got pretty young things throwing themselves at him, he's not interested in her."

I looked at Marley. "But you fucked her?"

He shrugs his shoulders at me and wipes his hand across his nose. "I was coked out my head, horny as fuck and she kept begging me for it. I caught fucking crabs off her and had to shave my pubes and avoid sex for a couple of weeks, dirty slut, I haven't been near her since, I don't know how she keeps getting a backstage pass, no one likes her."

I shake my head at Marley's little revelation, I don't care about the shagging, it's the coke that worries me, no wonder he looks so skinny, I've heard it makes you lose weight, that's why Ashley from school likes it. "Is that why you look so rough Marls? You been doing coke?"

"Well thanks for the compliment George don't mince your words." I shrug my shoulders.

"You look tired and skinny that's all, I'm worried, and Mum will flip when she sees ya."

He looks from me, then across to Sean and shrugs. "This tour has been hard work for all of us, even wonder boy here has had to have a little help to get him through, and I ain't the only one."

My gaze swings up to Sean's, who is looking at Marley like he's about to kill him. "You've been doing coke?" I ask Sean. Now it's his turn to shrug; he looks around the room before he answers.

"Just the odd line every now and then, it's hard going out there, we've all needed a little buzz to help us along. It's nothing and everyone does it."

I'm not surprised; I'm just disappointed that he hasn't told me. The same as he had never mentioned how many groupies there were following them around. I knock back my drink and say nothing; Lennon appears in the doorway.

"Boys, come on, I need you for some photographs and a quick interview for this Spanish magazine."

Sean looks at me. "I won't be long, stay close to Jimmie." I nod and smile at him but it's half-hearted, I don't think I like this fame game, it's okay when I'm by his side but I hate that he's seeing, doing and experiencing so many new things without me. We've done everything together for so long that I can't help but get that horrible feeling that I'm losing him again.

"Let's get another drink," Jimmie says. "These fuckin' groupies are really starting to piss me off, they're our boyfriends but they're looking at us like we have no right to be here."

"Ignore them," I say to her. "Most of them will die of old age by the end of the week, they're so ancient." She laughs at that and we make our way over to the bar at the back of the room.

A few minutes later there's all sorts of talk and chatter as the stars of the tour Kombat Rock, or K R as their fans call them, enter the room. We lean back against the bar as they greet the competition winners, smile, pose for photos with them and sign autographs, the fans and all members of the press are ushered out and I watch as the groupies start to circle the stars. Rocco Taylor is the bands lead singer, he's okay looking but has nothing on Sean or Marley and he must be around twenty eight. Jimmie and I watch as he works the room, kissing some women, ignoring others, shaking hands with some of the suits and hugging others. The first supporting act are on stage and their set is being played through the speakers in the room, they're actually not bad for a bunch of local fifteen year olds but not as good as Carnage, by a long shot.

Suddenly Rocco shouts out, "Can someone turn this crap down? It's making my ears bleed." Everyone laughs, everyone except Jimmie and I that is, what a dickhead!

I bet his band weren't that good when they were just fifteen, I take an instant dislike to him and the look on my face must show it as his eyes skim past me and then swing back in my direction. "So people, what have we here, who are these two beautiful young ladies and why has no one thought to introduce them to me?"

"You're too late Rocco," Anna the peroxide calls out. "They're already the property of Carnage, unlucky."

He looks across as Anna. "Who asked for your opinion cunt?" He looked around at his entourage. "Somebody get that slut out of here."

There's a flurry of activity, security appear and ask Anna to leave. The air is blue with the language that she uses as she's escorted from the room.

Rocco Taylor comes and stands right in front of us. "So, you beautiful ladies are friends with the boys from Carnage. They're doing well, they'll go far."

He strokes his index finger up and down the back of my arm as he speaks, I want to tell him to stop but he's Rocco Taylor, one of the biggest rock stars in the world. "What's your name honey?" he asks me in his American drawl. I'm not sure where in America he comes from but he sounds like a cowboy to me.

I swallow hard before answering but my voice still comes out squeaky as I reply, "George, this is my friend Jimmie."

"Ha ha George and Jimmie. Well lookie here boys, isn't this just the prettiest George and Jimmie you have ever seen in your lives?"

Another bloke with long jet black hair and covered in tattoos comes and stands next to Rocco and leers at us as he chews hard on some gum, he throws his arms around the lead singers shoulder. "Well ain't they a pair of pretty young things."

I am actually shitting myself, I suddenly feel all of my sixteen years and eight months and not a day older, all of my usual bullshit and bravado has left me, these are real live rock stars, who are used to getting whatever they want from women. I feel totally out of my depth and I can't help but notice that goose bumps are popping up all over my body and the hairs on the back of my neck are standing on end and it's through fear, not because I feel any kind of desire towards this pair of freaks.

Rocco reaches out and strokes his index finger up and down, over my cheek bone. "Well I hope those boys from Carnage are happy to share their toys, coz I sure would like to have a little play with you."

I'm suddenly pissed off, I swipe his hand away. "I'm not any body's toy; I'm Sean McCarthy's girlfriend."

The room has fallen almost silent as everyone watches the interaction; who the fuck does he think he is, he's not even good looking and the other one, Wayne Allen or whatever his name is, I think he's the drummer, he's not only as ugly as fuck but he stinks of body odour too. I'm debating whether to tell him this when I hear Lennon call out. "Rocco, Wayne, leave my little sister alone and the other one is my girl so don't even think about it."

Before I have a chance to react, he grabs me by the back of my head and kisses me on the mouth, I push him away as hard as I can, and as I do, I hear Sean shout. "G, what the fuck are you doing?"

I look horrified from Rocco to Sean. "You fucking animal, keep your hands off me!"

I wipe my mouth with the back of my hand; Rocco narrows his eyes on me, Sean is now at his side and is looking at me like I have lost my mind. "Not her fault Maca, she just saw the hot rock star and couldn't resist, best get a lead and keep her under control."

What? My mouth fell open but no words came out, he says no more, just turns and walks away. What a complete and utter arsehole. I look back at Sean and I suddenly want to cry but not here, I won't do it here, in front of all these people and embarrass not only myself but Sean and the band as well.

Sean looks me over. "What happened?"

I take a deep breath. "He fuckin' kissed me, that's what happened, he's a creep, and I hate him."

Surely Sean can see how upset I am. "Fuckin' hell G, can I not leave you alone for five minutes?"

"What? I didn't do anything, he came over to me, I told him I was with you but he kissed me anyway."

"She didn't do anything Maca, not a thing." Jimmie backs me up.

He lets out a breath. "I'm sorry, I shouldn't have left you here, he's a fuckin' animal. Are you okay?"

No I'm not, I'm scared, hurt and humiliated but I'm not going to admit to all of that now, not in front of all these people so again I let it go and just nod my head.

"Wipe your mouth, your lipsticks smudged," he points to my lips as he speaks, I want to go to the ladies and fix myself up but I'm too scared to leave his side now. I suddenly wish I was twenty five and knew how to handle wankers like Rocco Taylor, I'd fucking show him then!

Marley comes flying through the doors of the hospitality room. "Woohoo Maca, that is some good shit man, where'd you get that stuff?"

Sean instantly turns back to me, great, tonight just gets better and better, I've never felt that there was an age difference between Sean and myself, but right now I feel like I'm just an immature little school girl and he's a famous rock star, which really isn't that far from the truth and it hurts, so fucking much.

CHAPTER 6

Lennon finds Jimmie and me a great place to stand in the wings. The venue holds around fifteen thousand people and is already three quarters full. I watch as the boys are given their guitars by the roadies and are wired up with what I can only assume are mics and ear pieces, the music that's been playing goes quiet and the lights go down.

Sean appears in front of me and says, "I love ya Georgia Rae, show us your tits." I don't hesitate and pull my top up and flash him my new black lacy bra.

"Fuckin' hell babe, I've gotta go on stage with a hard on now." He kisses me again and is then pulled away by a stage manager and put into position.

The opening song 'Show Me' is from the new album and so are the next two, after this Sean addresses the audience and says how nice it is to be in Spain, a pair of knickers fly through the air and land on the stage.

Sean runs over to Tom and grabs a spare drumstick and goes back and picks the red lace knickers up with it. He holds them up, hanging them from the drumstick. "Hey Marley, don't you have a pair like this, are these yours?" Tom does a b'dom cha sound on his drums to accompany Sean's joke and the crowd laugh and whistle.

I hear a female voice call out in broken English "Marry me Maca" and that evokes more whistles.

"Sorry ladies but I'm taken." He turns his head toward me and gives me a truly breath taking smile. I feel so very proud in that moment, he's made it, he's got this crowd eating out of his hand, it's what he was born to do and he looks every inch the star out there and he's mine, he's been mine since I was eleven years old and I love him beyond words.

The band belt out all of the songs from the up and coming album and also throw in a few covers, they thank the crowd and run off the stage as the audience goes wild and call out for more. Sean comes straight to me, wearing the biggest smile. "Were we okay?"

"You were brilliant, just brilliant babe, all these years of work are finally paying off, I'm so proud of you." He pulls the towel from off his shoulder that someone has put there and wipes the sweat from his face.

"Don't move from this spot, we have to do a quick encore." He gives me a kiss on the lips and is lead back out, I expect the rest of the boys to follow him, but they don't, the lights come back on and Sean is out on stage alone, sitting on a stool with his electric acoustic and my stomach goes over, if he sings Georgia on my mind, I will cry and completely embarrass myself in front of all these rock star types. There is a massive cheer from the crowd as the lights come on, he plucks out a few notes and the whole place falls silent.

"I want your babies Maca, take me home and make me pregnant," a lone female voice shouts from the crowd. Sean laughs and shakes his head, then looks up and smiles at the crowd.

"Darlin', do me a favour here, all you ladies in the crowd tonight have gotta appreciate the fact that I'm a one woman type of bloke and I love my girl; I've loved my girl since the very first day I set eyes on her and back then she was just a girl… but I have had the pleasure these past few years of watching her grow into an absolutely beautiful young woman and as much as I love touring and playing in front of you lot every night, I'm counting down the days till I'm back in England and in her arms."

There are a combination of boos and whistles from the crowd.

"This song people, this song is for all of you that are missing the ones you love, for all of you that, for whatever reason, can't be with that one person you love most in the world, this song, is for my girl, this song, is for Gia, I love you baby."

As soon as I hear the sound effects of waves lapping and a boats horn, I know what the song is and I can't stop the tears, Georgia is the obvious choice, but this, this is something he's come up with all by himself, it's The Jam 'English Rose' and I can't stop the tears and I don't care who sees them.

Len is at my side with his arm around my shoulder and says into my ear. "He's been practising this for days; he didn't think his voice was good enough."

I cuff my runny nose and shake my head at Len. "He's gotta be mad, he sounds better than Weller."

"That's what we've all been telling him, he just wanted it to be perfect for ya."

I nod my head. "It's better than perfect Len."

We stand and watch together, Jimmie joins us, standing with her arm around Len's waist. Sean stands from his stool, the rest of the boys join him on stage and they all take a bow, if this is the response they are getting as the supporting act in a foreign country, then I can't wait to meet the crowd when they are top bill in England.

Sean walks off the stage straight to me, his eyes are wide, his pupils dilated, I really want it to be the buzz of being on stage that's causing this, but something tells me that illegal substances are involved and it takes a little bit away from the beautiful song he just sung for me, but I hide my disappointment and wrap my arms around his neck as he lifts me off the floor in a hug.

"That was beautiful, thank you," I say to him as he sets me back down, he throws his arm across my shoulder and we make our way back stage, passing the boys from K R as they head on stage. Carnage accept congratulations on their set and wish the boys from K R good luck with theirs; we all head into the hospitality room so the boys can grab a beer. The room is packed with even more groupies now and I feel inadequate and uncomfortable around these sexy, experienced women, I want to leave but I understand Sean needs to be with the boys and to network, he barely takes a swig of his beer when someone from the record company speaks to Lennon and he in turn calls the boys away. Sean passes me his beer.

"Stay with Jimmie, don't accept a drink from anyone except the waiters, we have to go do some meet and greets and a few quick interviews, then we'll go back to the hotel, I promise, okay babe?"

I nod my head and smile at him, the boys head toward the door and I'm not oblivious to the eyes of the groupies on them. I hate it! I hate these women, do they have no self-respect? I also hate that I have to share him with his fans right now, I'm only here for three nights and then I won't get to see him for another two weeks. God I can't wait for my exams to be over, and then I can do as I like and my Mum and Dad won't be able to stop me.

Jimmie lets out a big sigh from beside me. "Well George, I think this is it, I think our boys are finally about to hit the big time, can you believe it? You're going out with a famous rock star."

For some reason I fill up with tears, I shake my head at her as she wraps her arms around my shoulders as she sees my distress. "He's not a famous anything, he's just Sean, he's just my boy."

"Don't get upset George, of course he's still your boy, he always will be, but things are gonna change, you wait till the album is released and the UK leg of the tour starts, the whole of England will be talking about them, it's what all these years of practise have been for, all the driving about in the transit, all the grotty pubs we've been to with them, all the rehearsals in your summer house. Now look at us George, we're driving about in a stretch limo and staying at the Ritz, fuckin' hell, we're a couple of sixteen year old school girls and look at the life we'll soon be leading." I smiled and nodded and pushed down the feeling of unease all this change was giving me.

We ordered ourselves a vodka each from the bar and stood and made up stories about some of the groupies hanging around the room, all obviously waiting for Kombat Rock to come off stage. Len came back about forty minutes later to check on us, apparently there were more interview requests than they were expecting so things were taking longer, as Lennon turned to leave I watched when one of the Suits from the record label stopped him and started saying something in his ear. They both looked over at me, not expecting me to be looking at them, my cheeks burned, Len looked down at the ground, their conversation was obviously about me, but why I had no idea.

Half hour later and the boys still weren't back and I was getting nervous. Kombat Rock would finish their set soon and I didn't want to be here without Sean when Rocco got off stage. I didn't like him, he made me feel uncomfortable but I didn't want to make things difficult for Carnage with the lead singer of Kombat

Rock, there was still two weeks left of the European tour, then a short break before the UK leg of the tour started, which meant another four weeks of gigs they would be playing together. If I caused problems, Rocco could get them kicked off the tour and with the album being launched before the UK gigs started, which is the last thing the boys needed so I would just stay out of Rocco's way as much as I could. Their set was being played through the speakers so I already knew they were just starting their encore. I looked toward the door, silently begging Sean, Marley or Lennon to come walking through them, but no, it was Rocco amidst a lot of whopping and cheering and surrounded by a squealing group of nearly naked women and young girls, one of which had her legs wrapped around his waist as he carried her into the hospitality room. Her top was pulled down and he was sucking on her nipple, his eyes locked with mine as he stepped through the door, I quickly looked away and turned and ordered Jimmie and I another drink from the bar, that's when I heard her voice.

"Well, well, if it ain't Maca's spoilt little princess. Isn't it past your bedtime, shouldn't you be at home and tucked up in bed with your teddy?"

Haley, what the fuck is she doing here? I turn around and realise that it was her nipple Rocco was latched onto as he came through the door; I look her up and down as she stands next to Rocco, and he has his arm slung around her shoulder.

"Oh its way past my bedtime but don't worry that little brain of yours, Maca will be back soon, then we will be off to get tucked up in bed together and the only teddy that'll be involved is the one Sean will be ripping off me." I smile sweetly at her. "With his teeth."

She glares at me for a few seconds, and then turns to Rocco. "You know they're not eighteen yet? They shouldn't be drinking."

"Yeah, I heard they were jail bait, this is a private party though, don't think the law counts here, otherwise most of us would be arrested for one reason or another, now, get me a beer, then get back here and blow me, I need to come in that dirty, dirty mouth of yours."

Jim nudges me and says loud enough for Rocco to hear. "Some things never change, Haley the whore, still on her knees and blowing her way backstage." She holds her glass up to mine, we clink them together and say "Cheers" in unison and both start to laugh.

"Fuck off you pair of sluts, you're just jealous Jimmie, you're boyfriends just a hanger on, not even a rock star." She turns her beady eyes to me. "And yours, yours will never be in the same league as my Rocco."

"Oh sorry, Whorely, Rocco's your boyfriend now is he?" I turn to look at Rocco. "Bet you can't wait to take her home to meet ya Mumma, you do know that she has fucked and blown her way through most of the male population of England? She makes Anna look like a nun and has twice as many diseases."

There are a few nervous laughs from the hangers on, Rocco looks at me with a sneer on his face. "Well it's a good job I like my women dirty like her and not stuck up little cock teasers like you." He licks up the side of Haley the whores face, yuck, he's such a pig. "Want some?" he asks me.

"Not if my life depended on it," I reply.

He looks me up and down and moves away to the leather sofa. "Get me a beer, Whorely, and then get back here and get on your knees."

Like the idiot that she is, 'Whorely' does as she's told, with a look of nothing, but pride on her face. In that moment, I actually felt a little bit sorry for her, poor deluded girl. I notice Rocco is staring at me, he scares the crap out of me but I tilt my chin and stare back at him defiantly.

"You're just a bit too big for your boots little girl… but I'll show you, I'll show you whose fucking king around here," he sneers at me.

I shake my head and look toward the door as Marley comes walking through, Billy is behind him and as the door is held open I notice Sean and Lennon outside and it looks like they're arguing, I start to head toward them, but Marley wraps me in his arms and gives me a big cuddle. “Baby sister, I’ve missed you, I cannot wait to get back to England, you smell like home.”

He gives me a kiss on the cheek, this is my big brother, this is the Marley that I have idolised since possibly the day I was born, he didn’t look as spaced out now and he didn’t seem as speedy, “I’ve missed you too Marls, I can’t wait to have you all back.”

Sean’s arms slide around my waist from behind and he kisses the top of my head. “Let’s get the fuck out of here babe.”

I turn around and look at him as he speaks. “What’s wrong, you okay?” He nods but I can see that he’s pissed off.

I turn out of Marley’s arms and wrap my arms around Sean’s neck. “I’m ready to go whenever you are. How are we getting to the hotel?”

“There’ll be cars waiting outside the exit, the drivers just hang around until everyone leaves and drop us wherever we want to go, the label supplies.”

“Well let’s go then.”

Sean shakes hands with all the boys from his and the other bands, I kiss my brothers and Jimmie and we head off, not before I notice Rocco glaring at me as he’s getting a blow job from Haley the whore.

There’s champagne on ice when we get back to our room and rose petals all over the bed; a bath has been run and is full of bubbles and we strip naked and jump straight in, with a glass of champagne in hand. Because the taps are in the middle of the huge bath we are able to sit at each end facing each other. We sit in silence for a while, just watching each other and sipping from our glasses. Sean gives me his lazy lopsided grin as his chocolate eyes roam over my body.

“What are you thinking?” I ask him.

“I’m thinking that I wanted to undress you slowly and look at you in all that sexy underwear but I’m glad that you’re here, naked, in this bath with me; I’ve missed you so much Gia. I can’t wait to get back to England. Is your Dad going to be okay with you touring with us over there?"

I smile at him, despite how long we've known each other, I still blush when he says anything sexual to me, I know we've been doing it for a long time but I still really don't know a lot, only what he has taught me and I love that I'm enough for him, he has all these women throwing themselves at him but it's me he wants, me he misses, me he can't wait to get back to England to be with.

"I think my Dad will be fine, he let me come here so I'm sure Manchester or Liverpool won't be a problem. I'll be the perfect daughter for the next couple of weeks, you know my Dad, I can usually get my way, especially as I have Mum on my side too."

He bites down on the left hand corner of his bottom lip. "Come up here," he orders, fuck, his voice is all sexy and his eyes are partially closed, I love the feeling I get in the bottom of my belly when he looks at me like that. I walk on my knees toward him and kneel between his open legs.

"You know that thing, that we talked about, that you said we could try, that you said you would try for me?" I blush the colour of a tomato and nod my head. "Well I was thinking that seeing as I haven't seen you and you'll be going on Monday and I won't see you again for another coupla weeks and seeing as I'm here and all nice and clean."

"Yes."

"Yes?"

"I promised you a blow job when I got here, pour me some more champagne and you'll get your blow job." I sound confident but I'm so not, we have talked about this but I've never been brave enough to do it, I don't know why but to me it just seems so much more intimate than sex. Sean's kissed me, down there, lots of times, he seems to love it and I most definitely do but I've never been brave enough to return the favour, but I'd already decided before I left England that tonight was going to be the night and what with the wine we had at dinner, the vodkas backstage and now the champagne, I'm feeling like I could suck for England, or do I blow, shit, I actually have no idea what I'm supposed to do.

"What's the matter G, what are ya thinking?"

"Can we get out of here, I'll drown if I try and do it here."

Sean laughs and kneels up to meet me, he puts his hand to the nape of my neck and pulls me in for a kiss "I love you Georgia Rae Layton, I love you so fuckin' much, I can't wait for you to finish school so we can be together all the time. So we can go to bed and wake up together every night and day, so you can come with me, wherever I go in the world, I want you with me G, by my side, always." He kisses me gently on the mouth as I swallow back my tears.

He breaks our kiss and looks down at me. "Now get your sexy arse out this bath and give me a blow job."

"Charming," I reply as I shake my head at him.

We spend the rest of Friday night and most of Saturday morning, with me practising my blow job technique. I soon learn, after Sean can barely contain his laughter at my first attempt, that despite their name, they have nothing to do with blowing whatsoever. I think I will forever glow crimson when I think of the moment I held his dick in front of my mouth and just blew on it, like you would a hot cup of tea, if only it *was* that easy!

CHAPTER 7

The boys are busy Saturday afternoon with interviews and stuff so Sean gives me his bank card and sends me shopping with Jimmie, silly boy! By the time we get back to the hotel, loaded with bags, containing shoes, bags, perfume and a few bits for Sean and Lennon, it's almost six and the boys are back. Sean's sitting on the end of the bed, elbows on his knees, hands clasped together; he looks up at me worriedly as I come through the door. My first thought is that he's pissed off with the amount of money I must've spent as he takes in all of the bags from the designer shops but he did tell me to spend what I like.

"All right babe, did you have a good time?" He smiles up at me but it doesn't reach his eyes.

"It was great, you should see all of the designer label shops they have here, my Mum would just love it, I got you some t-shirts, I spent about five hundred pound, is that all right?"

I rake my teeth over my bottom lip as I wait for his answer. "Yeah, that's fine, I told you to spend whatever you wanted."

"Yeah, I know but I didn't wanna go too mad. What's wrong?"

"What? Nothing."

"Don't lie, what's up?"

He looks up at me through his thick brown lashes and my stomach does a little somersault and my heart picks up speed, he looks sad and I don't think I'm going to like whatever it is he's got to say.

"Come and sit down G." I drop the bags and sit next to him on the bed.

"Sean, you're scaring me, what's wrong?" He takes my left hand in both of his.

"Babe the blokes from the record label that were at the gig last night." He lets out a deep breath. "They didn't like me telling the crowd I was off the market, they want us, they want girls to like us so they want us all to keep quiet about our girlfriends so they don't want me talking about you on stage and dedicating songs to you. I mean, I can sing them and I can say, this song is for Georgia or whatever, I just can't say this song is for my girlfriend, well I can but they would rather I didn't."

Well that's no big deal.

"Okay, well, that's fine, I don't expect you to dedicate songs to me every show I attend and if you want to, just say this song is for G, I'll know what you mean, it doesn't matter, honestly".

His eyes meet mine and I know that there's more,

"What else?" Another big sigh.

"They don't want you in the hospitality room before the show, when the press and the fans are all in there."

"Why, the groupies are all in there, why can't I be?" I remember the suit talking to Lennon and looking in my direction last night now, I bet that's what they were talking about, and I bet that's what Sean and Len where arguing about after the show.

"I know, I know G and I told them, if you've flown all this way to see me, then there's no way that you're not coming backstage but he still said no way, backstage was now for wives and fiancés and family members only."

He turns his head toward me, his brown eyes, with their tiny flecks of amber and gold look deep into mine, through mine, into me, my heart, and my soul. "What is it Sean, what? Tell me?"

He slides off the bed and kneels in front of me; oh God, what's he done, is he about to beg me for forgiveness for something? "I went to the shops too while you were out G."

"Did you?" My words come out as a whisper, I can barely breathe, I'm so scared of what he's about to tell me, from beside him on the bed, he lifts a box and opens it.

Fucking hell.

I want my Mum.

"I was going to wait and ask your Dad properly and do this once we are back in England but I'm not having you barred from the hospitality rooms before the show, we always knew we would do this, this is just a bit sooner."

I want my Dad.

I want to cry.

"Georgia Rae Layton, I've loved you since the very first day I set eyes on you and your pink polka dot knickers, you are my world. I know we're young, but I love you Gia, I want to make beautiful babies with you. I know people are going to be against this but they don't know what we know, they don't feel what we feel, I want to grow old with you G, I want to marry you. Please, would you do the honour of becoming my Wife?'

It's a ring.

It's a big fat fuck off diamond ring.

He's bought it.

For me.

He wants to marry me!

I wipe a tear from my cheek that I didn't realise had escaped; I look from the ring up to his eyes and nod.

My Parents are going to kill me.

Then my brothers will probably kill me too.

And then they will kill Sean.

Shit, my Dad and my brothers.

Will kill Sean…

"Georgia?"

"Hmm?"

"I'm shitting myself here G."

"Yes, yes, yes, of course I'll marry you, yes!"

I wipe more tears from my face as he slides the solitaire diamond ring along my shaking finger, it fits perfectly. I look down at my hand.

"Do you like it?"

"I love it, is it white gold?"

"No, it's platinum, two carats of diamond."

"Two carats? Sean, it must of cost a fortune."

"It fucking did!" He laughs, I don't know why he laughs but I laugh with him.

He brushes my tears off my cheeks with the back of his hand and pulls me down onto his lap so that I'm straddling him and kisses me gently on the mouth. "But I love ya G so it was worth it, especially now you've become so good at BJ's, we have about fifty minutes before we leave for the venue, any chance of a quick shag?'

"I reckon two carats of diamond has got to be worth a quick something."

We have the quickest quickie ever, shower, change and make it downstairs to the bar only ten minutes late; the rest of the boys are waiting and moaning about us being late. We have decided to tell no one except the rep from the record label about our engagement. Sean wants to get back to England and speak to my Dad before he tells my brothers or anyone else and I'm fine with that. I'm more than fine, I'm crapping myself at what my brothers are going to say so the longer we can keep our news secret, the better as far as I'm concerned.

CHAPTER 8

The record label rep isn't impressed with Sean's news and has asked if it can be kept quiet until after the album launch, which suits us fine, he in turn agrees to keep it quiet from the rest of the band and allows me back into the hospitality room, before and after any shows.

The rest of our time in Spain goes far too quickly and all too soon we are back at the airport; the band are leaving for Germany that afternoon and Sean has promised to call me tonight to let me know they've arrived safely, we kiss, I cry and eventually Jimmie and Lennon drag us apart so that we can board our flight. I desperately want to meet up with him in France next weekend but we have our English O level exam on Monday morning so I know there isn't a lot of chance my Mum and Dad are going to say 'yes', but I can try. If not, it will only be one more week and the boys will be home for two whole weeks before they start the UK tour and the album is launched, and in between all of that, we will announce our engagement. Engaged! I'm sixteen, about to leave school and I'm engaged, to be married, to Sean McCarthy, the only boy I have and will ever love.

By the time I get home Monday, I'm exhausted, I chat with my parents at the dinner table, I don't really want to eat but my Mum has gone to a lot of trouble and cooked salmon, my favourite, so I make the effort. Eventually I make my excuses and go up for a shower, I wash myself as quickly as possible in case Sean rings and I miss it, I throw on my jarmies and lay on top of my bed with my music playing down low so I can hear the phone. We're lucky in our house, we have four phones but none of them are in my bedroom, the nearest is on the landing, a whole five steps away. I keep my bedroom door open and try to do the same with my eyes but I must lose the battle as the next thing I remember is waking up to bright sunlight, on top of my bed with a blanket over me, my bedroom door is closed. I turn and look at my clock radio, it's six thirty eight in the morning. I jump up and run down stairs, my parents are both sitting out on the patio drinking coffee.

"Morning Princess," my Dad says looking up from his paper, he folds it and holds his arms open for me to go and sit on his lap. It's a routine we've followed for my entire life but he's rarely here in the mornings now as I get up so much later. I wrap my arms around his neck.

"Morning Daddy, Mum, did Sean ring last night?"

"No babe, we came to bed about eleven and you were soundo, so I turned off your music and covered you with a blanket." She tilts her head and looks at me. "Marley or Lennon didn't call either; perhaps the boys were just tired after all the travelling and had an early night."

"Yeah, perhaps." But I knew they hadn't, even then, I knew something wasn't right but until the call came, I had no idea how very far from right things actually were and how wrong things would now always be.

I heard nothing at all until Thursday night; I'd given up waiting for Sean's call for another night and was just at the top of the stairs on my way to bed when the phone rang, I stared at it for a few seconds before picking it up.

"Hello."

"Georgia?"

"Sean, what's wrong?"

"I love you G."

He was crying.

"Sean, what's wrong?"

"I'm so sorry G, I love you, just know that, just hold on to that fact, I love you, I will always love you."

"Sean, you're scaring me, what's wrong…?"

I was crying myself now and almost screaming in complete panic at him down the phone.

"I love you G, always, wherever I am, whatever I'm doing, it will always only ever be you."

"Sean, Sean?"

The line went dead.

I held onto the phone as I slid down the wall, my legs couldn't hold me up, my heart was pounding so hard I could feel it throughout my entire body; I don't know how long I'd been sitting there when my Mum slid down the wall next to me, I became aware of the phone bleeping, still in my hand. My Mum took it from me and placed it back on the hook.

"What's wrong George, what's wrong with Sean?"

I shook my head at her, and then I shrugged. "I don't know but I have a feeling it's something bad. Mum, can Dad get the number of the hotel and talk to Lennon, something's wrong and I'm really scared." I threw myself into her arms, I felt sick with fear and I just wanted my Mum.

"Shush baby girl, what did he say? Frank, can you get up here."

My Dad was there in an instant. "What the fucks wrong, who was on the phone, Georgia, who's upset ya Princess?"

"Daddy, please phone Lennon, I can't remember if they are in France or Germany or in a hotel or on the bus, I can't remember but something's wrong, something's not right, Sean was crying and saying sorry, find out for me Daddy, find the boys and sort it out for me, please."

My Dad was kneeling in front of me and I was gripping his shirt in my fists, I had tears but I wasn't actually crying, I was hysterical but I had no idea why!

"Calm yourself down Princess, I will make some calls and see what I can find out, you know the boys, they've probably had too much to drink and are just messing about, go and get into bed and I'll have it all sorted out by the morning."

I shook my head. "No, I want to wait up, I won't sleep, I need to know he's okay, that they're all okay."

My Dad cupped my face in his hands and kissed my forehead, he was my Dad, I was his Princess, he would make everything right, he always did.

I curled under a blanket on the sofa with my Mum, my Dad made calls for what seemed like hours, at about two in the morning he came and sat in his favourite armchair with a coffee in his hand. "I've left messages everywhere George, with the record label and with the lawyers, they landed in France this morning, they have a night off tonight and I've called the hotel but none of them are in their rooms. If there was anything wrong, with any of the boys, Lennon would have called, I know he would." I nodded at him, despite what he said, I still had this horrible knot of dread pulling tight in my stomach.

"George, let's go and get in bed, Dad will wait up for the phone and come and get us when someone calls." My Mum looked exhausted but I knew she wouldn't go to bed unless I did, she held out her hand to me and I took it, following her up the stairs to my bed, we both got in and I laid with my head on her chest like I used to when I was a little girl and let the slow steady rhythm of her heartbeat and the familiar smell of her Dior perfume soothe me to sleep.

I woke to the sound of my Dad shouting, the sun was streaming through my bedroom window and I blinked a few times as I looked around my room. Glancing at my clock I noticed it was just after eight fifteen, I'd actually managed to sleep quite a long time, I suddenly heard what sounded like my Mum crying and my stomach lurched. I flew out of bed and down to the kitchen, it was full of my Dad's blokes, I don't know exactly what they did but they'd all been working for him for as long as I can remember. My Dad was talking on the phone and pacing the kitchen floor, the lead stretched from the wall past Marcus, my Dad's lawyer where he was sitting at the breakfast bar, Nick was sitting next to him. He drove my Dad around sometimes, standing talking to him was Tony who looked after security at a couple of pubs my Dad had recently bought and standing in the middle of the room, with his arms wrapped around my Mum as she cried into his chest, was my Dad's brother, my uncle Fin. The whole room fell silent when I walked in.

"Mum?" My Dad's eyes shot up to meet mine and he looked me up and down, I'd jumped out of bed in such a hurry and not expecting a house full of men, I hadn't thought about the fact I was wearing just a t-shirt and a pair of knickers. I blushed as I knew my

Dad would be angry, he was very old fashioned about what I wore, even around the house.

"For fuck's sake Georgia, go and put some clothes on!"

"What's going on, Mum, why are you crying?"

My Dad raked his hand through his hair, I noticed he was still wearing yesterday's clothes and he hadn't shaved. "Get some clothes on George, we'll talk then."

I turned to walk up the stairs and as I did I heard Marcus say, "What are you going to tell her?"

"I have no fucking idea," Dad replied and the knot of dread and fear pulled even tighter in my belly.

I threw on a pair of joggers and an old sweatshirt of Sean's that I'd never washed, it smelt more of me now than it did of him but I refused to let my Mum wash it regardless. I was back down in the kitchen in less than a minute, everyone's eyes were back on me as I re-entered the room; my Mum was sitting down at our big dining table drinking a cup of tea, my Dad gestured with his chin. "Sit down George, we need to talk."

I shook my head, I was so scared, my feet were rooted to the floor, so many thoughts were rushing through my mind. "Daddy, did one of the boys die, is Sean or Marley dead Daddy?"

He rushed toward me and held me in his big arms and I sunk into his chest, he squeezed me tight, then walked me over to the dining table and sat me in the chair next to my Mum, she reached out and held my hand, I looked from her to my Dad, who was now sitting the other side of me. I wanted to hear the words, I wanted someone to tell me what had happened but at the same time I didn't, if they were going to spoil my perfect life, my perfect love and my perfect future, then I didn't ever want to hear them, I could see my Dad was struggling, he rubbed his hands over his dark stubble continuously.

"Georgia, there's been some trouble… "

"NO!" My Dad roared at Marcus as he started to speak, "I will do this, you keep the fuck quiet."

My Dad was a big man, six feet three or four I couldn't remember which, I just knew that whenever I bought him a shirt as a gift he needed an eighteen collar to fit his chest, he was a big man but until that moment, I'd never, ever in my life been scared of him, he took my free hand in his. "Look George, there's no easy way to say this, there's been some trouble on the tour, the boys got into Paris yesterday, checked into their hotel and ended up having a bit of a party around the pool, things got a bit wild and it ended up back at Marley's and Sean's room, some allegations have been made and Sean and Marley have been arrested"

"What?"

"Things just got a bit out of hand, I'm gonna fly over there this afternoon with Marcus and some legal geezers from the record label and try and sort this mess out."

"Arrested for what, what did they do, was it drugs?" My Dad looked down at our joined hands and I followed his stare, my Mum reached over and put her hand on top of Dad's so the three of us were touching, I looked back up at my Dad and he shook his head.

"Rape, Georgia, they've both been charged with rape and a few other lesser things."

Rape?

"What, rape? Na, na, no way, this is Marley and Sean Dad, they wouldn't rape any one. Why would they? Why would Sean?"

"I don't know all the details, they're not telling us much over the phone, that's why I need to get there with the briefs and sort things out."

Rape. I was numb, what on earth could have happened that would've led to a rape charge? "I'm coming with you."

"NO!" My parents both said at the same time.

"No George, I need you to stay here and look after your Mum, we'll have this sorted in no time, once we do, then we'll get you over to see them, besides, they're holding them in cells at a Police station right now. Let me go and get it all sorted, then perhaps you can fly over next week, once your English exam is out of the way."

He rubbed his thumb over my cheek, then lent forward and kissed my nose, before standing and heading off to the shower. I sat at the dining table, staring blankly at my Mum's hand holding mine, I felt sick, I felt scared, I felt a little bit angry and for the first time ever in my life, I doubted my Dad's ability to be able to make everything right. The front door bell rang and I jumped, my Mum stood from the table, squeezing my shoulder on her way to answering the door.

I could hear my Mum talking quietly to someone, then Jimmie appeared in front of me. "George," is all she said as I stood from the table and we hugged.

"What a fucking mess George, I didn't know until early this morning and I didn't want to call, in case you hadn't heard, she's a fucking bitch, I don't believe a word of it."

My stomach hit the floor and my heart stuttered in my chest. "Who Jim?" She looked from me to my Mum and frowned.

"Who Jim?" I repeated.

"Haley the whore."

"It's Haley the whore who's saying she was raped. How? Why would she say that, was… was she in their room Jim?" My best friend steps toward me and in my head I'm begging her not to lie to me but in my heart, I'm begging her to protect me from the truth.

"Let's go up to your room George." I let out a deep breath and follow her up to my bedroom, I'm freezing so I climb under the quilt and Jimmie joins me.

"I won't lie to you George, this is what Lennon told me; the boys left Spain Monday after us, they had no gig that night and all went to a party that Rocco threw in his room, Len said it was madness, women, drugs and drink, the usual KR sort of a do, the room was trashed and everyone was suffering the next day."

"Including Sean?" I don't know why I ask, I know what the answer is going to be.

"Including Sean and the rest of the band," she nods as she speaks. "They played so bad that night that Len orders them straight back to their room Tuesday night and bars any calls from being made from their rooms so that they can't order in booze or drugs or girls. Wednesday they are on lock down and only allowed to rehearse and sound check, then straight back to the room after the show. They flew into Paris Thursday morning and Marley and Lennon have a big bust up. Marls goes straight to the bar with Rocco and the rest of KR, Sean joins them after a while, they take over the pool area, Rocco calls up girls from everywhere. Apparently Haley flew in around lunch time and started partying with them and was all over Sean and Marley, and they all went back to their room at about seven o'clock, they were all pissed and all off their tits on Charlie, whizz and trips. Next thing Len knows is Haley's on the landing, screaming the place down, stark bollock naked and saying that she wants the Police called because Sean and Marley have taken it in turns to rape her. Hotel management call the Police, everyone makes statements and Maca and Marls are taken away."

She's still talking as I jump off the bed and into my bathroom and throw my stomach contents down the toilet, Jimmies behind me, holding my hair back, then rinses out a flannel and puts it on the back of my neck. I stay on my knees for a few minutes and wait for the room to stop spinning and Jim passes me a glass of water, I rinse my mouth and spit into the toilet, before sitting back down on my bed.

"Why was she in their room?"

"I don't know George, I only know what I've told ya, nothing else, Lens gonna ring here as soon as he knows anything, he's not been allowed to speak with the boys yet but he said the label are flying their lawyers out there."

I nod. "Yeah, my Dad's going too."

"Why was she in their room Jim, I just can't see why she needed to be there? Unless they were all shagging."

"Don't George, don't do this to yourself until we know all the details, this is Whorely we're talking about, she would do anything for her five minutes of fame, you know that."

"Yeah and I also know that she's been after Sean forever and I also know that Sean should never have had a girl in his room, if Marley bought her back, then he should have gone to Len's room, not stayed there with them, with her."

I was angry now, fuck him, if he wanted the rock and roll life style, then fuck him, he could have it but there was no way I was going to sit at home like the dutiful little wifey while he shagged whores and snorted lines of coke. Serves him right if he was locked up, there was no way I was flying out to be with him now, let him sweat a bit. I went over to my bedside drawer and pulled out my engagement ring and held it up to Jimmie. "He proposed Jim, Saturday night before the show, he asked me to marry him, we were keeping it secret until he got home and could ask my Dad and we could do it properly."

I looked from my best friend to my ring. "Oh my god George, it's huge, put it on."

I couldn't, not now. I shook my head. "No, no way, until he's stood in front of me and gives me his version of events, until he looks me in the eyes and tells me nothing happened with that slut, then I don't want to talk to or hear from him."

"Don't be stupid G, you don't mean that." She laughs nervously at me.

"Oh I fucking mean it Jim, this is only the start, they've not even made the big time yet and already there are problems with whores and coke, if that's the life he wants, then he can take it, I won't be waiting at home for him while he does all that shit."

"George, he wouldn't, he loves you, he wants to marry you, fucking hell, don't be so harsh, it was probably all Marley's fault anyway, you saw him at the weekend, he's so charlied up all the time, he doesn't know what he's doing." Even as she spoke I could feel the little man in my chest, with his trowel, his bricks and his little pile of cement, he was building a wall around my heart, to protect it from what was to come.

The next few days were horrible, the worst I had ever endured in my short life, days that would change me forever.

My Dad and the lawyers had the boys out of custody and performing on stage by Friday night. I heard nothing from Sean all day Saturday, my Dad phoned Saturday afternoon to tell us that Haley had withdrawn the allegations and had actually admitted to being the owner of all the drugs that were found in the room. The boys had no gigs until Wednesday night in Stockholm so straight after the show Saturday night, they were going to fly back to England for a couple of days, I thought Sean would have phoned before they left but I heard nothing and was becoming more and more pissed off with him.

My Mum, Jimmie and I went for an Indian Saturday night and drank two bottles of wine, Jimmie and I were fine but my little skinny Mum, who wasn't a big drinker, was absolutely hilarious when we got home and started playing records. The three of us danced around my parent's front room and sang into whisks and spoons before collapsing on the sofa in a fit of giggles. I was barely hanging on, I was heartbroken, I was sad, I felt like Sean had abandoned me for this new life but I refused point blank to let anyone know how I was feeling and just pretended that my tears were from laughter and not because my heart was shattered.

Our front door unlocked at about two thirty that morning, my Mum was sleeping in my Dad's armchair and Jimmie and I were on each end of the sofa when I felt soft lips brush against mine, my eyes fluttered open and it took me a few seconds to realise he was really there and I wasn't dreaming. I don't know why I did it but for some reason I pushed myself by my heals away from him, backing myself into the corner of the sofa, his beautiful face fell and he held his breath for a few seconds, his face still close enough for me to watch as he closed his big chocolate eyes and to marvel at his long, dark lashes that fanned his cheeks.

"Georgia, I'm so, so sorry." I folded my arms across my chest and nodded at him. My Mum stood from the chair gave a cuddle to my Dad and Lennon, Marley had gone into the kitchen area and was sitting at the breakfast bar, I watched as my parents exchanged a look, then both looked at my brother, I stood and gave Len a cuddle, but I ignored Marley.

"Well, now you're all home safe, I'm going to bed, night, night."

"Georgia wait, we need to talk." He looked tired and delicious and I loved him so much but I was hurt and angry.

"Do we?"

He turned and looked at my Dad. "Frank, dya mind if we go up to Georgia's room so we can talk?"

My Dad's eyes shifted to mine, "George?" he asked with eyebrows raised.

"Fine," I huffed, I knew I was behaving like a complete brat but basically, that's what I was, a sixteen year old brat, a really pissed off brat.

I threw myself on my bed, scooted up and sat with my back against the headboard; Sean lent on my closed bedroom door. "I didn't do it G."

"I didn't think you did."

"So why are you so pissed off with me?"

"Why was she in your room Sean?" He looks down at the floor and shakes his head.

"I was so drunk G, I'd done a couple of lines of coke, Marley wanted to get hold of her but she wouldn't come back to the room unless I went."

"Why?"

"Why what?"

"Why did she want you to go back with them?"

He takes a few steps toward my bed, "George."

"Why Sean, tell me why?" He sits on the edge of my bed and looks at me.

"She wanted a threesome." I wanted to be sick, I wanted to punch him, and I wanted to kill her.

"And you went?' He nodded.

"I'm so sorry G, I was off my face."

"You were drunk and off your face and you went back to your room with Marley and Haley the whore for a threesome?"

"I didn't know what I was doing G, I went back so that Marley could get hold of her, then I was just gonna leave them to it…" he trailed off.

It suddenly struck me, I wasn't crying, I hadn't cried since he called me Thursday night, I was hurt and angry and emotional but I didn't cry, I just let that little man keep building that wall, higher and higher, one course at a time.

"So what happened?" He drags his hands through his hair and I want to do the same but I won't, I can't, I need him to look me in the eye as he explains what happened, I need him to tell me that he didn't touch her, that he never laid a finger on her. I sit and stare at him for a few long moments and notice that his hair is almost perfectly straight now, the curls that he had when we first met have gone, he's wearing it longer again. When did it grow? When did his curls disappear? It's a simple observation but one that makes me realise he's changing and because he's not with me, I'm not noticing, I'm not part of his everyday world, this boy who's skin I have known as well as my own these past few years has grown and changed and he's done it all without me.

"I was so drunk."

No! Please no.

"As soon as the door slammed shut behind us, she was on me."

Oh Sean!

"She was on you?" He nods as he covers his face with his hands, his elbows resting on his knees, he's sitting on the edge of my bed, angled toward me, his skin looks tanned, obviously from the time he's spent in the sun these past few weeks, in the sun, around a pool, without me. Every single beat of my heart hurts, it echoes through my body and wherever it reaches, it causes pain, I don't want it to hurt, I don't want it to feel, I would rather it just stopped.

"How, how was she on you?" This time he shakes his head.

"Rocco had these pills, I only had one, Marley had a couple, they were, they made me feel fantastic, we danced for ages down by the pool, everything just felt good and I just felt so horny."

"No, no, no! Get out, get out Sean, I don't want to hear this."

My stupid, stupid, naive, sixteen year old heart has now ceased to exist and something hard, harsh and cold is slowly taking its place but before it does, I need him to shut up and I need him to leave. Now!

"I love you G, you, no one else, no one else ever, please listen to me, it was the drugs, I just couldn't stop, I couldn't…"

Now it was time for me to cover my face with my hands, I wanted to scream, I wanted to cry, I wanted to die. I slid off the bed and took my engagement ring from its hiding place and held it out to him.

"What are you doing? I don't want that, it's yours, I bought it for you G, I spoke to your Dad on the flight, he's fine with it, he knew, he was expecting it, put it on, put it on and we can go down and tell everyone. G, put your ring on please." He's talking so fast but all I can hear is the phone ringing and my Dad shouting, then Marley's shouting and the front door slams. My Dad and Marls are still shouting at each other and I just stand there, with the stupid, ugly ring between my thumb and index finger. I've barely eaten a thing all week and I feel light headed, the room is swaying and I want to be sick. Then my bedroom door flies open and Jimmie is there, she looks from me to Sean.

"What did you do, what did you do? You stupid fucker!" She launches herself at him, punching and kicking and screaming and I just continue to stand there holding the ring out to him.

Lennon comes in and pulls Jimmie off of Sean. "Leave it Jim, let them sort it out, it's between them."

"There's pictures, there's pictures you fucker!" Jimmie screams as she tries to fight her way out of Lennon's arms. Sean stands up from where Jimmie knocked him back onto my bed and looks at Len.

"What, what are you talking about, what pictures?"

"She's got pictures of what you were doing, pictures of you and Marley snorting Charlie off her tits and she's sold them to the papers, you're all over the Sunday papers you fucker!"

My world stops spinning, the little man lays his last brick and my heart stops beating the way that it used to, it's enclosed safely behind a wall now, so it doesn't feel, it doesn't love, it doesn't care anymore, it's only use now is to keep me alive and I really don't care if it even bothers to do that. Sean's big brown eyes with their flecks of gold turn and meet mine but I can't focus, I feel my legs give way and the floor starts to come toward me.

CHAPTER 9

I don't pass out cold completely, everything just becomes hazy and I have no control or strength in my limbs. I'm aware of lots of shouting, Sean lifts me onto my bed, my Mum is crying, Jimmie is shouting and my Dad is arguing with Sean right over my head, as I look through it all, the noise, the faces, all I can see is Marley, standing in my bedroom door, sobbing. It's a sight that will stay with me till the day I die.

My Dad tells Sean to leave, which eventually he does but only because Len drags him out of my room. I don't know if he's gone home or just down stairs, I don't care, I just can't be near him now. My Mum makes me drink hot sweet tea and it does actually make me feel a little better.

Everyone except Jimmie and my Mum finally leave my room, I lay on my side, curled into the foetal position, not making eye contact with either of them. My Mum is fussing around me and talking too much, finally she kneels down in front of me and strokes my hair. "Can I get you anything Georgia, a drink, something to eat; do you want your music on?" I shake my head.

"No Mum, I'm fine, could you just leave me on my own, thank you for looking after me but honestly, I'm fine, you need to go and get some sleep."

She shakes her head back at me. "Oh George, there'll be no sleeping here, the sun's nearly up and your Dad has sent Tony and Nick out for the first editions of the papers so he can see what the damage is." Jimmie fidgets next to me on the bed, she knows I don't want to talk, hear or see anything to do with what the papers are saying, the story, the charges or events of the past few days.

"Mum, you can do one thing for me."

"What's that George?"

"I don't want to see those newspapers, I don't want to know what's in them, I don't want to see, or hear about them ever and I do not want to see Sean."

"Georgia, babe, don't you think you should wait and find out first? It could be nothing; you know how the papers like to make things up."

"Mum, please, I know Sean, I know him inside out and something went on in that room, I'm not saying the boys raped her, I don't believe that for a second, but he couldn't look me in the eye last night, he didn't tell me something did go on but he couldn't tell me that it didn't and I can't live with that Mum. If he's having threesomes with girls in hotel rooms now, what's it gonna be like when they're really famous? It's done, we're over, he can go and live the life he's been dreaming of and working so hard for all these years, he's let me down and I don't trust him, I don't want to see him again, please Mum, I can't see him."

I amaze myself by not crying, my Mum kisses my cheek. "Oh Georgia, I'm so sorry, I wish I could make it all better for ya babe."

"You can make it better by hiding it all away from me Mum, I don't want to talk about it, I don't want to talk about the band or their music or what they're doing, and as far as I'm concerned they don't exist."

She lets out a big sigh. "I'll do my best George but with your brothers being so involved, it won't be easy but I'll try."

She stands up and heads out the door. Jimmie has said nothing from where she's sitting on my bed behind me, I know she thinks I'm being harsh and over reacting but I've got to, it's the only way I know how to protect myself.

"George?" she whispers, as if she's been listening to my thoughts.

"Yeah?"

"I love you George, I'll do my best to not talk about this or the band or the boys but it's going to be so hard and I don't want to lose you as a friend if I slip up and say something by mistake."

I shake my head. "You won't lose me as a friend Jim, you're my best friend and you always will be and I understand if this makes things difficult but please just do what you can to save me from this. I can't see him Jim, it hurts too much, I can't see those pictures, I don't want to know what happened that night, ever, so please, as my friend Jim, as my best friend, would you please try and help me with that."

"Of course I will, forever G, I'll keep it from you forever, unless you ask me otherwise."

"Thank you."

We lay on my bed, spooning, until eventually we must drift off to sleep as the birds start singing.

The next few weeks of my life were a complete nightmare; by Sunday afternoon we had the press hanging about outside our house, trying to get pictures of Marley at first, then trying to get pictures of me, because somehow they had been tipped off that I was Sean's girlfriend. I finished the last of my exams with Tony driving me to and from school, other than that, I never left the house. Sean sat outside for the few days that they were home, he hid in his car so the press wouldn't see him, I have no idea what he thought it would achieve. He rang my house almost hourly, even when they flew to Sweden for the last few shows of the tour before coming back to England. In the end my Dad told him not to call anymore otherwise he would get the number changed.

Whoever came up with the phrase 'No publicity is bad publicity' wasn't wrong; the boys album launch was a worldwide success, on the back of all the newspaper headlines, they shot straight to number one. We had more press than ever camped outside the house, as well as the silly little fan girls; the label had to hire minders for the boys and as they were now back in England before the UK leg of the tour kicked off, there was absolute pandemonium down our street every time Marley tried to leave the house. I received untold amounts of hate mail through the post and even had an envelope full of dog shit shoved through the letter box addressed to me. All the crazy little fan girls hated me, they either thought I was still Sean's girlfriend or they hated me because I had apparently broken his heart, I was paying the price for the bands fame and reaped none of the rewards. I had continuous offers from tabloids and magazines to sell my story to them; they wanted to know all about my life as the sister and girlfriend of one of the biggest bands in Britain right now. I even had offers to pose topless, my Dad hit the roof and I became an absolute recluse. I knew the very little I did about the bands success because they received so much airtime on the television; I had stopped listening to the radio so as to avoid their songs. In fact I had stopped listening to music all together but I couldn't make the whole family stop watching the telly, my parents were good and would quickly turn it over or the radio off if I came in the room if something was playing or being mentioned, other than that, I pretty much managed to avoid all contact with anything band related. I didn't look at the papers, I stopped reading my magazines, I rarely left my room and that's how it stayed the entire summer. I didn't see much of Jimmie as she travelled around Britain with the band so that she could be with Lennon. I was jealous, incredibly so, but that was my issue and I knew it was wrong of me, I tried to be upbeat and chatty whenever she called but I was dying inside and so, so lonely; I hadn't spoken to Marley since we left Spain, on the rare occasions he did come home. I would wake up sometimes and find him standing in the doorway of my bedroom, I would then get up silently and close it in his face, I had nothing to say to him, as far as I was concerned, he had ruined my life, my beautiful, perfect life, that Sean and I had planned out together was over, all because of Marley, Haley The Whore and drugs and I wasn't yet ready to talk to my brother about any of it.

My parents desperately wanted me to go back to school in September and start my A levels, I got outstanding results in my O levels and knew that my A's would be no problem. The problem was, I was terrified of going back, I didn't know how I'd be received and I would be all alone for the first time in my entire secondary school life, I would just be Georgia Layton and not Sean McCarthy's girlfriend and I knew there would be plenty of nasty little bitches that would be over the moon about that.

I finally agreed with my parents that I would go and give it a try and as it turned out, the years of not being a bitch to the other girls at school paid off, there were a few spiteful comments but mostly people were still okay with me just because I still had links with the band. I spent the next two years studying for my Maths and English A levels, as well as a business studies course. I threw myself into my studies and completely shut out the rest of the world; the only person I really had anything to do with at school was Ashley. She had stayed on to re-sit her maths and English O levels as she had failed them miserably last year, we weren't in any classes together but it was nice to have at least one person to talk to around the school, she asked me to go out with her practically every weekend but I always said no.

All of my time was taken up with studying, going to the gym that my Dad had just bought in Brentwood or helping my Mum out in the shop my Dad had bought for in the local high street. My Mum had always had fantastic fashion sense and absolutely loved clothes so when my Dad came home and told her he'd helped out a mate by taking his struggling business off his hands, she barely listened. My Dad seemed to have so many businesses on the go it was hard to keep track, but then my Dad happened to mention that it was a frock shop as he called it, my Mum was all ears.

The following day was a Saturday so my Mum and I went down and had a look, it was a good sized shop in a fantastic location but it had a terrible range of stock. We lived in an affluent area, the shop had a high end hairdressers and beauty salon on one side and a bespoke furniture designers on the other, the shop itself sold absolute crap, cheap, nasty 'fashion' items; just the name 'Hollywood Fashions' would be enough to put off most of the women who would frequent the shops either side.

By that afternoon, my Mum had one of my Dad's draughtsmen who worked for his building company around, giving her advice on the changes she wanted to make. It took her around two months to have the place re-fitted, re-named and stocked with an up to the minute range of designer labels, by the time I'd finished with college, between us we were running a very successful business and had extended into the furniture shop next door. My Dad having somehow convinced the owners to relocate to another shop he owned, further down the high street. I'd been on numerous buying trips with my Mum, spending time in Europe and Asia and in the summer of 1987 we opened our second shop in Chingford; while my Mum took over the opening of the new store, I took up the reins of the Brentwood store. Not only were we selling clothing but we now offered a full range of accessories, including, shoes, handbags, scarves and sunglasses and had seven girls working for us. Despite the fact that I had zero social life, I was always busy and had little time to think about how dead I was inside; it had been over two years since I'd seen or heard from Sean but it still hurt like it was five minutes ago. I'd come to terms with the fact that it would probably always hurt but I still wasn't ready to face the world. I'd barely spoken a few words to Marley in that time and that was only because I was being polite at the Christmas dinner table last year, a few days before then, Lennon had asked me if it would be okay to invite Sean to have lunch with us as he had nowhere to go. I apologised to Len but explained that I just couldn't, just the thought of seeing him made me want to vomit, not because I disliked him but because I still loved him so very, very much, Len said that he understood, but I doubt that he actually had any idea.

Finally in the August of '88, I ended my self-imposed social isolation and went for a drink after work with Ashley; she was working for us now, we had three shops and were due to be opening a fourth before Christmas in Epping, we had managers in all of them and my Mum and I spent most of our time with buyers and now some small independent designers, who made stuff exclusively for us. Our range now including a few lines for men and underwear for both men and women, I had an office above the Brentwood shop and would soon be moving into my very own flat there as well. The tenants that were already in place had given notice and I'd convinced my Dad to fix it up and let me move in, Ash wanted to move in with me but I wanted to live alone, that way I could control the TV and the radio and anything else that might bring me into contact with Sean and the band, something that had become a complete obsession with me. The band were now world famous, my parents had sold our family home and bought a farm house in the countryside just outside of Brentwood, Lennon and Jimmie had bought their own place and were getting married next year and Marley had bought a place in the city to crash, whenever the band were in the country and I very rarely saw him. Jim and Lennon were only living around the corner so finally I got to see her on a regular basis again; she was working alongside Len as part of the management team for the band and so got to travel with him whenever she wanted to. I had dinner and caught up with them at least three or four times a month and they were always good in avoiding any mention of Sean and the band if possible, I had called Jim that afternoon and invited her for drinks tonight and she was going to meet us there.

My palms were sweating and I felt absolutely sick as we walked into the wine bar that night. I was glad we'd come somewhere up market and swanky as this, it was as far removed from the sweaty pubs I used to go to with the band as you could get. Full of big hair, shoulder pads and yuppies and yet, here I was, still thinking about him. I was almost twenty and still fucked up over a boy I met when I was eleven. I heard a loud squeal as we headed for the bar and saw that Jimmie was already here. She jumped up from her stool at the tall round table as she spotted us; she knew what a big deal this was for me. I'd driven my parents insane with worry these past few years and I knew they'd asked her to do what she could to get me out of the house but Jimmie knew nothing would work, she knew I'd do it in my own time and she was right, the time was now and here I was.

She threw her arms around me and whispered into my ear, "I am so fucking proud of you Georgia Layton, so fucking proud." I almost teared up, something I hadn't allowed myself to do since that fuck awful week my world fell apart.

Because Thursday was our late night, we hadn't closed the shop up until seven, by the time we had touched up our makeup and titivated as my Dad liked to call it, then walked up the high street to the wine bar, it was around seven thirty. The place was now packed full of the after work crowd from the city, double breasted suits and mullets, so not my type! We joined Jimmie at the table, as she poured us a glass of wine each from the bottle she had in a cooler, we sat and chatted and caught up, knocking back the first bottle in ten minutes.

Ash got up and went to the bar to buy another and as soon as she left, Jimmie grabbed my hand. "George, I really need to talk to you and it's about the banned subject." My stomach lurched.

"Is it about him or the band or something different?"

"It's about 'that' night. I found a few things out today at work, things I really think you should know."

"Will it change anything, will it fix this horrible fucking pain I have in my chest Jim, will it make it possible to hear his name, say his name even, without me wanting to pass out."

"Oh George, is it still that bad?" I nod my head.

"Yep, every second of every day." She reaches out and squeezes my hand.

"Then you need to hear what I have to say, because he's in exactly the same state you are."

Fuck!

"What?"

"He's a mess G, a complete fucking mess, he gets up on that stage or in front of a camera and he's big bad Maca but as soon as the show is over, all he wants is you. He does the interviews, smiles for the cameras, stays for five minutes at the after show parties and then he goes home, he still loves you George and he misses you so much."

My hand instinctively reaches up to the delicate silver necklace I still wear, it's the only part of him that I've allowed to stay in my life and that's only because I can't actually see it, well I can if I look in a mirror but it's been there so long now, that I don't really notice it, it's part of me, of who I am, exactly like he is.

"Why didn't you tell me this before?"

My head is spinning and it's not because of the wine.

"Because it's what you wanted, because, until today, I thought you were right, I thought you had every right to stay away from him, I thought it was the right thing for you but now I'm not so sure."

Ashley came back at that moment, with another bottle of wine and a bottle of champagne, which she waved in front of her. "This ladies, is compliments of the gentleman at the bar."

A barman appeared at our table with three champagne flutes and proceeded to pop the cork and fill the glasses. We thanked him and turned around to thank the blokes at the bar; there were four of them. One looked like he'd just come from the golf course, one looked like he'd just come from the gym and the other two from the office, one in a suit, one in a pair of dark fitted trousers and a white shirt, his sleeves rolled up to the elbows, he had his back to me and I couldn't see his face but I could see he had a lovely arse and shiny black hair It was quite long but not cut in the mullet that everyone seemed to be favouring at the moment, just long and pushed back, he was tall, very tall, with a broad back and shoulders. I smiled politely at all the others, mouthed cheers and tilted my glass toward them, just as I was about to look away, he turned and his eyes met mine.

Fuck!

My heart gave a little judder, it was like after three years, it was letting me know it was there and capable of doing more than just keeping me alive but I didn't want it to, I wanted it to focus on just one job, doing nothing *but* keeping me alive. I didn't want it to feel and I certainly didn't want it to react. His brown eyes remained locked on mine as I took a swig of my drink and as I did, he smiled, very slightly at me with his soft, full lips and once again, my heart stopped for a split second and then picked up its rhythm in my chest.

Fuck!

Fuck!

And fuck!

"Fuck G, he's nice." Jimmie nudged me and I almost spat my drink out as she said out loud, exactly what I had been thinking.

I noticed that he laughed as he watched me wipe champagne from my chin and his eyebrows rose slightly as I sucked it off the side of my finger, he shook his head and looked away and for the very first time in three long years. I felt the stirrings of desire, deep down in my belly and I knew that I had to stay the fuck away from this man; because there was no way that I would ever get involved with anyone who stirred that kind of reaction in me again. Ever.

After drinking the bubbly and the bottle of wine, Ashley stayed at the wine bar with some friends, while Jimmie and I jumped in a taxi and went back to her house. Lennon was in front of the telly watching a video of the band and as I stepped through the living room door, there, filling the screen, in all his glorious beauty was the love of my life. The room swayed as I quickly closed my eyes for a few moments but something inside me forced them to open and take just one more look, as soon as Len looked over his shoulder and saw me, he ejected the video, then stood as I finally dragged my eyes away from the now blue screen, I noticed that he was smiling at me sadly.

"Sorry George, I didn't realise you were coming back here."

I shrugged my shoulders and let out a deep sigh. "It's okay Len; it's not your fault."

He held out his arms and I walked straight into them; my brothers were all tall, like my Dad and I loved how safe I felt when they wrapped their arms around me, sadly Sean was the one monster my Dad and my brothers weren't able to save me from, I was just going to have to carry on fighting this one on my own. "How are ya George, you really need to put on some weight."

"Yeah thanks Len, good to see you too." He kissed the top of my head.

"Shut up, it's always good to see ya you know that, I just wish that I got to see more of ya, more often. How many times a week are you hitting the gym now?"

I shrugged. "Well we've been busy with work, the new shop opens in Epping at the end of September, so we've been buying in stock and recruiting new staff, so in the last couple of weeks I've only managed a couple of hours three times a week."

"Three times a week, is that all? You need to eat more and gym and work a bit less."

I go to speak but Jimmie comes out of the toilet where she's been since we got back. "Leave her alone Len, she looks fine, you look fine G, skinny as fuck but fine."

I sigh wearily again and shake my head as I sit down in the armchair. "So put the kettle on then Len and get the biscuits out, I'm starving."

I kick off my shoes and tuck my legs under me; Jim sits in the armchair opposite me and does the same. Their house is an old 1930's detached place that my Dad's firm extended and fixed up for them, it has big bay windows to the front and French doors to the back looking out over the huge garden. Their wedding was all booked for June next year and they were going straight in for a baby. I hate to admit that I was jealous but that's the only thing I could think was causing the ache that I felt inside when I thought about the domestic bliss they shared.

"So… " I tried to sound more upbeat than I felt. "What do you need to tell me?"

Len looked over from the open plan kitchen at Jimmie. "You told her?"

"Not yet but I'm about to." She looks warily at me and takes a deep breath.

"I was chatting on the phone today with a girl from Kombat Rocks management team, Carnage are going to tour the States next year and the record label wants KR on the bill for some of the shows. Anyway, Rocco being the wanker that he is, is refusing to be classed as the supporting act, although technically, that's exactly what they'd be doing but he wants it worded something like a double headline concert. Anyway this Carla I'm talking to on the phone is telling me how Rocco is such a knob and how nobody likes him and they can't believe the label would put the two bands together after the way Rocco set Maca and Marley up before, so I'm like, what dya mean, set them up?"

Then she proceeds to tell me that Rocco deliberately got them on ecstasy that day because he knew it would get them horny and off their nuts, then he convinced Whorely to get them back to their room so she could cry rape, he would be there, waiting and taking photos of it all and… it was all, to get back, at you."

I close my eyes and swallow down the bile that keeps making its way up my throat. "The rape cry was just to get the Police involved so that Carnage would hopefully get kicked off the tour. Whorely never had any intention of going through with it so when your Dad turned up and offered her ten grand to drop the charges; she was over the fucking moon, that was just…"

"Whoa, whoa, whoa, back up, my Dad paid her ten grand?"

Lennon puts three cups of tea down on the coffee table, I lean forward and pick mine up, I know it's going to be too hot but I need something to do while I try and absorb all of this info; Len stands in front of me with his hands on his hips and says, “Yeah, didn’t you know that?”

I shake my head. “No, I didn’t, anyway, carry on Jim.” I nod toward her to keep talking.

“Well you know the rest, Rocco sent copies of the pictures to the press and assumed that the images, along with the rape allegations would get Carnage off the tour and would split you and Sean up.”

She shrugged her shoulders. “He had half his wishes come true, the other half had the complete opposite effect, meaning Carnage are now bigger than KR and Rocco is thoroughly pissed off.”

She looks at me and shrugs, I don’t know what she expects me to say, yeah I’m well and truly pissed off that Rocco and Whorely plotted and schemed and got their wish in breaking up Sean and me, but at the end of the day, he did what he did and for me, the issue was never about the rape allegation, I knew that was a lie. I just knew, but Sean going back to the room for a threesome that was the truth, her getting naked and letting them snort blow off of her body, that was the truth and that was what I couldn’t forgive him for.

“Well, thanks for letting me know Jim, I hope if you ever come across either one of that scheming pair of cunts you will smack them right between the eyes for me but at the end of the day, he was there, he was in that room, snorting blow off her tits, just four days after declaring undying love and proposing marriage to me and there are pictures to prove it so it doesn’t change anything. Nothing will change the fact that he was in that room, with that slut, all that’s changed are the circumstances that led to it and yes I am angry that they set him up, but that just goes to show how easy it was for him to go astray, how easily he was tempted.”

I lean forward and dig into the biscuit barrel; I find a Mcvities chocolate digestive and dunk it in my tea. I actually want to curl up in a corner and rock, but I do what I have been doing for the last three years, I shut down my emotions and carry on with my numb little life.

"Do you know how much he still loves you George? He's such a mess on the inside, he hides it well but I know, I've held him so many times now, when he's had a few drinks, the conversation always ends up about you and always ends in tears." I raise my eyebrows and look at Lennon.

"And there's been no other women, since we broke up, there's been no one else?"

Len pulls his head back and looks at me as if I'm mad. "I never said that G, there's been sex, of course there's been sex but it doesn't mean anything, they mean nothing."

"Well that's where me and him differ coz those birds he fucks, mean a lot to me, they mean he's moved on, while I can still barely leave the house. Tonight was my first girls night out in over three years, I don't even look at other blokes, I can't, it's pointless, because all I ever see is him and that's okay, it's my issue, not his and it's just something I'm finally learning to live with."

Lennon lets out a long sigh. "Would you talk to him, if I could get the two of you together, would you talk to him?" I shake my head.

"Len, apart from business trips and meetings, tonight is the first time I've socialised in over three years, I don't watch telly, I don't listen to the radio, I don't read magazines, all because, just the thought of someone mentioning his name, catching a glimpse of his face or hearing his voice is much too painful. But I'm getting better, it doesn't hurt any less, I'm just finally getting to grips with how I handle my feelings. Tonight was really hard for me but I did it, and I want to keep going forward and if I see or hear from him, it'll probably just set me back, so no, not yet, I'm not ready."

I look at both of them. "I know he'll be at the wedding next year and I'm gearing myself up for that to be the day that I am ready to see him again. I'm not promising I'll look at him, I doubt very much I'll talk to him but I will do my very best to be in the same room as him, because I love the two of you and I know it will make you happy."

CHAPTER 10

Over the next few weeks I went back to the wine bar with Ashley and every time I saw tall, dark and handsome there and every time, he would smile, nod and send over a bottle of champagne, but make no effort to come and talk to me. After about three weeks, Ash finally convinced me to go out clubbing after we had drinks; my Dad had bought into a club in the West End of London so I'd got him to put us on the guest list. I had no idea what to expect but was willing to give it a go. TDH, as Ash and I had nicknamed him, had sent over his usual bottle of bubbly and when we were leaving he clamped his hand around my wrist and gently pulled me into him. "Enjoy the rest of your night Georgia."

My head jerked back, not just because I was surprised that he knew my name, but because of the sensation that shot through me, caused by his hand on my wrist, the sound of his voice and the feel of his breath on the side of my face, neck and in my ear. I swallowed hard and looked him right in the eye, then over his face, he was bloody handsome and a lot older than me, I was about to turn twenty, he looked thirty-ish.

I don't know where I found her, but suddenly, confident little fifteen year old George appeared. "Thank you for the champagne, but whether I enjoy the rest of my night, has absolutely fuck all to do with you, now take your hands off me and don't touch me uninvited again… Ever!" I go to yank my wrist from his grasp when his hand clamps onto me tighter.

"Such an angry little kitten, with such sad eyes. Who hurt you Georgia? Who took the light out of those pretty blue eyes ehh?"

My first instinct is to slap him but he has a hold of my right wrist and I've drunk a bottle of Moet and two Southern Comfort and lemonades so I'm not sure how good my aim will be with my left.

"Let go of my wrist," I say quietly through gritted teeth, he does exactly the opposite and pulls me in to his chest and places his hand at the small of my back, pressing me into him. Fucking hell, he's got a hard on and its pressing right into my belly. I give out a little gasp - shit, shit, shit, he knows I can feel him.

"Next time you walk into my bar, me and you are going to find a quiet corner and sit and have a chat and you kitten are going to tell me all about the arsehole that made you so sad and so angry."

Shit, he owns the place? Explains why he can afford to keep dishing out bottles of Moet, I bet he does it to all the birds he fancies and there was me thinking I was all it and a bit!

I keep looking into his eyes. "Well, looks like I won't be walking into your bar again and best start looking for somewhere else to drink."

He takes a step back and looks me up and down. "You'll be back, if you're not, then I'll just have to come and find you; now do as I say, go and have some fun, I want those eyes to have some light in them next time I see you." He turns me around, smacks my arse and sends me on my way.

For two whole weeks I avoid the wine bar, forcing Ashley to drink in the pub down the road with me instead, it's not as nice and twice I have heard songs played in there that I think are by Carnage. I haven't heard any of their latest stuff but I would know Sean's voice anywhere. Both times I ducked into the toilets and waited long enough for the song to end but we never hang around there long, after the great night we had at my Dad's new place, I've decided I have a few years of clubbing to catch up on and we've been to three other clubs since then. Ash is still as wild as she was at school and loves a few lines of coke on a night out and I must admit to having joined her every time we've been out lately. I just love the instant rush and the confidence it gives me; the new drug of choice on the club scene is ecstasy, but I remember Sean and Jimmie telling me it makes you horny and that's the last thing I need to be feeling, more so than I already am lately. For the first time since I was of an age to think about boys in any kind of romantic or sexual way, my thoughts haven't all been about Sean, he's there, always, painfully so, but lurking in the corner now, with that smile on those soft lips and a spark in those warm brown eyes is Mr TDH. I still have no idea of his name and have no intention of going back to the wine bar to find out, not yet anyway.

It's a Thursday night in the middle of September, my birthday is this coming Saturday and I'm going out for drinks and then on to my Dad's club with Ash, Jimmie and a few of the other girls that work at the shop for us. I've been in the West End meeting with buyers all day with my Mum and have just called into the Brentwood shop to pick up my new dress I ordered in for Saturday night. Ashley and Lorna are the only two staff left as it's just fifteen minutes till closing.

I notice Ash looks terrible. "You okay babe, you look rough as fuck."

She takes a deep sigh, shakes her head and looks at me with a frown. "I came on this morning, my belly's cramping like a bitch, I need to go home, get my jarmies on and curl up with my Danielle Steele book and a hot water bottle."

Periods ergh, hate the bloody things, I suffer terribly with period pain myself and know it's no fun being on your feet all day when it feels like your womb is being ripped out of your fanny! "Go and get your bag and go home babe, I'll lock up."

"Ah George, you're a star, I'm not even gonna argue, thank you." She really is pale.

"Go! Open up at ten tomorrow, don't rush in, we're never busy first thing anyway, I'll leave a note in the window now, just to let the customers know." Ashley comes from out the back with her latest Louis Vuitton bag on her arm.

"Ash, you're spending more than you bloody earn on bags and shoes lately."

"Nahh." She smiles. "This is a fake, got it down the Roman the other week, good though ain't it?"

"Ashley Morrison, if my Mother sees that you will be out on your arse, do not bring fake shit into our shop, if trading standards ever came in they would go through our entire stock and our reputation would be ruined."

I don't mean to pull rank but fuck, my mother would absolutely flip. "Shit George, I'm so sorry, I didn't even think of that."

I shake my head at her. “Go home Ash, curl up with your book and get a lay in, in the morning and do not bring that bag back here again.”

She kisses my cheek and leaves. “Lorna, get cashed up and you can go too.”

I run up stairs to have a look at the work on my flat, everything is done except for the tiling in the kitchen and the painting. I’m just heading down the stairs when Lorna appears at the bottom.

“I called Dave to come get me early and he’s here but a customer’s just come in, dya want me to wait?”

“Na, you go, I’ll deal with them.” I make my way down the stairs as I speak.

“Okay, thanks George, don’t forget to leave the note about opening late in the window, thanks for letting me leave early, I’ll see you later.”

“Night,” I call after her. I’m so lucky with the team I have at Brentwood, we’ve had nothing but trouble with the team that run the Romford shop, but my Brentwood girls are great. We have no problems with bitching or sickness and the girls are always happy to work late or come in early if they’re needed. I head over to the handbags with a smile on my face, I can just see the top of someone’s hair as they bend down and look at something, at least it’s bags and not shoes, then I would be here all bloody night.

“Can I … What the fuck do you want?”

“Charming Kitten, is that how you approach all your customers?”

“Get out of my shop!” He completely ignores me.

“I want to buy a bag for my sister, it’s her twenty-first on Saturday, what’s the latest thing, Louis, Gucci, what are the girls into at the moment?”

What do I do, make him leave or make the sale? I could be kicking out a potential five hundred pound profit. Shit, fuck, bollocks, arseholes!

"The Louis, the one you were just looking at, it's new in this week."

"Then I'll take that one, I'd also like a pair of sunglasses and a scarf, whichever you think are appropriate for a twenty one year old."

I tilt my head sideways. "Your sister's very lucky." And very spoilt, I think to myself.

"She has three big brothers, I don't know if I would call her lucky."

"I would, I have three big brothers and I consider myself very lucky, I love them like nothing else." Except Sean. Why did I tell him about my brother's? Fuckeration, he needs to buy this bag and go! He looks over my face for a few seconds.

"Do you realise, how much your eyes just lit up when you spoke about your brothers?" I blush instantly. Ohhh, for God's sake, get a grip Georgia; I shake my head and look down at the carpeted floor of the shop but rear back as I feel his knuckle brush across my cheek.

"What happened to you kitten? Why don't you come over to the wine bar and let me buy you a drink, just a drink, nothing else, unless you want more?" I want to lean into his hand that is now cupping the side of my face, his thumb is gently brushing over my lips but I don't, I can't, I won't.

"What colour scarf were you thinking of?" He smiles gently at me and sighs, puts his hands into the pockets of his light blue denim jeans and rocks back on his heels.

"You choose the colour kitten, I'm happy with whatever you choose, you must be a similar age to my sister so she will like whatever you do." Closer in age than you could ever imagine I think to myself.

I instantly turn into my mother and become the perfect sales consult, helping him select a pair of Gucci sunglasses, a Chanel scarf and a Louis wallet to match the bag, He stands and watches me while I wrap his purchases in tissue with his hands dug deep in the pockets of his jeans. He's wearing a white t-shirt and a tan sued bomber jacket and he smells absolutely divine, I think it's Givenchy, my brother Bailey wears it, and there's a hint of something softer, florally almost, like soap powder or fabric softener, who does his washing for him I wonder? "So, will you come over and have a drink with me? It's just a drink Georgia, nothing else, we've drunk at the same bar lots of times, this time we'll just be together."

"Why do you want me to have a drink with you? Why do you always buy me champagne, do you do that for all your female customers?"

"Of course I don't, I'd be fucking bankrupt if I bought every bird that walked through the door a bottle of Moet."

"So why me?"

"Because I want to, you always look so sad and that first time, when I gave the bottle to your friend, the loud one, Ashley, who works here, when you were drinking it, you smiled at me, then you laughed and spilt your drink on your chin and for a split second, you looked happy and I just wanted to see that spark in your eye again."

I don't want him to know it was him that I was thinking about that night, that I smiled because I was thinking about how good looking I thought he was, and Jimmie read my mind and stated my exact thoughts out loud, I don't want to hear this, I don't want him to be nice, I don't want him to care, I want him to be a complete arsehole but he's not, not at all.

"Why do you care whether I'm happy or sad, what difference does it make to you?"

"Because I own the bar and I like my patrons to be happy, now are you gonna come for a fucking drink with me or not?" He sounds harsh but the look on his face is anything but, he raises his eyebrows and leans away from the till point where I'm wrapping his purchases.

"Come on, you know you wanna." I do, I really do, dare I?

"One drink Georgia, one drink and lots of talk." I raise my eyebrows at him.

"Or no talking, one drink and no talking, if that's what you'd prefer." He's so nice and so fucking sexy; I swore I wouldn't get involved with someone that stirred those old but familiar sensations inside me. I had enjoyed a few snogs lately with completely random blokes, I'd even let one of them touch my tits as we kissed waiting for my taxi to arrive, Rick or Nick I think his name was, but I felt nothing, it stirred nothing but just standing here, in a shop, with a counter between us, was doing things to my insides and I really wasn't sure what to do about it, but for some reason, my big fat gob went into action before it engaged my brain.

"One drink, I have my car out the back, but I'll need to drive it around, I'm not walking back here later on my own."

He has the biggest smile on his face; it makes him look so much younger… Aaaaand off goes my mouth again. "How old are you?"

He laughs and shakes his head. "Where are your keys Georgia, I'll pull your car around the front while you lock up."

I fold my arms across my chest as I look him up and down, knowing full well I'm not going to get an answer. Shaking my head, I bend down under the counter and get my keys out of my bag and throw them to him, wait till he sees what he'll be driving, I nod towards the back of the shop. "Through there, turn left onto the back ally, it's one way."

I follow him to the back doors. Hilda, my burnt orange and black Triumph Herald is parked right outside, I watch him as he swings the keys around his fingers, stops dead in his tracks and shakes his head. This is obviously a habit of his, I expect him to turn around and say something to me, but he keeps walking towards my car. I lock the back door behind him, set the alarms and head out the front of the shop, where he's already waiting at the curb, looking like a giant as he leans against my little car with his long legs crossed in front of him, his hands once again in his pockets. As I walk toward him, it suddenly occurs to me that I don't even know his name, well he hasn't offered and I'm not going to make him think I'm interested by asking. He silently opens the passenger door, lets me in, and then closes it behind me. My car now smells of a mixture of me and of him and I don't like it, it unnerves me for some reason.

We drive in silence for the two or three minutes it takes to get to the wine bar, he parks next to a Mercedes Sports car in a spot marked reserved and is out and around at my door before I've even got my seatbelt off. He pulls my door open and holds out his hand to help me out, I ignore it and climb out unaided, holding my hands out for the keys as I do, I lock my car and he takes my hand in his as we walk into the bar. Once again it's pretty busy for a Thursday night; we walk over to the bar, where one of the bar staff immediately comes over to him, he hands over his bags containing the gifts for his sister and asks the barman who he calls Steve, to go and put them in his office and to make sure it's locked up. He then goes around the bar and proceeds to pour himself a Jack Daniels over ice and without even asking, makes me a Southern Comfort and lemonade, I want to tell him I want a vodka, just to be awkward but I manage to stay quiet.

He comes around the bar with our drinks, talking to one of the bar staff and saying hello to customers as he does, he nods to an empty spot over in the corner and I follow him. We sit ourselves on the stools that face the ledge around the wall and once I'm settled he turns my stool so that I'm facing him and pulls it closer, so close that my knees are touching his stool, in between his legs, which are open and straddling mine, he looks at me, as though he's daring me to object, so I say nothing.

Steve appears with the keys to the office and a pile of papers. "You have a pile of messages Cam, most of them from Tamara but there are a couple that are business and one from Tory"

He takes them from him, puts the keys in his pocket and looks through his messages, shakes his head and shoves them all in his pocket. "Sorry about that."

I shrug. "Not a problem, business is business."

"Sure is," he says with a smile.

He swirls his drink over the ice in his glass and says, "Well Georgia, you dragged me here, are you going to talk to me or what?"

I smile inwardly at his cheek but again say nothing; I don't want him to know I'm amused. "What would you like to know, Cam?"

He raises his eyebrows, obviously surprised that I know his name. "I'd like to know about you Georgia. Where were you born? Where did you grow up? How long have you been manager of the shop over the road?"

I correct him. "I'm not the manager of the shop over the road."

"Oh sorry, I just thought the way you spoke to the girls, you were their boss."

"I am." I reply. "I own the business that owns the shop, over the road."

He leans back on his stool, studies me for a moment and then knocks back all of his drink and puts it down a little too hard on the ledge. What's his problem I wonder?

"I thought Frankie Layton's Misses owned that place." How does he know that?

"She does, I'm her business partner." His frown disappears. What! Did he seriously think that I was married to Frank, to my Dad? "And I'm her daughter."

His mouth actually drops open, oh fuck, this news does *not* please him. "You're Frank's daughter?"

"I am." He sighs deeply and runs his big hands through his hair.

"Oh fuck," he almost whispers as he once again shakes his head.

"Is that a problem?"

"Drink your drink Georgia, I have work to do." He pulls the bits of paper out of his pocket and starts looking through them again, totally ignoring me.

Instant rage takes over; I stand from my stool and throw my drink in his face. "Fuck you!" I say, turn and walk out of the bar.

I don't know what happens to me that night, I lost my grip on my own self-worth, I assumed Cam didn't want to know because of some piece of gossip he'd read in a Sunday tabloid, regarding me and Sean. There'd been a few spiteful stories about underage sex, drink and drugs, all involving me, once again. Sean and that band had interfered with my life and I was so sick of it. I went out on Saturday night and celebrated my birthday by snorting a couple of lines of coke, popping one ecstasy tablet and going back to the flat of a bloke named Tom in Lewisham and fucking his brains out, it was awful but he loved it. When the cab pulled up outside at ten on that Sunday morning, he was begging me to stay and he was begging for my number, so I gave it to him, I saw him five times over the next two weeks and on the fifth date, he told me he loved me, so I ended it. I absolutely loved the power I felt, so much so that for the next six months, this behaviour became a habit; I would be off my face Thursday till Sunday, meet a bloke, spend a couple of weeks giving them the best sex they'd ever had, doing everything I possibly could to get them to say those three little words and as soon as they did, bang, I dropped them like a sack of shit. The other thing I liked to do was to take my dates to Kings, the wine bar Cam owned, I always waited until I knew for sure that I had them by the balls, that way they would always be all over me and I always made sure that I sat or stood right in full view of Cam.

I had only met this bloke Lee, the Saturday before but he was already making me feel sick with the way he kept telling me how beautiful I was. I must've been getting better at this gig; he was the third bloke I'd bought into Kings in three weeks.

Cam was always polite to me, always said hello and always asked how I was, my response was always the same. "Fuck you!"

But it didn't put him off; week after week he would watch me walk in with my latest conquest with a certain kind of sadness in his eyes. I stood at the bar with Lee waiting to be served, when I noticed Cam come out of his office, he saw me straight away and walked toward me. "Georgia, how are ya?"

I turned away but Lee had heard him, he looked from me to Cam and said, "Fuck off mate, she's with me."

Cam totally ignored him. "Georgia, how are ya?" he repeated.

Lee had just been served and had our drinks in his hands, he put them down on the bar, turned to Cam and said, "Look mate, do yourself a favour, this one's taken, she's with me so fuck off."

I know it was a horrible thing to do but at this stage of my life I was a horrible person so I looked at Lee, then turned to Cam and wrapped my arms around his neck and said, "I'm good Cam, how are you babe?"

Lee pulled me back by my shoulder so hard, that I spun around and was facing the bar, I didn't really see what happened next, I assume one of them threw a punch. I heard glass breaking and people seemed to move in all directions, I turned back to see two of the bouncers grab Lee by his arms and start walking him toward the door.

"Georgia!" he called out to me.

"Fuck off Lee, we're done." I called back. Next thing I knew, Cam had a hold of my hand and was pulling me toward his office. I tried to dig my heels in and stiffen my legs but he was too strong, so I tried to yank my hand from his grip.

"Get off me!" I screamed but he just gripped tighter and pulled me harder, almost throwing me inside his office.

He slammed the door and locked it behind us. "What the fuck are doing? You fucking idiot."

He actually scares me when I look at him, he looks so fucking angry; he stalks over to the his desk and pours almost half a tumbler of JD from a bottle, he stands still for a few seconds, breathing heavily, his eyes narrowed and fixed on me, he puts the glass to his lips and drinks the whole lot. Shit I think, that's got to burn. “What I’m doing Georgia, is trying to keep both you and me the fuck out of trouble.”

“Well thanks and all that but I can look after myself.” He lets out a little laugh and does his usual head shake.

“Why, tell me why kitten, every other week, you waltz in here with a different little play thing in tow, licking your boots and panting all around you. Why, why do you do it? Are you trying to piss me off, or are you trying to prove something to yourself?”

“Like I told you before, what I do has fuck all to do with you and why would me coming in here with a bloke piss you off anyway? You don’t give a shit, you made that clear the night you dragged me over here for a drink with you, then totally ignored me when you found out who I was so don’t fucking start with me about trying to piss you off.”

I keep my back to the door of the office but reach behind me and turn the handle, it’s locked and he must have the key, I lose my temper completely, grab the handle with both hands, turn it, pull it and kick the door.

“Open the fucking door!” I scream. I feel his hand on my shoulder; he pulls me around and kisses me hard on the mouth. I grab his hair and pull it as hard as I can, despite the force of his kiss, his lips are soft and warm, he tastes of whiskey or bourbon or whatever the shit is that he drinks and he smells delicious; I’ve had months of mindless, faceless sex and not one single orgasm but right now, I feel like I could come at any minute, just from his kiss. I bite down gently on his bottom lip and he moans into my mouth and my legs almost give way; his big hands run down either side of my body, his thumbs brush over my boobs as he drags them down from my armpits to my waist, he splays them over my hips, then over my arse cheeks as he pulls me into him and grinds.

“Fuck,” he moans into my mouth. I’ve been at a business lunch with my Mum today and am still wearing my work clothes, a Chanel skirt and jacket with a shell blouse underneath but it’s what I have on under my skirt that has got his attention now; his fingers are stroking the outside of my thigh, reaching under the hem of my skirt and I’m just waiting for it, in three, two, one.

"Fuckin hell kitten, you're wearing stockings?"

I smile at myself, what is it with men and stockings? "I sure am Tiger, what of it?"

He bends his knees so we are eye to eye, even in my heels; he's a good few inches taller than me. "Show me."

"What?"

"Pull your skirt up and show me your stockings."

"Fuck off."

"Don't swear Kitten, it's not nice, now pull up your skirt and show me what you're wearing."

"Fuck nice and no."

"Did you wear them for him?"

"Who?"

"That fucking idiot you walked in here with."

"Stop swearing Tiger, it's not nice and it's none of your fucking business."

He pulls me with him while he walks backwards and rests his butt on the edge of his desk, holding me at arm's length; he slides my skirt up my thighs to my hips, then seems to change his mind and pulls it back down again. My belly drops to the floor as that horrible, horrible feeling of rejection hits me and for the first time in almost four years, I think I might cry. He takes a step toward me, reaches for my hip, undoes the button and slides down the zip, because the skirt's fully lined and a little lose, thanks to the amount of cocaine I've been shoving up my nose every weekend for the past six months. My skirt slides silently to the floor and from somewhere, confident George appears. I step out of my skirt and away from him, shrug out of my jacket, pull my blouse over my head and stand in front of him in my pale pink La Perla lingerie. I put my hands on my hips, open my legs and look him square in the eye, his gaze doesn't meet mine, his eyes are looking over my body, and I feel a little self-conscious. I know I'm a little too skinny, too many drugs, too much gym, too much misery doesn't set you in good stead for a great appetite but judging by the tepee that's forming in his trousers, he likes what he sees. His hands are gripping either side of the huge oak desk and his knuckles are white, his eyes rest on my tits, which finally seem to have decided to stop growing, I'm five feet eight and only just filling out size eight clothes right now but I still need an E cup bra to fit my tits, making dresses an almost impossible wardrobe choice for me. Luckily working in the business, I just get things either tailor made or altered.

"Turn around," Cam's voice makes me jump as it rasps out, his gaze finally meeting mine, I turn very slowly, once I have my back to him, I pull the scrunchy out of my hair, shake it out with my fingers and let it fall down my back.

"Jesus fucking Christ Kitten." I look over my shoulder at him.

"What Tiger, what's wrong?" His brown eyes are almost glowing, they shine so brightly, his cheeks are flushed and I reckon he must have a whole tribe of red Indians sitting in that tepee judging by the size of it. I wink at him and he makes a sound in his chest that's almost like a growl and I have to control the little whimper that almost escapes my throat.

"Come here," he orders.

"Please," I say.

He stands up straight, he's so tall, he must be at least six feet five and broad and just so, so…

"Come. The. Fuck. Here… " Masterful. I turn all the way around so that I'm facing him again and take a step forward, then jump straight into his arms as someone bangs loudly on the office door.

"Fuck!" We both say together.

"Cam, you better get out here mate, this blokes going off his narna and smashing up your birds motor."

I look straight at him. "Hilda… I'll fucking kill him."

Cam looks at me totally confused. "Stay here, I'll sort the little prick out."

He looks me up and down, walks over to a cupboard in the corner and pulls out a sweatshirt. "Put that on and stay here."

He unlocks the door by flicking a catch on the handle. Well fuck, it didn't need a key after all, and marches outside. There's no way that I'm staying put while Hilda gets smashed up, I know it's no less than I deserve after the way I treated Lee but my Dad's blokes spent months finding the parts fixing her up and that's after the six months it took me and my Dad to actually find one that was worth fixing up. My Dad had begged me to let him buy me something new, like he had my brothers when they passed their test but for some unknown reason, I've always wanted a burnt orange and black Triumph Herald, with a walnut dash and a sunroof, and being the daddy's little princess that I was, I eventually got my own way.

I went over to the big oak wardrobe looking thing in the corner and found a pair of jogging bottoms, I spent a few more seconds being nosey, looking at the shirts and ties and giving them a little sniff as I did, I couldn't help it, he smelt so delicious. I could hear sirens outside and flew out of the office, the bar was quiet, with most of the patrons watching the show that was going on outside. I pushed my way through the crowd, I hadn't had chance to pull the joggers on but the sweatshirt came down to my knees anyway.

I assumed the pile that was on the floor with three of Cam's doorman leaning over it was Lee but I couldn't really see. Cam had his back to me, standing in front of my car, talking to a Policeman. It went quiet as I approached him.

I trod on something sharp and cried out in pain. I'd kicked off my heels to pull the joggers on and was now just stood in my stockings. Cam swung around as he heard my "Oww shit."

He dragged his hand through his hair and shook his head. "Excuse me a second, officer," he said very politely. He had a very strong East London accent, stronger than my Dad's and it sounded strange hearing him speak so nicely to the Policeman. "Kitten, I told you to wait inside, there's glass everywhere. Where's your shoes?"

"What's he done to Hilda?"

"Who the fuck's Hilda?"

"My car."

He laughed.

"What's funny?"

"Your fucking car's called Hilda?"

"That's not funny, that's her name. What's he done to her?"

Another Police car pulled up, Cam's bar staff started telling people to either head inside or head home. "Finish your drinks people. I'm closing up early, Steve will remember you all and you can have a free one on me next time you're in," Cam called out. Shit, he was going to lose money tonight and all because of me.

The doorman stepped away from the pile on the floor that was Lee, as two Policemen handcuffed him and picked him up, he had a split lip and a bloody nose. He spotted me straight away, more to the point, he spotted what I wasn't wearing and Cam's arm around my shoulder, he threw himself toward me. "You cunt, you fucking cunt, I loved you, you bitch, I fucking loved you. Why? Why would you bring me here and do this?"

I didn't know what to say, usually I blew them out and left or I did it over the phone, I never got to see the fallout, well I did tonight, in full blown Technicolor and I felt terrible, I had left ten different blokes in this kind of a mess over the past six months, all so that I could feel better about myself and now I felt worse than I ever had before. I felt ashamed, my parents would be ashamed of what I did tonight, my brothers would be ashamed, even Jimmie wouldn't back me up on this one. I looked down at the ground and followed the trail of glass to my car, my poor smashed up car, the windows were all smashed and the roof was torn, the bonnet and the sides were full of dents, my poor Hilda and as much as I knew I deserved it, my temper kicked in. "You bastard, what did you do to my car?" I launched myself at him, clawing and kicking but Cam yanked me back before I made any kind of contact, the Police started to drag Lee away.

"You're a slut Georgia, a two timing slut!"

"Yeah, well you're a shit shag with a little dick, no wonder I went looking elsewhere."

I stood looking at his back; I was barefoot, in a ten sizes too big sweatshirt, wearing stockings and suspenders underneath. I put my hands on my hips and watched as the Police took him away. When I turned back around to face Cam, he was standing with three of his doorman and two Policeman, they were all laughing their heads off.

"What?" I asked confused.

"It's not funny, look at poor Hilda, my Dad's gonna kill me!"

Cam instantly stopped laughing. "Shit." I heard him hiss.

"I think you'll find it's me that he kills kitten."

I cocked my head to the side. "Don't worry Tiger, I'll protect ya." I winked at him.

CHAPTER 11

After tiptoeing back to Cam's office, pulling on his joggers and spending half an hour giving a statement to the Police, I was ready to go home. I'd managed to get back there before everyone else came barging in and throw my clothes in the wardrobe, ashamed with myself for being so slutty with Cam earlier and taking them off. I had no idea where I was going with my little strip tease, it was most definitely not what I had been intending to do when he dragged me in here. I had wanted to claw at his face initially, not his back, but there was just something about him, something that I couldn't say 'no' to and I needed to get it under control. I wasn't ready to feel yet, that wall around my heart wasn't ready to come down. I doubted very much that Cam was interested in anything more than sex and I was so afraid I'd want more and I don't think my heart could be rebuilt if it were to be broken again.

I had noticed that as the Police were leaving that they had told 'Mr King' that they'd be in touch and I sat twirling faster and faster in the big leather chair behind Cam's desk while he showed the nice Policemen out. It occurred to me that he'd named his wine bar after himself, flash bastard, funny actually though, as the club my Dad had bought into was called Kings. I let these thoughts wander through my brain as I stared up at the ceiling whilst still spinning madly in the chair. It suddenly jolted to a stop and I was turned around slowly to meet Cam's brown eyes.

"What are you doing?"

"Twirling, you should try it, its fun." His lips twitched in the slightest of smiles; he pulled me out of the chair, sat himself down in it, pulled me into his lap and began to twirl us both around while he held on to me, a little too tightly, I lifted my legs up, put my feet on his legs and curled into him.

"You're right."

"I'm female, of course I'm right." He gave out a really big, loud, laugh, which for some reason made me smile.

"Oh Kitten, you do make me laugh."

"Why? I didn't say anything funny, I just stated a fact."

"Is that right?"

I nodded. "Yep."

He shook his head but smiled, reached out for the desk, grabbed it and stopped the chair from spinning anymore, we sat still and silent for a few seconds, blue eyes into brown, he stroked his finger over my cheek, circled it around my chin, and then traced the outline of my lips.

I forgot to breathe.

"You are all bullshit and bravado, why do you put on such a hard front kitten? All spitting and snarling, when I don't think that's really you at all." I bit his finger as it lingered on my lips, probably using a little more force than was necessary. He shook his head, again.

"Why are you always shaking your head at me?'

He strokes up and down my arm, over the curve of my shoulder. "Am I?"

"Yep."

"Perhaps it's because you frustrate me."

"You barely know me, how do I frustrate you?" I don't know if I feel hurt that he thinks this or happy that I have at least some kind of effect on him. Do I want to have some kind of effect on him? God I don't know, I don't know anything where he's concerned. My life might be a mess right now but it's a mess I have control over and that's the way I want it to stay. I don't want my emotions roller-coastering all over the place; in fact, I don't think I'm ready for emotions of any kind in my life right now. I've survived the last few years without them and I think that I'll manage without them for the next few.

"You frustrate me because you so obviously put on a front; I wish you would just be yourself, at least for me."

"Why, why does it matter who, or what I am around you?" He twirls my hair around his fingers, it's such a simple thing but for me, so intimate.

Yes I've had sex with men, ten of them in fact, over the last six months and some would say that's the ultimate act of intimacy, but not for me. For me, it was a cold and unfeeling act of power and control. I rarely let them kiss me, I gave them the best sex they'd ever had but just that, they got no part of me whatsoever. I didn't hold hands with them, unless they took mine and left me with no choice, I didn't stroke or lick or suck. I just fucked, but I did it so well that they couldn't get enough, just so that I could hear them say those three little words then have the pleasure of walking away, but this, him playing with my hair like this, was so much more intimate to me than anything else I'd experienced in the last six months. It was the most intimate thing I'd done with any man since Sean!

"Because I like you Kitten, I like you a lot and I want to get to know you, the real you, not the spitting, clawing alley cat you seem to want people to think that you are, and the first thing I want to know is what's made you like this? Who did this to you? What did they do… hmm?" He raises his eyebrows at me like he's actually waiting for an answer, well fuck that, I'm not spilling my guts to him so that I can get the pitying look I've got from everyone else these past few years.

"I need to go home; I'll get my Dad to arrange for my car to be towed tomorrow." I move to slide off of his lap.

"Don't go, don't run away Georgia, stay and talk to me." He holds me in his lap, his hands on my hips, his eyes looking right into mine, through mine, into me and I have to go, I can't have him seeing through me, into me, to the real me, I can't.

"I need to go Cam, please let me go." He shakes his bloody head at me again.

"You're shaking your head."

"Coz you're frustrating the fuck out of me. Would you have had sex with me, earlier, before little limp dick went all mental and started smashing things up? If we hadn't been interrupted, would you've let me fuck you?" My cheeks burn with embarrassment at the thought of my earlier behaviour, I shake my head very slightly.

"No Cam, you wouldn't have fucked me… but I might have fucked you." He lets out a deep breath, almost a hiss, through his teeth.

"Get your stuff, I'll take you home and don't worry about your car, I've got someone coming for it now, I'll get it fixed up for you."

"You don't have to do that, it's my own fault, I behaved badly, and I got what I deserved."

"Maybe." He shrugs. "But do you want to be the one to tell your Dad what happened and why? Do you want your Dad's blokes out looking for little dick, seems to me, the poor blokes got enough problems without Frank Layton putting a price on his tiny balls."

I actually laugh out loud at the thought of Lee and his little cock and balls being chased by my Dad; shit he's right, the least my Dad knows about the damage to my car the better. I chew on the inside of my lip.

"Okay but I want a receipt for the work, I want to pay the bill and make sure you tell them to be gentle with her, she's getting on and needs to be handled with love."

He frowns. "Who?"

"Hilda."

"Fuck, right, yeah, of course, Hilda the Triumph Herald, how could I forget?" He smiles as he speaks, he looks so young when he smiles and I wonder again how old he actually is. I'm guessing twenty-nine, thirty…

"How old are you Cam?"

"Old as my tongue, bit older than my teeth," he says with a shrug and looks away from me.

"My Nan always used to say that and she was like eighty or something when she died, are you as old as her?"

"Fuck off, let's get you home."

Cam dropped me off at my flat and we came to an arrangement whereby he would sort out the cost of the damage to my car as long as I agreed to go out for dinner with him Saturday night. I agreed. Of course I agreed there was just something about him that made me want to agree and try as I might, I didn't seem to be able to fight it.

Saturday morning I had a fitting for my bridesmaid dress with Jimmie, she was having three of us and her older sister was being matron of honour. Jim being the funky little soul that she was, had chosen fantastic fifty's style retro dresses for us, they were really simple, in a soft peach colour, with a strapless bodice a wide ivory sash to match the colour of Jims dress and then a full skirt that came just above our knees, with lots of petticoats underneath. Jimmies dress was the same style but where ours were strapless, she had lace over the bodice, with three quarter lace sleeves and a massive bow at the back of the sash around her waist, we all had little short veils for our heads, Jims was longer and covered her face, the whole thing was so her and I just loved it.

I got the usual telling off from Claude and Sally the dress-makers; I had to have my dress made slightly smaller every time we had been back for fittings, then my mother joined in the charge and started going on about how I spent too much time at the gym, at work or out clubbing, that I never ate and that I would never find a husband in a noisy, sweaty club.

"Actually, I have a date tonight and he's taking me out for dinner," I state loudly from where I'm standing on the podium while Claude darts the back of my dress where he wants it taken in.

A pin scrapes my skin, only just not piercing it. "Oww!" I complain, looking over my shoulder at him; we use Claude and Sall for lots of jobs for the shops and we referred lots of customers to them who wanted Bespoke tailoring so they were providing their services for free as a thank you to my Mum.

Claude looked up at me and rolled his eyes in an 'I barely touched you' expression. "Is there blood?" I asked.

"Oh do stop being such a drama queen Georgia, if you didn't shock me with that last comment then I might not have moved the pin too close. You are being serious I take it? You really do have a date tonight, with a real man? Don't go getting your mothers hopes up if you're just trying to placate her."

My family had no idea about the life I'd been leading these past six months, no idea I'd been leading men around by their dicks just for the pure pleasure of dumping them as soon as they mentioned the L word, as far as they were aware, I'd been a single party girl, living it up every weekend, which was also partly true and the story that I went with.

"Would I lie to you Claude, or my mother for that matter?" He stood with his hands on his hips; eyebrows raised and pouted his lips. Claude was the gayest straight man I'd ever met and the most amazing tailor, seamstress, maker of things, or whatever his title was, that I'd ever had the pleasure of doing business with.

"Probably yes," he said through a mouthful of pins. I nodded.

"Yea you're right but on this occasion I am telling the truth."

"Who's the date with? Anyone we know?" Jimmie called over from the other podium where she was being fitted, I looked across and smiled at her, dare I tell her, in front of my Mum, God, I was never going to hear the end of this, my Mum would be wanting to meet him and have him round for Sunday lunch, she was busy faffing around with Jimmie's sister Julie's dress with Sall so I took a chance.

"Mr TDH," I cringed at Jim as I said it. Her and Ash had given me shit for months about him and I told them all along that I wasn't interested and now here I was going on a date, out for dinner with him no less.

Jimmies jaw dropped. "Are you serious?"

"Yes I'm serious, why does everyone assume I'm lying today? Is it such a ridiculous concept that someone might actually want to take me out on a date?"

"No," my mother piped up. "The ridiculous concept is that you might actually say yes and want to go out on a date with someone. And who's Mr TDH?" Trust my mother not miss a trick.

"Oh Bern, you should see him, he is absolutely gorgeous, he's been after George for months, what made you finally say yes G?" I shrugged, shit, what was I going to tell them? "Aww, he spent two grand in the shop, it's the least I could do."

"The very least," my mother said.

"Well, who is he, what do you know about him?" I shot Jim a look; I didn't want my Mum knowing anything, yet.

"He's just a bloke we met in the wine bar, he bought me a drink, then he came in the shop and I helped him with some stuff for his sisters twenty-first after I'd sent Ashley home sick, I've not seen him in ages, bumped into him Thursday night and he asked me to dinner tonight… Okay, is that enough facts for everyone?"

Claude clapped. "Can't wait for the next fitting so you can tell me all about it, just don't go falling in love and not eating, I don't want to be making any more alterations to this dress, you're far too skinny right now Ms Layton."

I couldn't believe how nervous I was getting ready Saturday evening. I had my hair washed and dried at the salon next door this afternoon so I had a bath rather than a shower when I got home. There were nice clean sheets on my bed and I had lit a few candles about the place, I wasn't sure what would eventuate tonight because I knew full well that whatever I decided now, if he tried to, Cam would have me changing my mind and doing his bidding anyway.

I changed my outfit three times before settling for a seventies mini dress. It was A-line, in a gorgeous blue colour, with bell bottomed sleeves, I'd bought it at Kensington Market along with a pair of white sling back shoes and the two went perfectly together. I smoked a cigarette while I waited for Cam, I wasn't much of a smoker but I was nervous. I had had a couple of glasses of wine while I was getting ready, which had calmed me down and the cigarette did the same. My doorbell buzzed, I stood from the arm of the chair where I'd been sitting and counted to ten, didn't want to appear too keen if I could help it. I looked through the spy hole my Dad had insisted I install but all I could see was his back, I then proceeded to undo the three different bolts my Dad had also insisted I have and swung the door open.

He'd turned around, he wasn't facing away from me anymore, he was leaning on the door frame, filling my doorway, looking big and gorgeous and so fucking handsome. Just a pair of plain black trousers and a white shirt, rolled up at the sleeves to just below his elbows, I could see the hint of a gold necklace at his throat, amongst the dark hairs that I could also see there. Instinctively my hand rose to my throat and I touched my own necklace, the one that had sat at my throat for the best part of six years. Sean, no, don't do this to me, not right now!

Sean!

Sean!

Sean!

My brain screamed out at me.

They're all just like Sean, Georgia, all of them.

Fuck off, fuck off, fuck off!

I literally had to shake my head to clear the conversation that was going on inside it. He stood in complete silence, filling my doorway, just watching me.

"Hey," I eventually managed to say.

"Alright?" he replied, sounding like a right cockney geezer. He had the strangest way of talking. I'd been thinking about this last night whilst trying not to think about him, he had a strong East London accent, he dropped his H's but he used words that most blokes from our neck of the woods didn't. It made me wonder if he had received a private education, if he had attended a 'posh' school despite coming from where he did. Not that it mattered, coming from a working class background entitled you to a private education as much as the next person that could afford it, I was just curious, that was all.

"You look stunning," he smiled slightly as he said it.

"Thank you, you look… well fuckin' horny yourself."

"Kitten, really? You're all dressed up like a lady and talk like a brass."

"And how would you know what a brass talks like Cam?" He'd pissed me off now, I hadn't meant to swear, it just comes out. I grew up with three older brothers, they were just words to me, I managed to keep it under control at work, just, well most of the time, but out of work, they just slipped out and I was only trying to pay him a compliment.

"Because I've had to ask them to leave my establishments on more than one occasion, I don't mind them coming in for a drink but I won't have them turning tricks in my gaffs and they tend to get a bit lippy when asked to leave."

"And I sound like one of them?" He sighs and shakes that gorgeous head of his.

"No Georgia, you don't, I don't know why I said that, it's just that you look like such a lady and then you open your mouth and… " he trails off.

"Well this is a great start, you've only been here two minutes and already you're shaking your head and bollocking me for swearing." I fold my arms across my chest and tap my foot as I look him up and down.

"Dya wanna leave it and go and find a posh bird to take out?"

"No, I don't, anyway, posh birds swear too you know… come here." I shake my head.

"You want me, then you'd best come here Tiger."

"See, so fuckin' frustrating, no wonder I shake my head, do you ever do as you're told?"

"Nope." I shrug, raise my eyebrows and give him my best 'What?' look.

He gives a big sigh, looks as though he's about to shake his head, thinks about it for a split second, then stalks toward me, he reminds me of a wolf, his eyes narrowed as his big frame gets closer. He stands as close as he can without touching me, I deliberately keep my eyes straight ahead, staring into his chest, breathing in his scent, which just does unexplainable things to me, he uses his middle and index fingers to lift my chin, bringing my eyes level with his soft brown ones, I don't want to return his gaze but I can't resist.

"I'm going to kiss you Georgia, I'm going to kiss you and then we're going to leave, because if we don't leave the minute I stop kissing you, I'm going to drag you to your bedroom and fuck you senseless for the rest of the weekend."

I don't get chance to reply, shit, I don't get chance to think too much before his soft full lips are on mine, gently at first, he tastes minty and fresh as I open my mouth slightly, his tongue slides along my bottom lip and plunges deep into my mouth, dancing, stroking and teasing mine. I reach up and grab his hair in both of my hands and give out a little moan as he licks the inside of my bottom lip, my moaning obviously has an effect on him as he cups my arse and pulls me into him, grinding against me, I can feel his erection pressing into my belly and I moan again.

"Fuck off making that noise Georgia before I stop being responsible for my actions."

I want to do it again, I want to give out the tiniest of little moans but I don't know if I'll be able to resist if he initiates sex and I'm not sure if I'm ready to have sex with him. I want this to be different, I think I'm ready to try and have a relationship with him, if that's what he wants and I would rather we establish a relationship before we start shagging. I step away from him.

"Let's go." He stills, even holding on to his breath, what did I say I wonder? Then I get it.

"Out I mean, let's go out." He thought I meant let's go for it, bed, sex or whatever, shit that was close.

We drive into London and have dinner at a beautiful Italian restaurant in Knightsbridge, it's very posh and there are a couple of photographers hanging about outside so it's obviously somewhere that celebs hang out but the pap's aren't interested in the likes of us. The staff seem to know who Cam is though, greeting him by name and making a fuss while we are led to our table. We sit, chat and enjoy the food and the wine and each other's company; I learn that he has a flat above the wine bar, making us neighbours. He has a flat in Islington and a house out in Stock, near Billericay but he doesn't get out to it much because of work commitments. I'm not really sure what those commitments are as he's a little evasive when I question him. We talk about my work and I explain how mine and my Mum's business came about and how we got the name of Posh Frocks from what my Dad always called anything my Mum wore.

My heart began to hammer in my chest a little too hard when he asked about my brothers, it pounded in my throat, making it difficult to get air in and I thought I was going to have a full blown panic attack when he asked what Lennon and Marley did. I stared down at the table and tried to control my breathing, focusing on the food left on my plate, which is entirely the wrong thing to do, as the thought of food is adding to the nausea I'm starting to feel and the fear of being sick, starts adding to my panic. His hand reaches across the table to mine, where it's clenched into a fist, gripping hold of my napkin; he takes it and uncurls my fingers.

"Georgia, its fine." I slowly bring my eyes up to meet his and he dips his head slightly, shakes it and says, "It's fine, don't worry about it babe, tell me another time." His deep voice is soft and gentle and I nod slightly as my breathing begins to slow.

This is ridiculous; I've been apart from Sean for almost four years. I haven't seen him once in person in all that time and yet still, just the thought of explaining my brother's involvement with Carnage and the fear of being questioned about the band has me hyperventilating. Fuck you Sean McCarthy, fuck you and what you've done to my life. As is always the case when I think of him, Sean, my hand goes to my throat, to my silver G that's being held by angel wings. It sits there as a silent reminder of what was, what I had, what I lost. I need it, as painful as it is, I need to have that link with me at all times, a silent piece of him, as close to my heart as I've allowed anything to be over these past years. I pull my hand out from under Cam's, pick up my napkin and cover my mouth.

"I can't… I can't tell you, and I can't talk about it." He nods at me, slowly; I take a gulp of my wine, draining my glass. "I'm sorry."

He gives a little smile but it doesn't reach his eyes, he looks concerned and I just feel like a complete bitch, I'm out on a date in a posh restaurant and I'm almost in tears over a bloke that cheated on me four years ago and there's nothing I can do to stop it. I can't change how I feel, I still love Sean, I miss him, I long for him and I still can't talk about him. I only have a few more months before the wedding and I'll be standing in a church with him and then I'll be sitting in the same room at the wedding reception as him and no doubt, I will spend the whole day and the whole night, trying, forcing myself not to look at him. Just the thought of that day and how painful it's going to be has the blood rushing through my ears again and once again I'm swallowing hard, trying to stop the dinner I just ate, from coming back up and reintroducing itself to the plate it was originally served on.

"Do you want to leave Georgia?" Cam asks me very quietly. I nod. I don't want to speak, I don't think I can, my chest is so tight, I just wish I could cry, just once, if I could let go of the tears, then perhaps I could let go of some of the pain.

I don't even notice Cam gesture to the waiter but he must, he's there with the bill in an instant, Cam pays him in cash and then stands and helps me put on my jacket, the perfect gentleman. We wait for just a few seconds as the valet brings his car around, before he's even out, Cam has the passenger side door open and helps guide me in, before tipping the valet, taking his keys and sliding in beside me; he pulls silently into the Saturday night traffic of London's elite SW1 and we drive in silence until we are almost at my flat.

"I'm so sorry about tonight Cam, the restaurant was beautiful, and the food was fantastic, I'm so sorry my stupid behaviour ruined it."

He keeps his eyes on the road and says nothing, I've totally blown it, I like Cam, he's the first bloke since Sean to stir any kind of interest in me and I've just gone and fucked up any chance I might have had with him and I've no idea how I can try to make it better. Perhaps if we fucked? If we get the fucking out of the way first, it might help me to move on. I'm pretty sure that Cam would be good in bed, and I'm sure that he'd finally give me the orgasm I was so desperate for. I could DIY it myself no problem, I had invested in the perfect little toy that meant I could come in a matter of seconds on my own, but I hadn't come with a man in almost four years, since Spain, with Sean, Sean, Sean, fucking Sean. I let out a huff of frustration that I didn't mean to, just as Cam parked his car in the spot outside my flat, he finally turned and looked at me.

"Have you ever had help Georgia?"

"What? What kind of help?"

"Psychological help? Help to try and get over whatever it is that happened to you."

My hand instantly flew up to my neck. "Help to try and deal with whatever he did to you." He gestures with the tilt of his chin toward my necklace, where my hand still is, fucking hell; he thinks I'm mad, he thinks I'm insane, am I? I'm completely fucked up, I know that much but I don't know about insane, I choose to ignore the comment and the question.

"Would you like to come in for a coffee?"

"You really want me to come in?"

I nod, I do, I really don't want to be alone right now. I'm so sick of being alone and I'm so sick of being lonely.

When Sean did what he did in that room, not only did I lose him and the life that we had planned together, I also lost Jimmie, Lennon and Marley, I know I still got to see Len and Jim but we could've all been so much closer. I would have been involved with the band, touring with them, seeing my brothers and my best friend almost daily and suddenly, it was all ripped away from me. They all went off and road the fame wave with the band, whilst I quietly slipped off back to school, all on my own. While I'm lost in my own thoughts, Cam has gotten out of the car and come around and opened the door on my side, I stare up at him blankly for a few seconds, before I realise that he's waiting for me to get out, he takes my hand, puts his other hand on the top of my head so I don't bump it and guides me out of the car and up the stairs to my flat.

My Dad had insisted on two lots of security doors when his blokes worked on the refurbishment. You unlock the first door, walk along a short corridor and before reaching the front door that eventually lets you into my place; it's not huge but it's mine and I've decorated it exactly how I wanted to. My Mum wanted florals and dado rails, I wanted plainly painted walls and a leather sofa, a chesterfield in fact, it reminded me of the summerhouse, just the smell of the leather alone would make my belly flip every time I came home; my parents still had that old sofa, Sean and I had had sex on it, more than once. Sean, Sean.

"I think you need a drink not a coffee, what do you have in?" Cam's concerned voice interrupts my inappropriate thoughts.

"Sorry, what?" I'm sitting on a stool at my breakfast bar and I've no idea how I got here.

He doesn't wait for an answer, he just starts opening cupboards until he finds the bottle of Drambuie I always keep for when my dad comes over, he pulls two whisky tumblers from the shelf above the drink and pours two large measures into both, then adds ice from the freezer. Placing both the glasses down in front of me, he stands on one side of the bench top, and leans forward on his elbows, facing me as I sit on my stool on the other side. He tilts his glass toward me.

"Cheers?' It's a question not a toast. I pick up my glass and tap it against his and nod slightly.

"Cheers," I state.

He looks at me for a long while but I just know he's going to talk and I know he's going to ask questions and rightly so, I've behaved like a complete head case tonight. He took me out to a nice restaurant; he's behaved with impeccable manners and has shown the patience of a saint, so he's more than entitled to ask questions if he feels inclined; whether I'll answer them without having another complete meltdown is another thing.

"Why do you wear it if it causes you so much pain?"

What is he talking about?

"The necklace, why wear it?" I raise my hand, and then put it back down, he's very perceptive. My belly flips upside down and then feels like it's trying to turn itself inside out.

"I really like you Georgia but I need to know what I'm up against. I want to know who I'm up against?" He's quiet for a few seconds. "I'm not some kind of a cunt, if it's a bloke and he's still about, if your still involved, I will walk away and leave you to it. I want you George, fuck do I want you but I want you to come to me willingly and I want you to come to me single, I don't share."

I sip at my drink, enjoying the warmth as it slides down my throat and lands in my acrobatic belly, I watch as he drains his glass and pours himself another. "Are you with someone?" Ha, am I? Sean, yes I'm with Sean but only in my head, in real life, I'm alone, so fucking alone. "Georgia?"

"No, no I'm not with anybody; I haven't been with anybody for years. I'm very single."

"What about all the blokes you came into the wine bar with? You were with them."

I shrug my shoulders. "No I wasn't, they were with me, but I was never with them."

He closes his eyes and takes a deep breath. "I wish you'd tell me, if you told me, who, what, I mean give me a fucking clue here, even about us George. What do you want? Why did you come out with me tonight?"

"You looked after me the other night, you're getting my car sorted, I like you, I wanted to go out with you but I just can't talk to you about him."

"So it is a bloke then?" I nod slightly; he drags one hand through his dark hair.

"Well that's a start at least. George look, I may be way out of line with this but I've gotta ask… This ain't nothing to do with your brothers is it?"

My stomach is now doing a pirouette as well as back flips, how does he know that?

"They've never done anything, I mean, your brothers have never done anything, they've never touched you or anything have they?"

What?

"What, no, no, fuck no, my brothers are my, I love my brothers. What the fuck are you saying?"

"Every time I mention them, I mean, the younger two, you freak out, I thought it had something to do with them, I thought they'd done something to ya. I'm sorry if I'm wrong but I had to ask."

"Fucking hell Cam, what sort of a family do you think I come from? What sort of person dya think I am? It's nothing like that, nothing."

"Then what for fucks sake? I'm fucking lost George, everything I say is wrong, everything I say sends you off somewhere, I lose you for a few seconds or you look like you're about to hyperventilate and I have no idea what it is that I've said that has caused that."

I feel terrible, I like him, I really do like him but I have no idea how far I'm willing to take this, if I'm willing to take this any further than a few dates and a few fucks, I'm just a mess and he deserves better.

"It's a bloke and I'm not over it, I'm not over him, I don't know if I ever will be, no one else has ever come close. The others, Lee and the other nine I've strung along for the last six months were just…" I shrug and look around the room while I try to think of a word. "They were revenge, they were payback. They were me, trying to make myself feel better. They were me being a bad person."

"And is that what this is? Is that what I am, revenge? You trying to make yourself feel better?"

"No!" I almost shout, because it's not and I don't want him to think that.

"No Cam, that's the problem, I like you, you're the first." Fuck, I think I might actually cry, for the first time in four years, I think I might actually cry. I swallow it down. "You're the first since him that has made me feel anything, the others were nothing, I felt nothing. But you, you're different and I'm struggling, I've never let anyone one in, I've not allowed myself to feel, I've never even cried… since him, not once."

He looks at me confused. “When was this, how long ago?”

“Almost four years.”

“You haven’t cried in four years?”

“No,” I say quietly and shake my head.

He comes around the breakfast bar and stands in front of where I’m sitting on the stool, he opens his legs, placing them either side of mine so that he can get closer and wraps his arms around me, pulling my head to his chest. “What the fuck did he do to you baby girl, what did he do? I want you to know, I want to make it better.”

I tilt my head back so I can look at him. “Cam, I really do like you but you need to know, you need to understand.” I pause and shrug, trying to think of how to explain this. “There’s only him, it will always be him, there’s no room for anyone else, wherever we go with this, you need to understand that, my heart is sealed and there’s only him that’s locked inside.”

He closes his eyes for a split second too long, like what I’ve just said has caused him physical pain. “But you don’t know me Georgia; you haven’t had a chance to get to know me. If you let me, I will blow your mind baby.”

He smiles at me, a full on sexy smile and I’ve no doubt that he is more than capable of blowing my mind, whether he can blow that wall down that’s around my heart is another thing.

CHAPTER 12

As horny as Cam makes me feel, he doesn't stay over Saturday night; we talk for a bit longer and arrange to speak during the week. I've given him the number to the shop as well as my home, he has no idea what a big deal that is for me, I don't give any blokes my number, none at all.

I head over to my parents for lunch on Sunday and groan when I see my Mum sweeping the porch as I pull up in the taxi I've had to book. Jim picked me up for the dress fittings yesterday so I've been able to hide the fact that my car is off the road, until now. My Mum stops what she's doing and leans on her broom while she watches me pay and get out of the cab.

"Where's your car George?"

"Hello Mum, these are for you." I hand her a bunch of carnations, her favourites.

"Oh thanks babe, mmm, they smell beautiful. Where's your car?"

"Oh I left it at a friend's last night, because I had too much to drink. He's going to drop it back later. Is Bailey here?" I ask, noticing my brother's Range Rover in the drive. I start to head into the house before she can say any more about the car.

"Yeah, he's in there somewhere, talking business with your Dad."

The house my parents now live in is a barn conversion, it's absolutely beautiful, high ceilings and exposed beams; they had to adhere to all kinds of building regulations to get the job done and bring in a few specialists but the end result was spectacular. My favourite thing about it was the galleried landing that ran all around the upstairs, part of the flooring down stairs were the original flagstones and part was timber, it was sleek and modern but warm and cosy at the same time. I headed to my Dad's office as this is where I could hear his and Bailey's voices coming from, I put my head around the door, they both had their bums perched on the edge of my Dad's huge desk. Thoughts of Cam and what we had almost done in his office Thursday night popped into my head and my cheeks instantly flushed, my Dad was sipping from a whisky tumbler, Bails was inspecting a shot gun, probably the latest edition to my Dad's collection. He always kept guns and enjoyed shooting, game and clays but he had got into it even more since they moved. This house was on five acres, he had deer, pheasant and plenty of rabbits out the back, a huge pond and stables where my Mum kept here two horses, well one was mine, but I'd been very negligent lately and hadn't ridden in weeks.

"Ello Princess," my Dad said as soon as he spotted me, he held his arms open and I walked right into them, breathing in the smell of him deeply. Drambuie and Tabac aftershave, no matter how many different designer aftershaves people bought him, my Dad always resorted back to his old favourite and I'm so glad that he did. To me that smell was home, safety, love and security, that smell was, when I was a little girl, how I assumed all Dad's smelt and I loved it. He held me tight and breathed me in. "Fuckin' ell Georgia, you're skin and bone. What have you been doin' to yourself? Your mother really needs to fatten you up."

"Thanks Dad, I love you too." I pull away and give Bailey a cuddle and my head spins as I take in the smell of his Givenchy aftershave. "Big brother Bailey, how are you? I've missed ya, you smell lovely."

He squeezes me so hard I can hardly breathe. "Baby sister Georgia, how the fuck are you? It's been way too long. Fuck, you're skinny."

"Bailey, language please, it's Sunday." We all turn and laugh at my Mum; her and my Dad both grew up in Plaistow, my Dad still had a real cockney accent but my Mum spoke much nicer and had always corrected us on our grammar. I never dropped my H's or said ain't, grub or gissit… instead of give me it… around my Mum. When we travelled on business most people assumed we came from London but they had no idea which part and would never have guessed at my mother's working class roots. I most definitely wasn't posh but around my Mum, I wasn't common either, away from my Mum and work was an entirely different story.

"Mum, what difference does it make what day of the week it is, swearing is swearing, if your mate the Big G Man up there, don't like it, then he don't like it any day, not especially on a Sunday."

"His name is God, Bailey Michael Layton, or our holy father and you should be more respectful. Francis, talk to your son." My Mum was still a practising Catholic, my Dad not so much, we had all been christened in the Catholic Church and educated through the Catholic school system but none of us went to church, unless it was to make my Mum happy.

Jimmie and Lennon's wedding was being held at the Catholic Cathedral in Brentwood and I knew from family weddings I had attended in the past that it was at least a two hour ceremony, well at least they always felt that long. This next wedding would be excruciatingly long; Sean and I, both of us, standing in a church, watching two of the people we love most in the world get married. Well it would be agony for me, he probably wouldn't give a shit but then again, Jimmie did say a while back that he did still ask after me and Len said he'd got drunk and cried. What hurt me more than anything was the way he'd given up. He called a lot in the beginning but only for a few weeks and he never wrote or came round when I knew the boys were in England. Perhaps if he'd tried harder to convince me he was sorry, maybe things would be different, maybe I would've come to terms with things a little better. I don't know, it was all too much to think about, I had gone to sleep last night wondering if my young, immature, sixteen year old self had just over reacted at the time. Were my expectations of fidelity and faithfulness way too high? I just don't know and for the rest of today at least, I wasn't going to think about any of it, or at least try not to.

Sunday lunch was as always when my Mum cooked it, absolutely perfect, later in the afternoon, Jimmie and Lennon came over, Bailey was living at my parent's at the moment as he had recently split with his long term girlfriend Donna and was looking for somewhere new to live.

Despite my brothers all living elsewhere now, my Dad had still had one of the stables converted into a soundproofed studio, it's where we all sat now. Me lying with my head on Baileys lap as we both sat on the old Chesterfield sofa. Len sat on a bean bag, strumming on an old acoustic guitar that had belonged to one of my brothers and Jim lay on the floor flicking through yet another bridal magazine. Bail's passed the joint he was smoking down to me and I took a long draw on it, getting stoned and chilling the fuck out with my brothers was exactly what I needed to do today. Len stood up and came and took the joint from me.

"How about you share the love baby sister?"

"Happy to share big bro, just can't be arsed to get up and pass it to ya."

"Lazy cow."

"Yep, that's me."

He plonked himself back down in the bean bag and smoked and strummed, the strumming started to turn into an actual tune. Jimmie rolled over onto her back then jumped up and took the joint from Len, I watched as she took a draw and shook her head at him slightly, the song was probably something by Carnage I assumed by her reaction but I was well on my way to being shitfaced so I actually didn't care too much. Jimmie must've known what I needed and passed the joint back to me, I took one more draw and passed it back to Bails.

"Oh my God, I forgot to ask, how did your date go?" Jim squealed from her spot on the floor.

Bailey turned my head with his hands so that I was looking up into his face. "You finally back in the game and dating George?" I shrug and blush.

"Who was your date with G, anyone we know?"

"I told ya, she had a date with the bloke from the wine bar," Jimmie replies to Len.

"What wine bar did you meet him in?" Bailey looks down and asks me.

"The one he owns," Jimmie piped up again, I sat up straight.

"Fuck me George, you said that without moving your lips," Bailey joked.

"Get you, going out with a bloke that owns a wine bar."

"It's a wine bar Len, not a rock band."

Len raised his eyebrows at my remark. “I wasn’t being sarcastic George.”

I shrugged, I don’t know why I’d said that out loud but it was true, it was just a wine bar, nothing to do with a rock band.

“Which one?” Bailey asked. “Which wine bar does he own?”

“Kings,” I reply.

“You’re dating Cameron King, seriously, fuck George, does the old man know?” Lennon asks. How does he know Cam I wonder?

“You are kidding Georgia; you aren’t seriously dating Cameron King are you?’

“Yes, well no, I went on a date with him last night, he took me to dinner. How do you two know Cam?” Bailey is standing up now and standing over me and I don’t like the way this conversation is going.

“Georgia, everybody knows Cam, you do know who he is right?” I shake my head and shrug my shoulders. “Cameron King owns half of London and most of Essex, he’s partners with us in Kings but only because his wife’s sister sold us her share and he couldn’t do anything about it. Does Dad know? He’s dangerous George, I mean it, he’s fucking dangerous.”

Baileys pacing the floor in front of me, I don’t understand what his problem is; Cam’s a nice bloke, from what I know of him. Why didn’t he tell me he was in partnership with my Dad? Why the fuck didn’t he tell me he had a wife?

“He’s married?” I swear Jimmie could read my mind.

Bailey shook his head. “He was she’s dead.”

What the fuck?

“What, how did she die?”

Bailey scratched at the stubble on his jaw. “I don’t remember all the details, she was pregnant and it all went tits up, her and the baby both died, he was a mess, he was completely fucked up by it all, he's only sorted himself out this last couple of years. Did you not know none of this?"

No I didn't, he'd mentioned that he knew my Dad; surely he must have guessed that I would find out. Did he want me to find out like this? I felt a little hurt but then at the end of the day, I hadn't been exactly forthcoming with the details of my past.

"It was our first date; it's not exactly first date conversation is it?"

Bailey stops pacing and looks at me. "No sorry it's not. Look George, I know this is bollocks but you really do need to stay away from him, he's bad news, Dad will go mental and he's way too old for you anyway."

"How old is he?"

"You went out with him and you didn't even know how old he was?"

I shrug and shake my head again. "Just tell me Bailey, how fuckin' old is he?"

"I'm not sure, he's older than me, I think he's about thirty-five, thirty-six, too old for you and Dad will not be happy when he finds out, I'm not happy George."

"What's Dad's problem with him?"

"Our paths have crossed his a few times, he owns a few bars and clubs, and he's got quite a lot of fingers in quite a lot of pies. He owned Kings with his wife, and when she died it went to her sister, I forget her name but she's a right bitch, hates him with a passion, and blames him for her sister's death. Anyway, she got her sisters share of the club, King wanted to buy her out but she wouldn't let him, she wanted to sell to anyone but him." He shrugs. "She just wanted to fuck him over, we heard she was looking for a buyer, put in an offer and she took it but as part of the deal, we can't sell on to him for at least ten years, he offered Dad all sorts but the club does well so why wouldn't we want in, he made a few threats at first but he was such a mess at the time that we didn't take them seriously. Anyway, he has nothing to do with the place, it's his in name only, pretty much the same as us, we own it but the club runs itself. We have people we trust in there and no doubt so does he but I'm telling you now George, Dad won't be happy if he finds out you're seeing him."

I don't believe this, my brain is running in slow mode, I'm too stoned to think it all over right now, I slump back down into the sofa and let out a huff, Jimmie throws herself down next to me. "Well that's fuckin' bollocks, do you like him G? You seemed excited yesterday, about your date I mean."

"Excited is pushing it a bit Jim, I fucked it all up anyway, he asked about what Lennon and Marley did for work and I went into meltdown."

Jim takes my hand in hers. "Oh George, I am sorry, all this time. I really wish you'd talk to him George, you're both so unhappy, if you'd just talk, even if you don't get back together, you might at least sort out some of your issues so you can both move on."

I look down at where our fingers are laced together; my other hand is at my necklace. "How is he Jim?" I'd never, not in almost four years, no matter how desperately I wanted to know, asked her this.

"He's sad George, he gets on with his days, he writes songs that are so obviously about you, he drinks too much, he snorts too much Charlie, he smokes too much weed, he fucks too many women but all just to try and forget you."

Lennon is listening to what we are saying, he passes the joint to me that he's just fired up. "I really wish you two would talk before the wedding Porge, I don't want the pair of you not enjoying the day because you're worrying about the other one being there."

"I'll be fine." I shrug. I won't, I'll be far from fine but I didn't want Jim and Lennon worrying about how I'd be handling their big day.

"You've been sayin' that for nearly four years G and look at ya, you're skinny as fuck and still can't bear to hear his name mentioned, this whole thing between the two of you is seriously fucked."

Bailey is lying on the floor with his long legs stretched out in front of him and his head resting on the bean bag. "I'm sorry George, I didn't realise you were still such a mess over Sean."

"Shush!" Jimmie glared at Bails. "We don't say his name when Georgia's here."

"You're fuckin' kiddin' me right?" His eyes looked between all of us, I shook my head.

"We don't say his name, we don't talk about the band, and we don't play music."

Bailey was sitting up now with his elbows resting on his knees. "Why Porge, why?"

My eldest brother hadn't been around to witness how close Sean and I had become over the years; he had no idea how deep our love had become. "Because I love him so much Bails, because it still hurts so fuckin' much, because I am still, just barely hanging on."

"Oh Georgia, I'm so sorry, I had no fuckin' idea, I'm your big brother, I should've been here instead of letting Donna keep me away, I'm so fuckin' sorry baby girl." He pulls me down onto the floor, into his lap, everyone in the room is crying, everyone except me.

"What the fuck is that?" I ask as I hear a rumbling sound coming from outside, Bailey frowns.

"I don't know."

"Oh fuck."

Lennon stands up and looks from me to Jimmie, she shakes her head slightly at him and they both sit down on the sofa. "Ha, it's a bike, it must be Marley, fuck I can't remember the last time we were all together."

"Marley has a bike?" I ask, I know nothing about the life of the brother I was once so close to, I didn't even know that he was in the country. I really need to start building bridges with him, there were less than three months until the wedding and I didn't want any kind of an atmosphere between us on the day. I'd been thinking about this for a while now and if he was here now, well today was as good a day as any to make a start. The sound of the engine had gone quiet.

"He'll go in and see the rents first, skin up Bails." Lennon stated, yeah I thought, skin up Bails, talking to my brother again after almost four years would be so much easier to do stoned, I actually giggled to myself as I thought this.

Jimmie looked at me and smiled. "You mashed Georgia?"

I giggle again. "Fuck Jamie, I think I am."

We lean into each other like we used to back in the day, the door to the studio swings open and in walks Marley, Sean, and two girls. My world stops turning and without any hesitation, consideration or thought of any kind I just look at him and say on a sob. "No, oh God no."

"Fuck Gia." He starts to move toward me.

"Get out!" Bailey roars at him.

"Georgia!" he calls out.

"Get the fuck out Maca!"

"No Bails, let me talk to her, G, please, can we talk G? I just wanna talk." I don't know what to do; my eyes just roam over his face, his eyes, his nose, his chin, his beautiful face that I have missed so much, so very much.

"What do you wanna do George, shall I fuck him off out of it or dya wanna talk to him?" I take a few deep breaths, trying to steady my voice before I ask him to stay.

"Who the fuck's she Maca?" The girl standing just inside the door asks, she's short and blonde, with massive tits. Haley, she looks just like Haley, I can't do this.

"Get out!" he shouts at the girl. "Get out, get out, get out!" She looks stunned but turns around and leaves, his eyes swing back to mine, pleadingly. "G, please baby, just talk to me, I miss you so much, so fuckin' much."

"Go," I whisper.

"No G, no, please, just five minutes, there's so much I need to tell ya, I love you so much Gia."

"Go Sean, go!" I scream. Bailey knocks me off his lap as he throws himself toward him.

"Get the fuck out, you've hurt her enough, no more Maca, no fuckin' more, else I swear I will kill you with my bare hands you cunt."

I stand up but the room spins so I sit, Jimmie is next to me on the sofa, she's sobbing, Len and Bailey are trying to drag Sean out of the door but he's fighting them and calling my name and there to the left is Marley, standing all alone and just sobbing and shaking his head and my heart try's its very hardest to break into even more pieces but it's packed so tightly together behind that wall, that try as it might, it's held in place, still and hard by all those bricks. I want to cry, I want to go to Marley and tell him that I don't blame him, I want to go to Sean and tell him its okay, I forgive him and I want to be with him. Instead I wrap my arms around myself and scream and scream at every one to go and then finally, after so very long, I cry, Jimmie holds me while I cry, then my Mum is there and I cry, there is so much commotion going on outside. I can hear my brothers shouting, I can hear my Dad shouting but above all, I can hear Sean shouting and calling out my name.

My Doctor said it needed to happen, that I had held things in for far too long and what happened over the next few days, needed to happen. Basically what I had was a bit of a breakdown; I spent a couple of days in my old room at my parents, doing nothing but cry, then another couple of days staring into space, finally on Thursday I got up and showered, I pulled on a pair of trackies and a sweatshirt that I had at my Mums and went downstairs. I looked a mess, I had barely eaten, my eyes were puffy and my face blotchy from all the crying but I actually felt okay. My Mum had given me a couple of Valium Sunday night and a couple more on Monday so those days had gone by in a blur. Jim had been and sat with me Tuesday; Ash came over for a while on Tuesday night. I'd asked my Mum if she would call Marley and ask him to come and see me on Monday but I hadn't heard anything from him. I'd fallen asleep around ten o'clock after Ash had come over again on Wednesday and when I woke at about two in the morning, he was there, sitting in the chair next to my bed, watching me sleep.

For some reason I was freezing, so I smiled at him and said, "Marley George Layton, would you please get in here and give me a cuddle, I'm freezing my fuckin' tits off."

He smiled back and said, "Fuck, it must be cold, coz you've got some fuckin' tits to freeze off there girl."

He kicked off his shoes and got into bed next to me, repeating an act that we had carried out throughout our lives, up until these past five or six years. We both lay on our sides and I spooned into his back.

"Don't you dare fart on me," I told him.

"Oh please George, don't make out, we all know you're the farter of the family."

"Yeah right Marls, anyway, at least when I fart it smells of roses, yours smells like something crawled up your backside and died."

"Hark at you, fuckin' Avon arse."

We both fell silent after trading insults, then I quietly said. "Marls?"

"Porge?"

"I'm so glad you're here."

"I'm so glad you wanted me here."

"Let's never not talk again."

"No problem."

"Porge?"

"Marls?"

"I am so sorry for everything."

"I know you are Marls, let's go to sleep."

I slept soundly the entire night with my brother there to look after me; when I woke in the morning he was gone but I now felt like I was done with the crying and ready to face the world again.

My Mum was sitting on a stool at the bench top, flicking through a magazine when I walked into the kitchen, the radio was playing and my Mum instinctively lent across to turn it off as I came into the room. “Morning, its fine Mum, leave it on, please.”

She beamed. “Are you sure George?’

“I’m positive Mum, what time did Marley go?”

“He left about five, he had a flight to catch, they’re on a chat show or something in Ireland tonight.” I proceeded to make myself a coffee, aware of my Mums eyes on me.

“Thanks for looking after me Mum, sorry for all the trouble.”

“Georgia, you’re my daughter, looking after you will never be any trouble, I’m your mother, it’s my job to look after you.” I give her a cuddle and a kiss on the cheek. “You’ve had a lot of calls here and at the shop and someone called Cam dropped your keys off, Ash bought them over with her; they’re on the hall table.”

Shit, Cam, I would have to get in touch with him and explain where I’d been all week. I nodded as my Mum reeled off the messages, they were mainly from the girls at work, then she said, “Sean has called a couple of times a day, every day, he begged to come and see you but your Dad and Bailey were having none of it, but what do you want George? Do you want to see him? If it’s going to set you off again, then I don’t think it’s a good idea.”

She watched me, waiting on an answer as I sipped some more of my coffee. “Seeing him won’t set me off, I don’t think anything will set me off like that again, I don’t know why I reacted like that but, it won’t happen again.”

“I do,” my Mum stated. “Because you bottled everything up, you can’t do that George, you need to open up a little bit, let us all back in, we love you and we all want to help you move on. Who’s this Cam? Ash said he’s really nice.” Oh shit, how do I explain this one? “He’s really nice Mum but I don’t know if he’s for me.”

“Why, you need to move on Georgia, you really do; Sean’s not spent the last four years sitting around moping, he’s in the paper nearly every day with a different girl on his arm, all of them stunning… slutty looking but stunning.”

“Mum! I said I was ready to see him, I don’t want to hear about his love life or the women he’s shagging and as for Cam, well Bailey’s not happy, he knows him and has told me I’m not to see him again.”

“Bailey said that?”

“Yes Mum.”

“Why, why on earth would he say that?”

“Because it’s Cameron King Mum, the bloke I went out with Saturday night is Cameron King.”

My Mum’s mouth actually fell open.

“Oh shit, fucking hell Georgia, your Dad will go berserk.” I let out a long sigh, my Mum just swore, that meant it was bad, very bad if it had made my Mum swear.

“Yes Mum, that’s pretty much what Bailey said but he didn’t swear.”

I looked at my Mum pointedly; I would have got into so much trouble for swearing like that. “Well, I’m sorry George, I’m just saying it like it is, I understand the attraction, Cameron King is bloody gorgeous but you need to stay away from him, he’s a dangerous bloke to be around, he’s involved in all sorts, he runs all these raves that the kids go to out in the middle of a field.” What was she on about?

“Mum, Cam runs a perfectly respectable wine bar, why would he be organising raves?”

“Because of the drugs Georgia, he organises the raves so his people can sell their drugs to all the kids, your Dad thinks I don’t know about any of this stuff but of course I bloody know I’m not stupid.”

“What has this got to do with Dad?”

"George, really, you are not stupid enough to think that our lifestyle is provided by your Dad's building firm and a couple of car fronts are you?" I look at her, totally confused.

"Well he's got the clubs and the pubs and the gym and the houses he rents out."

"George, they're all a front, well most of them are. Your Dad has many sources of income, all of those you just mentioned plus he's got a couple of brothels and a sex shop in Soho, he's into all sorts George, your Dad is a bit of a wheeler and dealer and it's made him very rich, I thought as you got older, you would have worked all this out." Shit, no I hadn't, how stupid was I?

"I thought he was an entrepreneur, that's what he told me when I was little, that he was an entrepreneur." Of course my Dad's dealings were dodgy, why else would he have a driver and at least one minder with him all the time, how else had he always been able to 'pull a few strings' to get things done, all of my life and how had I been oblivious to this fact?

"Well he is I suppose, it's just some of his ventures aren't exactly legal, that's why everything to do with our little business is in mine and your names only, there's nothing to trace it back to your Dad at all but anyway, aside from all of that, your Dad's dealings have bought him into contact with Cameron King over the years. They've fallen out a few times but I think at the moment things are polite between them, they are businessmen from different companies to term it loosely, one company is always looking to take over the other, both looking to be head of the company or more to the point, Governor of the manor." She folds her arms across her chest.

"George, if Dad found out you were seeing Cam, things could get nasty and I'm not being overly dramatic when I say that."

Bloody hell, all this time… all this time I've not allowed myself to feel anything for anyone and the minute I do, it's someone my parents don't approve of and Sean just happens to pop up and make an unexpected appearance with a Whorely lookalike in tow. Added to all of this, is the fact that Cam must have known I'd find all of this out. Why didn't he warn me? Why didn't he let me know of his business connections with my family?

"Mum, it was just one date, it's not like we've booked the church for our wedding. We just had dinner."

My Mum tucks a stray lock of my hair behind my ear and runs her fingertips over the side of my face. "Well you obviously had an effect on him during that one date; Ash said that he has been in the shop twice a day, every day to find out how you are."

"How the bloody hell did he know I was sick?" Great, all I want is Cam knowing about my little melt down, he already thinks I have screw lose after my little performance Saturday night. I can't help but wonder if opening up just a little bit to him, was the catalyst for this little breakdown of mine.

"Well I phoned Ash to let her know that you wouldn't be about this week because you were sick. That was on Monday morning, then apparently Cam came into the shop Monday afternoon looking for you. He said he'd called at the flat Sunday night, had phoned you and was worried, she explained that you were sick and staying here, he hasn't called here for obvious reasons and instead called into the shop every morning and every afternoon to ask how you were doing."

She gestures toward the dining table with her head. "And they've been arriving every morning since Monday." I look towards the table, which isn't actually visible, due to the fact that there are around twelve vases of flowers covering it.

"Shit!" My Mum actually doesn't reprimand my swearing for the first time ever.

"Oh there's more." She gestures toward the fireplace. "I had to go out and buy more vases yesterday."

There must be at least another eight vases covering the hearth and mantle of my parents huge brick fireplace but these flowers are different, the ones on the table are big bouquets of mixed flowers, the ones on the fireplace are just white Arum lilies, my favourite flower, I get the usual head spin and belly roll the instant I think about him and I swallow hard but I'm okay; I look towards my Mum.

"Sean?" I don't know why I'm asking, because I already know. She nods her head.

"He's called daily, he really wants to see you George but your Dad won't hear of it, he thinks you need time, he wants to send you away on a holiday, a week in Marbella or Portugal, a bit of time away from work and all of this." She gestures toward the flowers. "Wait till he finds out about Cam, he'll be wanting to send you to Auntie Kath in Australia for a year."

A holiday sounds good but I need to try and get my head a little straighter first, what do I feel about Cam now that I know what I do and am I ready to talk to Sean? "Oh Georgia, you're so grown up in many ways and so naïve in so many others, I forget you're only twenty sometimes, everything that went on between you and Sean, you were both so young, I feel so guilty about it, I should have protected you more."

"Protected me from what Mum, love? How do you protect someone from love?"

"It's not the love that's the problem George; it's the heartache that goes with it. You were so convinced that Sean was the one, I just let you get on with it."

"Mum, please try and understand, Sean is the one, there is and never will be anyone else, he's been the one since the day I first clapped eyes on him when I was eleven years old and there's nothing, you or anyone else can ever do to change that fact."

"I know George… I know and it scares me, I'm scared for you. That you'll go through life, never loving like that again."

I shrug my shoulders. "I've survived the last four years."

My Mum shakes her head. "No you haven't George, you've existed and you've only just about done that and I want more than that for you. I want you to fall in love again, get married, have babies; I don't want you to just exist."

My Mum twirls my hair in her fingers and I think of Cam, Sean, Cam, Sean, Cam, it's making me bloody dizzy, still better than just being stuck on Sean, Sean, Sean all the time. "But in saying all that," my Mum continues, "I don't want you and Sean getting back together if he's going to carry on the way he is and for you to just accept it. I bought you up better than that George, I know that the money and the power that goes hand in hand with what your

Dad does attracts women, women that would give and do anything to be in my place and I'm not stupid, I'm sure that there have been times that your Dad has strayed but he's never done it openly or blatantly. I've never heard so much as a whisper of him ever being unfaithful and it's still my bed he comes home to every night but I don't know if Sean is capable of that, I don't doubt he loves you George, I think he loves you with a passion beyond reason but I don't know if he's strong enough to resist all the temptation that's put in his way, and I wouldn't want to see you go through that."

I let out a big long sigh, I've been so busy these last four years, concentrating on shutting everyone out, avoiding any kind of emotions, trying to just survive each and every painful day, that I have failed to notice the effect all of this has had on the people that care about me. I love my parents and hate the fact that I am causing them so much worry. "Mum, I have no plans to get back with Sean."

As much as I would love to. "I'd never be with him knowing he was shagging about, it would kill me, like you say, you've bought me up to be better than that. I hope that one day, I will be able to find someone that will love and take care of me but I will always have to be honest and up front with them, they will have to know from the very beginning that I will only ever love Sean, I can't change that, it is what it is. Please don't worry about me and you're right in what you said about this little episode, it needed to happen, it should've happened four years ago but it's happened now, I've finally managed to shed some tears over it and I am ready to move on, I'm ready to listen to music again." I smile at her.

"Hmmm, well that will be a feat in itself George, every other song seems to be one of the bands and most of them are about you."

WHAT??

"What dya mean they're about me?"

"Well they aren't called 'This Song Is About Georgia' but seeing as Sean writes most of them and I know him like I know my own children, I know they're about you. When you're feeling ready, listen to some of their music, listen to the words and you'll understand, especially I got it wrong and the other one, the one they got all the awards for." I shrug, I have no idea, I know nothing of the band and their achievements, other than that they are now very famous.

"With me… it's called 'With me' George, it's one of the few ballads they sing, it's beautiful, Sean's voice…" she trails off. "Anyway, when you're ready, give them a listen."

My head is spinning by the time my Mum drops me home with orders to take the rest of the week off and to have a quiet weekend. The first thing I plan on doing is confronting Cam, I have had this horrible little thought going around in my head and before I decide where my feelings are going with this man, I need to find out if he's just playing a game. Is he using me to get at my Dad? Is he trying to find out my secrets so that he can use them as leverage in some way?

I change into a pair of jeans and my Chucks that I bought in America on a business trip with my Mum, she hates them, and I love them and the fact that no one else wears them. I pull on a sweatshirt as it's a bit cold outside and put a bit of makeup on, a whole morning of not crying has improved my puffy eyes but my face is still a bit blotchy.

I head back down the stairs and have a look at my car, I had to ignore it when my Mum dropped it off, she has no idea it was damaged, or why and that Cam has had the repairs done. This is what I don't understand, why would he do that, if he was just using me to get at my Dad, wouldn't he find it amusing to let my Dad know that his daughter is a two timing whore and got her car smashed up because of it? I have all of this going through my head as I make the ten minute walk up the high street to the wine bar.

Cam's car is in its usual spot but the bar is locked, it's only four in the afternoon. Shit I hadn't thought about that. I knock on the door and it's opened by one of the bouncers, he looks surprised to see me. "Alright love? Come in, he's in the office, just give the door a knock before you go in would ya, he's been on the phone for the last couple of hours."

I smile up at the giant of a man, he's about the same height as Cam but a whole lot wider, he's bloody huge. The bar is empty apart from one barman restocking the shelves, Mr Big and another bouncer who are in the middle of eating something up at the bar, they all watch me as I come through the door but smile nicely and then carry on with their conversation as I head to the office at the back, as I get closer I can hear Cam talking and he doesn't sound happy.

"I don't care; he's a piss taking cunt… No, he's been given more than enough chances and more than enough time… No Eddie, people will think I'm going soft, I've tried to be fair but I want my money and I want it by Friday… Well take his fuckin' car then and whatever else he's got that adds up to thirty grand, and tell him he's an arsehole and he's fuckin' lucky I haven't charged him interest and that I'm leaving him with his balls still intact."

Shit, angry Cam is scary and so fucking sexy, I knock on the slightly open door. "Hang on," he says to whoever is on the phone. "Come in."

I push the door open slowly and his mouth drops open slightly as he takes me in, I ache instantly, right down low in my belly and my face flushes as I look at him. He's sitting in the big twirly chair, wearing grey suit trousers and a light blue shirt, the sleeves are rolled up to the elbows and his grey tie has been loosened and his top button is undone, his long legs are crossed at the ankles as his feet rest up on the desk. He was rocking back in the chair when I opened the door but he's now stopped and is still, without saying another word or taking his eyes off me, he hangs up the phone.

"Kitten," he sighs my name. I think I just had a mini orgasm, I smile at him, yes, this man definitely affects me, I really hope he's not using me; I pull gobby George from somewhere.

"How the fuck are you Tiger, miss me?"

"Georgia, really, language."

"Errrm pot calling the kettle black there I think, after what I just heard you saying on the phone."

His whole demeanour changes in a split second and he sits up straight in his chair. "And what exactly do you think you heard me say on the phone?"

Shit, I do not like this Cam… well maybe I do, a bit.

"I heard you swear, a lot, that was all."

He leans back in his chair as his eyes look me up and down. "You look skinny kitten, are you feeling better?"

"I know, I've lost some weight this week but I'm feeling much better now; were you worried?"

He doesn't answer my question but instead says, "Come here." I think about it for a second, he raises his eyebrows, daring me to disobey.

"Yay, are we gonna twirl?" He lets out the biggest laugh as he pulls me into his lap and sniffs my skin, right below my ear, my nipples are instantly hard and my skin is covered in goose bumps. The phone rings, he reaches around me, picks up, then puts it down again, waits a few seconds then takes it back off the hook and lays it on its side. He holds me at arm's length and looks over my face.

"Are you sure you're okay, you look tired and very sad." His words make my insides melt; I let out a long sigh as I remember why I'm here.

"Why did you take me out Saturday night Cam? Why have you bought me champagne in the past? Why did you get my car fixed?" He holds me around the waist with his right arm, his big hand is splayed over my belly as I sit sideways on to him, still in his lap, I can smell him, I actually blink to try and remain focused.

"I like you George, I've liked you since that very first night that you walked in here, I've told you this; why, why are you asking?"

"Are you using me?"

"What the fuck are you talking about, in what possible way could I be using ya? You ain't even let me fuck ya."

"Why didn't you tell me about your business relationship with my family?" He puffs his cheeks and blows out a big puff of air that makes his hair move. I can't take my eyes off those full soft lips.

"Kitten." he says very quietly, and then pauses for a second as he rubs his index finger backwards and forwards over his bottom lip and I almost sigh out loud… Focus Georgia!

"I didn't say anything, because I didn't know what you knew about your Dad's business dealings, I didn't want to be causing any trouble."

"Why would it cause trouble?"

"Georgia, your Dad's a very private person and I respect that, any information concerning his business affairs are up to him to divulge, not me." And here it is again, that posh words, common accent of his again.

"But I'm his daughter."

"Well yes, I fuckin' know that now don't I, but I had no idea who you were when I first bought you drinks. I only realised that the night you came over here for a drink with me, that's why I, that's why."

"That's why you ignored me, that night, that's why you went all weird on me?" Fuck and I thought it was because of something he might have read, shit, I threw a drink in his face for thinking that as well, oops.

"When you told me that night who you were, I… I just thought it would be better to walk away. I know your Dad George, he's private and very, very possessive of his family, I had no idea he had a daughter, knew he had boys but I've only ever met Bailey and he's exactly like your Dad. I take it your other two brothers don't work for the fam… Oh shit sorry, fuck, you don't like talking about them do ya, sorry."

I feel weirdly happy that, that thought had popped into his head. "Anyway, I couldn't get you out of my head but decided to stay away, I like my head being attached to my shoulders and knowing your Dad and brother the way I do I decided that the best way to keep it there was to stay away from you."

He strokes his knuckle over my cheek bone and I can't help but lean into it. "But I couldn't, every couple of weeks you would parade in here with a different idiot all fucking over you and it was all I could do to not knock them the fuck out, but I didn't want to cause trouble I didn't want to cause trouble with you and I didn't want there to be trouble between me and the Layton's and then last week, when you turned up with no dick, shit shag, I couldn't keep a lid on it anymore."

He looks me right in the eye and grinds his obvious hard on into my hip. "I've had a hard on for you Kitten, since the first time I laid eyes on you and when that little prick told me you was with him and then put his hands on you the way he did, I fuckin' lost it. Good job Benny was there to hold me back, coz I was ready to kill the cunt, I wish I fuckin' had now, seeing as what he did to your car just cost me two grand."

What?

"My car cost you two grand? Cam, you can't be paying that for me."

He totally ignores me; he seems to do that a lot when I say something he doesn't like.

"Why did you ask if I was using you? I still don't understand where that came from?"

I feel guilty now, should I tell him why I thought he was using me? I let out a deep breath.

"I thought you were using me to get at my Dad; Bails told me that you weren't happy about him owning a share of Kings, I thought perhaps you were trying to get at him through me, find out my secrets, tell them to him, tell him that you had fucked his daughter."

He throws his head back and laughs that big loud laugh of his "Kitten, do you seriously think I have a death wish? If I ever got to fuck Frankie Layton's daughter, the last thing I would ever do is tell him about it, he would blow my fuckin' balls off, and then feed them to me."

His big laugh is infectious and makes my giggle sound very girly. "Don't be ridiculous Cam, Bailey would do it before my Dad could get to you, and he's younger and faster." I deadpan.

He gives a small shake of his head. “Well I would rather one of them than that psycho uncle of yours.” He’s lost me now.

“Who’s that, not Fin?”

He looks at me wide eyed. “Yes Fin.” He stops whatever he was about to say and sighs deeply. “Kitten?”

“Tiger?”

“Where are we going with this?” he speaks into my neck, in that spot, right bellow my ear, my body reacts in an instant and I’m covered in goose bumps, my nipples harden and I shudder, and that ache between my legs, aches just a little bit more. God I need sex!

“Where would you like to go with this Cam?”

“Where I would like to go, is right over this desk, and then where I would like to go is upstairs to my bed but we’ll get there, eventually.”

“You’re very sure of yourself Mr King.”

“That’s because I generally get what I want Ms Layton and I have you in my sights.”

For some reason that makes my belly do all sorts of acrobatics and I’m lost for words. We stare silently into each other’s eyes, I don’t know what I’m looking for, I don’t know what I hope to see, perhaps it’s myself I should be looking at, perhaps it’s my own eyes I should be looking into for some answers. This man leaves me so confused, he’s so alpha male, so dominating, so different to what I’ve been used to of late, I’m always the one in charge and with him, that’s just not going to happen and I’m beginning to wonder if that’s exactly what I need, instead of planning and scheming on how to get a man to fall in love with me, how to get them to the stage where they can’t live without me. Why not let all of that go? Why not just let go and see what happens, dare I take that chance, can I take that chance?

Then there’s Sean, of course there is, there’s always Sean and as frustrating as it is, I know that there’ll always be Sean. I have just ten weeks until the wedding, ten weeks in which I have to get my head in a space where it can cope with being in the same room as him and I don't know what to do for the best, whether to just go with it on the day or to agree to see him beforehand so that we can talk. I know I'm making progress, I've proved today that I can now talk about him and I even listened to music but that's today, I haven't heard a Carnage song on the radio yet or seen his face on the telly, tomorrows another day and if either of those things were to happen, I have no idea how I will react. I know the majority of the population won't understand any of this, I didn't then and I still don't think I completely do now and unless you have ever experienced that all-consuming, obsessive, takes over every second of your life, kind of love, then you never will.

"Would you like to come over to my place tonight for dinner? I'll cook, we can talk, because I have questions?" I ask him and feel absolutely gutted when he shakes his head no.

"You've been sick, you come to my place, and I'll feed you Kitten." Oh good, that's good then.

"You cook?"

"Fuck no, I never said anything about cooking, I said I'd feed you."

"So you're going to feed me raw food?" He gives a toned down version of his usual laugh and a slight shake of his head.

"No, I won't feed you raw food, I have a perfectly good chef here, where we can order from the menu and have it sent up. If you have nothing to go home for, we can go up now."

"Well I'm not exactly dressed for dinner."

"You're dressed perfectly. I've always wanted to have a twelve year old boy with great tits over for dinner." He tries to keep a straight face as he speaks.

"Do you realise how wrong, on so many levels, what you just said is?" He tilts his head back and considers what he said for a few seconds and I laugh when his eyes widen.

"Shit, fuck yeah, no, no, I am not, in any way, attracted to twelve year old boys, even if they do have tits like yours, or look like you in any way. Fuck, I don't like any boys, of any age, or men, blokes, I don't find… "

"Okay, okay Cam, I get it, I was joking." He rakes his hand through his hair and those dark eyes burn right into me.

"Shall we go then, upstairs?" he asks, before I can answer the other phone on his desk rings, he picks it up. "Fuck off," he says and puts it straight down again. He stands and I slide off his lap.

"Sooo authorative," I say to him, rubbing his chest as if I'm impressed with the power he exudes, which is actually turning me on no end. He pulls me to him and grinds the erection he still has going on into me, it presses the seam of my jeans, right into my clit and I fight to control my bottom jaw as it drops open, I clamp it shut and swallow hard.

"Oh Kitten, you have no idea."

His breath is hot and right in my ear and on my neck. I grab his arse cheeks and pull him into me tighter, I am on absofuckinlute fire inside and I know that I'm getting wet, he pushes his fingers through my hair and holds onto the back of my head and looks down at me. "Don't tease me Kitten, coz I will take you, right here, right now, right over this desk if it's what you want but you are pushing me to stage where I won't ask again, I will just take what I want."

My head swims with his words. How can just words have that kind of effect on me? I bite down on my bottom lip, I do want him, now, on this desk but I need a clear head, I have some questions I need answering before I take this further, because being the sad little compulsive person that I am, I'm afraid I won't care what the answers are once we have sex and I need to save myself from that fate.

CHAPTER 13

Cam led me out to the bar by my hand, the bouncers were still sitting at the bar talking and both turned to look at us, I watched as their eyes remained on my hand in Cam's.

"I'm taking the rest of the night off Ben, take any calls and keep an eye on things, I don't want to be disturbed unless it's an absolute emergency."

"What about the meet with Eddie?" Giant monster man asks… Ahh so this is Benny.

"I've spoken to Eddie on the blower, I want my money Ben, I let it go because I didn't want to see him lose his house but his Misses has left him now she's found out about his other bird, so fuck him, I want my dough." He looks at me, then brings my hand up to his lips and kisses the back of it, Benny just stares, and the other bloke's eyes almost pop out of his head and I wonder why that is.

"I'll ring down in a bit for some food, I'll call the bar phone." He looks at me. "Let's go."

"What, wait, you're going upstairs?" Benny asks.

"Na Ben, I'm going to fucking Mexico. Of course I'm going upstairs, I don't expect someone to deliver me food elsewhere." Benny's eyebrows rise up, they would be hidden by the hair of anyone else but Benny doesn't have any, he's as bald as a babies arse and just as pink.

"Okay," he says with a shake of his head.

Cam leads me to a door behind the bar, we go up a flight of stairs then he unlocks another door and we are in a hallway, this leads through into a large open planned living, dinning and kitchen area. Everything is white, except the sofas, which are black leather. The fireplace is huge, white marble Adams style, with a black marble hearth.

He lets go of my hand and goes over and flicks a switch and it roars to life, he turns and looks at me. "See how good I am at turning things on," he says with a wink and I cannot think of a single comeback.

"Park your arse; what would you like to drink? I've got a couple of Aussie wines in the fridge I need to taste for the new restaurant if you wanna give one of them a go?" he calls out while I watch him open a fridge that's full of wine.

"I'll give it a go," I call back.

The kitchen is all white with a black marble bench top that matches the hearth, I watch him as he puts the wine into a cooler and turns to head toward me with two glasses in his hand, he smiles when he sees that I'm looking at him. "Was you looking at my arse Kitten?"

I shake my head. "I was looking at all of you actually." He smiles.

"Good girl, honesty is always the best policy you know."

"I don't tell lies Cam."

"No? You don't give fuck all away either, do you Kitten?" I sigh and shake my head, not sure if I'm ready to go there yet.

"What dya fancy eating? The menu's over there." He gestures toward the coffee table. I pick it up and have a look through.

"What do you fancy?" I know what I've said before the words leave my mouth but I keep looking at him innocently, waiting for his answer. He sits back into the corner of the sofa, drapes one arm across the back, the other that's holding his wine glass, he rests on the arm, he's kicked off his shoes and his right foot is resting on his left knee, he brings his wine glass up to his lips and without taking his eyes from mine he takes a sip.

"What I fancy is you, naked on my bed, legs wide open so that I can see how wet you are. I want your hands tied to my bed head. I want you so turned on that when I stand at the end of the bed to look at you, I'll be able to smell you, I'll be able to smell how turned on you are, I'll be able to smell how much you want me to lick, suck and fuck every square inch of you." He takes another sip of his wine, while I struggle to not jump up and straddle him. "But what I will have is the steak, rare, with a fully loaded jacket potato. What do you fancy Kitten?"

Fucking hell, I've forgotten everything that I just read was on the menu. "Salmon," I reply.

He frowns and takes the menu off me. "There isn't salmon on the menu."

"Oh, shit, sorry, I just always have salmon, I just assumed…"

"No, no, don't be sorry." He picks up the cordless phone that's lying on the coffee table and dials. I sip my wine, wondering what he's doing. "Get Gino… Yes it's me, get Gino."

He looks me over. "How's the wine?"

I look at my glass, and then back at him. "It's delicious, very clean and crisp, a bit dryer than I usually drink but it's nice."

He nods his approval. "Good girl, well done."

Shit, I didn't know it was a test, I would've swirled it and sniffed and mentioned peaches and grass if that's what he was after, still, he seems happy enough with my answer.

"Why do we not have salmon on the menu?" he asks whoever is on the other end of the phone, I'm assuming its Gino. Who Gino is, I have no idea. "Well look harder, I want salmon on the menu, in fact I want a couple of fish choices, not just prawns, I don't know, you're the fuckin' chef, do your job, this might be Essex but I want more than prawn cocktail, sirloin steak and black forest gateaux on the menu… No, don't take all of that off the menu, I said I want more than that, hang on."

He looks toward me. "How dya like your steak?"

"Medium rare," I reply.

"Two steaks, one rare, one medium rare, both with jacket spuds fully loaded, spuds, spuds, potatoes, learn some fuckin' English will ya." He disconnects the call and throws the phone down on the coffee table.

“Sorry, we’ve only just started doing food, this is just a trial menu, I’m expanding the wine bar into the shop next door, we’ll have a full a la cart restaurant up and running by September and bar food available in the wine bar.”

“That’s great.” I raise my glass to him. “Here’s to Cameron King and his ever expanding kingdom.”

He smiles at me and his eyes sparkle. “I’ll drink to that.”

He clinks his glass against mine. He leans forward and my heart pounds hard against that brick wall it’s encased in. He reaches for the wine bottle and tops up both our glasses with a slight smile on his lips, fucker, he knows I thought he was going to kiss me, I thank him for the wine and turn and angle myself toward him. “How old are you Cam?”

I don’t know why I asked that. I’m curious, I know he must be at least thirty, he’s been married, he almost had a family, I won’t ask about that though, it’s too soon, I’ll let him tell me when he’s ready. “Why are you so concerned about my age? You haven’t told me how old you are.”

“I’m twenty, it’s not a secret.” He spits his wine everywhere and I mean everywhere, coffee table, sofa, carpet, me. “You’re only twenty?”

“Well yeah, didn’t you know that?” He doesn’t look happy, he gets up and goes and gets a tea towel from the kitchen and wipes the sofa and the coffee table and then leaves the room, leaving me sitting there. Fuck, what does that mean? Am I too young for him? How fucking old is he then? He returns with a t-shirt in his hand.

“Sorry about that, throw this on, I’ll put this in the drier.”

He’s standing right in front of me, between the sofa and the coffee table, as I stand up, there are only a couple of inches between us. I pull my sweatshirt over my head and face him in just my bra, he struggles for a split second, then loses the battle and looks down at my chest; he reaches up with his three middle fingers and drags them over my throat and down into my cleavage. My nipples are so hard they are painful, I look down to where his touching me, he cups my right boob and drags his thumb over my nipple, he leans in and sucks on my left, through my bra and I can’t help but throw my head back. “You have a fantastic pair of tits for such a skinny little thing.”

Before I get chance to consider what is the appropriate answer to that, a buzzer sounds and I jump out of my skin and launch myself toward him.

“Bollocks,” he whispers looking down at me, he kisses the top of my head and says, “Let’s get you fed.”

The food is great but I only manage to eat half of what’s on the plate, Cam complains that I haven’t eaten enough, then dives in and finishes it off for me, he opens a second bottle of wine and we go and sit back down on the sofa.

We are sat at the breakfast bar to eat and as I look across the room, I notice a vase of flowers on the dining table. “Oh, thanks for the flowers by the way, they’re beautiful, my Mum had to go out and buy more vases to put them in and my car looks good too, I haven’t looked at it properly but what I did see looks good.”

He smiles at me. “You’re welcome Georgia, I wanted to call to make sure you were doing okay but I was worried about your Dad answering the phone, I didn’t know… I wasn’t sure if you’d said anything to him about us.”

I shook my head. “No, my brothers know, well Bailey and Lennon do, I haven’t said anything to Marley yet.”

His lips curl in the slightest of smiles. “What?”

“I love the way your eyes spark when you talk about your brothers.” I can’t help but smile at the thought of my brothers, I’m so glad Marley and I are on talking terms again, I really do need to arrange to spend a day with him.

“I love my brothers, we’ve always been really close. It’s just,,, it’s just been a shitty few years. Bailey was living with Donna and she wasn’t a big fan of how close we all were and he stopped coming over for dinner but they’ve split up now and he’s back living at the barn with my Mum and Dad in Shenfield. Lennon I see a bit of each other now that he’s not travelling so much, he’s marrying my best friend in June, I’m being bridesmaid for that, they want to start a family straight away so he won't really be travelling anymore."

"What does he do?" I can answer this. I *can* answer this…

"He's the manager of my brother's band but he's getting into the agency side of things now so that he doesn't have to tour with the band and Jimmie, his girlfriend, she works for them too so she's been able to travel with him but if she has a baby, that's not what either of them want."

He nods as he listens. "I can't believe your brothers are called Lennon and Marley, who's the music fan?"

I laugh as I think about the times I've explained our names to people and for some reason I think about sitting on that old Chesterfield sofa in the summer house and explaining to the cutest brown eyed boy I had ever seen, a tear rolls down my cheek and I wipe it away quickly.

Cam doesn't say a word; he just waits for my answer. "My Dad. My Dad loves music, all music, any music, he encouraged all of us, and my brothers are all good musicians, with great voices. I play guitar and sing, I had piano lessons but I'm not very good at it, but our names, well Bailey's named after a bloke who makes guitars, my Dad met him at a festival in the sixties and remembered his name. Lennon and Marley, well that's obvious and me because Georgia on my mind is my Dad's favourite song and it's sung by Ray Charles, I'm Georgia Rae."

I feel embarrassed as I finish the story behind mine and my sibling's unusual names.

"It's a beautiful name." He leans in and tucks my hair behind my ear.

"Thank you," I reply.

He leans back into the corner of the sofa. "So your other brother, Marley, he's in a band then?"

For just a split second, my heart stops beating, my blood stops flowing and my brain stops functioning, just for a split second, then I pull myself together. "Yeah, they're doing… " I shake my head, I actually have no idea how they're doing, I know they're famous but I have no idea how famous because I've avoided all information about them for almost four years but I know from what little information I have heard, that they are big. "They're Carnage; my brother's band is Carnage."

His mouth opens but nothing comes out for a few seconds, I think he must have heard of them. "Fuck, fuckin' hell, your brothers *that* Marley, shit, I had no idea. My sister loves them, she's been to see them a few times, I've got a couple of their albums here, they're really good."

I nod in agreement. "Yeah, they've done well, I've barely seen Marls these past four years, we, I, I've had a few problems and we haven't really spoke but he came over to my Mum's and stayed last night, I think we've sorted things out now."

My heart is hammering in my chest; I can't believe I'm talking about this. "Is he the one that hurt you George, did he buy you the necklace?" He gestures toward my throat and I realise my hand is there, over the letter G at my throat. I drop it down into my lap and shake my head.

"No, no he didn't, not on purpose, it's complicated, I just, I'm not ready to go there yet."

It suddenly occurs to me that he still hasn't told me how old he is. "How old are you Cam?"

He blows out a deep sigh and looks around the room. "I'm thirty, I had no idea you were only twenty, fuck, no wonder Bailey went mental, I didn't realise you were only twenty, I had you pegged at about twenty five."

"Is it a problem then, is my age a problem?" He shakes his head; he suddenly looks very young and very vulnerable as he looks up at me through his lashes.

"Does my age bother you?"

I shake my head. "No," I say it like it's the most ridiculous statement ever.

"Will you tell me a bit about your family now?" I ask.

"What dya wanna know?"

I think about this for a second. "What's your sister's name?"

He folds his arms across his chest and rests his wine glass in the crook; I'm not sure if this is a defensive stance or if he's just getting comfortable. "My sister's name is Tory; my brothers are Robbie and Josh, nothing as unusual as your lot. My Mum's Scottish so they're all a bit traditional."

"I like them, they're nice names. How old are your brothers?"

"Robbie's thirty four; Josh is twenty eight and Tory's twenty one."

"Yeah, I remember Tory's birthday, the twenty fourth of September."

"How'd you know that?" He asks, frowning.

"Because you came in the shop and bought her a shit load of stuff remember? You told me it was her twenty-first on the Saturday."

"Fuck, you've got a good memory."

"Not really, it's my birthday too."

"What is?' He narrows his eyes as his frown deepens.

"My birthday is the twenty fourth of September, the same as your sister's."

"Really?'

"No, I lied; just to make conversation coz you're boring the fuck out of me." I hold a serious face for about five seconds. "Of course really you twat." I laugh. He doesn't.

"Oh Kitten, you will fuckin pay for that." Oh shit. He puts his glass down and then takes mine from me; he takes my hand and pulls me along the sofa and between his legs. I lace my fingers across his chest and look up at him. "Are you going to let me fuck you tonight or what? Because I am just about ready to explode here."

"I thought you were punishing me for calling you a twat."

"Yeah I am, I will, I just need to know if I'm gonna get a shag tonight first."

"Well seeing as you asked so nicely, no, no you're not."

"What, why?"

I don't know why, if we'd just gone for it, I probably wouldn't have been able to stop but because he's asked and I'm actually thinking straight, I know that I'm not actually ready.

"I'm not ready."

"Fuck Kitten." He looks all around the room but not at me. "I need to get you home then."

Well that hurts. "So just my company isn't good enough for you, if I won't shag you, you don't want me around. Cheers Cam, that's nice to know and there I was, thinking that there's more to you than the flash cunt that's always on display downstairs."

I go to stand up but he grabs at the top of both my arms and it hurts. We are both kneeling, facing each other, in the middle of his sofa. "I need to get you home because I don't want to be up on a rape charge."

I shrink back at his words, rape charges and every horrible memory those words conjure are forced to the front of my mind.

"Let me go," I say through gritted teeth.

"What the fuck is wrong with you Georgia?" he shouts at me. "You're sitting there all fuckin' sexy in my t-shirt." He scratches at his head. "I don't know where I fuckin am with ya, I'm a thirty year old bloke, I don't play games Darlin', if you want someone to mess with, then fuck off back to the dickless wonder you swanned in the bar with last week and stay the fuck away from me."

I twist away from him while he has one hand still in his hair but he grabs at me again, pinning both my arms to my sides.

"Let me fuckin go Cam, let me go!" I screech at him as I throw myself about trying to get away from him.

"What dya want, what do you fuckin want from me?" He pulls me to him and looks down into my face.

He looks so angry, nobody has ever grabbed me, pulled me about like that or shouted at me in my life; I was a princess, I was spoilt and pampered, I had grown up getting basically, anything and everything I wanted in life, except for Sean that is and the only way I knew how to react to being shouted at in this way was to spit and snarl my way out of it. I tried to head butt him first, he reared back and looked at me, eyes wide with shock at my actions. "What the fuck are you doing?"

His voice was all high pitched and incredulous and as I realised he was trying not to laugh at my futile attempts to escape his grip and to inflict pain on him, the more determined I became. I threw myself backwards and he couldn't help but fall on top of me, I bring my knee up and knee him in the balls, I'm thrashing from side to side and screaming at him, I must make contact as he doubles up and rolls onto his side, giving me room to roll out from underneath him, I start to head toward the door but he's too fast and grabs me again.

"Stop." He shakes me by my shoulders. "Fuckin' stop, what the fuck is wrong with you?"

I slap him around the face and almost faint in shock when he slaps me back, it's not hard, it's barely a tap, but I've never been slapped, except by my brothers, in my life.

"Is that what you want?' he asks. "Is that what you like? Is that what you're into?"

He pushes me slightly in the chest and I take a step back. "Give me something, give me something for fuck's sake Kitten, you totally baffle me, we were having a lovely night, one of the best nights in a woman's company I've had in years and then, then you just flip. Who did it? Who fuckin' broke you? I have to know who broke you before I can start putting you back together again so who,

who was it?" he's shouting and getting in my face and every step I take back, he takes one forward.

"Fuckin' tell me." he suddenly roars and I don't know why, despite his size, his strength and his absolute maleness, I'm not in the least bit afraid of him, all I feel right now is anger, anger and sadness at the fact that the boy I love so much is still fucking up my life so badly.

"Sean!" I scream back at him. "Sean," I sob as I drop down to my knees. "It's Sean, it's all Sean."

I sob harder, big heaving, out of control sobs; he's on the floor with me and pulls me into his lap. "Thank fuck." he says into my hair, he kisses me, my head, my hair, my cheeks, my tears.

"Let it out Kitten, let it all out, it's not good to keep it all in like that, believe me, I know, just let it out." And I do, I thought I had cried all the tears I had in me at my Mum's all week, but apparently not, this is different, I cried alone at my Mum's, here, I was crying with someone and admitting to that someone, who my tears were for, I was facing up to my demons and not just brushing them aside.

"I love him Cam, I love him so much, and it hurts so bad, I just don't know if I can live the rest of my life like this."

He kisses my hair some more. "I know, I know but we'll make it better, I promise, we'll make it better."

He stands without putting me down and carries me to his bed. He lays me down and starts to unbutton my jeans. "Cam," I say on a whimper. "I'm a mess, I don't want sex."

"Shush, shush baby, I'm not gonna touch ya, I promise, I just want ya to be more comfortable… okay?" I nod, too exhausted now to speak; he pulls my jeans off, then takes off his own clothes and slides in beside me in just his boxers. He pulls me tight into his chest and we spoon, my brain doesn't get the chance to even form any more thoughts before I am drifting off to sleep.

CHAPTER 14

Exactly like I did with Marley the night before, I slept soundly in Cam's arms. I woke on Friday morning to the smell of coffee and opened my eyes to the delicious sight of Cam walking through the bedroom door wearing nothing but a pair of light blue boxers, he looked at me warily and I felt guilty and ashamed of my latest meltdown in front of him last night. He put the coffees down on the bedside table without saying a word, I sat myself up, taking in the sight of his bare arms, chest, abs, legs, every naked bit of him and I've got to say, there wasn't a single bit of him that I didn't like, he was just an absolute, perfect specimen of maleness.

He lent forward and tucked my hair behind my ear. "Good morning Kitten, please don't lick your lips like that, otherwise I swear to God I will not be responsible for my actions."

I blushed and smiled at him, I was actually amazed he was being so polite and hadn't kicked me out on my arse considering my performance the night before. "Thank you for my coffee."

He shrugged. "You're welcome; I didn't know how you took it." He smirked at the double entendre then carried on. "So I made it the same way as mine, strong, dash of milk, a little sugar."

"Perfect," I replied.

"Gee thanks, you're not so bad yourself Kitten." He wiggled his eyebrows at me and I couldn't help but laugh and wonder what it was exactly that my family thought was so scary about this man.

"So, I best make the walk of shame and get home."

He threw his head back and I knew then I was going to be treated to his big booming laugh and he didn't disappoint, when his eyes met mine he said, "Fuck Kitten, if we had been doing anything shameful here, you wouldn't be capable of walking anywhere, I'd make sure of that."

"Oh you are so sure of yourself."

He shrugged his big shoulders, making my eyes flick from his face, down to his chest and back again. "What can I say, I've never had any complaints and they always come back begging for more from the Love King."

For a split second jealousy flashes through me but I kick it's arse till it leaves my head and say to him. "'The Love King', you seriously just called yourself 'The Love King'? That's almost as creepy as fancying twelve year old boys."

He shakes his head. "Fuck, you're never gonna let me forget that one are you?"

I smile and shake my head. "Hmmm, I'll keep quiet, as long as you're nice to me."

He looks at me without saying a word for a few seconds, he reaches up and brushes his fingers gently over my left cheek, then leans in and kisses me very gently on the lips. I close my eyes and keep them closed even after he's taken his mouth from mine. "I want to be more than nice to you Kitten, but we'll get there."

I open my eyes slowly as he speaks. "Are you going to work today?" he asks

"No, my Mum's banned me from work till at least Monday, I was gonna get some washing done today."

"Wow, life on the edge, dya fancy living dangerously and coming out for lunch with me? I want to have a drive out to a pub in Horndon, they get great reviews for their food and I want to see what all the fuss is about."

* * *

We have a lovely lunch together, Benny drives us in an old car, which I find out is a Jag XJ something, something, it's all leather and walnut inside and very old manish, I keep this thought to myself, seeing as he seems to be a bit touchy about his age, or my age, or, is it the ten year age difference between us? I'm not really sure. Our lunch is delicious and we share a couple of bottles of wine and at no stage during the day does Cam mention my escapades of the night before, we discuss countries we have visited, countries we would like to visit. I learn that both his parents are dead, he lost his Dad when he was eighteen and his Mum when he was twenty five; this reminds me of what I've been told about his wife and child but he doesn't mention them and I don't pry. He's eloquent and articulate but with a cockney accent, he's well-travelled and seems to be well educated. He's sexy, so fucking handsome and I enjoy every minute of his company and all of this terrifies me. The thought that finally, I might be able to move on with my life has my heart galloping like a race horse; I'm not saying that I'm falling in love with Cam, or anything remotely like that, but finally, I've found someone who has stirred an interest, someone I want to spend time with. He sets my skin on fire with just his words and I almost combust at his touch, finally I have met someone I want sex with for all the right reasons but I know I have to be very sure of this fact. I've spent the last six months being a serial user and abuser of men, I've slept with them for all the wrong reasons and with Cam, when it happens, I want to make sure that it's for all the right ones.

I have no idea where Benny waits while we enjoy our lunch but the second Cam goes to use the gents he's at my side. "We need to get him out of here as soon as possible, get your coat on and be ready to leave the minute he gets back out."

I frown as I look at him and my heart rate picks up when I notice the beads of sweat on his top lip. "Why, what's wrong Ben?"

"Just do it please Georgia, there's a crowd just walked in here, that we really don't want him bumping into, believe me." He walks back out to the bar at the front of the pub, sits on a stool and turns to look at me, he gestures behind me with his chin and I assume that Cam is heading back; I stand and start to put on my jacket.

"You in hurry to get back and wash all those dirty knickers of yours Georgia? I was gonna suggest having a drink at the bar before we leave," he speaks into my neck and the sensation of his breath on me makes me shudder; I remain facing away from him, I'm a shit liar and I don't want him guessing that's exactly what I'm doing when I reply.

"I'm absolutely stuffed Cam, I couldn't eat or drink another thing but thank you, the food was amazing, you really should think about poaching the chef for Kings." He turns me around to look at him, he has a frown on his face, which causes a little curve on his forehead, just above his eyebrows, almost like a smiley mouth, I want to reach out and touch it but something in his eyes tells me that he's not impressed with my last comment.

"What the fuck is wrong with Gino, my chef? He has the reputation of being the best in the southeast, it was the menu I came here to try, not the standard of the cooking."

Jesus, competitive much?

"It was a joke Cam, 'poaching' the chef… Geddit?" He closes his eyes for a second, gives his customary headshake and lets out a long sigh.

"That's a terrible joke Georgia."

"No it's not, it's fucking hilarious, you're just too old to get my humour." Shit, the wines kicked in and my brain is no longer communicating with my mouth.

"Are you trying to really piss me off now Kitten? Coz I tell you what, its working." He kisses me, a little too hard on the mouth, grabs my hand and leads me out to the bar where Benny is waiting.

As we reach Benny, he stands and sort of walks sideways, as if he's shepherding us toward the door, he steps in front of Cam and holds the door open for us, I just start to step outside when I hear someone call out. "Oi King, there's no need to leave on our account, stay and have a beer, we owe you at least that mate."

His hand instantly squeezes mine so hard it's painful and he stops dead in his tracks.

"Cam, leave it," I hear Benny growl, I turn and look at Cam, there is a nerve twitching in his jaw, he's looking down at me but he's not seeing me, he's looking straight through me and I suddenly feel scared and I just know that we need to get out of there.

"Cam, let's go Tiger, you can come and help me wash my knickers." He doesn't flinch. From the other side of the bar I watch as an older man approaches, he's in his fifties maybe, grey hair, pushed right back off his face, which is craggy, with a huge scar running down the right side of it, he's wearing an expensive suit which somehow doesn't match his face or the earring in his ear, he has a cigar in his mouth but is still managing a sneer on his lip.

“Get her in the car,” he says between gritted teeth.

“Cam, please…” I start to say.

“Do as you’re fucking told and get in the car Kitten, else I swear to God I will drag you out there.”

“Cam, Robbie and Josh are on their way, let’s just go, we can deal with this when we’ve got the numbers but not like this, not on your own.” He doesn’t move his head, just his eyes shift to Ben’s.

“Get her, the fuck out of here.” I know I’m not going to win; the grey haired man slaps Cam on the back.

“Cam, what you doing in this neck of the woods? Not your usual stomping ground.”

“Get your fuckin’ hands off me Terry.”

“Well that’s fuckin nice, not seen ya in…” He doesn’t get to finish, Cam’s hands are suddenly around his throat, he picks him off of his feet and pushes past me and Ben as he carries him outside to where the Jag is waiting, he keeps hold of the man’s throat but leans him back against the bonnet of the car, he pins him with just one hand as the man uses two to try and prise Cam’s fingers from his throat. I stand and watch in shock as Cam pulls a gun from the back of his jeans and forces it into the man’s mouth.

I know my mouth is hanging open, I cannot believe what is unfolding in front of me, two other men come flying out of the door of the pub and Benny puts out his arm like a barrier to block their way. “You really don’t want to get yourselves involved boys believe me.”

My eyes lock with Benny’s; surely he’s going to do something? Surely Cam won’t shoot him? He’s talking into the man’s ear, his teeth are still gritted and he has froth at the corner of his mouth. He suddenly pulls the gun from his mouth, lifts him once again by his throat and throws him onto the concrete of the car park, then shoots him twice, once in each knee.

I'm frozen to the spot. Benny unlocks the car, Cam guides me into the back seat and we roar off at speed. I suddenly realise that I'm going to be sick. "Stop the car, stop the car Ben."

"Keep driving Ben, she ain't getting out."

"I'm gonna… " Too late, my lunch comes up all over the leather seat and all over the floor.

"Shit!" I hear Benny say.

"Keep driving Ben, we'll deal with it when we're back on our manor, I'm not stopping here."

I back myself into the furthest corner of the car, away from my own spew and away from him. What the fuck did I just witness back there and how does he think he's going to get away with shooting someone in broad daylight? He's fucking mad and he's just involved me in a crime. Is this what my Dad does? Is this what being an entrepreneur involves? No wonder Bailey and my Mum said he was dangerous if this is his usual behaviour and what if they get to hear of this, what if my Dad and Bailey find out what Cam did and that I was there? My stomach roils again and I can't hold it down and this time I can't stop the cry that comes from me either, I've just watched someone get shot, fucking shot, right in front of me.

Cam goes to slide across the seat to get closer to me but I put out my hands. "No, no, don't touch me, don't you dare touch me."

I'm amazed at how calm I am when I speak, I don't feel calm, I can barely breathe and I can't bring myself to look at him. We drive in silence the rest of the way home, Benny pulls around the back of the shop so I can go straight up the stairs to my flat. I don't wait for him to open the car door; I can't wait to be out of there, as I run to the stairs that lead to my front door. Ben and Cam are both out of the car, I turn to Benny about to apologise for the mess I've made in the car when I see Cam handing the gun over to him, I turn back and shove my hand in my bag looking for my keys, as I pull them out, Cam snatches them from my hand. "Give them back, you're not coming in."

He totally ignores me, unlocks the front door and pulls me inside by my hand; he unlocks the second door and pushes me into my living room. I launch myself at him. "Get out, get out of my fuckin' house. How dare you involve me in that!"

I scream and scratch and kick at him; he grabs my arms and pins them to my sides and drags me through to my bedroom, throws me on the bed and lays on top of me, my arms still pinned to my sides. He looks straight into my eyes. "You can scratch and snarl all you like Kitten but I'm not letting you go and I'm not leaving here until we talk, or at least I talk and you listen."

He looks down at me, his eyes dart all over my face and I watch his Adams apple move as he swallows hard, I feel calmer now but he shot someone, I just can't get my head around it and by the way he did it so casually, he's obviously done it before. Fuck he was carrying a gun; does he always carry a gun, why?

"I'm so sorry you had to witness that today, I should've walked away, I should've taken your safety into consideration, and I should never have put you in danger like that. It was possibly the most stupid thing I've ever done in my life but when you're calm and when you're ready to listen, I want to tell you, I want to explain the reasons I reacted the way that I did but I am sorry, nonetheless." He rests his fore head on mine. "Please don't be scared of me Kitten, I'd fuckin hate that."

I'm actually not scared of him, I never thought for a second at any time today that he would hurt me, I never even thought about the fact that I might be in danger at all. We lay in silence for a while, I can feel his heart beating against my chest and it comforts me, I love that he's that close, I would have been a mess if he'd left me on my own this afternoon. Does that make me a bad person? Is it wrong to want to be in this man's company after what I witnessed him do this afternoon?

"If I let go of your arms, are you gonna scratch my eyes out Kitten?"

"No… but if you don't let go and get off me I might just piss everywhere, I seriously need to whaz."

"Georgia! That is so unladylike."

“Oh sorry Tiger, I didn’t realise that sticking a gun in a bloke’s mouth and then kneecapping him with two bullets in a pub car park was so fuckin’ gentlemanly.”

“You have such a smart fuckin’ mouth Kitten; it’ll get you into trouble one of these days.” Before I get a chance to reply, he grinds himself into me. “Especially with me, because for some reason, that mouth of yours makes me so fuckin’ hard.”

I don’t know why I do it but I kiss him, very gently on the left corner of his mouth, his eyes flutter closed and then open, locking onto mine. “Kitten,” he whispers and it sounds so fucking sexy that without hesitation. I grind my hips into him, then kiss the right side of his mouth, then right in the middle where I know his perfect cupids bow is hiding underneath the dark stubble that’s covering his top lip and jaw, he didn’t shave this morning and that two days’ worth of growth looks just about perfect, so perfect that I want to run my tongue over it.

Very gently, he kisses me back, his tongue runs along the seam of my joined lips, gently at first, then with a little more force, encouraging me to open and allow him access to my mouth and when I do, oh God, I spend the next five minutes being kissed like I’ve never been kissed before. He lets go of my arms and my hands instantly go to his hair, I wrap my legs around his hips and he grinds hard against me, his hands run up and down the sides of my body, from my arm pits, down to my hips and around to my arse cheeks, lifting them, forcing me into him harder. “Georgia, if you’re gonna tell me to stop, then tell me now because I won’t be able to in a few more seconds.”

“I don’t want you to stop,” I pant. I don’t, do I? Am I really going to do this? Well shit! “Cam?”

“Yes Kitten?”

“I really need a wee.”

He laughs quietly and rests his forehead back on mine, then rolls off me. “Go, have a wee but don’t be surprised if there’s nothing but a big pile of spunk here when you get back, because I will fuckin’ explode in a minute, I swear.”

"Eww, Cam, that's gross." He lies beside me on the bed, staring up at the ceiling.

"Go to the toilet Georgia and hurry up, I need to be inside you."

Fucking hell.

I climb off the bed and head into the en suite and go to the toilet, then I have a quick freshen up and clean my teeth, God knows how bad my breath must be after throwing up like I did, then I decide that as I know I'm wearing nice undies… I'm my mother's daughter after all... that I will go back to the bedroom without my clothes on. I look at myself in the mirror, my cheeks are flushed and I look the healthiest I have since my little meltdown last Sunday. Fuck, that's all I seem to have had this week, meltdown after meltdown. I tip my head upside down, my hair is due for a perm, but I was trying to leave it until as close to the wedding as possible so it's more wavy than curly right now and because the curls are lose, it hangs further down my back and over my boobs, I position it to hide them and head out to the bedroom wearing just my bra and knickers.

He's turned one of the bedside lamps on and drawn the curtains, it must be late afternoon by now and it's just starting to get dark, he's taken off all of his clothes except his boxers and is lying back on my bed, leaning on his elbows. I could probably stand right here and with a few rubs in the right spot, make myself come just by looking at him, he is just so big and manly and sexy and bloody hell, just, my brain can't think of a word, it can't think of anything, not even how to put one foot in front of the other as it would seem I've now come to a complete standstill.

"Come here." He beckons with his finger. Left, right, left, right I think in my head. I head toward where his long frame is spread out on my bed and I straddle him, I sit up on my knees as he sits up to meet me; he licks from the middle of my cleavage, up my chest, throat, under my chin and then plunges his tongue into my mouth. He unclasps my bra at the back and I let it slide down my arms, he pulls it off and tosses it on the floor, I watch him as he takes each of my breasts into his hands and sucks on first one nipple and then the other. I throw my head back and allow a moan to escape. He holds me under my armpits as he rubs my nipples with his thumbs “You are so fuckin’ beautiful kitten, you have the most beautiful skin, I want to lick every part of your body.”

“Do it then,” I grind into him as I speak. “Lick me Cam, lick me, suck me and then fuck me, I want you.”

He throws me down on to the bed on my back and kneels between my legs and pulls off my knickers. He bends my legs at my knees and positions my feet so that I am spread wide for him; he lifts my left leg and drags his tongue along the inside of my foot, then kisses up the inside of my calf, then drags his teeth all the way up to the top of my thigh. “I can smell you Kitten, I can smell how much you want me. I’m going to taste you now.”

He drags his index finger through me and then sucks on it, he repeats the action but this time he puts his finger into my mouth. “See how good you taste.” I nod.

“Don’t move,” he orders. Like I would want to be anywhere other than here right now.

He stands next to the bed and pulls down his boxers. Fucking hell, I’ve never, in all my days seen a dick so big, I suppose it stands to reason, seeing as the rest of him is so big. He takes his cock in his hand and kneels on the bed in front of me, between my still spread legs. “Touch yourself; rub right in the spot that turns you on the most.”

I do exactly as he says and use my middle finger to rub my clit, I can’t take my eyes from what he is doing to himself, as he strokes, I notice the head of his cock become shinier and wetter and I want to taste him, I haven’t done that for any man other than Sean, fuck, get out of my head, the last thing I want to do is start thinking about him. Yeah, fuck you Sean, I can do this, I can move on. I sit up and lean forward and take him in my mouth, he sits back on his heels “Oh fuck Georgia that feels nice. Oh fuck that’s good.”

Both of his hands are in my hair but he lets me go at my own pace; I only take the tip of him in as I know I will gag if I take any more, he releases my hair when I’ve had enough, then pulls me to him and pushes his tongue into my mouth, he pulls away and looks at me with a little smirk on his lips. “That’s my new favourite taste in the world.”

He doesn't wait for me to ask what, he plunges his tongue back into my mouth. "My spunk, in your mouth, nothing will ever taste that good to me again."

He winks as he pushes me back on the bed and buries his face between my legs. He pushes his tongue inside me and I moan, but that's nothing compared to the noise I make when he flicks his tongue over my clit and pushes two fingers inside me, I buck into his mouth. "Fuck, Cam!"

He looks up at me from between my legs, his stubble is wet and glistening with me and I don't feel the least bit embarrassed about it. "I want you to come in my mouth Kitten, I want to feel you tighten around my fingers and I want to feel your clit throb while you come all over my face." Fuck me!

"Are you ready for this Kitten? Coz I'm about to spin your world off its axis."

He pushes a third finger inside me and curls them all, he flicks his tongue over and then flat down onto my clit and I explode, I writhe and buck and lift my hips off the bed, I want to close my legs but he won't let me and it just seems to go on and on and on. I have never had an orgasm like it; I actually didn't even know they existed. Before I have chance to recover he's sliding up my body, kissing, licking and sucking, just above my pubic hair, across to that soft and sensitive area in the crease at the top of my leg, over my lower belly, he flicks his tongue inside my belly button and I squirm, then up to my breasts, paying attention to my nipples with his tongue then his teeth, then finally my mouth, his face and stubble are wet and smell and taste of me.

"My second favourite taste in the whole wide world." He twirls his tongue inside my mouth. "Your cunt, in your mouth, put there by my mouth."

"And how does my cunt taste?" I ask between kisses.

"It tastes fuckin' perfect and don't say cunt, it's not ladylike."

"You said it."

"Kitten, I am not a lady."

"Tiger, right at this moment neither am I."

He gives me a little head shake and a slight smirk and sits up to kneel between my legs. I watch him as he reaches for a condom that he must've left on the bedside table earlier, he tears open the foil packet and my eyes are glued to his actions as he rolls it down the biggest cock I've ever seen. I swallow, hard. He must notice the look on my face.

"We'll take it slow; I swear I'll be gentle."

"I don't think that's going to fit."

"We'll make it fit, believe me, slowly Kitten, I'll slide inside you slowly, you're so wet, it won't be a problem."

I give a slight nod of my head, still not convinced. He positions himself on top of me and uses his hand to guide himself to my entrance, I try not to tense up and fail miserably, there's no way that thing is going to fit inside of me without doing some damage. He kisses me very gently on the mouth. "You're beautiful Georgia; we are going to fit perfectly together."

He very gently pushes inside me, then moves his mouth from mine to pay attention to my jaw, my neck, my breasts, until I'm so turned on that I lift my hips to meet him, taking more of him in. "Fuck, Kitten, you feel good."

He pushes in further, it takes a few seconds to get used to how I feel with him inside me, it's not uncomfortable, not at all, it is different though, I've never felt so full. He starts to slowly rock in and out of me and I know it's not going to take much to make me come again, we rock our hips together and find a rhythm that suits us both; his mouth and teeth are all over me and I can't help but moan, fuck, it feels good. "Cam."

"I know, I know Kitten, just let it go, just give it up for me."

I don't really know why but I sob, I suddenly feel very close to tears as I call out his name. "Cam, please, I can't, I, I… " I shut up, because nothing I'm saying is making any sense anyway. We rock and grind against each other for a few more seconds, then he looks down at me, right into my eyes, all the while he's grinding right on my clit, while filling and stretching me inside.

"I'm gonna come now Kitten, you feel too good, you're gripping my cock too tight, and I can't last any longer. Are you ready, can you come again for me?" I nod my head and wrap my legs around him tighter, he slides his hands under my arse cheeks and tilts my hips up to meet him, all without breaking eye contact.

"Yes?" he asks, I nod. I'm not sure if I'm exploding or dissolving, I nod again, even though he hasn't asked me a question. "You feel it Kitten, can you fuckin' feel it?"

I can feel him jerk and throb inside me as my own orgasm rolls from the tips of my toes to the tips of my hair and then repeats itself over and over again and I cling to him and sob. I can't help it, four years of frustration, hurt, self-doubt mixed with every other emotion I have held at bay for so long. I don't know, I'm not sure of anything right now but I can't stop the tears and Cam is just perfect, he just holds, kisses and strokes me, he tells me how perfect our lovemaking was, how beautiful I am and eventually, I fall asleep in his arms.

CHAPTER 15

I don't know what makes me wake up, perhaps just the sense that someone was there; I'd been dreaming of Sean, we were driving through the countryside on a motor bike, it seemed so real, I could feel the wind in my hair, I could feel my arms wrapped around him but the most vivid part was his smell. He had started wearing Paco Rabanne the last few months we were together and I could smell it as I rested my head on his back as we rode, every now and then he would squeeze my hands where they sat low on his waist as I held on and when he did that, I would squeeze him tighter and breath him in deeper but something had woken me, something had dragged me from the absolute, perfect contentment I was feeling in my dream and I wasn't impressed.

I laid curled on my side and remained still for a moment, I could hear someone breathing lightly and I could feel an arm wrapped around me, there was a large hand splayed over my belly and a chest pressed into my back; the scent of Sean that I had woken up thinking was so real was replaced by something else, Cam, Cameron King was in my bed. We had had the most amazing sex last night, just the thought of it made me want to grind my bum into him but I didn't, I remained still, contemplating how I felt, I felt pretty good actually, I hadn't used him in any way, other than to achieve a couple of excellent orgasms. I had no desire to make him fall in love with me and then dump him, he was nice, I enjoyed his company, and he was the first man since Sean whose company I enjoyed, purely for the pleasure of his company. The fact that he looked like a Greek God and could fuck for England were a tip top bonus, he didn't seem to be looking for anything too serious and I most certainly wasn't, which meant, we seem to be pretty well suited. And then my belly does a little back flip; he shot someone, I stood in a pub car park yesterday and watched as he shot someone. I roll onto my back and am met with a very handsome face and a pair of golden brown eyes looking down at me; he smiles, ever so slightly and it stirs something deep in my belly, never again will I wait four years to have an orgasm with a man, I feel like I could quite happily lock myself away for a month with this man, let him fuck me senseless and still be left wanting more. Whore!

"What time is it?" I ask, my voice sounding raspy from sleep.

"Dentist o'clock." he replies. I lean my head back into my pillow and look at him for a few seconds.

"What are you talking about, what's dentist o'clock?"

"Two-thirty."

"What?'

"Tooth hurty… Geddit?" I groan loudly and it has absolutely nothing to do with sex.

"Fuck off Cam, even my Dad's jokes are funnier than that, are you sure you're thirty and not fifty two, because that was a proper, lame, Dad joke."

He stares at me blankly for a few seconds, I watch as his Adams apple bobs in his throat as he swallows hard, for a split second I think he's going to cry because I didn't laugh at his joke, when he says, "Her name was Chantelle, she was my wife."

My eyes widen as I realise this one of those moments where I need to keep my mouth shut and listen. "Our parents were best friends, I was two years older than her, and it was just always assumed that we would end up together. Her Dad owned a few businesses, my Dad owned a few. She was an only child so her Dad had no boys to take over the reins. Robbie was too old for her, Joshie too young. When my Dad was killed, Colin, her Dad, stepped in and helped us out, he made sure nobody came in and tried to take what my Dad had built up while Rob and I established ourselves." He takes a moment to sit himself up and leans back against the headboard, I sit up and tuck the quilt under my arms and sit cross legged next to him and listen to the rest of what he has to say.

"Georgia, I'm assuming you've worked out by now that not all of what I do is entirely above board, entirely legal?" I nod my head and just make an mmm sound.

"Me and your Dad are very similar in the way that we do things, the way we run our business, we're both very fair with people, we don't take the piss and we always try and help people out when we can but if you cross us, we will fucking break you." I nod some more. "Chantelle wasn't my girlfriend or anything until I was twenty five when Colin got diagnosed with cancer, it all happened so fast, there was so much going on. There's a family called the Riley's, they used to be faces around the East End in the sixties, then they moved out to Basildon way and made a name for themselves there. When my Dad was killed, they tried to make themselves busy, tried to take over a couple of the doors we run security for in Romford and Harlow, they would send people into the clubs to cause trouble, then report the bouncers to the Police, that and a few other things, anyway, it died down once they realised we had Col on board and that me and Rob weren't just a pair of kids to be fucked around with. So then Colin gets told he's only got months to live and he wants to see his daughter married, I know what I have to do, I did love her but she was just, she was more like a mate but I was prepared to give it a go. Colin lived a bit longer than we thought he would and Chantelle was six months pregnant when he died, this triggered all sorts of problems, she had had a bit of high blood pressure during the pregnancy, I… " He looks up at the ceiling and I can see he's struggling.

"I'm no angel Georgia, never have been, never will be, but I'm sorry for how I treated her when we first got married, I stayed out all night, getting off my nut on Charlie, fucking other women and she wasn't stupid, she knew, but she loved me, she fuckin' worshiped me, she always had, always did." He stares blankly right at me but I'm not there, he doesn't see me.

"Anyway, she's a mess after her Dad dies and I realise that I need to step up, she's on complete bed rest to try and keep her blood pressure down and I'm trying to deal with her and the Riley's who've crawled out of the woodwork again and are causing us problems."

I watch as his hand comes up to his jaw and he rubs with his thumb and index finger, he seems to study me for a few long moments, I think he's debating whether or how to tell me whatever it is he's about to say next. "I went out George, I went out on the Friday night, I was off my tits and pubbed, clubbed and fucked my way through Friday and Saturday night, I didn't call her, not once George, not once did I give my sick, pregnant wife a thought during that weekend, not until I pulled up Sunday lunchtime, back at our home."

He rakes both of his hands through his hair, then drags them down his face. "We had bought a place in Shenfield, not far from where your Mum and Dad are now. The first thing I noticed were that the gates were open, Chantelle would never have left them open. I had them put in especially for her and the baby's security, then when I pulled up outside, I could see that the front doors had been smashed in, I went running in, calling out her name, I found her in the bedroom, she was tied to a chair, blind folded, with an alarm clock left ticking and tied to her, she'd… " He shook his head, not the little head shake he does when I piss him off but a no, no, no kind of head shakes.

"She'd thrown up all over herself and was totally confused, I untied her and laid her on the bed, then called for an ambulance, she hadn't been touched, not raped, not beaten, what they had done was terrify her. Her blood pressure was dangerously high, they delivered my son by emergency caesarean, and he was still born. Chantelle started fitting on the operating table, her blood pressure was so high that it was causing seizures, eventually all of her organs shut down and she died, she died, my baby died a large part of me died. I should've died, not them, they were good and pure and innocent but they died because of me."

He has tears but he doesn't appear to be crying, he's just talking, telling me his story, with tears rolling down his cheeks. I go to him and sit myself in his lap, curl myself into his big body. He holds me, wraps his arms around me and kisses into my hair. "The man I shot yesterday, he was one of their firm, he didn't come to my house that day, if he had he would have been long dead but he was known to us as one of the faces causing us trouble in the clubs, then he got banged up and I just let it go. I had no idea he was even out so yesterday, yesterday he finally got what was coming to him."

I sit quietly comprehending all that he's told me. "It was the Riley's then, who'd come to your house."

"Yeah, we caught up with one of their firm later that night, didn't take much to get him to grass, but he did; all of those involved had done a runner over to Spain, all trying to lay low, they got in touch, pleaded that they had no idea it would cause her blood pressure to go up, they didn't want any trouble, they were sorry." I feel him shrug his shoulders. "I'm a nasty bastard Georgia, I've done lots of bad things in my life but I have rules, most people I deal with, your Dad and your uncle, your brother, we all live by the same rules, you do not involve people's families, whatever grief you have with someone, you do not involve family, especially not pregnant wives."

He sighs deeply. "They got what was coming to them, I didn't have to do anything, everyone else was so disgusted, so appalled at what they had done, that as soon as they surfaced, they were taken out, all but one, Chris Riley but I found him, I found him and I took a lot of pleasure in dealing with him. Terry was the last on the list, he's lucky I was with you and in such a good mood yesterday, I let him off lightly."

Fuck!

My Dad, my Uncles, my brother, my family are all involved in this, in this lifestyle and I had no idea. I sit silently in his lap, my head resting on his bare chest, he has one arm around my waist, the other wrapped around my shoulder, while he traces patterns over my back with his fingertips. I have no idea what to say. What do you say? Is this a conversation that anyone, has sat naked and had before I wonder?

"Would you like me to go?" He looks down at me as I look up at him. Do I? I suddenly feel incredibly tired again and just want to go back to sleep.

"I don't know, do you think I should want you to go?"

"Probably."

"Do you want to go?"

"No, I want to stay. I want you to tell me what you're thinking? What you think of me now that I've told you all of that?"

Bloody hell, this is all a bit deep and heavy for three on a Saturday morning, then thoughts start popping into my head. "How did your Dad die?"

"He was murdered."

"Like, Kray gangster style murdered?"

"Yeah, he was shot, on our doorstep, my little sister saw the whole thing, she had run and opened the front door ahead of him, and they pulled out a gun and put a bullet between his eyes."

"Fuckin hell Cam."

"Now dya want me to go?"

"Will you shoot me if I don't give the right answer?"

"That's not funny Georgia."

"And dentist o'clock was?" Before he answers his belly growls loudly, my heads still pressed into his chest and I hear the sound echo around his insides, I look up at him with a grin.

"Are you hungry Tiger, have you worked up an appetite?"

His mouth is on mine before I even finish what I was saying, I twist around in his lap and straddle him, the duvet is between us but I can feel how hard he is regardless. I tangle my hands in his hair and he does exactly the same to me. My lips feel sore, burnt almost where his stubble is scratching over them; I pull away and look up at him, we went to sleep with the lamp on earlier, it's just enough light to be able to see the glint in his eye.

"I thought you were hungry?" I ask with one eyebrow raised.

"I'm Hank fuckin Marvin Kitten but would much rather be inside you"

"Do you have another condom?"

"Are you not on the pill?"

"I'm on the pill but I don't know you well enough Cam, no condom, no sex, sorry but that's my rules."

He looks thoroughly pissed off for a few seconds. "I'm clean Georgia."

"Says you."

"What, do you think I would lie, about something like that?"

"Cam, I, no, I don't think you would lie but I don't have sex without a condom."

"What if we were in a relationship, would you still make me wear a condom?"

"I… we would… no, probably not."

"Would you like to be in a relationship, with me I mean?" Oh fuck, here we go and I thought he was different.

"Cam, look, we've just had sex for the first time tonight, we could be sick of each other in a week, can't we just see how we go with this?"

He bites down on his bottom lip and still doesn't look happy. "I don't share Georgia Layton, if we're sleeping together, then I don't expect you to be sleeping with anyone else."

I feel a little bit ashamed, he has every right to think that I'm a two timing whore, I want to get off of his lap, I want to have a little hissy fit and order him to go but how can I, how can I when he knows exactly how I have behaved these last six months?

"There's no one else Cam, there will be no one else while I'm seeing you, I won't fuck you about." I don't want sex now, the whole moment has gone.

"Would you like me to make you something to eat?" I ask.

His forehead is pressed against mine. "I would love for you to make me something to eat now please Kitten, and then when we are done, we find a fuckin' condom somewhere and we will fuck again."

And we did twice more.

CHAPTER 16

The next few weeks were busy; I went back to work on the Monday and helped out at the Brentwood shop, we were half way through March, people were now looking for summer wedding and Royal Ascot outfits. My Mum and I tried to be hands on at this time of year, spending a day a week at each store, making our customers feel special, which they were and giving them the personal touch from the management always made them feel extra special.

Cam and I were now in an exclusive relationship, he was a workaholic but he always made time for me, we would go out to dinner in the week or meet for lunch. Sometimes I'd come over to the wine bar and sit at the bar chatting to his bar staff and the bouncers, while I waited for him to finish meetings and phone calls in his office or for him to turn up if his meetings were elsewhere, later we would have food sent up to his place and I would spend the night there. Other nights he would come to my place once he had finished with all his business dealings, he would let himself in with the key I'd given him, either way, when we were alone together, it usually resulted in us having amazing sex, and it was amazing, toe curlingly so, he was a master in the bedroom, dominant, inventive and considerate. I loved the fact that when I was with him, I didn't have to think, I could just shut down my brain and enjoy the experience. Time spent with Cam, was time spent *not* thinking about Sean. Not that that was the only reason I spent time with Cam, not at all, I really did enjoy his company, in fact I enjoyed it more with each time that I saw him. The problem was, as always, Sean. I know I shouldn't compare the two, as my mother has told me on numerous occasions, no one will ever compare to my first love. She was lucky; she got to marry her first love. While mine was ripped away from me and I had never recovered from what I felt for him, and as handsome and hot and sexy and caring as Cam was, he didn't make my heart race like it still did when I thought of Sean. I didn't ache for him when we were apart, the way I used to whenever I was apart from Sean. I was beginning to care for him, but I knew from the second I set eyes on Sean that he would always have my heart and to this very day, he still does and there is nothing that I can do to change that fact.

Cam was usually busy on a Friday and a Saturday night and I really didn't mind, it meant that I could still go out with my friends on the weekend, which I generally did. Fridays we would club, Saturdays could go either way, we would sometimes club again or sometimes just go to the wine bar, then for an Indian. Sometimes I would get back to my place at dawn to find Cam in my bed and I was fine with that, it worked for me but by May, I noticed that if I wasn't at his place, then he would always be at mine. We'd gone from seeing each other three or four times a week to six or seven nights a week and he had started to complain about the fact that I still went to my parents every Sunday for lunch, and if my brothers were there and we all ended up in the studio, stoned or drunk, I would stay over till Monday.

I really liked Cam, I wasn't really comfortable with what he did for a living, but I wasn't a hypocrite either. I had, it turned out, been raised on money gained mostly by illegal means, so I could hardly call Cam on how he chose to earn a living.

We'd danced around the topic of moving in together but I felt for me, it was far too soon, I was too young. I was in the best place mentally that I been in for just over four years, I wasn't fixed, I still spent most of my time with my chest hanging on to that last little breath, because I knew, that if I let it all the way out, the panic would set in. I was better, much better. I was listening to music but not theirs. I still couldn't bring myself to listen to his voice, to hear him sing words that might tell me his thoughts, his feelings, it was still painful, my heart still hurt as much as it always had but I'd just gotten better at coping with it. Every now and then I would wonder if I'd go through my whole life like this. Sometimes I had suicidal thoughts and thought that perhaps I would rather be dead, than live with the hollow, emptiness I had inside, but since Cam had come along, I coped better with it all, I was grateful to him but I wasn't ready to move in with him.

The other issue between us was my Dad, he still didn't know about our relationship; at least I don't think he did. Both my Mum and Bailey had been on my case to tell him before he heard it from someone else but I still wasn't sure where we were headed. I liked Cam, a lot but he was giving me the distinct impression that he liked me a lot more and my old instinct of running as soon as I heard those three little words was beginning to surface.

I was out having dinner with Cam on a Thursday night at the beginning of May when he asked what my plans were for the coming Saturday. "Actually, its Ashley's birthday, we're going to Kings, my Dad's sorted out the VIP bar for us, we have a stretch limo picking us up, then there are about fifty people coming to the club."

He puts his knife and fork down. "Why didn't you ask me?"

"I thought you'd be working." Shit, I didn't want another night of walking on eggshells around him, he'd been really hard work for over a week now, and never seemed happy with anything I did.

"No, why didn't you ask me to sort out the VIP bar for Ashley's party?"

"Well, because…" I really didn't need this, was it going to turn into a pissing contest between him and my Dad over who had what power at the club?

"If I had asked you to sort it out for me Cam, my Dad and my brother would want to know why I hadn't gone through them, then my Dad would want to know how I know you, my brother is already on my case about seeing you and it would all just get complicated… So I just took the easiest option, the option that would cause me the least grief, at least I fuckin' thought it would."

"Do you really need to swear to emphasise your point?" Right, he's just patronising me now.

"Don't be so condescending Cam, you sound like an old fart." I put down my knife and fork and stare him square in the eye.

"Why haven't you told Frank about us yet?"

I shrug my shoulders. "I was just waiting to see how things went, if this was going to go nowhere, then what would be the point in stirring up trouble between you and him?"

"And is it?"

I raise my eyebrows, unsure of what his question means. "Stirring trouble?"

"No Georgia, going nowhere. Are we going nowhere?"

I shrug my shoulders. "I'm having fun, it's working for me. I don't know what your thoughts are, other than that you seem thoroughly pissed off with me tonight."

He gives his regulation shake of the head and his eyes meet mine, he lets out a long breath and reaches his hand across the table to take mine. "Sorry Kitten, I'm not pissed off with you, I just feel a bit gutted that you didn't come to me, didn't even mention to me about Ashley's birthday."

Okay, now I feel bad, I can see how that could be hurtful, it would be like him coming into the shop and asking one of the other assistants to help him and ignoring me. I let out a long breath and try to explain why I didn't come to him. "Ashley spoke to my Mum about it, before I had a chance to talk to my Dad my Mum had done it for me; it's really not a big deal Cam."

My eyes wander over his handsome face. "Why don't you come, surely you're entitled to a Saturday night off once in a while, or do the rounds and then come after?"

He knocks back his glass of wine. "Yeah, I dunno, I might feel a bit out of place, seeing as I'm such an old fart."

"Now you're just been facetious."

"Hmm, I'm impressed, big words from such a little girl." I don't know why but that statement really pissed me off, I felt like he was talking down at me, like I was a child. Did he think I wasn't capable of long words? I pulled my napkin out of my lap and slung it on the table.

"I need to go; this little girl is tired and has a headache." I pushed my chair back way too loudly for the posh restaurant, grabbed my jacket and headed for the door.

I didn't hear Cam's chair move so I'm assuming he remained seated. The instant I stepped outside, I saw Benny start the Jag up in a car park across the road. He pulled up next to me with his window open. "All right Duchess, jump in."

I had lit up a cigarette. I hadn't smoked in ages but he had pissed me off tonight so I felt the need. "Fuck off Ben, I'm not in the mood, I've had to sit through dinner with your boss acting like a prick, again, I don't need to be patronised by you as well."

"Fuckin' 'ell George, was only 'avin a laugh wiv ya, ignore him, he's got a lot on his plate right now."

"Not interested Ben, not interested." I stepped into the alley at the side of the restaurant and smoked my cigarette, I put it out and waited for five minutes but Cam didn't come out. Well fuck him, if he thought I was going to hang about and wait, he had another thing coming. I looked down the alleyway and could see that it led out to the next street but was blocked by a bollard to stop cars cutting through, so I quickly headed down it. Ben couldn't see me from where he was sat in the car and I walked quickly, as soon as I stepped out onto the main high street I was lucky enough to be able to hail a cab straight away. I jumped in and gave them Jimmies address and hoped that she didn't mind me turning up uninvited.

I got the cabby to stop off at the off license and I grabbed a couple of bottles of wine, if Jimmie wasn't up for a drink, then I would just go home and get plastered by myself.

I rang the doorbell and stood with my forehead pressed against the door, I was so busy going over tonight's conversation with Cam and his shitty attitude toward me that I didn't hear the door being opened, I fell forward and face planted right into someone's chest and I knew, in an instant, in a millisecond, exactly whose chest it was.

He grabbed me by the shoulders at first and I panicked and thought he was going to push me away, but then he wrapped his arms around me tightly, sniffed my hair, kissed the top of my head and said into my ear." I love you Georgia Rae, show us your tits."

Everything fell away, the floor from beneath me, the wall around my heart was gone in an instant, the person that I was, the person that I'd become over these past four years crumbled to dust and was gone, disintegrated, decimated.

I had a bottle of wine in each hand, I didn't let them go but hung on to them, I gripped them so tightly that my hands ached but

I needed to hold on to them, they were real, all the time I had them in my hands, I knew that I had some kind of a grip on reality. I wrapped my arms around his neck and pressed myself into him, taking deep breaths of him in. I thought that perhaps I was dreaming, or perhaps the front door had opened and I had fallen and bumped my head, so I moved the wine bottles that I was squeezing and my brain registered the chinking sound of the glass knocking together.

"Do you know how long I have waited to have you pressed up against me, how long I have wanted to bury my face into your neck and just breathe you in?" I can't speak, I'm terrified that if I do, I will scare away the magic and it won't be true, he won't be here, with his arms wrapped around me "Do you, do you know Gia?"

My insides curl in on themselves at the sound of him, calling me, that name, nobody, only Sean has ever called me Gia, nobody has ever even thought to.

"Four years G… four years and eleven days if you want me to be exact and every single moment has been absolute hell." He reaches round and using his index finger, he lifts my chin, I close my eyes, I can't look, I can't take that chance. What if I have finally had the meltdown of all meltdowns and completely lost the plot and this is all in my fucked up imagination? In that instant, I've never, ever prayed so hard to be mentally insane. "Open your eyes G; I need to see those beautiful blue eyes of yours."

"I can't," I whisper, my voice barely audible.

"Why G, why can't ya, I need to see them, I need to look into them, to see us, when I look into your eyes, I want to be able to see you and me and I need to know that we're still us, Sean and Georgia. Are we, are we still us G?" Very slowly I open my eyes, hoping for heaven, fearing all that I will get is hell but they're there, those dark brown eyes with their flecks of gold, my very own personal piece of heaven is staring right back at me.

"There's my girl." He smiles that lazy lopsided grin down at me and I whimper. He's so much taller than I remember, not as tall as Cam but he must be well over six foot now. "Can I kiss ya G, I want to kiss you. I need to kiss you G. Can I?"

I nod my head, which was at that precise moment not attached to my shoulders and was instead spinning off somewhere in the stratosphere and before I can think any more, his mouth is on me, soft and gentle at first, his tongue dancing with mine, gently, then deeper, tasting me, his lips harder on mine, he groans, I groan. He reaches behind me and takes the wine from my hands but doesn't stop kissing me, he wraps his arms around me and the bottles clang together, reminding me that this is all real. He's here, I'm here, we're kissing, we're here, together, Sean and Georgia; we finally stop kissing but stand with our mouths together, just leaning into each other, mouth to mouth, while we look into each other's eyes, he has tears rolling down his cheeks and I realise that I do too; I reach up and touch his face.

"God, Gia, I've missed you so fucking much."

"You never came back for me Sean, you just let me go. You didn't fight for me."

He frowned and lent away from me, then put the bottles down on the hall table; he turned and looked back at me, his eyebrows drawn together. "Georgia, I came to your Mum's but they wouldn't let me see you, so I sat outside the house in my car, all day, all night but then I had to go back on tour, so I called you, all day, every day, for weeks I called and I wrote and wrote, I sent letter after letter. I sent you the songs that I wrote for you, I wrote down every thought and feeling that I had for almost a year, I made videos of the songs so you could hear them, I sent it all to you G."

I can't believe what I'm hearing, to the point where I'm shaking my head. "No, no, where, where did they go?" I think I'm going to be sick. "Where did you send them? You must have got the wrong address."

Which was a ridiculous notion; he had spent more time at my house growing up than he ever had at his own house. He knew my address better than his own. Absolute panic is rolling in my belly, is he lying to me? Just when I suddenly had hope that he was here, with his arms around me, was he going to lie, was I going to lose it all again? He looks as devastated as I feel. "You sent them back?" But he's shaking his head; it's a question, not a statement.

“No, no Sean, never, I never got them, I never saw them so how could I send them back?” I’m shaking so hard that I can hardly control my jaw.

“They came back, unopened, with a note, saying, please don’t contact me again. All of it came back, the letters, the cards and poems, the videos, it all came back Georgia, you said you could never forgive me and to stay away.” He’s pulling at his own hair and sobbing as he speaks. “I wanted to die; I’ve wanted to die, every fucking day since. Every day, I’ve thought about it, dying, instead of living with this pain.”

He punches himself hard in the chest, into his heart as he speaks through gritted teeth. “I just wanted a chance G, just one fucking chance to explain, to say sorry, to tell ya, that, it’s you, it’s always been you, it will, only, ever, be you.”

I know that I’m pulling the ugliest of faces as I cry and try to speak and try to make sense of what he’s telling me. “No, Sean, no, I didn’t, I wouldn’t do that, I wanted to see you, I wanted you to come back to me, so badly, I almost died, my heart hurts so much, the pain, the pain, it’s killing me, it’s fucking killing me Sean.”

I’m shaking my head and gulping in air and my legs won’t hold me up any more. Lennon appears at the end of the hallway behind Sean. “Fuck… Jimmie!” I hear him call.

“I don’t understand then G, who, who would do that to us? Jimmie and Lennon knew how hard I tried, they knew how hard I tried to see ya, they knew about the phone calls and all the stuff I sent ya. Where did it go? How did you not know about it, surely not your Mum and Dad?” I can’t comprehend this, I just can’t get my head around it, all this time, all this pain and he wanted me back.

Jimmies suddenly at my side, I’m on my knees in her hallway, Sean is sitting cross legged facing me, with his head is in his hands. “Babe, what’s going on? Sean?”

She looks from one to the other of us. Sean looks up, he looks at me, and I think I’m on the verge of an anxiety attack. I’m gulping in air and making sounds that I’ve never heard a human make. “Gia” Is all that Sean says as he pulls me into his lap and holds me so tight it should crush me, instead I start to breathe slower. Air starts to reach my lungs, as I look up at him.

"Who would want to hurt us like that, who?"

Jimmies right down on the floor with us now, Lens pacing the floor behind Sean, then Marley appears. "What the fuck George, what's wrong?" He moves toward us.

"Will somebody please tell me what the fuck is going on?"

Jimmie is crying too and she doesn't even know what's wrong. "The letters Jim, all the letters, you told me that she got them?" Jimmie looks confused and frowns. "She did, you did, your Mum said that they upset you so much that we weren't to talk about them."

No, no, this can't be right, my Mum's one of my best friends, she wouldn't do that; she knew how much I was hurting. "No, no Jim, I never knew, I never saw a single letter."

"What?"

"She told me that Sean phoned for a couple of weeks and that my Dad had threatened him and he had stopped calling and that was it."

"Georgia, I swear to God, I called your house four or five times a day, I begged them to let me talk to you, I wrote letter, after letter, I begged you to see me." The hallway falls silent apart from the sound of breathing and sniffing. Sean continuously strokes at my back and my hair with the tips of his fingers and soothes me, calms me. I suddenly feel so tired, like I haven't slept in four years and now finally, I can.

Sean kisses the top of my head. "G, I love you babe but your arse is fuckin' bony and mine is going numb."

I look up at him and giggle. "You love me?"

"Of course I love you, how many times do you need telling, I meant it then and I mean it now, there's only you G, there will only ever be you."

He stands still holding onto me and carries me into Jimmie and Len's lounge; he sits down on the sofa with me still in his lap and says in my ear. "I have been without you for four fuckin' years. I'll never be without you again; I might just carry you around like this forever."

I smile and inside I feel like I did when I first wake up from one of my dreams about him, completely content, cocooned in his arms and his scent but then just like with my dreams, reality comes crashing in, my Mum, my beautiful Mum betrayed me.

Len passes me a glass of wine and what looks like whiskey to Sean. I take a long sip of my drink. "I need to speak to my Mum, I can't believe she'd do this to me, she knew the mess I was in. We've talked so many times and I've told her that I still love you, that I will always love you, I just don't understand."

I look across at Marley sitting in the armchair. "You okay big brother Marley?"

"Gotta say little sister Georgia that I'm with you, Mum just wouldn't do that, surely Mum wouldn't do that?" He shakes his head, and then carries on, as if he's talking to himself. "I don't know if I'm just over thinking things, but now I am thinking about it, she has gone out of her way over the years to stop you two from having any kind of contact. I just thought it was to protect you George and then after that Sunday the other month."

I feel Sean hold his breath and squeeze me just a little bit tighter. "After the way you reacted that Sunday, I thought she'd done the right thing but there have been a few times when she's sort of been a bit irrational about things, the way she told me not to give you our address and she was really pissed off when you found it out. It makes me think now she had her own agenda? What if there was more to it than just protecting you? Perhaps it was about hiding what she had done, I don't know, I'm just surmising."

I'm totally confused and have no idea what he's talking about.

"I don't understand Marls, what dya mean, giving me our address, I don't understand?"

"Ours, mine and Sean's, she told me not to give you our address because she was worried that you would just turn up unannounced. She said you'd been trying to find out where we lived so that you could stalk Sean." I'm floored and now, I'm also starting to get more than just a little pissed off.

"Marley, I have no fuckin' idea where your place is and I had absolutely no idea that you and Sean lived together."

Everyone seems to stop what they're doing, even breathing.

"George, did you never go to the boys place and try and get past the reception area, did you not go there and scream abuse at the security guard and try and kick the doors in?"

I look around the room at everyone; I look up at Sean, who looks at me horrified. "I didn't know about this babe, you came to our apartment?" What on earth is going on here?

"Are you all deaf, or just fuckin mad? I have no idea where Marley lives and I had no idea that Sean lived with him, no fuckin' idea. Where is this coming from, who told all of you that I had been there causing trouble?"

There's silence for a long moment as my brothers and Jimmie all look at each other, Jimmie shrugs her shoulders. "Your Mum, George, your Mum told us."

My bottom jaw quivers as I try to hold onto the hurt and betrayal that I am feeling inside, this is at least equal or maybe even worse than how I've felt about Sean's apparent misdemeanours for the past four years. I burrow into him and look up into his face. He looks pained and kisses my temple, very softly whispering, "Oh babe."

"Why Sean?" I look around the room at all of them, pleadingly. "Why would she do that to me? Why would she do that to us?" I can't control the sobs as I speak and once again, Sean pulls me into him and soothes and calms me down.

Eventually I resign myself to what needs to be done, I stand up and miss the closeness of being next to Sean instantly. "I need to call her; I need to talk to her."

I look at Len and Jimmie. "Can I ask her to come here?"

They look at each other. "It's ten o'clock George, dya think she'll come out at this time?"

I shrug my shoulders. "I won't give her any choice."

I have this little ball of anger burning in my belly now; if my Mum did this, if my Mum could have prevented the pain and heartache I've gone through for the last four years by even a fraction and didn't, even worse, if she has in fact been behind keeping us apart all this time, then I think my relationship with her is over, without hesitation, I will walk away from her and the business if I find out that she did this, this hurtful, spiteful thing.

I go out to the kitchen, take the phone off its base and with a shaky hand; I dial my parents' number. My Dad answers. Did he have a part to play in this I wonder as I speak? "Alright Dad, sorry for calling so late, is Mum there?"

"Hello, treacle, how you doin'? Yeah, she's right here babe, love ya."

"Love you too Daddy."

I hear him tell her it's me, I swallow and lick my lips but I don't seem to have any moisture in my mouth. "Evening Georgia, what's wrong?"

What's wrong, what's fucking wrong, where would she like me to start? I want to scream, I want to drag her down the phone line. I decide instead, to get straight to it. "Mum, I need you to come to Jimmie and Lens and I need you to come now, it's urgent."

"Georgia! Whatever's wrong, is someone hurt?" Is someone hurt, is someone fucking hurt? Hurt like you have no idea mother! My finger nails are digging into the palm of my hand so much it's painful.

"Yes Mum, someone is hurt. I don't want you to panic but I need you to get here as quick as you can."

I end the call before she can say any more and put the phone back on its base and stand and stare at it; Sean's arms wrap around me and he kisses me in that perfect spot right below my ear, my head swims and I can't help but give a little sigh and lean back into him. "We have so much to talk about, so much we need to sort out but I swear to God Georgia, I promise you here and now, I will spend the rest of my life making up these last four years to you, regardless what's happened since. It all started with me, me and my own stupidity, I will never put you through anything like that again, I want you back G, I want you with me, and I want it how it should have been all these years, Sean and Georgia."

I turn around and look at him, He looks down at my hand, it's at my throat, and he reaches out and moves my hand out of the way and brushes his fingers over my G. "You still wear it?"

He brushes his knuckles, gently over my cheek and smirks. "Are you blushing Georgia Rae?" He licks his index finger and runs it over my face, making a sizzling noise, like my face is frying him.

"Yes, I still wear it; it was the only piece of you I've allowed into my life these past four years. I wanted you near, I wanted to feel you but I didn't want to look at you and be reminded of what I had lost." He closes his eyes as if what I am saying is painful, he nods his head slightly.

"This is so fucked up G, you won't believe this." He pulls his t-shirt over his head, he's so much bigger than I remember him but he was only just eighteen then, he's a grown man of twenty-two now and ripped and toned to fuck; he lifts my chin with his finger. "Eyes up here G, this is what I wanted to show ya, not my abs, although I'm happy to show them later too."

He winks at me as he speaks. "But look, look at this." He points to the tattoo on his chest; it's the exact replica of my necklace, the letter G, being held up by angel's wings. "I wanted a piece of you, a piece of you to always be with me but I couldn't have it where I could see it all the time, it hurt, every time I looked at it, every time I caught a glimpse it served as a reminder of how badly I'd fucked up and how much I had lost."

I cover my mouth with my hand while trying to hold in a sob, it's pointless, I've held them in for far too long, four years in fact, he pulls me into his arms. "Hey, hey hey, it's okay, we're here

G, we found our way back to each other, we're meant to be G. They won't break us, not now. I'm never losing you again."

I kiss his bare chest and lick my tears off of him, he looks down at me. "This one's for you too." He tilts his head so that I can see the tattoo he has around his neck, it curls from his throat, around the top of his shoulder.

I read it out loud. "There's no one else. There never was. It's still only ever you." I touch it ever so gently with the fingers of my right hand and look up at him.

"It's from 'With Me'." I draw my eyebrows in together.

"What's that?" He frowns at me and smiles, and then shakes his head.

"Our biggest seller, the one that went platinum." I swallow hard and look down at the floor.

"I don't know any of your songs Sean, I couldn't listen, I couldn't listen to any music until a couple of months ago, but I've never been able to listen to yours. I couldn't bear to hear your thoughts or your feelings, I stopped reading magazines, I stopped listening to the radio, I used to hide in the toilet if your songs came on in the pub." I feel like such an idiot now, admitting to all of this. "It just hurt too much to hear or see anything related to you." I swipe at my running nose.

He grabs at me and pulls me in so tight to him. "Fuck baby girl, fuck, I'm so sorry."

I stand and let him hold me, my head spinning with everything that has happened so far tonight. I have no idea what to think right now, is that it? Without a word, without any kind of discussion, am I just going back to him? Am I just going to allow him back into my life? Before I get any further with that thought, the front doorbell rings.

He looks down at me. "Sean and Georgia, they'll never break us again." He kisses me on the mouth and then pulls his t-shirt back over his head, takes my hand and leads me to sit back down on the sofa.

CHAPTER 17

We all look at each other as Len goes to answer the door. I'm squeezed in to Sean's side as tight as possible, he has one arm along the back of the sofa behind my head, the other is stretched across his lap and his hand is holding mine, we both have sweaty palms.

I hear them talking in the hallway and I hear my Dad asking what's going on and if everyone is okay, then I hear Baileys voice as he walks in the room first, he frowns and looks around the room at everyone and then swings his eyes back to rest on my hand in Sean's. He tilts his head slightly toward me. "You okay?" he asks quietly. I nod. "Maca," he says quietly to Sean and sits down next to me.

My heart stops, then leaps up to my throat, down to my stomach, then back up to my chest as my parent walk into the room, there is absolute silence. My parents look around at all of us, checking us all over for any sign of injury, my Dad narrows his eyes at me and Sean and tilts his chin up slightly and asks, "What's going on Princess? What's happened? You've scared your mother half to death."

"Can I get either of you a drink?" Len asks.

I can't take my eyes from my Mum, I knew, the instant she looked at me and Sean holding hands that she had an idea of what this was all about and my heart froze, the wall hasn't gone back up. It hasn't gone back into hiding from any feelings or emotions, this is something entirely different. I have an anger burning hot in my belly now, what was a little glow earlier, is now a raging bon fire and I'm struggling to contain it, I really want to lash out at someone and I can feel my breathing become erratic.

"Hey," I hear Sean say next me, I look up at him. "Calm, the fuck, down. We've got this okay, we're Sean and Georgia, remember, they won't break us again," he nods as he speaks to me.

My eyes wander back to my parents; they sit on the two seater as Len passes them both what looks like whiskey. I can't wait any longer. I have to speak before I explode.

“Did you do it?” I ask my Mum. I don’t shout, I keep my voice at a reasonable level and I think I sound pretty calm, my Dad looks at my Mum and then at me, my Mum stares into her lap.

“What’s going on George?” He looks back at my Mum. “Bern?”

“Did. You. Do. It?” I ask louder this time and emphasise every word. My Dad is still looking at my Mum.

“Bern, what the fuck is goin’ on?”

“Shall I tell him?” I ask, finally her eyes swing up to mine.

She knocks back all of her drink and takes a deep breath. “I did what I thought was right.” I fly out of my seat but Sean and Bailey pull me back. “How could you, how fuckin’ could you?” I scream at her.

“That’s enough Georgia, will someone please tell me what the fuck is going on here?” my Dad roars.

I bring my gaze to meet his. “Did you know, were you a part of it?’

“*No*,” my Mum shouts.

“Part of what George? I ain’t got a Scooby what you’re on about love.”

“Did you keep Sean’s calls and letters hidden from me? Did you pack them all in a box and send them back to him with a note, supposedly from me, saying do not contact me again? Did you tell everyone that I had been to Marley’s and tried to smash my way in? Did you, or was it just your lying, deceitful, spiteful wife?”

My Dad didn’t know he has no idea what I’m talking about; he looks to my Mum. “Bern?”

My Mum holds her head in her hand and shakes it; she looks up at me and Sean. “It wasn’t like that, at first I wanted you to get back with him, I wanted you back together but you were so broken George, you needed time, I couldn’t let you talk to him, you wasn’t strong enough and you refused in the beginning anyway.”

Lennon goes into the kitchen and comes back with a bottle of Wild Turkey bourbon and tops up everyone's glasses, Bailey has his hand on my knee, Sean has a hold of my hand, and we're all on the edge of our seats. I take Sean's glass from him and take a swig of his drink. Len sits back down and my Mum continued.

"I'm your Mum George, my job is to keep you safe" she looks at me wide eyed, and then turns to Sean."You'd only sent a few letters at that stage." She swallows hard and closes her eyes for a long moment. "After a few days, I was going to let him talk to you, I thought once the band were back on tour and you could only talk on the phone, that it would be safe, the distance would keep you safe"

She gestures to Sean as she speaks. "Then one day when George was at school, doing one of her last exams, this girl knocks on the door; I had no idea who she was… Anyway, she wants to talk to you George, she said that she needed you to know that Sean had been two timing you with her for years, that he'd only stayed with you because he was scared of being kicked out of the band and that as soon as they made the big time, he was going to break up with you and start a new life with her."

She swallows and licks her lips, I can see in my peripheral vision that Sean is shaking his head next to me.

"Na, na, na, what girl, who was she?"

"Sean," my Mum sighs out his name. "You had just broken my daughters heart into a million pieces, I didn't, I just believed what she told me, I didn't check up on her story, I just believed it, you weren't my favourite person at the time." She sips on her drink. "I didn't tell anyone else about her because I didn't want to cause any problems with the band so I just decided to keep quiet, Georgia seemed to be getting better so I had all post addressed to her, diverted to a Post Office box. I thought after a while it would stop coming, or at least slow down but it didn't. In the end, I packed it all in a box and sent it back to Sean with a note saying, please don't contact me again, I'm moving on with my life, you should too," She shrugs as she says this and I want to punch her, I want to cause my own mother physical harm.

"I didn't hear from her, the girl, for a long time, then a couple of years ago, when you boys bought the warehouse between you, she phoned up and said that she had heard through some friends that Georgia was trying to find out where it was and that she was asking a lot of questions about Sean, I was so worried, she was doing so well, you, were doing so well." She looks at me. "Everything was going well with work, you were gaining confidence but when she called, I got worried that you might have been heading for some kind of breakdown so I panicked and just told all of you lot not to mention that the boys had a place together or where it was." She shakes her head. "I thought I was doing the right thing."

My Dad reaches across and holds her hand. "You should have told one of us, you should have said something Bern."

"To who? If I had told you or Bailey I was worried what you'd do to Sean and if I'd told Marley, Lennon or Jimmie, I was worried about this other woman having an effect on the band."

"What about me, did you not consider talking to me about it?"

"No, no I didn't George, you've been so fragile for so long, I just couldn't take a chance on setting you back, you're my daughter, you were so badly broken when you thought he'd been with that girl in the hotel room. I thought that if you found out he'd been two timing you for years that it would kill you. I needed to protect you at all costs. I'm your Mother, it's my job is to protect you".

"Well you fucked right up there then didn't you? All you've managed to do these past four years is cause me untold misery," I spit back at her; I take Baileys glass and drain the contents.

"What I don't understand though, is all this about George going to the boys place and trying to get in?" Jimmie asks.

"Well that's when alarm bells should have started ringing for me and I don't know why they didn't. Do you remember when there was that big article in one of the magazines about your wedding last year and they asked you about George being bridesmaid and if it was going to be awkward with Sean being there?" I watch Jimmie as she nods, I had no idea Jimmies future wedding had made the news, bloody hell, were the band that famous?

"Well a few days after that, this Mandy, the girl that had said she was Sean's secret girlfriend, she called the house and said that Georgia had found out where the boys lived and had caused all sorts of trouble trying to get up to the loft and that she had convinced security not to call the Police. She said that George was obviously in need of psychiatric care and that she needed to be kept away from Sean at all costs, otherwise she would have no choice but to tell him and that she would make sure that he would press charges."

"I swear to God, this has nothing to do with me," Sean protests from beside me. My Mum scratches at her head, it's a most unlikely action from her, she's always so composed and perfect, doesn't fidget, doesn't scratch, doesn't yawn, a perfect lady.

"George, you were out clubbing all the time, you had lost so much weight and your behaviour was a little bit erratic, I just thought that you were slipping again, I wondered if the thought of the wedding and seeing Sean had caused it… so… " She lets out a long, long breath. "Again, I told everyone to keep quiet about it, I discussed with Jimmie and Marley and we all decided to wait and see if you mentioned it to us George, we were just worried about you."

Sean runs his hand through his hair, and then looks at Marley. "Why didn't you say anything to me?"

"Because I thought you would go straight to her and I didn't think that was what she needed, I thought she was fragile, the same as my Mum, I was just protecting her, my Mum never mentioned a girl though." Marley looks at my Mum. "You said the security guard called you."

"Well I couldn't tell you about Mandy, she swore me to secrecy, she told me that her and Sean were still together but they were keeping it quiet until after Jimmies wedding as they didn't want to tip Georgia over the edge, I thought she was being considerate." My Mum gives a bitter little laugh as she finishes speaking. She looks at Sean. "When you turned up at my house that Sunday with the girls on the bikes, it struck me that the girl you was with, looked a lot like this Mandy but what I couldn't get my head around was, if you was so in love with this Mandy, why were you at my house with her lookalike, then I realised it was her that Georgia had the problem with."

She moves her eyes across to me. "All you kept repeating George was that she looked just like *her*… That got me thinking that perhaps you already knew about this Mandy, so I went through all the scrap books, I made them for you George, every piece of news about the boys, I kept and put into a scrapbook, in the hope that one day you would be able to look at it." She wipes tears from under her eyes and my bottom lips trembles as I watch her do it and I hate myself, I hate myself for caring that she's upset and I hate myself for being the one that's made her cry and I'm beginning to feel sick, because I think that I'm beginning to put this puzzle together. I cover my mouth with my hand as I can feel it start to water, the way it sometimes does before you vomit.

"I kept the good stuff and the bad stuff, the pictures, articles, song lyrics, you name it, I've kept it all and I sat and went through it until I found her picture and that's when I realised what an almighty fuckup I'd made."

I shake my head continuously. "Oh no, no, no."

I look across at Jimmie, she looks at me incredulously. "Whorely?" She asks me. I nod my head, then turn and look at Sean, he hasn't joined the dots.

"It was the girl from the rape charge." My Mum continues. Sean is instantly on his feet. "No, no, no fuckin' way, I have not clapped eyes on that girl since that day, there was never anything between me and her, never G, I swear on my life."

I shake my head at him. "I know, I know, I believe you."

I look around at everyone in the room. "Fuck, wow she really does hate me, because she's gone all out to ruin my life and keep us apart all this time. I need a drink."

I am so angry, angry to the point where I can't think or see straight, I need a drink, I need a cigarette, I need a joint and I need my Mum out of my sight while I try to make sense of all of this, my head right at that moment, feels like it's about to explode.

CHAPTER 18

The problem with open plan houses, is that you can't make a grand exit, you can storm off in indignation but there are no doors to slam, which, let's face it, is what you really need to do to get your point across and to let everyone know just how pissed off you are. The other problem is that there are no rooms where you can lock yourself away and have a good cry when the need takes and I think that right at that moment, that's perhaps what I need to do.

I go into the kitchen and retrieve the wine glass I left there earlier, I pour myself a drink and lean back against the work top and look across to my family all gathered in the lounge area. I watch Len, Jim and Marley, all deep in conversation. I watch Bailey, pat Sean on the back, say something to him and shake his hand, then begrudgingly my eyes go over to my parents, they are sitting side by side. My Mum seems to be trying to explain something to my Dad, he has her hand in his and I watch as he brings it to his lips and kisses the back of it, he nods in agreement at whatever it is that she's saying and they both look up at the same time toward me. She stands and the room falls quiet as she heads in my direction; I take a long chug on my wine and watch as she approaches.

"We really need to talk Georgia, I really need you to understand that what I did, I did out of love and concern for my daughter. What I did, I did to protect you." I don't want to cry, I want to be strong and defiant and nasty to her, I want to say spiteful, hurtful things, instead I just say what comes into my head as I really don't have the capacity to think too much right now.

"I understand all of that Mum but what you also forgot along the way is that you're my friend and friends don't keep secrets from each other, even if they think it's going to cause pain, they tell each other the truth, they share and then they're there for you, then they help you to pick up the pieces and move on."

"Well Jimmie lied to you too; you don't seem to be angry with her."

"Oh no, no, don't even go there, Jimmie was asked, by you I might add, not to mention something. She didn't blatantly, barefaced lie to me." Sean appears from behind my Mum and comes and stands next to me, taking my hand in his. "Mum, I've had the night from hell, I really don't want to talk about this anymore, I need to think, I need to get my head around the fact that for the last four years, someone has gone out of their way to fuck up my life and you helped them to do it."

She goes to say something but I hold my hand up to stop her and shake my head. "Please just go, I'm going to take tomorrow off and maybe next week too, I'm sure you and Ash can cope."

"Don't do this George, please talk to me."

"I can't right now Mum, just give me some time."

"One day Georgia, one day you will be a mother and then you will totally understand my actions."

I shrug and look at her. "Who knows?"

She lets out a deep sigh, then turns and walks away. My Dad gives me a cuddle. "Don't be so hard on her Princess, she loves you more than life, she thought she was doing the right thing."

"I know Dad, I know." Is all I can come up with, I just don't want to argue right now, not with anyone.

He shakes Sean's hand. "Look after her Maca."

Sean puts his arm around me and pulls me in tight, kisses the top of my head and says, "I will Frank, I will."

My parents leave and I just want to go and throw myself down on the sofa but Sean pulls me back as I go to walk away from him, I wrap my arms around his neck. "We need to talk G."

"Not tonight we don't Sean; I'm exhausted, I just wanna flop."

He bends his knees slightly so that we are at eye level. "Okay but tomorrow, we talk."

"Fine," I agree; he holds my hand as we walk back into the lounge and I sit down next to Marley, I lay down and put my head on his lap. Sean lifts up my legs and puts them in his lap, he pulls off my boots I was wearing and throws them on the floor, then starts to massage my feet; Marley looks down into my face.

"Eww George, you have the biggest bogies up your nose, they're like boulders." I smile up at him and shake my head.

"Well I can't see anything up your nose; your nostrils are hairier than Dad's."

His hand flies to his nose. "Fuck off; I do not have hairy nostrils."

We stare right at each other for a few seconds. "That was horrible, what just happened with you and Mum, intense and horrible, I love you and I'm so sorry, this all started with me getting off my nut and wanting to shag."

"No." I say quickly. "Do not say her name."

"Well whatever George, I'm just saying, I should never have dragged Maca into it, and then none of this would ever have happened." I sit myself up as Sean scoots up and sits in tight next to me.

"Marls, how many times do I need to say this, we were both at fault, neither of us should have gone back to that room with her, we both knew…"

"Enough, enough. That bitch has fucked with my life for long enough, it ends now, I don't want anyone blaming anyone for any of this anymore, including yourselves, what's done is done. I hate her and if I ever get my hands on her, I will kill the bitch but I'm not letting her actions eat away at me anymore, she's taken all she's getting from me." Baileys lying spread out on the two seater my parents were sitting on earlier, his long lanky legs hanging off the end. "I can't believe the bitch got away with it all for so long."

"Bails, I just said I didn't wanna talk about it."

"I can find her if you want George, let me have her name and I can get a trace on her."

"Bailey, will you leave it," Lennon snaps. "Just leave it, like George said, we all need to move on."

Bailey huffs and folds his arms across his chest. "Well if you don't want me to do it, ask your new boyfriend, he's pretty good at tracking people down."

Cam, fuck! He hadn't entered my head once since I fell through the front door; I realise the whole room has gone silent, Sean is completely still next to me, I'm too scared to turn and look at him.

"Bails, you really do need to rein in that big gob of yours tonight, these two have got enough shit to sort through, without you stirring the pot!" Lennon says to him.

My skin prickles and the hairs on the back of my head and neck stand on end, I just know that he's looking at me but I don't look round. "For fuck's sake, is anyone gonna skin up tonight or what?" Marley jumps off the sofa and heads out to the kitchen, returning with Lennon's stash box.

"Help yourself Marls why don't ya."

"Cheers Len, I will." He winks at Len as he proceeds to roll a joint on the coffee table in the middle of the room, he lights it up, takes a huge draw, then passes it to Bailey and continues to roll another.

I manage three hits before I feel the effects, then it hits me like a ton of bricks and all I want to do is sleep. "Can I stay here tonight Jim?" I ask.

"Of course babe, your usual rooms all made up."

I don't dare go home; Cam will be going absolutely mad and is probably waiting at my place for me right now. Cam, what am I going to tell him, things had been going perfectly until these past couple of weeks but now there was Sean? Sean who I love with all my heart. I feel whole, complete, fixed, just by being in the same room as him but we have a whole shed load of shit to sort through and if we have the slightest chance of ever getting back to together, then it's only fair that I end things with Cam, while I try and fix things with Sean.

At some stage, I must have fallen asleep as I feel myself being carried up the stairs, I open my eyes slightly and see that I'm being taken to the spare room, I know that it's Sean that's carrying me, I can smell him. He lays me down and kisses my forehead and then sits down on the edge of the bed and strokes my hair off my face, I open my eyes and look into the eyes that I have missed so much. "Don't leave; I don't want to be on my own."

I barely finish speaking, when he stands up and starts taking off his jeans, whilst toeing off his shoes. "Thank fuck, because I don't want to leave ya G."

"No sex though Sean, I just want to cuddle."

He stops and looks at me. "Gia, I wasn't, I didn't think, that's not what I wanted to stay for." His eyes look all over my body, the dress I'm wearing has ridden up my legs but they are covered by the thick black tights I have on, I watch as he adjusts himself through his boxers. "Okay, what I mean is, you're as horny as fuck and of course I've got a fucking hard on."

He shrugs and smiles at me. "You know me and what I'm like around you G, I just can't help it, and nothing's changed there." I can't help but smile at his honesty. "But that's not what this is all about, I just want to be with you, I won't even touch if you don't want me to but I hope you do, coz I do, really wanna, really, really wanna touch ya, but I get it, you've got a boyfriend now, I just…"

He looks around the room, struggling to get out whatever it is he wants to say. "Fuck G, please don't tell me I'm this close but I'm gonna lose you again." He sits back down on the bed next to me, the only light is what's coming from the old fashioned street lamp Jimmie and Len have on their drive, it bathes him in a soft golden glow and I unconsciously reach out and touch his hand, just to make sure he's real.

"I can't believe you're here," my voice is barely a whisper as I speak. He laces his fingers with mine. "I can't believe we're together, in the same room, touching."

My belly feels like it has batwings flapping about in it, I've had a few wines and I'm slightly stoned and all I really want is to curl up and go to sleep with him and think about the reality of it all in the morning, when I have a clearer head. "Draw the curtains and get into bed, I'm taking my dress off and putting your t-shirt on, so don't look."

He tilts his head to one side. "I'm the one that's taking their top off G, so don't you be looking, I saw how your tongue was hanging out of your head in the kitchen when I showed ya me tats."

"Don't flatter yourself rock star, I was admiring your ink, that's all… besides, you ain't got nothing I haven't seen before."

He smiles at me as he stands up and pulls his t-shirt off and yes I do stare, because he's fit and toned and standing right in front of me in just a pair of boxers. He hands me his top and I stand and take off my dress and pull off my tights. I never wear tights, I only ever wear stockings, especially for Cam, he loves them, I actually think they drive him a little bit insane when we go out and he knows I'm wearing stockings and suspenders underneath my outfit, he actually growls ever so slightly every time he brushes against me, just like a real tiger. Unthinkingly I take off my bra, then realise what I've done and quickly pull Sean's T over my head. God it smells divine, this is the smell that I've been dreaming of for so very long; I pull the quilt back and climb into bed, Sean climbs in beside me, the room is now in complete darkness, but my eyes do gradually adjust.

"Come here," he whispers, I curl into him, my head on his shoulder, his arm around me, our bare legs tangled together, in an instant, it feels so right, so perfect, like we'd never been apart. It would be so easy to just go with it, so, so easy but I'm not a naïve little sixteen year old, I'm almost twenty-one and I know that's not old by many people's reckoning, but I bet there are forty-year olds out there that haven't been through what I have in my short young life and the one thing I've learnt from all the drama of the past few years, is that the only person you can ever really rely on in this life, is yourself, and I'm not about to let me down, I have to protect myself from whatever tomorrow may bring.

Sean pulls me in tight to him and whispers in to my hair, "I love you Georgia Rae, good night, sleep tight." I close my eyes and drift into a deep, contented, dreamless sleep.

When I wake up, it's still dark, there's no clock beside me so I know I'm not in my own room, my belly does a few flips as I remember where I am and who I'm with. Sean, I'm in bed with Sean, my boy, my beautiful boy, who I've loved, missed and longed for these past four years. I turn and face him. I can just make him out in the dark and I first study his face, he's more handsome than beautiful now, his features much stronger than I remember, his boyish good looks are still there but his jaw is stronger and he has more stubble. I suddenly have the overwhelming urge to touch; he's lying on his side facing me, one arm folded under his head, one around me. I reach out and using just my fingertips, I trace across his brow, over his cheek and outline his lips, he sighs softly and grinds his hips into me, then I'm totally amazed as he whispers, very, very gently, "Gia."

I think for a moment that he has woken up but I lay still and stop touching. I realise that he's still sleeping; he's sleeping and dreaming of me. My heart suddenly aches as I think of the time that we've wasted, nights I've laid in bed and dreamt of him, even nights I've been with other men, it's still Sean that I've dreamt of. I wonder if it's been the same for him, despite all the beautiful women he has no doubt spent the last four years shagging. I wonder if all the while, he was dreaming of me. I wonder if they heard him whisper my name. I wonder if they wondered who Gia was. I don't want to obsess too much about the other women but I know I will ask. I don't want to know but I need to know. I don't know if that's a woman thing or if it's just my nature.

"Tell me about your boyfriend." Shit, I didn't even notice he had opened his eyes and was watching me. It's creepy that what was going through my mind was pretty much what was going through his.

"Is it serious?" What do I say, is it serious, was it serious? I think it was important more than serious. Cam was important to me because he had helped me move on.

Sean rolls away from me and puts on the bedside lamp, then rolls back to where he was, we mirror each other, side by side, one arm folded under our head, the other draped across each other's hips.

"I need to know G, if you're in love with this other bloke and, we're… if all of this…" He looks all over my face as he tries to think of the right words. "If it's too late for us G, then I need to know now, before I get my hopes up, before I start... "

He pauses again and closes his eyes; he moves his hand from my hip, to the back of my head and pulls me toward him. He kisses my forehead and then rests his against mine. "Just tell me G, are we too late? Please tell me it's not too late. I fuckin' love you, so much, but if, if, fuck, I can't even say it."

I take his face in my hands. "Sean, like the tattoo says, 'There's no one else. There never was. It's still only ever you.'"

He repeats my actions and takes my face in his hands. We're so close that I can see the little flex of gold sparkle in his brown eyes. "I love you Georgia Rae Layton, so fuckin' much, I'm gonna give you the world, the whole fuckin' world but first, first G, I'm gonna kiss ya." And he does, so, so, softly, so gently, all over my closed mouth, then he pushes inside with his tongue, he tangles it with mine, then swipes it over my teeth, the insides of my cheeks, like he's trying to taste every bit of my mouth; he kisses, licks, sucks and gently drags his teeth over my lips, my jaw. He rolls over and kneels between my knees, then pulls me up to straddle him, I go to wrap my arm around his neck, but he puts them back down at my sides. Then pulls his t-shirt over my head and throws it on the floor, he uses the fingertips of both hands to trace over my face, jaw and neck, and he brushes so gently over my collar bone that I shudder. I don't take my eyes from his, he mostly studies intently what he's doing, but every now and then his eyes flick up and meet mine and my heart threatens to escape my chest with the way he looks at me, love, lust, desire, it's all there. His fingers travel over my chest, then over my breasts, he circles my nipples a few times, and then cups them, he looks up at me in absolute wonder. Before he moves his mouth to suck on my right nipple, I arch my back, offering them up to him, he switches his attention to my left, except now it's his teeth I can feel, he doesn't bite, he just drags his teeth and his tongue over my nipple, all the while, pinching and rolling with his fingers, the right nipple that's been abandoned by his mouth. I arch my back and tilt my head as I look up at the ceiling; I wrap my legs around him and grind against him. He moves his hands to underneath my arse cheeks and lifts me as he stands up from the bed, before lying me gently back down.

I'm lying sideways across the bed; Sean stands in front of me and takes off his boxers. I want to look but I don't take my eyes from his, he leans in and takes off my knickers, he bends each of my knees up as he pulls them down, I go to close them and lay them back flat on the bed when he says, "No, no G, leave them up and open them, I want to look at you."

I don't hesitate, this man has kissed every part of my body, he's watched me throw up, he's watched me wee, fuck, he's actually held my arms while I've squatted in a bush when we've pulled over at the side of the road. He's bought tampons to me in the toilet when I've unexpectedly come on, he's seen me drunk, he's seen me stoned, my heart suddenly hurts as I realise exactly how much we have shared. All of the memories I have locked away for so long suddenly come rushing forward, he's suddenly there, right between my open legs, looking right into my eyes. "I've dreamt about this so many times G, how you would smell, how you'd taste but now you're here, it's all so much better. I wanted to take my time, I wanted to make this last but now, I just want to be inside you, fuck Georgia, I really want to be inside you."

I can't speak, I reach out my hand to him and he holds it as he crawls up my body, not taking his eyes from mine he laces our fingers of both hands and places them either side of my head and slides straight inside me. I let out a little rush of air and I feel my eyelids flutter. "Gia, that feels so fuckin' good, so right, so perfect."

He kisses me softly on the mouth, our lips and tongues the only parts of our bodies moving as we lay completely still, kissing, and just looking at each other, our breathing in complete synchronisation. "I've missed you, I've missed us, I've missed this, so fuckin much G, this is all I want, all I've wanted for so long, just you and me, it's like coming home."

I give him a small smile. "Welcome home."

He kisses my nose and gives a little shrug. "They say that home is where the heart is and mines never been anywhere other than with you, always G, forever and always my heart is yours and will be with you no matter what."

I bite down on my bottom lip and try so hard to hold the sob in, but I can't. My tears are already running down onto my neck and into my ears. He kisses both my eyes, and then licks the tears from each side of my neck. The room sways and I feel myself clench around him, he presses his forehead against mine and chuckles, it's the most amazing sound. "Did you like that babe, my tongue on your neck?"

I can feel myself blush, he tilts his head and licks from the hollow of my throat, out across my left collarbone, then back and across my right, I squeeze my internal muscles again. "Georgia, you keep doing that and I will come without even moving, I swear to God baby that feels good."

I look over his face and eventually into his eyes. "Sean?"

"Gia?"

"Would you make love to me please?"

"It would be my absolute pleasure Georgia, my absolute pleasure."

He rocks his hips very slowly into mine and I rock back, we find our rhythm instantly, I tilt my hips so that I can feel him deeper inside and I love the sound he makes when I do this. He slides his hands around to my hips, his fingertips dig into my arse cheeks, his thumbs press onto my hip bones. I dig my nails into him, his shoulders, his back, then his bum, I pull him by his bum, into me, I want him as far inside me as he can get, no space, I want no space between us, so tight together that there's not even room for air, nothing, just me and him, Georgia and Sean, Sean and Georgia.

My orgasm starts as heat warming my core, then spreads, my blood, my skin, my internal organs, everything burns, everything, every single part of me is on fire but there is no pain, just absolute pleasure. I feel it in every cell, in every hair follicle, pleasure like I have never known, I'm calling his name and telling him I love him and I can hear him saying similar things to me and then at the exact same moment we are both silent and just look at each other. At the exact moment I feel him come inside me, he whispers, "Gia," and my second orgasm hits me, entirely different to the first. It's short, sharp and unexpected and I whimper and I just know that I have tears again and in a whisper that I can barely hear, he sings a song to me, a song that came out not long after we first met, when I was just a girl and he was just the boy that I knew I would always love. A song that I haven't heard in such a long time, it's just the two lines but we change the words slightly, like we always did and sings the first line of Dire Straits Romeo and Juliet, then waits for me to sing the second, it was just a thing, that we did.

"Georgia Rae, when we made love you used to cry… " He waits for me to sing my bit, I try to swallow down a sob but I end up singing through it…

"I said I love you like the stars above, I'll love you till I die."

And it's suddenly all too much, he cries, I cry, we cling to each other and everything is just as it should be, Sean and Georgia, Georgia and Sean, us against the world.

We fall back to sleep with our arms, legs, bodies, hearts and minds completely tangled up with each other, no telling where one starts and the other one ends.

CHAPTER 19

We spend Friday morning lying in bed at my brother's house talking. Well Sean talks, I listen as he tells me about the huge success that the band has had, the places he's been, the people that he's met. He tells me about the warehouse him and Marley have bought in the old docklands area of East London and with the help of my Dad's firm, they have had converted into eight luxury apartments. Sean and Marls now share the penthouse on the top floor, complete with a roof garden. He tells me how he's back in contact with his Dad and they now seem to have a pretty good relationship; he does ask me about my life and my work but oddly enough, he already knows everything that there is to tell. It would seem that we've handled our separation in the exact opposite way to each other, where I shut everything out and wanted no reminder of anything to do with Sean or his life, he has sort out every piece of information that he can about me. He knows about my work and how successful we've been, he knows about the countries I've visited, he even knows that I finally got to own my dream car and then says something really strange.

"You have no idea how hard it was to find one in that colour, I knew you wouldn't settle…" he trails off.

"How do you know what colour my car is?"

"You always said you wanted it burnt orange and black, ever since we saw that one down the Kings Road years ago, remember?"

"Yeah, but how do you know that's what I've got? What did you mean about it took ages to find one that colour."

"I bought you the car."

"What?"

"I bought you the car, alright?"

"But, how, why? I don't understand."

"You were what, thirteen, fourteen when we first saw that car and you told me that was the car you wanted. I swore back then, that if the band… if we were doing okay and I had the money, then

I'd buy you that car, I never said anything, I never told you, in case I couldn't afford it."

He looks up at me, we are naked, his head in my lap, my fingers are raking through his hair, exactly the way I used to, we are, exactly the way we were and yet, so entirely different…

"Jim told me you had passed your test and were driving around in a Beamer your Dad had given you and I just knew that you'd be hating it. Then Jim said that Frank was looking for some old car for you and was having trouble finding it." He looks away for a second, as if debating something.

"Then she told me that your Dad wasn't really looking too hard because he didn't think an old car was safe, he wanted you to have something German or a Land Rover or something similar." He shrugs his shoulders. "So I found your car, that disgusting colour you wanted, the soft top and the tacky fake walnut dashboard and got it delivered to your Dad's car place in Epping and they fixed it all up and…" He shrugs again. "The rest is history."

I'm gobsmacked! "You did all of that for me, but you didn't come for me, you never thought… you never just thought fuck it, I don't care if she wants to see me, I'm gonna see her anyway?"

"A million times G, more than a million. I sat outside your Mum and Dad's old house and almost broke in one night. I was gonna break in and just sit and watch you sleep but then I remembered that Frank has a gun and I didn't want him to shoot me." As sad as I feel, I still manage a small smile.

"I went to the shops once, I waited outside for a bit and then just as I plucked up the courage to go in and speak to ya, you came walking along with your Mum, you looked…" He closes his eyes and smiles. "You looked so beautiful. So grown up. You had a cream suit on and sling back shoes, you reminded me of Audrey Hepburn, all elegant and ladylike."

His eyes sparkle as he looks up at me. "Nothing like the Georgia I remembered in her monkey boots, camouflage trousers and Sex Pistols t-shirt. Anyway, once I saw your Mum was there, I knew it was pointless, I knew she wouldn't let me near you." Again I'm floored by what he's just told me.

“I know that day, I remember wearing that suit to a business lunch with my Mum and she had told me to put my hair in a beehive because the suit was very Hepburn. Sean that was only last year, less than that, last summer sometime.”

“I know when it was G, there’s been other times since then but that was just driving past, I just didn’t know what to do. I had the note remember; it told me to stay away, to never make contact.” My belly goes over and then ties itself into a complete knot. “Babe, you’re pulling my hair.” I look down at my hand, twisting a handful of Sean’s hair, I release it.

“Sorry, sorry, that’s what thinking about her and what she’s done to us does to me, I wanna kill her Sean. I should’ve done it years ago, I should’ve done it that night she licked your face.” He throws his head back and laughs, his shoulders shake in my lap.

“What’s funny?”

He has tears rolling down the side of his head. ”You were, that night, you beat the crap out of her, there were handfuls of her hair everywhere, and I’ve never seen you move so fast.”

I don’t know why he’s laughing, I wish I had stomped on her head and as if reading my thoughts he says, “G, don’t even think about it, just let it go. If we keep going over it, it means she’s won. killing her is not an option so let’s just ignore her, we’re here, we’ve ended up right here, naked, like this, talking like this, loving each other like this, despite everything that she’s done, we’re right where we were always meant to be, together.”

I shake my head at him. “You are such a song writer, hark at all this shit.”

In one swift move, he throws me down on the bed, pinning me underneath him. “What I just said is not shit G; I mean every word of it. One way or another, we’re gonna find our way back to each other. One way or another I was gonna fight and win you back, even if I died doing it.”

He rakes his hand through his hair and his fingers meet mine. “Fuck G, the things that have gone through my mind, the things I've thought of doing to try and see ya and then, everything else, the band, touring, the fuckin' press up my arse all the time. It's been a nightmare. There've been times, when I seriously thought that I was gonna go mental, that I was actually gonna end up in the nut house."

My eyes wander over his face, hating but at the same time feeling overjoyed that he'd pretty much gone through the exact same emotions I had for the last four years.

We eventually make our way down to the kitchen around midday and that's only because Sean is complaining that he's starving, my stomach is still too all over the place to even consider food; there's a note taped to the fridge.

Morning young lovers

Help yourselves to food, shower, whatever.

Stay as long as you want, you know that you're always welcome.

Don't do anything we wouldn't do, although,

Judging by the sounds coming from the bedroom in the early hours of this morning, the deed's already been done.

We love you both so very much and truly hope you can work things out.

If you need to hide out here for a while that's fine with us.

George, ring me, Maca, I've cancelled all your appointments until next Wednesday.

Luv ya's

J & L

x

For some reason, the note made me teary but I managed to swallow them down as I pulled out a frying pan to make Sean some fried eggs on toast. It was just a natural thing to do. I made his tea exactly how he liked it, strong, no sugar; he liked his yokes runny and his toast well done, three eggs, three slices of toast, well-buttered and a dollop of HP sauce on the side, oh and white pepper and salt on his eggs. White pepper, never black on his fried eggs.

He sat in silence as he watched me prepare his food, his lips twitching up into a smile at every individual thing that I remembered; when I set it all down in front of him, he said, "Come here."

I walked around to where he was sat at the breakfast bar, he opened his legs and pulled me between them, he wrapped his arms around my waist, and I wrapped mine around his neck. "Do you have any idea the affect you remembering all of that had on my heart?"

I smile at him and shake my head. "No, but I can feel the affect that it's had on your dick."

He's still only wearing his boxers and I'm still only wearing his t-shirt. He slides his hands underneath it and grabs my bum cheeks and pulls me in closer to him. "Georgia, baby, you cooking me eggs on toast has fuck all to do with my hard on, the fact that you exist is enough to do that."

He tilts his head and gives me that lazy lopsided grin, the one that had me falling head over heels in love with him, nine very long years ago. "But you remembering exactly how I like my eggs on toast, right down to the white pepper and HP sauce, that's got my heart beating in a way that it hasn't in four very long and lonely years."

I don't know why I say it, but it's out before I think too much about it… "Oh I'm sure you've had no shortage of women to make you eggs on toast and to make things hard for you over the last four years and I bet those years have been anything but lonely."

His face falls and I instantly regret what I've just said, he swallows hard and strokes over my cheekbone with the back of his hand. "Oh Georgia Rae, you have no idea, no fuckin' idea."

He pulls me in and takes a big sniff of my hair. "I smell of fried egg," I complain.

"Na, you smell like Gia, you smell like home, you smell like exactly where I want to spend the rest of my life."

I swallow back the next round of tears threatening to escape and just say. "Eat your breakfast before its stone cold."

He smacks my arse as I turn and go to fetch my cup of tea from where I left it over by the kettle. I come back and sit on the stool next to him and watch him eat as I sip my tea. "Why are you not eating G?'

I shake my head. "I don't think I could keep anything down."

"Why, what's wrong?" He asks with a frown.

"Nothing, just... " I shrug, "I don't know, just all of this."

I gesture between us. "You, me, my Mum, the circumstances, it's just got my head spinning and my belly back flipping, I really don't think I could keep anything down right now."

"Just a bit of toast?" he asks.

"No." I shake my head.

"G, baby, please don't take this the wrong way but you really need to put on a bit of weight." I don't take it the wrong way; I know that I'm way to skinny. I'm not short at five feet eight and the last time I weighed myself I was just over eight stone, a whole stone lighter than I was a couple of years ago. I'd gained a couple of pounds these last few months since I'd been seeing Cam, but I still needed to gain more.

Cam, shit, I need to speak to him, he'll be worrying himself sick about where I am, but I also need to end things between us. Don't know how he'll take that and oddly enough, I'm not really sure how I'm feeling about it either.

"G, you okay, I haven't upset you with that have I?" Sean brings me back from my Cam dilemma.

"What? No, no. I know I've lost weight, too much work, gym, clubbing." I shrug. "I was skinnier, but Cam's been good for me, I've put… " I stop as soon as I realise what I'm saying.

"So is Cam the boyfriend?" he asks, looking right into my eyes, I nod.

"I'll have to call him today, he'll be worried."

"Don't let me stop ya." His eyes have lost their spark.

"Please don't, I need to call him and I need to see him, he's a nice bloke and he'll be worrying about where I was all night."

"You live together?"

"No, no but he's got a key. I was out with him last night, we had a row, I stormed off and left him in the restaurant and jumped in a taxi and came here."

"So I have Cam to thank for you falling into my arms last night?" he asks with a smirk.

I suppose he does. "If that's the way you want to look at it, then yeah, you do."

"G, where you and he are concerned, I don't want to look at it at all, but, ya know, we've been apart, it's been four years, I get it." He shrugs his shoulders. "I hate the idea of it but I get it."

He reaches out and brings my hand to his lips and kisses first the back, then turns it over and kisses my palm, then licks and kisses the inside of my wrist. He lets go and stands from his stool and takes his plate and cutlery over to the dishwasher. I know Sean, I know him inside out and I know exactly where he's going now, even before he says, "I need the bog, you make your calls then come and join me in the shower."

I smile and shake my head. "In one end and out the other, some things never change do they babe?"

He grins a cheeky grin at me and shrugs. "What can I say G? It's the way I'm made."

I watch him as he walks out of the kitchen, a few seconds later, he's back and stood between my legs as I still sit on the stool, he tucks my hair behind my ears and my belly and my eyelids both flutter at his touch. "When you speak to Cam, be gentle with him." He looks over my face and gives a slight nod. "I know first-hand, how fuckin' awful it is to lose you." He tilts his head, kisses me gently on the lips and turns and heads for the bathroom.

I sit for a moment longer and look over at the phone; my mind is in a complete whirl, for some reason thoughts of my Mum's tumble drier come into my head. When we all lived at home, it always seemed to be full of socks, lots and lots of socks, different sizes, different colours, all going around and around and that's exactly how my head feels right now and every one of those socks represents a thought and each of those thoughts are scrambling for attention in my brain and I have no idea where to start. I swallow down the last of my tea and pick up the phone, I call my flat first and see if Cam picks up but there's no answer. I let it go to answer phone and call out for Cam to pick up if he's there but still no answer, I call his flat but there's no answer there so I leave a short message on his machine. I knew he wouldn't be at either of the first two places, I'm just delaying the inevitable, it's one o'clock on a Friday afternoon, there's only one place he'll be and that's the office at the wine bar. He picks up on the second ring.

"Speak." Charming, he's so not in a good mood.

"Cam?"

"Kitten? Fuck, where the fuck are you? Don't you ever do something like that to me again, you fuckin' hear me. I've been worried sick, where are you?"

"I'm sorry, I'm fine, I should've called you last night. I didn't mean to make you worry."

"Where are you? I'll come and get you."

"No, no, that's fine, I don't need collecting."

“You okay? I missed you, I stayed at yours last night, I needed to be able to smell you, I fuckin’ hated sleeping in your bed alone, and waking up alone.” My heart gives a little stutter, now that the hard protective brick wall is down, it’s affected by more than Sean it would seem and this little revelation seems to rush over me like a tidal wave. What does that mean? Has Cam always had the ability to make my heart do strange things, if I’d have let him?

“Georgia, you still there?”

“Yeah, yeah, I’m still here. Look Cam, we need to talk, not on the phone, I need to see you.”

“Well I just said I would come and get you now but I only have an hour, I have a flight out of City Airport to catch at four thirty, and I won’t be back until Monday.”

“Well, I’ll just wait and see you Monday then.” Monday’s good, gives me a bit of breathing space at least.

“I’d really like to see you now Kitten, Monday’s a long way off and I want to show you how sorry I am for being such a prick last night.”

“I can’t Cam, you don’t have to keep apologising, you shouldn’t have behaved like a prick, and I shouldn’t have stormed off like a diva. Go catch your flight and give me a call on Monday, once you’re home.”

He’s quiet for a minute and I feel really mean, I would actually like to see him now, the fact that he’s flying off somewhere I assume is overseas makes me feel a little pang of jealousy, he hadn’t mentioned this trip to me all week and he hadn’t said anything about it last night when I told him to come to Ashley’s party. I start to feel a little pissed off, we argued over Ashley’s party, when he knew full well he wouldn’t be able to come anyway.

“If I could get out of it George, I would but something’s come up with some business I have going on in Amsterdam and I need to fly over and sort it out, I only found out myself a couple of hours ago that I was going.”

“It’s okay.” I lie “You go and sort out your business. I’ll talk to you Monday.”

"I miss you George, have a good weekend."

"You too Cam, bye."

"George, I… nothing, I'll see you Monday." I end the call and wonder why, once again, I want to cry?

I walk quietly into the bathroom and watch Sean in the shower, he's standing with his back to the water, it's hitting the top of his head and bouncing off his shoulders, his head is tilted up to the ceiling, his eyes are closed and he's singing. I shudder and close my eyes as the desire I feel at the sound of his raspy voice unfurls between my legs, making my muscles tighten and my heart speed up as I listen to him sing. I've never heard of the song but as I listen to the words, I think I know what it is.

I tried, I really tried but it was only ever you.

All these years, all the tears, it's still only ever you.

What we did, the things we said, they're still always on my mind.

There's no one else, there never was, it's still only ever you.

The sweetest smile, the bluest eyes, the taste of you, on my tongue.

You're in my heart, you're in my head, right where you belong.

All the others, they never mattered, they don't come close to you.

Wish you was here, wrapped in my arms, my heart aches just at the thought of you.

All the others, they never mattered, none of them come close to you.

The things they write, it's all bullshit and lies

Because it's still only ever you.

You're the only one that can make me complete but I let you down, I fucked it up

Our lives were planned and with one stupid act, I blew it all away.

My lies were white, my heart was black

I got just what I deserved when you never came back

But still…

You're in my heart, you're in my head, right where you belong.

I want you here right by my side, I want you real, a distant memory just ain't the same

There's nothing left, my life's gone to shit and I've only got myself to blame.

I get on stage, I sing my song but all I want, all I need, is to have you back, where you belong

With me…With me…Always…With me.

I undo the shower screen door and step in beside him, he opens his eyes and looks at me, the water is bouncing off of him, his shoulders, his broad chest and I sway with the emotion of it all.

He pushes my hair off my face and sings in a whisper, "Where you belong, with me, with me, always, with me."

His mouth comes down hard on mine, he spins me around and pushes me against the hard tiled wall of the shower, he slides up and in me all in one move, I wrap my legs around him as he holds onto my bum cheeks and presses me between the wall and his hips. Still kissing me hard on the lips; he breaks away and pushes my hair off my face. "Fuck I love you Georgia Rae and I'm gonna spend the rest of my life proving it."

We have bed sex after we have shower sex so then I have to have another quick shower, which I insist on taking alone so that the cycle doesn't start again. We strip and remake the bed, then jump into Sean's white Range Rover and go to my flat. He calls Len from there and thanks him for letting us stay and arranges for us all to go out tonight, apparently it's been a while since the boys were all in the country at the same time so they want to catch up, that's what last night was supposed to have been about and it was, till I fell through the front door. Sean then calls Marley to see if he would like to join us for dinner, which he does. You would think that being the world famous, jet setters that they now were, we would be heading to some swanky restaurant in the West End or the city but no, this is Sean and my brothers and all they want to do is head into Upminster to their favourite Indian, which is the very same Indian I go to most Saturday nights.

Thankfully there's no evidence of Cam having been here, my bed has been made and there are none of his clothes hanging about. I throw on a pair of jeans with a smart blouse and a pair of heels, put my hair up in a messy bun and put on some makeup, and then we drive into the Docklands area of East London. The whole place is like a huge building site, with redevelopment work going on everywhere, we pull up at what looks like a huge warehouse on the edge of the water. It's a three story building, built from old stock bricks. Sean takes my hand as we head toward a set of wooden and glass doors, he taps a code into the machine and we walk into a lobby area where there is a concierge come security guard sitting behind a sort of hole in the wall. He's an older man, maybe in his sixties but very tall and muscular, he stands from where he was watching telly as we walk in.

"Alright Ronnie, how's things?"

"All good here Maca, all good, Marley's home, I ain't seen him go out nowhere t'day."

He smiles and nods his head toward me as he speaks in his gruff cockney accent. "This is my girlfriend Georgia, Ron, I'm gonna sort her out with keys and the key code, just in case you see her coming in and out and wonder who she is."

My belly does a little twirl and my heart swells as I hear him call me his girlfriend, Ronnie steps out from his little room and comes over and shakes my hand. "Nice to meet ya Georgia, 'bout time he settled down wiv a decent bird, still, he ain't as bad as

Marley. I don't know where he gets the energy from, two and three at a time I've seen him take…" He trails off as I think Sean is glaring at him from beside me.

"Nice to meet you too Ronnie," I smile as I speak. "And I will be having a word with my brother about his lose morals, don't you worry about that."

He looks from me to Sean with a frown; Sean pulls me into him by my waist. "Georgia is Marley's little sister Ron, you just dropped him right in the shit."

We turn and head for the lifts as Ron mumbles something I don't quite catch. The lift is the original old fashioned metal box, with a caged door that you have to pull across and close by hand. There's also an old fashioned wrought iron spiral staircase if you don't want to take the lift, Sean informs me.

The apartment is fantastic, nothing like you would expect two, twenty-two year old rock stars to live in. It's all exposed brickwork and timber. I notice the sofas are the exact replicas of the old Chesterfield from the summerhouse, in the exact same colour too. Marley's lying on one of them as we come in. He's playing some kind of a game with a controller, it looks like a werewolf, running riot in ancient Greece and I don't think Marley's doing too well because he throws the controller down and sits up as we come in.

"Big brother Marley, how are we, you got any dirty birds stashed up here that I need to kick out?"

"What the fuck are you talking about little sister Georgia?" he asks as he stands, stretches, then pulls me in for a cuddle and kisses the top of my head.

Sean heads off in search of clean clothes and shouts, "I just introduced G to Ronnie. He told her about the amount of birds you bring back here, before I had chance to tell him she was your sister."

"Nice one Ron," Sean mumbles as he sits back down on the sofa.

"Anyway, cheeky fucker, who said the birds I bring back here are dirty?" Marls shouts loud enough for Sean to hear.

"Err, actually, you did, don't you remember, you threw one out a few weeks back coz you said she had a smelly twat," Sean shouts as he heads back in to the open plan room.

My mouth drops open, he's wearing black jeans, with a white v necked t-shirt; he has on a black suede jacket, and is wearing wooden rosary beads and a cross around his neck. He looks every bit the world famous rock star that he is and I suddenly feel inadequate as I look at his perfection.

He smirks as he walks toward me and wiggling his eyebrows he asks, "Wanna see my bedroom?"

I stand and roll my eyes at him as he pulls me in for a kiss. "Not if you want to leave here any time this century."

He kisses me on the mouth and squeezes my arse cheeks. "Suits me, I'm only going where you go for the rest of my life anyway."

"Oh please, I'm gonna spew, is this how it's gonna be again, you two all over each other like it used to be?"

"Fuck off Marls, we've got four years to catch up on, you're just jealous coz you can't keep a bird."

"No Maca, I don't want a bird, look at the fuckin' mess you've been in the past four years, writing shitty love songs and crying in ya beer every time you have more than two drinks."

I bite on my bottom lip as I try to contain the smile this news induces, well good, I'm glad he suffered, makes me feel a little better about what I've been through.

Sean raises his eyebrows at me. "What you laughing at?"

"Nothing." I shake my head and grin.

* * *

We finally make it back into Essex and are seated in the Indian Restaurant by eight o'clock. I don't know when the table was reserved, but it was and it's right at the back, tucked around a corner. Despite this, the boys still end up signing autographs for half the night. We laugh, joke and talk in the way that we always have, five lifelong friends catching up. There's no rock stars amongst us, it's just my two big brothers, my best friend and my boyfriend, until we head outside to our cars and all hell breaks loose. Somebody has obviously called the press and as I walk out of the restaurant first, looking behind me as I chat to Marley, I'm first knocked in one direction and then the other as cameras flash in my face. There's suddenly chaos all around me as I'm asked my name, my relationship to the band, am I going home for a threesome with Marley and Sean. I hear Sean roar at them all to fuck off from somewhere behind me, then Marley tucks me under his arm and walks me to Sean's car as it bleeps and is unlocked by someone I am assuming is Sean, behind us. Marley pushes me into the passenger seat and then goes back to help Sean out, as he is now being mobbed by pap's, reporters and a bunch of screaming girls. I jump as I hear a loud crack when a camera lens is pushed up against the window of the door, I lock the door quickly and just try and keep my head down and ignore the questions. Sean makes it to the car but then can't get in because I've locked it; he scrambles for his keys, jumps in and locks the door behind him.

I know as soon as I look at him that he's angry. "Fuck G, you okay, they didn't hurt you did they? Fuckers." He looks me over.

"I'm fine, it just freaked me out, fucking hell, they're aggressive."

"Tell me about it and they're getting fucking worse, you sure you're alright? I'll knock them the fuck out next time, they're pigs some of them."

The commotion is still going off all around us, cameras flashing, people banging on the windows asking for autographs; he starts the car and moves slowly forward.

"Move you stupid fuckers!" he shouts and punches the hooter on the steering wheel. "I swear these people have a death wish."

I don't know why but I get the giggles and by the time we escape the 'stupid fuckers' we're both laughing at absolutely nothing.

"Where's Marley?" I ask when I realise he's missing.

"Gone with Len, he's gonna stay at their place tonight."

My belly goes over as I wonder what that means for us, he looks from the road to me and then back to the road. "I wanted to take you to mine but them wankers know where we live, they'll probably be there waiting for us."

I keep staring ahead; he reaches across and takes my hand. "Would it be okay if we stayed at yours? They'd never know to look there."

"Of course, it's not as flash as yours and I don't have a Ronnie at the front door." He brings my hand up to his lips and kisses it.

"As long as you're there G, I don't give a fuck if it's even got a front door."

I laugh at that. "Ah, now that I do have, in fact I have two, my Dad's boys did the refurbishment, it's something that he insisted on and I'm sure if he thought that he could get away with it, he would also have got me a Ronnie."

He throws his head back and laughs and the sound makes me smile. We drive back to mine without being followed and spend the rest of the night making love in my bed, which smells of Cam. I fall asleep in Sean's arms, dreaming about lights flashing and being pulled in different directions by two tall, dark haired, dark eyed men.

I'm woken in the morning by my phone ringing. I look across at my clock radio, shit, its eleven forty-five. Sean is wrapped all around me and hasn't stirred at the sound of the phone. I wriggle out from underneath him and grab the phone from its base and walk out to the kitchen and put the kettle on as I answer.

"Hello." My voice is dry and raspy from my long sleep.

"I'm sorry Kitten, did I wake you?" For some reason, guilt washes over me as I hear Cam's voice. I look down at my naked self and think about all the different ways Sean fucked me in my bed last night.

"Mmm, yeah, you did," I say as I stretched, trying to disguise the guilt in my voice.

"Did you have a late night baby?"

"Not really, just needed the sleep." Lie.

"What did you do last night?"

"Went for an Indian." Not a lie.

"Right, who with?"

"Jimmie." Sort of not a lie, Jimmie was there.

"Oh right, no Ashley?" Shit, I nearly always go out with Ash on a Friday night. Double shit, it's Ash's party tonight at the club, shit, fuck, bollocks, I have a hair and makeup appointment at three.

"No, no Ash, she's saving herself for tonight."

"Ah, right, yeah, her party at the club."

"Yeah." There's a few seconds of uncomfortable silence.

"Okay, well seeing as you don't seem to want to talk, I'll hang up. Sorry for waking you up Kitten."

I feel terrible, evil. "Cam."

The instant I say his name, I realise that Sean is behind me, I turn to see him standing naked, his arms above his head as he reaches up to touch the top of the door frame, he isn't as tall as Cam, but at around six foot, he's still tall and he's nowhere near as broad but he's still beautifully defined. That's exactly what Sean is, from his dark hair, which is a long mess right now, his dark skin and eyes, all the way down to that perfect V thing men have going on, to his toned legs and sexy brown feet, he is just beautiful, my beautiful boy.

"Kitten?"

Shit, Cam. "I'll talk to you Monday," I say. He hangs up without saying any more. I turn and look at Sean who now has a hard on that's almost touching his belly button, I walk toward him, wrap my arms around his neck and kiss him, he slides his hands underneath my bum cheeks, lifts me up and carries me over to the breakfast bar, where he sits me down but remains standing between my legs.

"Shit," I complain as the cold surface hits my bare arse. "It's freezing."

He gives a little smile but it doesn't reach his eyes. "I thought you spoke to him yesterday."

My stomach jumps to my throat and I swallow it back down before I speak, "I did, he's away on business, I want to talk to him face to face but he's not back till Monday so I'll talk to him then."

He slides me forward so that I'm pressed against him, he's standing, I'm sitting on the breakfast bar, both naked, my legs wrapped around his hips. "I'm jealous; I don't want you to see him Monday."

"Why are you jealous? I'm seeing him to break up with him." He shrugs his shoulders and rubs his thumb over his bottom lip.

"I don't know, just the thought of you with him." His hand rubs at the back of his neck. "I'm being a twat ain't I?"

"You're being a complete twat babe."

He smiles that beautiful, lazy, lopsided smile of his. "I love you." Is all that he says, and then he carries me back to bed.

Later, I explain to him about Ashley's party tonight at my Dad's club and ask if he would like to come with me. Jimmie and Lennon are going so we call Marley up and ask him to come along too, despite the fact the party's in the VIP area. Sean calls up his usual security guards and arranges for them to work tonight. Later Sean heads over to Lens to pick up Marley and they go home to get ready for tonight. They'll meet us at the club later as I'm going in the limo with the girls. The instant he's gone, I miss him, miss him to the point that I stand for a few seconds and hug myself as I think of the mad events that have happened over the last forty eight hours. I'm bought back to earth by my buzzer going off, Sean had insisted that I lock both doors after he left, he's worried about reporters finding out who I am and coming over here, although why exactly they would be interested in me, I have no idea.

"Hello," I call into the intercom.

"Get the door G, my arms are breaking here." It's Ashley; I had completely forgotten she was getting ready here. She will freak out when I tell her who I've invited along tonight. She loves Carnage. I've got her tickets for their shows a few times but never the back stage passes that she's begged for. I couldn't, I hated the thought of her seeing Sean when I couldn't so I always made up some excuse, well today, I would make up for that and give her a birthday present to remember.

I buzzed the bomb/riot/nuclear war proof door my Dad had insisted was installed, open and went to my front door. Ashley not only had a garment bag and holdall with her, she also had a case of champagne. I helped her in with everything and we hug.

"I've been worried about you babe, your Mum said you was a bit under the weather, I thought you was gonna bail on me. I belled a couple of times but you didn't pick up. What's up babe, dodgy guts or summit?" Ashley had the kind of Essex accent that made my Mum cringe, she was careful in the shop to never drop her H's or to use slang but once she was out of the shop, she spoke like a typical Essex girl, the way I would have spoken if my Mum hadn't been around to always pick me up on my pronunciation. I slipped occasionally but never to Ashley's degree.

"Ash." I held her by the shoulders and looked at her, she was as blonde as I was dark but we both had blue eyes, she was as tall as me but much curvier and whenever we went out together, we turned every head in the place.

She frowned and looked at me. "George."

"I have some news."

"Yeah, right, am I gonna like it?"

"Not sure, you will definitely like some of it."

"Fuck's sake George, jus spill will ya."

“I’m back with Sean.”

“What… Rock star Sean, Maca, from Carnage Sean?”

“Hmm mmm.” Is all I can manage while I nod.

“Fuck, what about TDH.” Okay, that wipes the smile off my face. I let out a deep sigh.

“I know, I feel really bad, he’s away till Monday, I’ll see him then and call things off.”

“Wow, babe, back with Sean… Shit, was that you in the paper with him this morning, coming out of a restaurant last night?” No, the pictures were in the papers?

“What, what papers, what did it say?”

“Ha, well actually it’s really funny now I know it was you, you’re looking down at the ground and Marley’s on one side with his arm around your shoulders and Sean’s on the other, pushing a pap out the way and the headline says something like ‘Looks like another Marley and Maca threesome was on the cards for the Carnage boys last night’. How funny is that, they had you down as shagging your own brother, which, yeah anyway, so, wow.”

She realises that I’m not impressed by the look on my face. I grab my phone and dial the number that Sean wrote down on a piece of paper for me earlier, Marley answers. “It’s done; we dumped the body in the Thames.”

“Very funny Marls, one day that will get you in deep shit.”

“Hello little sister Georgia, it’s been what, two hours since you seen him and your already on the phone, you sad little individual.”

“Is that Georgia? Gimme the phone,” I hear Sean say in the background.

“G?”

“Sean, those pictures from last night made the papers; apparently I was going home for a threesome with you and Marley.”

"Fuck, Norman, the doorman said we were in the papers when we got back here but he didn't say what it said. You okay G?"

"Not really but what can I do?"

"Nothing really, I told ya, they're pigs most of them, I'll sort you out some security, if they see us together again, it'll only get worse and then…" he trails off.

"And then what?

"Look, don't freak out but some of our fans are a bit… possessive, any girls, any of us have ever been linked with generally get abuse of some kind. But don't worry, I'll get Milo onto it, I'll get you the best close protection, I ain't having anyone getting near ya G."

"I need a body guard, seriously?"

"Yes G, I ain't taking no chances, there's some fuckin' nutters out there and I ain't risking one of them getting near ya." I don't really know what to say to that.

"I miss ya, can't wait to see you tonight," he says quietly into the phone.

"Peeerrrleeease, you've just left her, you'll see her again in a few hours!" I hear Marley call out.

"Shut the fuck up Layton you dick." I smile at a conversation I have heard so many times between these two. I look up to see Ashley watching me with a grin on her face.

"I miss you too."

"What time you leaving?"

"The limo picks us up at nine, get ready and come back here if you want."

"Na, you enjoy your girl time, we'll just meet ya at the club."

"Okay, see ya then."

"I love you Georgia Rae, show us your tits," he whispers into the phone.

"Maca, I can hear you, that's my little fuckin' sister, you perv."

"I love you too Sean." I stand and grin into the phone for a few seconds, listening to him telling Marley to shut up again.

"Go get yourself tarted up, can't wait to see ya." I hang straight up; otherwise we'll be there for hours, just like we used to be.

As soon as I end the call, Ashley is on me. "George, I've gotta say babe, I've never, ever, seen you look so happy, you're proper in love with him ain't ya." She sounds amazed, like this is a revelation, has no one been listening to me these past nine years. I love Sean McCarthy, always have, always will, nothing will ever change that.

"I love him Ash, I've always loved him." She didn't say anything for a while and then surprised me by giving me a cuddle.

"You know what babe, I believe ya, it's written all over ya face, you look different, like the light has been switched on somewhere."

I smile back; I know exactly what she means, because that's exactly how I feel. "Ash, look, I hope you don't mind but tonight I sorted of invited Sean along."

"Oh my fuckin' God, George, are you serious. Sean McCarthy is coming to my birthday party, really, did he say yes, is he really coming?"

"Yes Ash, really and Marley's coming too." She screams so loud, it actually hurts my ears.

"Georgia, oh my God Georgia, the boys from Carnage are gonna be at my birthday party. Fuck, you are the best friend ever." I think she's happy!

CHAPTER 20

By eight o'clock that night I was dressed in a short black leather dress and knee high leather boots, my hair was a long and bouncy mass of curls and my makeup applied by professionals to perfection. I had downed three glasses of champagne and snorted two lines of coke, Ashley's brother had supplied her with some top notch class A shit along with a few ecstasy pills that we would take later in the night. By eleven o'clock when we walked into Kings, I was buzzing and felt on top of the world. I loved turning up here when there was a queue and walking straight past everyone to the front.

My Dad and Bailey had done me proud, the room was decorated exactly as I had asked them to, in Ashley's favourite colour of purple, matched with silver, there was a small table with nibbles on and waiters and waitresses on hand with champagne. Jimmie had come in the limo with us and had told me that the boys had a driver and would be leaving from her place about now so to expect them within the hour.

Bailey appeared at my side and gave me a cuddle, I could see the eyes of Ashley's friends light up as they looked my eldest brother over. "How you doing little sister Georgia? See you got papped last night outside the Indian. I've called in a few extra doormen in case there's any problems tonight."

"Thanks big brother Bailey, the boys are bringing their own blokes and thanks for all this too, it looks great."

"Not a problem, Mum's been here all afternoon organising all of this, you know what she's like but I've gotta admit, it looks nice, she does have a good eye." My stomach lurches a little bit at the mention of my Mum and I feel guilty, despite everything, she still came here today and did this for my friend.

"How is she?" I ask him, he shrugs.

"She's actually really pissed off with herself; she can't believe she believed that girl without checking out her story."

"That's just typical Mum though Bails, she only ever sees the good in everyone, she thinks we're all as nice as her."

He nods in agreement. “Exactly, that’s why you shouldn’t be so hard on her, she fucked up. We all do it at least once in our lives, most of us even more.”

“Yeah, I know, I’ll sort it between us, I promise.”

“Make sure you do, right, enjoy yourselves and behave, your pupils are already like saucers.” He narrows his eyes at me. “I’m watching you Georgia, no doing any of that shit in public, you never know who might be watching, especially as you’re practically famous now.” He kisses my hair and Jims cheek and leaves.

“Shit George, your brothers are so fuckin’ good lookin’, even your Mum and Dad are still hot.”

“Eww, Ash.”

“Well it’s true and then look, your brothers marrying Jimmie and she’s gorgeous, you lot are gonna produce the next generation of beautiful people between ya’s.” Jimmie and I just shake our heads and laugh, Ashley’s buzzing. We call her machine gun lips when she’s on one, because she talks so fast.

The VIP bar has its own dance floor overlooking the main dance floor, with the same music pumped in through a hidden sound system. Friday nights are always dance music nights and I can’t keep still, I love dancing, after so many years of not listening to music, I found that when I first started coming to clubs with Ash, that I just couldn’t stand still. I don’t know if it was because I was pretty sure I wouldn’t hear a Carnage song in a nightclub and I just relaxed enough to enjoy myself or maybe it was the drugs but I just had to dance and tonight it didn’t matter either way, in fact I would love to hear a Carnage song, just so that I could dance my arse off to it.

Ash, Jimmie and I headed down to the main dance floor as no one was dancing up in our section yet. We had arrived early so that Ash was there to greet her guests, but most wouldn’t arrive until after midnight, which is when we usually turned up. We dance for four or five songs and when we get sick of fighting off the unwanted attention of sweaty men, we head upstairs; as soon as we enter the bar. I know that Sean is there, I just feel it, feel him, it was like, long fingers of electricity reached out from him, toward me, even if they didn't quite touch me. I could still feel the current, the pull and I think it worked in reverse for him, at least I hoped it did.

Ashley had warned all of her friends that the boys would be here tonight and she had asked them all not to ask for autographs and just treat them as normal blokes on a night out, which I should've realised to some women meant that they could chat them up as they would any other good looking blokes. I spotted Marley first; he was taller than Len now, who he was stood next to. Sean was right at the end and seemed to be receiving the most attention from Jill and Coral, Ashley's two friends who had arrived in the limo with us, they were both dressed like cheap, nasty sluts and had not shut up about Sean and Marley all night. I had reminded them earlier that Sean was my boyfriend and they had given me an 'of course he his sweetheart' patronizing type of smile, why would they believe me? If all they ever read were the newspaper stories about him and Marley. Why would they believe he suddenly had a girlfriend? Why would anyone? Suddenly that old familiar rage I used to feel, back when the band were just starting out, started to burn inside me and I clenched my fists, Jimmie didn't miss it, not for a second.

"George, no trouble." I didn't even look at her, I just walked over to where they all stood, Jill had her hand on Sean's chest, so I grabbed it and bent it back as far as I dare, she yelped out in pain. "Get your fuckin' hands off him."

"Whoa, whoa, Georgia." Lennon jumped in and pulled my hand from hers.

Sean just smiled at me. "Georgia baby, you are such a bad girl."

His eyes are glassy and he stinks of whiskey and I love him so very, very much. Milo the bouncer from Spain steps out of thin air and escorts Jill and Coral away. Marley passes me a glass of champagne and says, "Little sister Georgia, what are we gonna do with you and that temper of yours?"

He shakes his head as if he's telling me off. "We're not gonna do anything with that temper of hers," Sean says. "Because she makes me so fuckin horny when she gets all green eyed, I fuckin' love it."

Lennon and Marley both shake their heads. “You two are a fuckin’ nightmare.”

Len looks at me. “We just had to practically sit on him when he saw some bloke touch you on the dance floor.”

I smile up at him and wrap my arms around his neck. “Did they baby, did you get jealous?”

“Yes, I told you this morning I get jealous; I hate the thought of you even talking to other blokes, let alone them touching you.” I kiss him, hard on the mouth. “You look stunning G, fucking gorgeous.”

Before I can answer, Ashley calls out. “Oi George, you gonna do the honours or what babe?”

I smile at her bluntness. “Of course, sorry, how rude of me.”

She comes over and stands beside me, we link arms. “Ashley, this is my boyfriend Sean and this is my brother Marley, Lennon you already know and Jimmie is just Jimmie… Boys, I don’t know if you remember Ash from school, think you might have already left by the time she started, but anyway, this is my good friend, work colleague and birthday girl Ashley Morris.”

“Happy birthday Darlin’,” Sean says and gives her a kiss on the cheek.

“Wow, I mean thanks, thank you and thanks for coming. Love your work by the way, sorry, I know it’s your night off but just wanted to get that out there.”

Sean just smiles and says, “Not a problem and thanks for the invite.”

But Ashley is no longer listening, she’s looking at Marley and Marley is looking at Ash, with his mouth almost hanging open to the floor. Sean uses the back of his hand under Marley’s bottom jaw and closes it.

Marl’s eyes wander over to me and he swallows, then says to Ash, “Happy birthday Ashley, you’re beautiful.”

"Okaaay," Jimmie says and grabs my arm, I in turn grab Sean's and we all turn in the opposite direction and leave the love/lust struck couple to chat. Sean and I stand and talk with Jimmie and Lennon and the continuous flow of people that come over and talk to us. There are a few people from school there, some Sean remembers, some he doesn't but they all remember him and Marley, who is still at the end of the bar drooling over Ash.

After about an hour, Sean grabs my hand and says into my ear, "Come and dance with me." He pulls me to the dance floor, where one of my favourite songs is playing, Soul 11 Soul's 'Back to life'.

Sean and I have only ever slow danced together, this song is too fast for a slow dance but too slow for a fast dance, but we manage. Sean pulls my back into his chest and I grind into him, he holds me against him by splaying his hand over my belly, with his other hand, he moves my hair off of my neck and scrapes his teeth over my bare shoulder, all the way to my nape. I lift my arm and curl it backward around his neck as I grab at his hair and grind my arse right into his rock hard cock.

"Fuck Gia, I need to be inside you, is there somewhere we can go?"

I turn around to face him and pull his hips into mine, I grab his hand and go in search of Bailey, luckily his office is upstairs and I don't have to drag Sean through the crowd downstairs.

I knock on Bailey's door and open it before he replies, he looks up from paper work and I give him my best smile. "What?" he asks, he knows the look I'm giving him means I want something.

"Maca." He nods at Sean.

"Big brother Bailey?"

"What dya want George?"

"This room."

"What?"

"This room, can we borrow this room for like…"

"Twenty minutes," Sean jumps in. Bailey looks from me to Sean and back to Sean again.

"You're seriously asking to borrow my office, to fuck my sister in Maca? You've got some balls."

"Bails please, we've got a lot of making up to do, I'll owe you big time, pleeease," I whine.

He sighs, stands from his desk and throws me the keys. "Fifteen minutes, don't make a mess and I want ten tickets with back stage passes for your next concert."

"Cheers mate, not a problem, you can have twenty, fifty even," Sean shouts as Bailey leaves. I lock the door after him.

As I turn around Sean is on me, his mouth slams onto mine, his tongue inside, hungrily seeking mine, he unzips my leather dress and because it's strapless and fully lined, it slides down my body to the floor. I'm not wearing a bra so I'm now stood in the office that my Dad shares with my brother in my knee high boots and black lace knickers. I step out of my dress as Sean watches me.

"Fifteen minutes G, what can we manage in fifteen minutes dya think?" He licks up the inside of my arm and sucks on the inside of my elbow and I shudder.

"Bend over that desk and put your arse in the air." I shudder again, this time just from pure desire. Coke always makes me horny and tonight more so than ever. It takes me just three steps to reach the desk, but the sensation, the friction caused by my thighs rubbing together, by the lace from my underwear, all off it pushes me closer and closer to an orgasm. I ache so badly, I just want him inside.

I do exactly as Sean requested, I lean forward on the desk and put my arse in the air, and I spread my legs and wait. I hear his zip undoing and groan quietly and can't help but gyrate my hips toward him. He leans over me and wraps my hair around his hand and pulls it, just a little, but just enough to make me moan, he bites down on my shoulder and then says, "I'm gonna fuck you G, I'm gonna fuck you hard and fast and make us both see stars and then later, when I get you home, in bed, alone, I'm gonna make love to you. I'm gonna worship you and start making up for the past four years but right now, right now, we both need this."

He pulls my knickers to one side and I buck and grind into him, I can feel his cock at the top of my arse crack and I panic for a minute at what he thinks he's gonna do to me and let out a little whimper. "Shush baby, just relax."

Every time he speaks, every word he says, just edges me closer and closer. He slides his finger out and drags them back, they hover over my arse. "I want this." He taps. "But not here, not now, but I want it, I want you in every way G, every fuckin' inch of ya."

As he finishes speaking he yanks on my hair and rams into me, his arm slides around my front and his middle finger pushes down on my clit, I push back, taking all of him inside me, then I grind forward onto his finger, he moves his hand and pushes his fingers inside me along with his cock and I feel like I'm being ripped open and it drives me insane. When he pushes the heel of his hand onto my clit, I'm done, I explode and my legs, quite literally go from under me. "Fuck!" Sean roars in my ears and I feel him come, hot and deep inside of me.

Sean and I have never had sex like this before, until this week, I was only sixteen the last time we had made love and that is exactly all that we had ever done, made love. Sean had always been gentle and considerate, he'd taught me, but never forced me and he had definitely never been rough like he had tonight. Tonight was fucking, pure and simple, lust fuelled fucking and I think I loved him even more than I did at the beginning of the night. The fact that he couldn't wait till we got home, that we needed that connection so bad that I had had the cheek to ask my brother to use his office, it made me love in a way that made not just my heart but my whole body to ache.

I was spread; face down, with Sean still buried inside me over my brother's desk. I groaned as Sean pressed against my back. "I can't believe we did that, my brother's got to work on this desk, I'm such a slut." I could feel Sean's laugh rattle inside him, I could feel his chest and shoulders move and his hot breath in my ear but he didn't say anything, his hand reached out in front of me and he dragged a box of tissues toward us, pulled a handful out and passed them to me, he grabbed another handful, kissed my shoulder and pulled out of me.

We used the bathroom in the office, cleaned ourselves up, got dressed and unlocked the door. Bailey was sitting on a stool at the bar, talking to someone. Sean had my hand in one of his and the keys in the other, he dangled them over Bailey's shoulder and said, "Cheers mate, we owe you big time."

Bailey turned on his stool, his eyes slid to mine and at first I couldn't make out the look in them, then two things happened at once, Sean kissed my temple, and then said. "You wanna drink baby?" Just as the person Bails had been talking too stood up.

Cam!

Everything in the room stopped, the noise, the people, it either stopped or faded away or it was all just too much for my brain to deal with. Never for as long as I live will I forget the look on his face, he started to smile, then his eyebrows drew in together as he watched Sean kiss me and call me baby. His mouth dropped open slightly, as he looked between me and Sean, he looked at Sean's hand in mine, then from my face to Sean's and that's where it stayed for a few seconds. My gaze moved to Baileys, he was looking panicked; I needed to say something but my mouth was so dry I didn't think I could.

"Gia?' Sean was looking at me. "What's wrong?" The affection and concern in Sean's voice was unmistakable.

Cam's face completely fell, as did his shoulders, his eyes closed for a few seconds before they shifted back to me and the hurt that they expressed was tangible, he started to turn to leave. "Cam?" He swung back around to face me. Bailey jerked slightly, unsure of what he was going to do. Cam looked from me to Sean, and then put his hand out to Sean.

"Cameron King, joint owner of the place."

Sean obviously hadn't missed the name or the atmosphere. "Sean McCarthy," he hesitated as if he was going to say more but he didn't.

Cam nodded his head, as if everything was suddenly becoming clear. "You're Sean, the lead singer of Carnage, of course."

Sean nodded slightly back and then looked at me. “Do you need a minute, to talk?” I couldn’t have been more grateful or loved him more at that moment; I gave a slight nod as he kissed my cheek. “Ten minutes, then I’m coming back, I don’t care, how big he is, ten minutes.” He turned back to Cam and Bailey. “I’m gonna get a drink from the other bar.”

He didn’t pretend, he didn’t say nice to meet you, because obviously, it wasn’t, he just turned and walked back into the VIP bar, “I’ll leave you two to talk.” Bailey kissed my cheek and got up and left.

“Cam, I’m so sorry, I didn’t want to tell you over the phone, I thought you were away till Monday, I wanted to tell you then, face to face.” My heart was pounding so hard I could feel it in my throat and in my head.

“I came home early to surprise you, I wanted to see you, wanted to tell you, show you how sorry I was for my behaviour Thursday night. Thursday night Kitten, you remember that? Two nights ago, when I stupidly thought you were in a relationship with me.”

“I was, I was, I… ”

He knocked back the drink he had in his hand, then looked at me and shook his head. “Sean McCarthy, now why didn’t I work that one out, I knew all about Sean, I just didn’t realise it was that Sean. I didn’t stand a chance did I? Me or a twenty-two year old fucking rock God?”

“Cam, please, it’s not like that, I’ve known him since I was eleven, he was my boyfriend from the age of thirteen, he’s the only boy I’ve ever loved.” He looked thoroughly defeated when I said that.

“Thanks Kitten, thanks for that.” Then he turned and walked away. I stood until I couldn’t see him anymore, then feeling like the worst person on earth I went to find Sean.

Ash and Marley were practically having sex on the dance floor when I walked back into the VIP bar, the only thing missing was actual penetration but nobody seemed bothered by it. Sean was at the bar talking to Lennon, Jimmie, and Bailey, he didn’t look happy. I grabbed a glass of champagne from a waitress and made my way over to his side.

"Hi," I said as I slipped my hand inside his.

"Cameron King? Cameron fucking King babe, that's your Cam? Thanks very much for the warning; so what, do I need to start wearing a bullet proof vest now? Should I expect a horse's head in my bed?" He'd let go of my hand as he talked.

"I thought these two would have had the sense to keep you away from a bloke like that G, for fuck's sake babe, he's fuckin' dangerous."

I lost my temper, I don't know why I felt the need to defend Cam, I knew what he was, I had seen first-hand what he was capable of. "Is he Sean, more dangerous than a fuckin' rapist, a two timing rock star, who enjoys threesomes with my brother, or am I safe with one of them?"

His eyes didn't leave mine, I'm not sure what it was that I saw flash through them, but I knew that I'd said too much. "Touché, Gia, touché." He tilted his glass toward me and knocked back whatever it was he was drinking, walked away from me, grabbed Jill by the hand and pulled her onto the dance floor.

"Way to go George, anyone you haven't pissed off tonight?"

"Fuck off Len, he wasn't here, it's got fuck all to do with him who I was seeing while we were apart but if that's the road he wants to go down, I'm sure I can start going through the scrap books Mum kindly made for me and dig dirt on some of his fuck whores he's been shagging for the past four years." I grabbed another drink from a passing waitress.

"Yeah, coz that's gonna help the pair of you move on ain't it," Bailey adds his tuppence worth. "I'll tell you, exactly what I've just told him, if you two stand any chance, any chance at all of making things work between the two of you, then you both need to let the past go, forget what you had before, forget whatever went on while you weren't together and focus on what you have now."

I know what Bailey is saying is true but I don't want to listen. "Well I thought that was what I was doing by finishing with

Cam. Sean's the one with the issues when he has no fucking right to."

Bailey and Lennon both shake their heads but Lennon has more to add. "Just for once George, just for once let it go, stop trying to punish him. Calling him a rapist was a low fuckin' blow, just leave it, just leave the past in the past and move the fuck on, for all our sakes. You two being apart affected all of us, we all love both of you and we all hated watching the pair of you in such misery but we stayed out of it because we all thought that one day you would sort your shit out and get back together, now it's happened, please try your hardest to make it work."

I chewed on the inside of my bottom lip, Jimmie has stayed quiet and I look at her with a 'Well aren't you going to say something' expression. "Dya love him George?"

"Of course I do."

"Can you live without him?"

"You know I can't."

"Then get over there, get that slut's grimy mitts off him and let him know."

I turn toward the dance floor, Jill has her hands all over Sean, he keeps laughing and moving them off of his arse, then his face, then his arse again, she's grinding into him and steps closer every time he steps away, his eyes meet mine and he looks at me desperately, I raise my eyebrows and fold my arms across my chest.

"Na," I say to Jim. "Let him suffer for a bit longer."

Jill suddenly lunges at him with her mouth, that's when I move. "Oi!" I yank her away by her hair. "You're taking the piss now love."

She shrugs and walks away. "Come on, can't blame me for trying," she calls over her shoulder but I'm not listening.

Gloria Estefan's 'I don't wanna lose you' starts to play and he grabs my hand and pulls me into the middle of the dance floor.

"I'm sorry," we both say at the exact same time.

"I'm a jealous fucker, it's done, you've finished with him, I won't mention him again, and I love you." He kisses me, softly on my mouth.

"I shouldn't have said what I said, it was spiteful and not what I think, I love you too." I kiss him gently on the mouth.

He smiles at me. "Then listen to the words G, listen to the words of this song, I don't wanna lose you again, ever and no matter what, we will get through this somehow, because this, what we have got, blows all of the others out of the fuckin water, Romeo and Juliet, Bonnie and Clyde, Sandy and Danny, even Baby and Jonny, they can't touch us. They couldn't write our story, what we have, there aren't even words invented yet to describe it."

A lone tear runs down my cheek and he licks, yes licks it from my face. "Shall we go home so you can show me your tits?" he asks with a grin.

"You're such a charmer Maca." He gives me his full on, rock star on the front cover of a magazine, smoulder.

"Yeah, you think, am I good enough to get into your knickers later?"

"Erm babe, you did that about an hour ago, over my brother's desk."

He looks horrified. "Aw shit, was that you? Sorry, I thought that was some random bird, throwing herself at me."

I stop dancing and put my hands on my hips. "That's not funny."

"I'm joking, I'm joking, come on, say goodbye to your mates and let's get out of here."

"Mine or yours?" I ask.

"Well I'm assuming Marley won't be leaving without Ash so let's go to yours."

We say our goodbyes and leave the club by the back doors as apparently there are number of reporters waiting out the front. Milo walks us out and jumps into the front of Sean's Land Rover that's waiting outside for us. I'm introduced to Dave our driver and we're driven through the night back to my flat, me trying to keep Sean's hands from sliding into my knickers all the way there.

CHAPTER 21

My Dad had this lame saying that he used to quote to my brothers; it was usually when my Mum asked who had made the mess in her kitchen. De Nile is not just a river in Egypt, it never failed to make us groan but I had had that saying going around in my head for two weeks now and I was unsure why. Well I wasn't, not really, I knew why and if De Nile was just a river in Egypt, I was drowning in it, I had drowned in it, for two weeks, I had felt like I had stones tied around my neck and I was firmly weighed down and on the very bottom of that river and the reason being was the guilt I felt over Cam. Not for what I had done, not for the way things ended but for the fact that I missed him so much. I loved Sean; I love Sean with a passion that defies logic. We have spent every spare moment together this past two weeks and he's been in my bed every single night, we've woken up together every single morning, we've talked and talked and talked, we've decided not to waste time, we're already looking for our own place. The press haven't worked out where I live yet but they know who I am. Last weekend one of the Sunday tabloids run a front page and a whole double spread inside about mine and Sean's 'Great Love Story'. How we were childhood sweethearts and how we were ripped apart by his fame, they didn't mention the rape incident because the accusation was withdrawn, charges dropped and the press threatened with legal action if they ever mentioned the incident without making it perfectly clear that it was a fabricated story so it was just never mentioned but because the press knew who I was they had camped out at the gates of my parents drive and the house had been bombarded with phone calls and post for me, lots of the calls were abusive from fans, lots of the mail were hate filled threats for me to back off. Sean was theirs and I needed to stay away. Some letters were actually really sweet, telling us that what we had was something special and wishing us well. Some were just plain weird, pictures of blokes' dicks, with notes telling me I was beautiful and that they bet Sean wasn't as well-endowed as they were. In the end, everything sent for me to my parent house was put in sacks and sent to Sean's personal assistant Andrea. She siphoned through it and only sent us the things she thought we would like to read, which wasn't much. All of the publicity had done wonders for trade at the shops, lots of new customers coming in, buying something small, just to see if I was there but I had stayed away.

My Mum and I had met for lunch on the Tuesday after Sean and I got back together, we talked through everything and I told her I forgave her. I'm not entirely sure that I did but I did understand her motives, I had said then, that I would carry on with work as normal but now, two weeks into my relationship with Sean, it was becoming apparent that this was going to be impossible so after a meeting yesterday. We had promoted Ashley as area manager and put a new full time manager in all six stores that we now had, and we had taken on an admin team consisting of a personal manager, staff in charge of accounts and orders and two new buying assistants, basically, my Mum and I, were part of the business in name only.

The band were touring the states next year and Sean had asked me to go with him, because of Len and Jimmie's wedding they had taken the whole of June off and were only committed to a few television appearances over the rest of the summer. They were back in the studio in August to start recording their new album, due to be released in March as the U S tour kicked off. Sean and Marley had written a few new songs for the album but they would start getting together more regularly in July so that they were prepared to start laying down tacks by about September. All of this meant lots of free time for Sean and I to spend together but when he got a song in his head, he was gone, off with Marley to do their thing and as I was too scared to go out because of the press. I stayed home and had too much time to think and to feel guilty about the fact that I was missing Cam and that's exactly what I was doing on this Friday lunch time, almost two weeks after I had last seen Cam. I'd just finished talking on the phone to Jimmie, her hens do was in a week's time, twenty six women, all off to Marbella in Spain for five nights, friends, Mums, sisters, cousins, ranging in age from eighteen to sixty five and I couldn't wait. Hopefully Marbella was going to mean anonymity for me, five whole days of nobody knowing who I was, I had only experienced two weeks of this fame game and already I was over it.

My buzzer on the intercom went and my belly went over, I was worried all the time that the press were going to find out about our little love nest. They had besieged Sean and Marley's place and were totally confused about Sean's whereabouts as he hadn't been back there, he's had Milo bring his clothes and toiletries and guitar here and here we had hidden away for two weeks, waiting for the ridiculous amount of interest they had in me to die down, which so far, had failed to happen. My palms were instantly sweaty as I stood up on the intercoms second buzz.

"Hello," I said nervously.

"Georgia?"

"Who's that?"

"Georgia Darlin', it's Benny, Cam's Benny, dya think I could come in and have a chat babe."

What on earth did Benny want? I was suddenly nervous, had Cam sent him to kill me, would Cam kill me, did he despise me that much?

"What's wrong Ben, why do you need to chat with me?"

"Georgia, look Darlin', its Cam, I don't wanna do this over the intercom love, I just need five minutes." I thought about it for a few seconds. Dave had been assigned to look after me when Sean wasn't around and was sitting outside in a big Toyota four wheel drive when I looked this morning.

"I'll come out," I said to Benny.

"Sweet." I heard him reply.

I looked out of the window onto the parking space below, Dave was out of his car and was obviously watching Benny and looked a little bit unsure of what to do. I went out and opened the door to Ben and stepped outside, I put my hand up to Dave to let him know that everything was okay and then turned to talk to Cam's minder. "What's up Ben, what can I do for ya?"

"Georgia, look this is a bit embarrassing, I know you're with that pop star an' everything now an' I'm sorry an' all that but the boss is a mess an' I don't know what to do. His bruvers an' his sister av bin an' tried to sort 'im out but he ain't 'avin none of it, 'is hittin the bottle and he could keep an army marchin' for a month on the Charlie 'is snortin an' it's all since you left 'im."

He looks at me pleadingly. "I'm scared love, I'm really scared 'is gonna neck 'imself."

Shit, I really don't know what to do. I know what I want to do but Sean will go mad. I could *not* tell him I suppose, shit. "Ben, if he's in this mess because of me, then I'm probably the last person he wants to see."

"Na, ah fink he wants to see ya, I fink he just needs to see ya, he won't listen to no one else, you need to tell 'im to sort 'is shit out, else they're gonna put 'im in rehab again."

"Again, Cam's been in rehab before?"

"Yeah, yeah he has, twice before, when he was younger and then again after he lost Chantelle. He was a mess for a long time after that, then 'is brothers took charge and he ended up in rehab for nearly six months. He hated it, nearly killed 'im and that's what they're talkin' about doin' now, they're givin' 'im a week to sort 'imself out, then they're gonna lock 'im up, they got a court order before, he 'ad no choice, he 'ad to stay."

Jesus, what a mess.

"Where is he?" I can't believe I'm even considering this.

"Up the flat above the wine bar." I nod, I owe him this much, he saved me from myself, now I need to see if I can return the favour.

"Let me get some shoes on." I run back inside and slide my feet into a pair of flip flops, grab my keys and head back out. I follow Ben down the stairs, run over to where Dave is leaning on his car and tell him I'm just popping out to see a sick friend, that I won't be long and that I don't need him with me. I jump into the Jag and five minutes later, Ben is unlocking the front door to Cam's flat.

Music is blaring and I hesitate in the doorway, Ben juts his chin forward. "You go in, I'll wait here, he ain't gonna be 'appy 'bout this but I dint know what else to do." I must look nervous as Benny adds. "I'll be right here, I won't go anywhere."

He nods as if to reassure me, I walk down the hallway, the place is lit up like Christmas, and every light appears to be on. As I enter the open plan living and kitchen area, I'm struck by the mess. There are bottles everywhere, whiskey, wine, beer; the coffee table is covered in them, along with lots of little empty bags that coke was obviously once in. There's a tray on the floor with two lines ready to go on it, along with a rolled up fifty pound note. The place smells awful, stale alcohol and vomit mainly and a hint of cigar smoke. The song that's been playing has just started to play again, its Fake, by Alexander O'Neal, he has a couple of his CD's that he plays in the car. I look over to the kitchen; there are a couple of plates with mouldy food on them, a pizza box and more bottles.

I head toward Cam's bedroom and can hear the shower running; I head into the bathroom quietly. The door to the shower cubicle is open and Cam is sitting inside on the floor, the water is bouncing off of him and out of the open door, making the floor wet. There is a pile of vomit on the tiled floor beside the shower and another beside the toilet. I throw a towel over each pile, he doesn't notice because his eyes are closed, his legs are out in front of him, arms slumped at his sides, his head is hanging forward and he's completely naked. He looks… small, which is ridiculous as he's six foot four and a big strong man but right at this moment he looks small and frail and I feel so bad that I have caused this. I stand and stare for a few moments, my hand covering my mouth as I try to control my sobs, I go back out to the front door and tell Ben to grab some bags and to start clearing away some of the bottles. I go back to the bathroom and shut the door; I go over to the shower and turn off the water. Cam mumbles something and lifts his arm in front of him and reaches for something… someone, me? I straddle his lap and dry his hair and his face. He almost has a full beard growing, it's dark but with a few flecks of grey. I raise my hand and gently touch his face, his eyes flutter open but he can't focus, he sucks on his own cheeks, probably trying to moisten his mouth, then he opens his eyes again and tilts his head to the side and gives me a little smile.

"Kitten," he whispers, very, very softly. "I love you."

I let out a sob, I can't help it, I hold on to each side of his face. "Oh Tiger, what have you done to yourself?"

"I love you," he whispers again, he grabs a handful of my hair, not roughly, just enough to tilt my head and make me look at him, he nods his head and says it again, "I love you."

I don't know what to say, my heart is telling me to tell him that I love him too but my head is telling me not to be so fucking stupid. He shivers and I realise I need to get him out of the shower and into bed. I move his shoulders off of the wall and drape a dry towel around them; I'm afraid that he will slide over and hit his head so I call out for Benny. The music goes quiet and I can hear talking, I call Benny again. Cam whispers, "No, no Benny, just you, just you Kitten."

The door that separates the bathroom from the bedroom opens and Cam's absolute double is standing there. "I… I'm sorry, I'm Georgia, I was… he's cold, I don't know how long he's been in here. I can't lift him."

Cam's double is wearing a suit; he takes the jacket off and throws it behind him onto the bed. "Mind out the way. Benny, get your arse in here."

I step out of the way of who I'm assuming is Cam's older brother but that's just a guess as he hasn't introduced himself. Benny comes through the door, just, his huge frame fills it; he must've been working hard at cleaning up as he's sweating and his bald head is shining. "Mind the spew Ben," I say as I walk out of the bathroom, there's not enough room for all of us and I don't feel particularly welcome anyway.

Thankfully Cam's bed doesn't look as though it's been slept in so I don't have to put clean sheets on it, I just throw the cushions that we bought to match the new bedding we shopped for just a month ago, onto the floor. My heart stops, starts, sidesteps, and then carries on its normal rhythm at that thought.

"They're cushions George, we bought cushions and bedding together, we didn't get married, get a grip girl," I say out loud to myself. Benny and Cam's double come into the room with an arm of Cam's each draped around their shoulders, his feet are dragging along the floor and the way he's being held, the way he looks, reminds me of Jesus on the cross, just for a second, just for a split second. They drop him unceremoniously onto the bed and I lift his legs and cover him with the duvet.

"You gonna stay here and look after him?" Cam's double frowns as he looks at me. I look around the room, purely for affect, I know full well it's me he's talking to.

"Me?" I ask.

"Yes you! Are you gonna fuckin' stay and help put right this mess you caused."

What? I shake my head. "Who the fuck are you and who the fuck do you think you're talking to?"

"I'm Robbie, Cam's brother and I'm assuming you're Georgia and if I assume correctly, then I'm talking to you."

"Yes, I'm Georgia, but I didn't cause this, he's done this to himself." He puts his hands on his hips and nods his head in a stance and a gesture that is so much like Cam that I want to weep.

"You fucked him over Georgia, you're the first woman since Chantelle died he's allowed himself to get close to. You're the first woman he has openly admitted to me that he's in love with, he was so happy and then you fucked him over. You blew him out for your rock star and you broke him, he's more broken now than when he lost his wife and baby and you fucking did it, so yes, you are the cause of this mess!"

I feel ashamed, I did cause this, not intentionally and I didn't know Cam loved me. "I didn't know."

"You didn't know what?"

"I didn't know he loved me, he never said, he never told me."

"No, because apparently you have a history of doing a runner when blokes tell ya that shit so he was waiting. He knew you was coming round to the idea, he had it all planned, he was taking you away, for two weeks in June, after your brother's wedding. He was gonna take you away and show you, make you realise that you did love him." He stops talking as Cam mumbles in his sleep. "Are you staying or not sweetheart, that's all I wanna know?" He was taking me away, he knew I was falling in love with him, he knew, I didn't, did I?

"I can stay for a couple of hours." He didn't acknowledge my reply so I went and sat on the bed next to Cam. "Right Ben, I'll arrange a cleaner to come through, but for now, can you just check all the cupboards and drawers in here and in the bathroom, anywhere he might stash gear or booze. I'll get someone over to put some locks on the door and we'll work out shifts between me, Josh and Tory to watch him. He hated rehab, we haven't left it so long this time so what I'm thinking is we get a doctor over here to check him out and if it's okay, we do his detox and rehab from here."

Benny nods in agreement. "Good, that's good Rob, you're right, he hated rehab, it'll kill him if he goes back there."

"I don't understand this, is Cam an alcoholic or a junky or both?" Robbie's whole demeanour changes as he comes and sits down on the bed and looks down at Cam.

"Not really, I don't know, I'm not a professional, Cam usually stays away from drugs, but he does do the odd line of Charlie and he likes a drink as much as the next bloke but he always knows when to say enough's enough, apart from when he's not coping. When he's not coping he uses them to escape, he loses himself in a bottle and when that's not enough he makes himself feel like he can deal with anything by snorting line after line of coke and that's what he's doing now." His gaze turns to me and he looks me over, like he's seeing me for the first time.

"I'm sorry alright, about what I said, he told me you had never said that you loved him, he told me you had admitted from the start that you were in love with someone else. He just didn't expect you to get back with the other bloke."

"Neither did I," I say quietly. "I never wanted to hurt him, I wanted to tell him to his face about Sean, but he went to Amsterdam and I arranged to see him when he got back so that I could tell him to his face but he came home early and…" I close my eyes as I think about Cam's words.

"Thanks Kitten, thanks a lot." The look in his eyes when he realised who Sean was. I start to cry.

"He turned up at the club and I was there with Sean and I never meant to hurt him, I am so sorry, I haven't stopped thinking about him for the past two weeks. I just don't know, I don't understand what's going on with me. I think he might be right, I think I do love him, I think, I don't know."

Robbie looks at me with eyes so much like Cam's. "Well that's something only you can decide Georgia and until that time please don't go getting my brothers hopes up, because if you decide that you're wrong or if you leave him again, then I think that would actually kill him."

I have no reply, I don't know what to think, I don't know what to feel. I'm left alone with Cam as what can only be described as a military operation goes on around him, his flat is cleaned, bolts and locks are put on the bedroom door. Benny comes in and goes through every draw and cupboard in the bedroom and bathroom, all while Cam sleeps. I've noticed beads of sweat are starting to appear on his forehead and top lip so I go into the bathroom and run a face cloth under the cold tap and come back and wipe his face, he stirs and mumbles but doesn't wake so I go out to the kitchen to fetch a bowl that I can fill with water so that I don't have to keep dripping the face cloth from the bathroom. The whole place is now spotless and smells fresh and clean. Robbie is still here, talking on the phone, Benny and another bouncer from the bar are sitting on stools in the kitchen, eating burgers. My belly rumbles because I've not eaten today.

"What time is it Ben?"

He looks at his watch. "Ten past six." Shit, I've been here since twelve, I need to get home.

"Ben look, Cam's starting to sweat, I'm gonna give his face another wipe, then would you take me home, I can't walk, I have the press up my arse at the moment." Robbie has ended his phone call and is looking at me.

"Go wash his face and I'll take you. The doctor will be here to give him something for the sweats and shakes." I nod, then fill the bowl with cold water and go back to the bedroom.

This time when I wash Cam's face he opens his eyes, they are a lot more focused now and he looks over my face as he licks his lips, which are dry and cracked. "Kitten," he whispers in a croaky voice.

"Would you like some water?"

I ask him, he shakes his head. "Scotch."

I give a little laugh and shake my head. “No can do Tiger, water, tea, coffee, them’s your choices?”

“You’re mean.”

“I know.”

“I love you.”

“I know.”

“Do you?”

“Yes, would you like some water or some tea?” My heart is banging so hard in my chest that it’s giving me a headache.

He sighs. “Will you serve it to me naked?”

“I’ll pour it over your dick if you don’t simmer down.” He gives a little chuckle.

“There’s my angry Kitten.”

“I’m not angry Cam, I’m sad. Why? Why did you do this to yourself?”

He closes his eyes, when he opens them, his look is cold and hard and it scares me for a second. “My head hurts, would you please get me some headache tablets and a glass of water?”

I don’t question his change in tone or the way he’s now looking at me, he’s hurt and he’s angry and I’m the cause of his suffering. I think that entitles him to look at me however he likes. “I can get you some water but no tablets, the doctor will be here soon and I’m not sure what he wants to give you.”

“What doctor, why?” He starts to get up out of bed but his legs are unsteady and he stagers and falls back down, I call out for Benny, but it’s Robbie that’s first through the door.

“Back in bed Cam.”

“You’re not locking me up again; I’m not going back to that place!” Cam’s shouting and Robbie’s trying to get him back into bed, Benny comes in and helps to hold him down.

"Don't hurt him," I shout at both of them.

"Get her out!" Cam growls. "Get her the fuck out of here, don't let her see me, Rob, don't let her see me like this."

He starts to sob, and I start to cry. "Please Rob, please don't lock me up."

Robbie holds onto Cam as he sobs. "I won't mate, I promise I won't, the doctor's coming. Joshie and Tor are on their way. We'll look after you here, I won't lock you up, and we'll get you better between us."

Cam stops fighting and just lets his big brother hold him, while I stand in the corner and cry, as I watch the outcome of my actions unfold. Robbie looks at me and gestures with his head for me to get out. I leave, I don't wait for a lift, I leave the flat and make the ten minute walk back home with my head down and hope that no one recognises me; as I come down the back ally, I spot Sean's, Len's and my Dad's cars all blocking my way. Fuck, I'm in trouble.

Dave is standing at the bottom of the stairs and lets out a sigh and then shakes his head as he sees me. "Thanks Georgia, I'm in so much fuckin' trouble coz of you." For fucks sake.

"I'm sorry Dave, but if it's any consolation, I bet I'm in more."

He nods his head. "I think your right there babe, Maca is doing his narna, I think they were about to call the Police." Shit, fuck, bollocks.

I run up the stairs and down the hallway to a welcoming party of my entire family plus Jimmie, Ash, Sean and Milo, the whole room falls absolutely silent for a split second. Sean has his back to me; he turns, looks me over, puts his hands on his hips and lets out the biggest sigh as his chin falls forward onto his chest.

"Where the fuck have you been George?" Bailey speaks first, my Dad rakes his hand through his hair and comes and gives me a cuddle.

"Princess, you scared the fuckin' life outta me, don't ever, ever do that again!"

I swallow. "I'm sorry Daddy." I look around the room at all the anxious faces, Baileys making a call.

"Fin, she's here, call the boys off… Na, she's fine, I'll bell ya later and let ya know, cheers." His angry eyes look me over.

"That close." He shows me a very tiny space between his thumb and index finger as he holds them up. "We were that fuckin' close to start banging down doors. Dave said you went off with bald Benny, said you wouldn't be long. That was seven hours ago George, seven fucking hours, no one's seen you, no one's seen King. You didn't call, we had no idea where the fuck you were. We thought he'd flipped his lid and gone psycho again, kidnapped ya, killed ya, we didn't know George, coz you being the selfish little bitch that you are, fucked off without a word. Dad was ready to start shooting people, Macas not far behind." He stops to draw breath. "Do you ever stop and think about anyone but yourself George, ever? You start running around with Sean when you're just a kid, getting up to God knows what. Then you spend four years acting like we should have you committed, then you start running around with one of the East End's biggest gangsters, whose wife just happened to die in very mysterious circumstances and then, finally, we get a two week window where we all think that we can finally breathe, you're back with Maca, finally right where you wanna be and then you pull this little stunt. What the fuck is wrong with you? What exactly is it you want, do you even know? For fuck's sake Georgia, you're nearly twenty-one, it's time to grow up and start being accountable for your actions and the affect they have on everyone else."

I stand, alone, mortified and let the tears roll silently down my cheeks, everything he has said is true, I'm a spoilt, selfish girl and I don't take other people's feelings into account as often as I should, as much as I should. I look around the room, at the worried faces of the people that love most in the world but I don't make eye contact with any of them. "I'm so sorry everyone, I didn't mean for anyone to worry, I was asked to help out in an emergency and I lost track of time. I'm so sorry, I should've called, I should've let someone know where I was or taken Dave with me but I didn't and I'm sorry."

I walk past every one, go straight to my bathroom and turn on the shower, I turn the water around to hot, take off my clothes and step under, adjusting the water so that it's as hot as I can bear it. I want to curl up in a ball and cry. I didn't mean to be selfish, and I didn't mean to hurt anyone or make them worry. I didn't know Cam loved me, I didn't know my family had been so concerned for so long but at the end of the day, is ignorance any kind of defence or am I just a stupid, spoiled twenty year old, who thought she knew it all?

I slide down the wall, bring my knees up to my chest and wrap my arms around them.

I'm not sure how long I spend sitting on the shower floor but when I eventually get out, Sean is sitting on the edge of the bath holding a towel. He stands and wraps it around me and just holds me tight, he grabs another from the rack and starts to rub my hair dry with it. I've stopped crying but my jaw is still quivering and you can hear it in my voice when I say to Sean, "I'm so sorry."

He pulls me in tighter and kisses the top of my head. "Let's go to bed," is all that he says. I climb into bed and sit and dry my hair as I watch him take off his clothes, he strips totally naked and climbs into bed next to me, pulling me to him. I feel safe, warm and loved, which is probably more than I deserve. "Dya wanna tell me about it?"

I shake my head. "Not yet."

"I was so worried G, I don't think I've ever been so scared in all my life. I didn't know what to do. I didn't know where to start and what scared me more was how worried your Dad was." Once again I remain silent.

"Sean?"

"Gia?"

"Make love to me?"

He kisses me gently on the mouth, his hands tangle in my damp hair, he pushes me gently over onto my back and slides down my body and starting with the soles of my feet, he kisses his way back up my legs, bending my knees and spreading me open, kissing, licking and sucking me into my first orgasm, then up and over my belly, onto my boobs, he bites down gently on first one nipple, then the other. He keeps climbing up my body, until eventually he's straddling my chest. I take his cock in my hand and stroke him. He brushes his thumb over my bottom lip as he looks down into my eyes.

"Squeeze your tits together," he whispers. He places his cock between my tits while I squeeze them like he told me, he strokes himself right down at the base, all the while, he's staring into my eyes. "God you look fuckin' beautiful right now."

I give him a small smile, I don't want him to be nice to me, I want him to be rough and cause me pain. "Fuck my arse," I say to him.

"What?"

"I want you in my arse, now." He stills for a few seconds, his eyes fully focused on mine, then rolls to the side.

"Turn over."

He climbs off the bed and goes into the bathroom, returning a few seconds later and puts something down on the bedside table. He lays down flat on top of me at first, just stroking up and down the backs of my arms, he kisses the back of my neck and my shoulders, then all the way down my spine, he pushes my legs apart with his. "Pull your knees underneath you babe, arse in the air, keep your legs open wide."

I do exactly as he says; his fingers gently stroke down from the back of my neck, down my spine, over each of my arse cheeks, then through the middle of them, he uses his hands to spread me open and I can feel the calluses on his fingers caused by years of playing the guitar and of all the sensations firing through me right now, it's that one that makes me groan, it's so Sean, so unique to Sean. He licks me, from back to front and then back again, his tongue flicks in and around my hole, while he uses his middle finger to rub my clit. "Fuck, Sean."

"That feel good G?"

"Yeah."

"We've got no lube so I'm gonna use Vaseline, keep still for me." I remain perfectly still while I listen to him unscrew the jar of Vaseline, then he's back, he starts with just one finger, he rubs it gently in circles, around and around.

"Open your legs wider baby, push your arse higher and relax, you look so beautiful right now, so fuckin' beautiful." He pushes one finger inside me, and then adds another. "That okay, tell me if it hurts?"

I'm biting down so hard on my bottom lip that it actually hurts when I release it, so I suck it to relieve the pain. "Gia, am I hurting you? Tell me baby and I'll stop."

"No, no, fuck no." He pulls his fingers out, and then rubs his cock up and down my arse crack; he stops and nudges against me. "I love you baby, please tell me you really wanna do this, you know I love you right? Don't do this if you don't wanna."

I look around at him from over my shoulder. "When do I ever do anything I don't wanna?" He gives me his 'front of a magazine cover pout' then winks at me; he wraps his hand around my hair and yanks my hair back roughly. "I fuckin' love you Georgia Rae, now I'm gonna fuck your arse and make you scream."

He eases inside me slowly as he talks, "Fuck, you're tight baby."

He pulls me up so that I'm almost sitting on his knees, his knees between my open legs from behind, he reaches around me and gently rubs my clit, his mouth is at my ear and I tilt my head to the side so that I can feel his hot breath on me as he speaks, "You're in control Georgia, ride me, go at your speed baby."

I grind gently onto him, enjoying the full sensation, it's different but it's nice. "You want my fingers in your cunt?" Oh

God, just him saying that word has me groaning and grinding back on him. "Do ya G? Tell me, else I'll stop."

"No, I mean yes, no don't stop, yes I want your fingers in me."

He chuckles in my ear. "You're a bad, bad girl Georgia Rae and I love the fuck out of 'ya, now come for me, coz I ain't gonna last, you're too much, I can't last."

He pushes his fingers inside me and it's the strangest of sensations, I feel full, stretched and when he pushes the heel of his hand onto my clit, it's too, too much, every muscle I have below my waist clamps around his cock and his fingers. I roll my head back as he bites into my shoulder, I moan and call out his name, trying to relieve the intensity of the orgasm that just won't stop rolling through me. In the end I have nowhere left to go and just take it, moaning and whimpering my way through it as I listen to Sean's words, "Fuck, that's good, I'm coming baby, only for you, it's only ever been you."

We collapse in a heap less than a minute later, he holds my back tight against his chest, kissing the back of my neck and my shoulders continuously; eventually we lay still and silent, I listen to him breathe and feel his chest move up and down against my back. I want him to talk, to ask me about today but I also want him to never mention it, he kisses the back of my head.

"Come and shower with me." I nod and he eases out of me, he pulls me by the hand and we walk to the shower, he doesn't wait for the water to heat up and pulls me in with him. I scream and he laughs, pulling me tight against his chest as the cold water makes both of our teeth chatter. It eventually starts to warm, he pushes my wet again hair from my face, then holds it with both of his hands, he kisses my eyes, my nose, then so, so softly my mouth, my chin, down through my cleavage, all the way down my belly. He kneels down on the floor in front of me, takes hold of my hands in his and says, "I love ya Georgia Rae, please be my wife?"

Oh my God, I stare down at him, not sure if I've just heard right. "I love you Georgia, more than life, I love you like the stars above." He raises his eyebrows at me and smirks, waiting for me to sing my line.

"I'll love you till I die," I continue and he breaks out his best grin yet.

"Like I told ya, Romeo and Juliette have got nothing on us baby. I don't wanna wait; if other people hadn't fucked us up we would've been married and probably had a couple of kids by now."

He's looking up at me, with those big brown eyes, with their little flecks of gold shinning so brightly in them. He's my life, he's my world and whatever feelings I thought I might have for Cam are now irrelevant. Perhaps I do love Cam, I don't know but it doesn't matter, because Sean will always have my heart, I have no control over that fact, it is what it is and no one will ever be able to change it.

I push his hair back off his face and smile down at him; I nod first, and then follow it up with. "Yes, yes of course I'll marry you."

We make love again in the shower before collapsing into bed and sleeping for a few hours, then he wakes me up as he slides himself inside me, we make love silently and afterwards, when he holds me tightly to his chest, I tell him about my day. I tell him about Cam, I tell him about how guilty I feel, that I didn't know Cam loves me and I tell him that I think I might love Cam a little bit and he tells me its fine, and that he understands. He's jealous, hates it, but he understands. Cam was there, right when I needed him and it's perfectly natural for me to have strong feelings for him, he tells me to go back and help him get better, support him in any way that I can, which just makes me love Sean even more. I cry and tell him how my heart feels like it's going to burst with how much I love him.

In the end, just as the sun is coming up and the birds are beginning to sing, we decide together, that perhaps it will be better if I don't see Cam again, it might just get his hopes up and then it might all be too much for him when he finds out that we are getting married. Sean's happy with whatever I want to do and I decide a clean break will be the best and fairest way forward. I fall asleep, happy, content and without guilt.

CHAPTER 22

AUGUST 1999

Sean and I were sat at a little café in Chapel Street Melbourne, Australia; we had just enjoyed an enormous fry up and were now sipping on our coffees and watching the very interesting sights and sounds of this part of Australia. It was an absolutely freezing cold, but a bright and sunny day; we had no idea when we arrived eight months ago, on a stinking hot thirty eight degree day that Australia could get so cold. We'd been travelling all around the country since our arrival, and had seen waterfalls in Kakadu, and watched the sun set and rise again over Ayers Rock. We'd dived with sharks, inside a shark cage in Western Australia, and we'd surfed at Bondi, spent New Year's Eve on a yacht in Sydney Harbour, driven along the Great Ocean Road, surfed again at Bells Beach and sat freezing on a beach on Phillip Island watching a colony of Fairy Penguins coming back to dry land after a day out at sea fishing. We spent the last three weeks discovering the city of Melbourne and its surrounding areas.

We'd fallen in love with Australia when Carnage had toured here almost two years ago and we vowed to come back and have a look at the whole country, not just Sydney and Melbourne where the band had played. The people were so friendly, the country and the scenery were stunningly beautiful and vaster than you could ever imagine. Victoria was the smallest state and yet you could fit the whole of Great Britain inside it.

Sean and I had been away from England and our families for almost a year now, we'd decided to take a year out, leaving the madness of Carnage and the fame that came with it behind us while we travelled, before coming back to England and trying for a baby.

After Sean had proposed to me, we kept our news secret until after Jimmie and Lennon's wedding as we didn't want to take any of the attention away from them or attract any more attention to ourselves. The press intrusion had been relentless, sometimes the stories they printed about us were half-truths, but mostly they were complete fabrication and often very hurtful. We mostly ignored them or had a good laugh over them. We'd been split up, according to the press on an almost weekly basis. Sean had had numerous affairs, quoted as being in places with different women, when he was in fact, at home, or even on a different continent with me. The best story was that the reason we hadn't had children yet was because our marriage was a sham and Sean was gay; that was the one that we laughed most about and the one that had caused Sean to have the most piss taken out of him amongst the band, my brothers and our friends.

The real reason we had in fact held off having children, is that we were simply enjoying life too much. We loved travelling; being on tour with the band was hard enough without adding children to the equation. We'd seen this first hand with my brother's kids.

Jimmie and Lennon had produced a son within a year of being married, and in keeping with Layton tradition, his name had a musical link. When little Jimmy was born, everyone assumed he was named after his Mum, until his little sister was born eighteen months later and named Paige, then along came Ziggy, named after Ziggy Stardust, not Marley but both worked, then last year Harley was born, named after one of my Dad's favourite singers Steve Harley.

Marley and Ash had stayed together, although their relationship was nowhere near as happy and settled as Jim and Len's. They'd split up and reconciled so many times over the last ten years I'd lost count, although they seemed much happier of late as the band were touring less and the press attention wasn't as intrusive. They'd never married, but had three children a boy called Joe, after Joe Strummer from The Clash and two girls, Connie after my Mum's favourite singer Connie Francis and Annie after Annie Lennox. Add to this Tom and Billy's kids, there were times that there'd been a total of ten children in tow whilst the band toured, most of whom I have to say, behaved better than the band members. Witnessing first-hand the stress of travelling with the kids and the limitations it put on what you could and couldn't do, the places you could and couldn't visit. We had just decided to wait, the same as we ended up doing with our wedding, which eventually happened in October of 1999. The band had just ended their American tour and the whole lot of us, all of my family, including my parents, Bailey and his new girlfriend Sam, Billy, Tom and their families, headed down to Florida for a much needed holiday, where we decided on the spur of the moment to get married.

Everyone we wanted to be there was in the same place at the same time for a change, so, we got in touch with a Justice Of The Peace, got ourselves a licence and were married just as the sun set on St' Pete's beach on Saturday the 27th of October. It was a simple service, we wrote our own vows, each of us struggling to get our words out with the emotion of the day bearing down on us. Sean being the lyrical genius out of the two of us had every one in tears in an instant.

"Georgia Rae, I love ya, I've loved ya since the day I saw you hanging upside down on the monkey bars, flashing me your pink knickers, you were eleven years old and you stole my heart from my chest and the breath from my lungs. I only ever feel complete when you're near, you own me Gia, heart, mind, body and soul, completely. I love you like the stars above and I will love you till I die, but these words, all that I tell you today, all that I declare before our friends and family today, they still aren't enough, because like I've told you before, the words haven't been invented yet to describe what you mean to me, what I feel for you. There's no one else, there never was, it's still only ever you and I will spend every minute of every day, loving you, worshiping you and doing my best to make you happy, doing my best to be the Husband you deserve. I love ya Georgia Rae, please be my Wife?"

He stopped twice to regain his composure, watching Sean cry as he declared his love for me in front of our friends and our family almost floored me, I pointlessly fought so hard not to cry. For me, the most amazing thing was, we hadn't read or even discussed our vows and was amazed at how we had thought along the same lines, mine sounded like a shortened version of Sean's, I spoke between sobs.

"Sean, from that very first day I set eyes on you, I've known you were my one true love, you own my heart, my mind, my body and soul and I will love you till I die. I'll spend each and every day trying to be the Wife you deserve. You make me a better person, and without you I'm lost, incomplete. Please, will you be my Husband because there's no one else, there never was, it's still only ever you, I love you Sean McCarthy, please marry me."

"What's up G, what ya thinking?" Sean looks across the table at me; he has the hood of his leather jacket pulled up. He shaved his beautiful hair off when we got here and amazingly, he had hardly been recognised the whole trip. In fact, on one occasion, it was me that was recognised and not him. I ended up signing autographs and having my photo taken with Sean's fans while he hid in a tourist shop on Sydney's Circular Quay, but he had let it grow since May now and we had started to garner the odd second glance from passers-by so Sean had taken to either wearing a hat or keeping the hood of his jacket up.

Sean's skin is so dark from all of the sun we've been exposed to, he almost looks Arabic, the way his hood drapes over his hair, framing his dark skin and eyes, my belly does a few forward rolls as I digest the fact that this stunningly beautiful man, who's adored, loved and lusted after by millions of both men and women around the world, is in fact, my Husband. And I'm under absolutely no illusion as to how much he loves me. We've spent almost a year in near isolation from anyone else, just Sean and Georgia, Georgia and Sean, as it should be and I can't help but smile.

"I was thinking about our wedding." His face lights up.

"The day or the night?" I shake my head at him, he's just turned thirty two and still such a boy.

"Our vows." He moves his chair closer to mine and puts his arm around me.

"I meant every one of them," he says, I give him a broad smile.

"I know you did and you've lived up to each and every one of them."

"And so have you, I couldn't be happier, could you?" I think about it for a few seconds, apparently a few seconds too long, my Husband can read me like a book and now his smile has vanished, his eyebrows pulled together in a look of concern. I have a confession to make and I'm not sure how he's going to take the news, it's something we have discussed, but as yet have made no firm decision on.

"What G, what is it?"

"I ran out of pills."

"Pills, what pills, you got a headache?" I laugh.

"No, contraceptive pills." His eyes widen.

"Ahh shit, right, well we can just get you in to see a doctor here and get you a prescription. I can't see that it'll be any hassle, if it is, I'll make some calls and get some Fed Ex'ed over."

"In June," I add and wait for his reaction, he looks totally confused.

"What, you don't need them till June?" I smile at him, I'm as nervous as shit at what I'm about to tell him.

"I ran out of pills in June, we've been having unprotected sex since June." He looks at me blankly for a split second, then his face lights up, his eyes spark with, everything that I hoped to see in them.

"You wanna make a baby?" Oh God that sounded so sexy that all I can do is nod and smile stupidly. He stands up, throws twenty dollars on the table, grabs my hand and pulls me out to the side of the road as he hails a taxi.

"What are you doing?" I laugh as I speak.

"We're going back to the hotel to pack, it's time to go home baby, I'm not having you flying long haul with my baby in your belly, it won't be good for either of you so the quicker we get home, the quicker we can get on with the job of making a mixed up version of you and me." He opened the door of the taxi and guided me in.

As soon as we are settled in the back of the cab and on our way back to our hotel, Sean is on his mobile to the private jet company and books us a plane for six that evening.

Just to make sure that I'm not flying pregnant, he makes the cabbie stop at a chemist on the way to the hotel and buys two pregnancy tests, luckily I need to wee pretty much as soon as we are in our room and we sit on the edge of the bath tub and stare at the little stick I hold in my hands.

"What if it's positive, you gonna make me stay here for the next nine months?" He grins his lopsided grin at me.

"Well first, I would kiss you till your lips were numb, because I would be the happiest man in the world and second, I… I don't know I'd just carry on being the happiest man in the world."

We stare as one line appears on the stick, not pregnant, I feel a little surge of disappointment, so I look at him and shrug. "The pill will take at least six months to clear my system, January, that's when we'll get pregnant, but let's get home and get trying any way."

He tilts his head to one side. "Naaa, let's get trying now."

He drags me back to the bedroom and jumps on me, but the look of disappointment on his face didn't go unnoticed, but I'm not worried, I've been on the pill for sixteen years, I'm not expecting to get knocked up yet, besides, I want to see in the new year with a bang. It's the first time in years neither Jimmie or Ash are pregnant over Christmas and we can actually all have a proper celebration in New York where the band are playing at a special New Year's Eve concert to see in the year 2000.

Around thirty long hours later we are back at our home in Hampstead, North West London. I call my Mum, Jimmie and Ash and let them know we are home. We spend the next week hardly leaving our bed, not because we are continuously having sex, although a lot of that does go on, but because we are so jet lagged from the flight and the time difference. Sean runs his business dealings from his phone whilst still in bed, I mostly sleep.

* * *

The following weekend is when we were due home and I'd completely forgotten the boys were off to France to play at some sporting event. I really don't feel like getting on another plane so soon after the trip back from Australia so instead I arrange a girls night out with Ashley and Jimmie, as luck would have it, the boys record label have invitations to a new club opening in Shoreditch.

We all meet up at the Docklands penthouse, the boys still own it and we all use it at various times after nights out in the city when we need somewhere to crash. It feels like years since we've all gotten ready together like this, probably because it is. We take forever as we talk and drink and have a general catch up, we've spoken on the phone almost daily since I've been back in the country but I haven't seen them in almost a year and there are a few tears as soon as we set eyes on each other. By the time we finally make it down to the car, where Dave is waiting to drive us, it's already eleven thirty pm and we're all well on our way to being legless.

The club is a warehouse conversion, pretty much like every other building in and around East London but it looks great, the sound system is pumping and the girls are desperate to dance. I did a pregnancy test this morning, just to make sure and as it was negative, I joined my girls in a couple of lines of coke before we left and I'm now feeling the effect and can't wait to hit the dance floor. The place is full of celebrities, actors, models, footballers, pop stars and the usual bunch of glamour models that always seem to get invites to this type of thing. The waiters and waitresses come around with an endless supply of champagne and there's a free bar for anything else. While the girls are still on the dance floor, I head to the toilets and on the way back decide to grab us a round of shots. I stand at the bar waiting to be served when a shiver goes through me, before I get the chance to wonder what could have caused it a deep voice says right into my ear.

"Good evening Kitten, hope you're well?"

My stomach hits the floor for a few seconds but then my cocaine enhanced confidence finds its voice and without even looking at him I say, "Tiger, how the fuck are you?"

"Really Kitten, that's so unladylike."

"Tiger, I think we established many years ago, that I'm no fucking lady."

He's quiet for a few seconds, in which time I finally turn my gaze to him, he looks *afuckinmazing*, he's wearing a black suit with satin lapels, a black shirt and a black satin tie. He's standing so close that I can smell him, he smells delicious, still wearing the same Givenchy aftershave that he always has, it instantly reminds me of my bed at my flat above the shop, and all the things he did to me in it.

"You look beautiful Georgia, absolutely stunning."

"You don't look so bad yourself Tiger, how ya doing? You look a whole lot better than the last time I saw you, that's for sure." I want to reach out and touch his face, run my hands over the beard he has growing there, it really suits him. "I love the beard."

He ignores my beard comment. "I owe you an apology and a thank you, regarding the last time you saw me."

I shrug and knock back the first of the three shots that have been placed in front of me. "No apology necessary, no thanks required, you would have done the same for me."

He nods his head slightly, in a way I remember so well. "I would and more, I would've done so much more for you, given the chance."

"Don't Cam, I'm so sorry the way things turned out, the way you found out, please don't make me feel worse than I've done all these years."

He puffs his cheeks and blows out a long breath; I feel it over the side of my neck and know in an instant my nipples are painfully erect. I need to get away from him, but before I can, he pulls me into his side; I look up at him, about to ask what the fuck he's doing when a camera flashes in my face.

"Cam what the fuck are you playing at?" I don't wait for his answer, I just turn and head back over to where I left the girls dancing, grabbing a glass of champagne from a passing waitress as I go. I've drunk it all down by the time I reach the dance floor, and I spend the next hour knocking back more champagne and dancing.

While I dance my mind drifts and I think about the life Sean and I have lead over the past ten years. We've been so lucky, we are lucky to have found our way back to each other; we're happy, content and still so in love. I hate being apart from him for any length of time; especially when he travels overseas and I don't go with him. Mobile phones have made things easier, but despite talking to him sometimes five times a day, I still miss him. That's why usually I go with him, but I just didn't fancy the flight this weekend and he will only be away for one night. It's a small sacrifice for the lifestyle the band's success has given us, not just the money and all the materialistic things it can buy but the doors it opens for you, the places we have been able to visit, and the people we have met. We've been to award ceremonies and sat at a table with Jagger and Richards, we've been to film premiers and been in the same room as De Niro. I had slow danced with the British Prime Minister at a charity event and then spent an hour talking about music to Nelson Mandela, who had the spark and wit of a thirteen year old boy and who to this day, remains my ultimate human being. Sean and I have appeared on magazine covers both together and apart, we've been interviewed about our lives and there has even been rumours that we'll soon be approached to not only write our autobiographies but to contribute to a film that's apparently going to be made, loosely based on our lives. Why people are so interested in me, I have no idea. Sean I can understand, but I'm just his Wife. I've done some work over the last ten years, mainly for various charities, but other than that, I've just been at Sean's side and I have loved every minute, I don't need more.

Despite all of these great and wonderful things, its nights like tonight that I've really missed, just a plain old simple night out with the girls, as plain and simple as it can be when the wives of one of the world's biggest bands embark on a night out. Dave drove us here and is lingering at the bar, just to make sure we are okay. He has just come over and advised us that as a lot of the celebs are now leaving, the doors will be opened up to the general public and perhaps it would be best if we went upstairs to the VIP area, where we won't be harassed. The weird thing is, I still consider myself part of the general public, I still get tongue tied when I speak to one of my idols, I nearly wet myself when I met Weller for the first time. Sean and Marley have a picture of me staring at him in wonder as he speaks to Lennon about something or another, I can't remember. I've never fancied the bloke, it's just that his music is something that I grew up listening to and I've always thought that he remains to this day, one of the greatest song writers England has ever produced.

I'm snapped out of my thoughts by a camera going off in my face.

"Fuck this," Ashley says. "Dave's right, let's go upstairs."

I gesture to Dave that we are going to the VIP lounge and the three of us hold hands as Jimmie leads the way; we were given wristbands when we first entered the club so just walk straight into the floor to ceiling glassed off area. I spot Cam at the bar straight away and groan inwardly; I haven't seen him once since the day I tried to help him, no contact whatsoever and yet he still has an effect on my body and I don't know why. I love my Husband, I'm in love with my Husband and I hate myself for having this reaction to another man. I have thought about him over the years; Bailey told me that he rang my Dad the morning after he ran into Sean and me at Kings and sold him his share immediately. Further down the track he'd told me that he had bumped into him and Cam had asked how I was doing and if I was happy. That information made my heart beat faster too at the time and now here he was, tall and handsome, leaning against the bar talking to a tall red head who I think was an actress or a television presenter, I'd seen her face somewhere before anyways.

'Shit G, Mr TDH is at the bar," Jimmie squeezes my hand as she speaks.

"Fuck," Ash adds. "He's still Mr TDH too; just look at him George, that man is sex on legs."

"Yeah, he spoke to me at the bar earlier, we got papped together, that'll be interesting tomorrow when I try and explain to Sean why I'm all over the Sunday papers with my ex."

We are offered more champagne by a topless male waiter and each take one, we find a tall round table and put our drinks down on it and stand and chat. I ask about my nieces and nephews, who I can't wait to squish and confess to the girls that I'm off the pill and that we are actively trying for a baby, they both shriek in excitement.

"Well it's about time," Jimmie says. "I thought perhaps there was something wrong and you just weren't telling us, I was going to offer you my eggs, my womb even if you needed it."

I'm stunned into silence; my eyes instantly fill with tears. "You'd do that for me?" I ask her.

"Of course I would, why have you left it so long?"

"You can have my eggs," Ashley adds. "But fuck being pregnant again; I wouldn't do it for myself, let alone any other fucker."

I laugh at Ashley's bluntness; along with me, she's rubbed shoulders with the worlds beautiful people, but she hadn't changed a bit from the wild child I'd met at school fifteen years ago, even motherhood hadn't tamed her.

"We waited because we love our lifestyle, no disrespect to you two, but I've seen how hard it can be when the boys are on tour and you have to either bring the kids or arrange babysitters. Now that things aren't so manic with the boys, I'm ready… we're ready. We've got that last bit of travel bug out of our system by taking this last year off and now we're ready to be grownups," I smile as I speak, unable to hide my excitement at the thought of becoming a parent, at the thought of Sean holding a baby in his arms, of a brown eyed baby boy with a mop of curls, just like his Dad's used to be. I can't wait.

"Well I'm really pleased for you both; you'll both be amazing parents." Jimmie gives me a cuddle.

"Fuck, a little MacBaby running around the place, that'll be one good looking kid G. I mean Maca's smoking hot and if I didn't like cock so much, I wouldn't kick you out of bed either babe."

"Thanks Ash, I think."

"What the fucks a MacBaby?" Jimmie asks.

"It's what you get after you have unprotected sex with McCarthy." Ashley winks.

"And if you're really lucky, you'll even get a MacGasm," She laughs as she speaks.

"Oh I'm more than lucky girls; I've been having multiple MacGasms since I was fourteen. I was an underage slut."

"MacSlut," Ash and Jimmie say together and we all burst into laughter.

God, this feels so good, a girls night with my sister in laws, who also happen to be my best friends, life doesn't get much better.

We all clink glasses and talk about this and that for a bit longer before hitting the small dance floor as tune after tune of eighties and nineties club classics are pumped through the sound system.

"I need to wee," Jimmie says.

"I'll come too," I add, obviously being girls, one in, all in but as we approach the ladies room in the VIP bar, we see that there's a queue, I go back to the bar and ask the bar man if there's a toilet nearby.

"Here, go out of here and turn left, use the toilet in my office." Cam holds a bunch of keys in front of my face; I turn and look at him.

"You own this place?"

"I do." I simply nod, take the keys from him and call to Ash and Jimmie to follow me.

Cam's office, is very similar to that at the wine bar, very old fashioned, gentleman's club looking and it smells so much like Cam; we all take turns using the bathroom and I can't resist spraying a squirt of Cam's aftershave onto the inside of my wrist after I find it sitting on the edge of the sink. We lock up behind us and start to head back toward the bar and that's when I see her.

I feel faint at first, light headed, it rolls from the tips of my toes to the top of my head, it stops me dead in my tracks I watch her as she pleads with security to let her into the VIP bar and then the light headedness is gone and I can see very clearly and think and feel even clearer, my rage doesn't even start at red, it's way beyond red, it's white hot and searing and I have to get to her. I drop the keys and my bag and I think that for a few seconds, I might actually fly, I move so fast. I think that my feet actually leave the ground, and I'm on her in what seems like a second. I vaguely hear Jimmie calling my name, then just a rush of air and my own heart beat in my ears. I grab her hair with my left hand and punch her with my right, she goes down onto the floor and I throw myself down on top of her, straddling her chest, I punch again and again. Then I lift her head by her hair and bang it into the ground. I don't see her face, I don't see anything, I don't feel anything, but I keep punching, clawing, pulling at skin and hair continuously, until I'm pulled backward, through the air. My vision comes back first, there are club security leaning over an unconscious woman. Dave has my arm on one side, Cam on the other; Jimmie is in my face telling me to calm down. Ash is just glaring at the woman on the floor, who is now moving, she starts to try and stand and I catch sight of her face and rush toward her again. I'm screaming something, but I've no idea what, I land a great right hook on her jaw and she flies backward, caught by the bouncer. I'm once again dragged back in the opposite direction and pulled into Cam's office. I scratch and spit and scream obscenities all the way. I've lost it. I scream at Cam to shoot her, to give me a gun so that I can shoot her, my eyes scour the desk and I spot the scissors and I make a grab for them, telling anyone that's listening that I'm gonna cut the bitches throat. Never in my life have I felt rage like it.

I'm pulled down into someone's lap. It registers that it's Cam after a few seconds, I can smell him, I stop fighting and try to calm my breathing, there's still a commotion going on around me, doors opening and closing, people talking.

"I need to get her out of here," I hear Dave say. "The fuckin' press are gonna be all over this."

"Is there a back door?" I hear Jimmie ask.

"Where is *she*, have you kicked *her* out? Cos if George ain't killed her, I fucking will!" Go Ash!

"Let's just sit tight for a minute, I don't know what state she's in and this one still needs to calm down."

I hear a door open and someone says, "She's saying she wants the Police called boss, what dya want me to do?"

"For fuck's sake," Cam says quietly.

"Where is she?"

"One of the barmaids is with her in the staff room."

"Keep her there, I'll go down and talk to her, see if I can change her mind." It's all quiet for a few minutes.

"If I let you go, do you promise not to go psycho on me again Kitten?" I nod and open my eyes, they slam into his, looking down at me. He has a slight smile on his face.

"You're a fucking mad woman Georgia, dya know that? I've never seen a girl punch like that."

"That's what happens when you're taught to fight by three big brothers," I reply, shakily.

He loosens his grip around me and I turn and look at everyone in the room, Jimmie is sitting on the edge of Cam's desk shaking her head at me, Ash is sitting on the leather sofa.

"Feel better George? I know I fucking do, that bitch had it coming, if you hadn't of chinned her, I fucking woulda. Mind you, I didn't recognise her, she looks about fifty. I've only seen the pictures from when she went to the papers but I swear she looked dog rough compared to then."

I look at Dave who's on his phone and does not look happy. "Do none of your husband's ever answer their phones?"

Sean always answers his phone, before I can speak Jimmie says, "Len always answers, no matter what time it is, in case it's an emergency with me or one of the kids."

"Marley never picks up, he's a fucking nightmare," Ash complains.

"Please don't ring them." I look pleadingly at Dave. "It's the middle of the night, Sean will just go off on one and so will Len."

"Georgia, if you're about to get nicked, I have to call him, he *will* have my balls if I don't."

"She won't get nicked, I'll sort it. Who's this bird anyway, what did she do to piss you off so much?" Cam asks.

"Whorely," we all reply together. Ash had never met her, but she knew the name.

“She accused my Husband and brother of rape, and then told my Mum a bunch of crap that kept me and Sean apart for four years.” Sadness is the only word I can use to describe the look that washes over Cam’s face.

I slide to my feet as he stands. “Wait in here, I’ll get rid of her, then you can leave out of the back doors.

Twenty minutes later he’s back. “Fuck Georgia, her face is a mess.”

“George didn’t do that, that’s how she looks anyway, ugly cunt,” Ashley pipes up and we all laugh, except Cam, who cringes at Ashley’s use of the C word.

“I’ve convinced her to leave the Police out of it, and I’ve offered her a lifetime VIP access to the club, but I have a feeling she’ll be billing you for a new nose.”

I shrug. “Well she can go fuck herself; she’s getting nothing out of me.”

“Kitten,” Cam says quietly. Dave shifts on his feet, obviously not comfortable with Cam’s term of endearment.

“Right, well, I’ll go and pull the motor round the back, you girls come down when you’re ready. Cheers Cam, thanks for sorting this out, I’m sure Frank or Bailey will be in touch.” He nods his head in Cam’s direction.

“You tell my Dad or Bailey about this and I will slap you Dave,” I tell him.

“Georgia, love, you did it in front of a fuckin’ audience darlin’, subtlety has never been a strength of yours. I don’t think I’ll need to tell anyone about this, the Sunday papers will do that for me. That’s why it’ll be best if you get hold of Maca and tell him yourself.”

Fuck. Shit. Bollocks. “Yeah, yeah, I’ll ring him; he can ring the label, or speak to the lawyers, whoever, see if they can do some damage control.”

I'm probably going to cause Sean all sorts of problems with my actions, but I don't regret it. I actually understand in that moment, the rage Cam must have felt when he shot that man in the pub car park in front of me, if I had a gun on me tonight, I could've quiet easily shot that bitch. I may have regretted it later, but only because of the trouble it would've gotten me in.

I'm not sure if it's the drugs, drink or adrenalin in my system but I can't help but feel a little bit of resentment toward Sean, this all started with him and if he has to clean up my mess and the repercussions of my actions tonight, then so be it. I suffered for years because of his stupid irresponsible actions.

"Say it was me, I don't give a fuck," Ash adds, bringing me back into the room I just shake my head at her.

Dave leaves and five minutes later, we make to leave, the girls say goodbye to Cam and thank him. I go to give him a hug when he says, "Can you give me a minute Georgia, and I'll walk you down in a sec. I just want a word?"

I make eye contact with the girls and nod. "I'll be down in a minute."

They leave and I'm left alone with Cam and my pounding heart, he bought me an ice pack for my aching knuckles earlier, bitch had a hard jaw, and I adjust it over the pain in my right hand.

"Despite the circumstances, it's been really good to see you Kitten." I smile at him.

"You too Cam." He takes the ice pack off of me and puts it on his desk, next to where he's leaning; he takes my hand and kisses my knuckles.

"Angry Kitten, you really need to learn to control that temper baby." My heart skips a beat at his words, at the sensation of his lips on my skin and I know it's time to leave.

"If he hadn't have come back, would it have been me, would you have stayed with me?" I pull my hand from his and shake my head.

"I'm not doing this Cam; it was ten years ago, I'm married, I'm with Sean."

"But I still affect you don't I? There's still something there, I feel it and you're lying if you say you don't." He's stating facts, not asking questions.

"It doesn't matter what I feel, I'm married to Sean. I love Sean. Thanks Cam, thanks for everything tonight, I'm sorry if it's caused any trouble for the club and I'm sorry for the past, I have to go." I reach out for the door handle.

"Did you love me Kitten, even a little bit?" I don't hesitate with my answer.

"Yes Tiger and I think I still do." I pull the door open and jump when it's slammed shut from behind me.

He pulls me around by my shoulder and his mouth is instantly on mine, his tongue seeking out, and then almost attacking mine. His hands are over me, they slide up my hips, over my waist, they cup my breasts and I offer no resistance to any of it. I just stand with my arms at my sides at first, then they are up and in his hair, grabbing, pulling him away, he starts pulling my dress up my legs and I stop pulling his mouth away from me and instead start pushing it toward me. My dress is suddenly up around my waist and Cam's grinding into me, I'm grinding back, he bites down on my nipple, hard, viciously almost, through the silk of my dress. I undo the zip of his trousers and reach inside, he's hot, throbbing and huge; he doesn't use his fingers on me first, he doesn't need to, I'm soaking wet already. He pulls my knickers to the side and rams into me. I cry out in pain, and… in absolute pleasure. He lifts me off the floor with each thrust, my head bangs back against the door, on just the fourth thrust I feel my orgasm start to grip me and everything begins to tighten.

"Fuck, Kitten, look at me, fucking look at me." I stare straight into his eyes as we fuck, hard, nasty, dirty, adulterously fuck against Cam's office door. "Come, come with me, now Kitten, come." He rams roughly into me a few more times, my legs now wrapped around him, I grind back, once, twice and explode. I make a noise that's not quite a scream, not quite a sob, not quite a moan but a mixture of all three. Cam comes, spurting hot inside me, with tears in his eyes, I drop my legs to the floor, move away from him and pull down my dress and stand and stare at him, panting.

"Oh God, oh God, what have I done, what have I done?" I sob. I grab my bag and leave but he's right behind me, tucking himself in.

"This way… this way Georgia." He pulls me roughly by the arm, back toward the emergency exit sign, he pulls me down a flight of stairs, then stops in front of a door "Let me have your number, we need to talk."

"No, no number, we don't need to talk, not about this, not ever, it should never have happened."

"You fucking love me Kitten, you know you do." His hand rakes through his long dark hair, he must be in his forties now but he's still so handsome, still so very alpha male.

"I know that, I fucking know that, but it makes no difference, I'm with Sean, I love Sean. This was a mistake that will never happen again. Stay away from me Cam, do not try to contact me, just stay away."

Once again I've caused that defeated look on his face, I push past him and outside to the Range Rover, where Dave and the girls are waiting, I slam the door behind me.

"Let's go." I call out. We drive back to the penthouse in silence, the loudest silence I have ever heard in my life.

CHAPTER 23

Dave drops us off in front of the building and comes up in the lift, seeing us in; he heads home once we are safely delivered but reminds us that he's on 24 hour call if we need him for anything.

Jim and Ash haven't said a word to me all the way home and I'm shitting myself that they know what I did with Cam. I need to get into the shower, I smell of sex, dirty, filthy, adulterous, guilty sex and I smell of Cam and I need to wash him away.

"I'm going to shower," I tell the girls.

"George, wait, we need to talk to you," Jimmie calls out. I turn and finally look at the pair of them.

"What's wrong?" I ask as nonchalantly as possible.

"George, I'm really worried, Lens still not answering his phone, even Milo's not answering."

"Stop panicking," Ash jumps in. "They're probably drunk in some French bar or something and just can't hear their phones."

My stomach does a nervous back flip, the last time I couldn't get hold of Sean, was the night Haley had made her accusations. Haley the fucking whore, my fists clenched at the thought of that slut, despite venting my rage on her earlier, there was still so much more damage that I'd like to inflict, if Cam hadn't been there to stop me.

Cam, the enormity of what I did starts to hit me. I swallow down the bile with my tears, which Jimmie mistakes for worry over the boys. I am worried, of course I am, chances are, Ash is probably bang on with where they are and what they are doing and I have absolutely no right to feel angry at what they might be getting up to.

"Ash is probably right Jim, it's nearly morning now, they have an early flight home anyway and the planes landing at City airport so they'll be here after lunch, let me have a shower and then we'll make some more calls. We'll call the hotel and wake them up if we have to, serves them right for not answering their mobiles."

The second I step into the shower I let my tears go and I allow my brain to start trying to make sense of my actions, but I can't. Why would I do that? Why did I do that? What a stupid, selfish thing to do. If this ever gets out, no I can't even think along those lines, I have to put it all away, I have to never think of it again and carry on. I love Sean, I want to be with Sean, and nothing at all has changed there. My life is with Sean, we're planning on starting a family next year and I won't let my actions tonight come in the way of that.

Then it hits me.

Oh God.

No.

How could I be so stupid?

I'm not on the pill.

What if Cam's made me pregnant?

What if, right at this minute, his sperm are heading toward my ovaries?

I grab the sponge and force it up inside myself, twisting it around inside of me, washing away every last trace of Cam from my body but knowing full well that I may already be too late, I may already have a piece of him and a piece of me forming, developing, dividing inside me right now.

I stand with my eyes closed, my face up to the ceiling, letting the water hammer down on the back of my head and hope that it can wash away my shame and my guilt and if it doesn't, then I'll just have to live with the consequences of my unforgivable actions tonight.

The door to the shower cubical opens and I'm startled out of my thoughts. Sean is standing naked in front of me, wearing a grin and an enormous hard on. Without saying a word he leans in and sucks on my left nipple, then looking up at me, he says, "Good morning Georgia Rae, I fucking missed you baby."

I laugh and wrap my arms around his neck and breathe him in. “How are you here so early?’ I ask.

“We just wanted to get home, Len rearranged the flight so we could fly right back after we played, but they didn’t have a pilot available so we had to hang about for a bit but we’re here now, six hours earlier than we should be. You not pleased to see me?” He’s kissing my neck and my jaw as he speaks.

“Of course I am.”

“Show me; show me how pleased you are.”

So I do.

* * *

When I wake up later that morning, the sun is shining through the wide open windows and a warm breeze is blowing on my bare back, I’m lying across the bed, alone it would seem. As I climb out of bed, I’m amazed at how well I feel; no hangover at all but a mouth that’s as dry as a nun’s crutch, I head for the kitchen in search of coffee and from where I can hear talking and laughter, as I walk out into the open plan living area. Ash is sitting on Jimmie’s chest, obviously demonstrating what I did to Whorely last night.

I pause for a second then say in my croaky morning voice, “You punch like a girl Ash, I hit her so much harder than that.”

All eyes turn to me, Marley starts a slow clap and says, “Here she is, our very own battle queen She Ra, well done George, you’re all over the papers.”

I let out a big sigh and fold my arms across my chest. I’ve pulled on Sean’s boxers and the t-shirt he was wearing last night and nothing else. I look at Len, my sensible brother. “I’ve been onto the lawyers; they’re doing what they can with regard damage control. You really do need to think about anger management classes George.”

“Like fuck she does,” Ash says. She climbs off of Jim and comes over and gives me a kiss on the cheek. “That bitch got what was coming to her. If G hadn’t of smacked her, I would’ve.” She drapes her arm around my shoulders. “She’s my fucking hero and she's got the best legs and tits and if I didn't love you so much Marls, I would totally bang your sister."

"Fuck baby, you've just made me totally hard. Is that wrong, that the thought of you banging my sister has made me hard?"

"Yes," we all say together. My eyes meet Sean's and he holds his hand out to me, I walk over to him and he pulls me between his legs as he sits on a stool.

"One night G, I go away for one night and look at the trouble you get into." I suddenly feel nauseous and swallow down the bile that rises to my throat; he has no idea exactly how much trouble I got into. No one does, except me and Cam. The colour must leave my face as he adds, "I'm only joking babe, don't stress about it, I just wish I'd been there to watch you give it to her."

"I bet," Marley adds. "Bitch fights are the best. I always get horny when I watch them."

I shake my head at my brother as Ash slaps him in the chest. "You are one sick individual Marls dya know that?" I ask him.

"Yep, just the way my woman likes me, nothing wrong with getting excited about a bit of girl on girl action, it's fucking hot, hey baby?" Ashley blushes and looks mortified.

"*What!*?" me and Jimmie both shriek together, Ash just shrugs. "Oh shut up you two, don't judge, we were smashed and this bird come on to me and Marls got all excited so we just went to a hotel for a bit of fun."

"Fucking lot of fun baby, it was a whole lotta fun." I'm intrigued and oddly turned on, I lean back into Sean's lap and realise, he is too.

"But were you okay with that Ash, Marley with another bird I mean?" Jimmie asks.

"Oh she didn't touch Marley. No fucking way was I having that, although they sort of did, but only 'cos they were both fighting over me," she grinned as she spoke.

"*Shit!*" Sean says a bit too loudly.

“See, I told ya Maca, it’s fucking hot, all that shit we’ve done before is bollocks compared to watching another bird with your misses. It was fucking incredible. Don’t get me wrong, I could never let a bloke go there, no fuckin’ way but watching her with a bird was fuckin’ mind blowing, for both of us, ay babe?” Ashley just nods as she looks at us all, waiting for a response.

I turn and look at Sean with raised eyebrows. “All the shit you’ve done with birds before?”

“G,” he sighs out the letter. “It was over ten fuckin’ years ago and anyway, what about this?”

He reaches behind him and holds up one of the Sunday tabloids and there, half a page big, is a picture of me looking up at Cam. Alongside the head line – “Rock star Macas Wife hooks up with East End bad boy! Could this mean Carnage for the golden couple?”

I felt sick, I could feel my cheeks burn and my mouth was so dry I was incapable of speech, which was a good thing anyway as my brain was incapable of forming a sentence.

“Aw Mac, she was bloody lucky to have TDH there last night, calmed the whore down and stopped her from getting the Ol’ Bill involved, G was only saying thank you to the bloke.” Sean looks past me to Ashley.

“TDH?” Shit!

“Tall Dark and Handsome, come on Maca, you might be a bloke but you’ve gotta admit, he’s a fucking good looking bastard, even for an old bloke.” Jesus, Ashley digs me out, then drops me right back into an even bigger pile of shit every time she opens her mouth. I don’t know whether to kiss her or slap her.

“That true?” Sean asks.

“What bit?”

“Did he stop her from calling the Police?” I nod.

“I had no idea he owned the place, I haven’t seen him for years, he probably wanted to avoid the Police getting involved as much as I did." My heart is pounding so hard in my chest, I worry that Sean will hear it, but he says no more.

We all eventually shower and dress and make our way over to my parents' house for a Sunday BBQ in the sun, they have babysat all seven grandchildren all night but don't look in the least bit phased when we eventually arrive. Bailey and his new girlfriend Samantha, a glamour model, join us. It's the August bank holiday weekend in England and none of us have to be anywhere on the Monday as it's a public holiday so we all end up staying up, laughing and talking, drinking and getting stoned until the sun comes up, enjoying our first time all together as a family in over a year.

I spend the next three weeks like a cat on hot bricks as I wait for my period to arrive. Carnage are getting ready to record a new album so the boys are in the studio at the end of our garden from about lunchtime every day, sometimes finishing up at four, sometimes not till nine and even then Sean is usually off in his own little world, working on lyrics. I feel a little bit lost, it seems like ages since I've had this much spare time and each day seems to drag as I wait for my period to arrive and having so much time to think, brings me to a few conclusions.

I love our house in Hampstead, you would never know that we were so close to the city but I'd decided that when we did finally have a baby, I wanted to be closer to my Mum and the rest of my family, who all lived within a five mile radius of each other. So I had started to look for houses for sale in the Essex countryside near where my parents lived. I had left my number with a few agents with a list of specifications on what we were looking for. Sean's success had meant that we had homes in several countries. We were lucky, we didn't really live a lavish lifestyle but we had the money to do anything we really wanted to in life, so telling an estate agent that we had no limit on our budget for a new home had them calling me almost daily.

"Hello." I picked the phone up as I stood deciding what to where and what to do with my day on this boring wet Wednesday.

"Good morning, may I please speak to Mrs McCarthy?" I was always wary when answering the phone. We'd been caught out before by journalists looking for a story and by crazy fans that had somehow gotten hold of our home number.

"Who's calling?" I asked.

"It's Vera White, from Blackthorn White and Co Real Estate." I liked Vera, she was very proper but swore like a trooper, she was in her fifties and had made me laugh from our very first meeting when she told me that I was a lucky bitch and that despite being happily married, she would gladly jump my Husband's bones if he ever decided he needed some attention from an older woman. She was also one of the few agents who'd actually shown me through the houses that had ticked most of our boxes. Although, as yet, we still hadn't found 'The One'. Like our home in Hampstead, I knew that I'd just know when we found the right house.

"Hi Vera, this is Georgia, what can I do for you?"

"Oh, hi Mrs McCarthy. Look, I have a property that's just come on the market that you may be interested in."

"Okay, can you give me some details?"

"I sure can, it's a completely refurbished Georgian style farm house. It's set on twelve acres, behind security gates and high fences all the way around, six bedrooms all en suite, plus two more bathrooms, five receptions, a cinema room, a gym, a sauna, an indoor pool, a games room, paddocks and stables for six horses and there's a fully detached three bed roomed cottage on the grounds. I can email you a floor plan and some photo's if you're interested?" She asks hopefully.

"Wow, that's a lot of house."

"It is," she replies. "And the best part of all is that it's only three miles from your parents place."

Now I'm definitely interested. "Okay, when can you get me through?"

"How does this afternoon sound?"

“Perfect but I’m sorry Vera, I’ll probably bring my Mum along with me, not Sean, he’s busy in the studio right now but if I like it, I promise I’ll bring him along next time.”

“Good girl, grab a pen and I will give you the address…”

Two hours later, I am walking through ‘The One’ with my Mum and Vera. It’s absolutely perfect, it’s big and spacious but not sprawling, there’s plenty of room on the grounds for Sean to build a studio and I love the fact that it already has stables. I had just taken up riding lessons again and was desperate to own a horse of my own; my Mum still had hers, but had gotten rid of mine years ago. I knew I wouldn’t be able to ride when I was pregnant but I didn’t plan on being pregnant permanently. We walked through the house twice and let Vera give her spiel on the property, the original part of the building had been built in the early eighteen hundreds and had been extended and renovated over the years and had undergone a major refurbishment ten years ago. It needed a more modern kitchen and the bathrooms needed updating but other than that, it just needed a lick of paint and new carpets. I loved it, it felt right, and it felt like home.

We stood in the kitchen, discussing the pros and cons of the property and the price. I was trying not to show too much enthusiasm as I wanted to be able to negotiate on the asking price, although all things considered, it was pretty reasonably priced. As we stood talking, we all became aware of a door closing and footsteps coming down the hall.

“Do excuse me; I wasn’t aware anyone was going to be here.” Vera turned to meet whoever the footsteps belonged to, when Cam appeared in the doorway.

You have got to be fucking kidding me!

Cam!

Cam in jeans, a t-shirt and a pair of flip flops, looking larger than life and as hot as holy hell, I actually swayed on the spot as the air left my lungs and refused to allow any more to enter.

“Oh, Mr King, I’m so sorry, I wasn’t aware you would be home today, I was just showing… ”

His eyes met mine, he looked at me like he wanted to eat me, right there and then, in front of the estate agent and my mother, the yearning, longing in his eyes was unmistakable and I had to hold on to the marble bench top as he whispered, "Kitten" in that deep voice of his.

"Excuse me?" Vera asked and I nearly laughed. Did she think he was talking to her?

His eyes left mine and were on Vera's then my Mum's. "Mrs Layton, how are you, hope Frank's well?"

My Mums eyes flicked from Cam to me and then back to Cam again. "I'm very well thank you Cameron, we both are."

"Good, that's good, please give him my regards."

"I will do."

He nodded his head, his eyes back on me, while he spoke to Vera. "I'm sorry Vera, I didn't realise you would be showing someone through so soon."

"Yes, well you did say we could move on it straight away."

"I did and you are that's good."

"And what a coincidence that you all happen to know each other."

None of us say anything for a moment, my Mum being the first to speak, "Vera, why don't you show me the pool again, that's going to be just perfect for when the baby gets a bit bigger."

My Mum looks back at me as she speaks and shakes her head, my Mum's not stupid, anyway, you would have to be deaf, dumb, blind and thick as shit not to notice the silent interaction between Cam and myself and my Mum was none of those things.

Cam stalked toward me. "You're pregnant?"

He looks like he was going to cry, I shake my head. "No, but we're hoping to be, next year." I cannot give him a clue, that I may already be and that the baby could be his.

He reaches out and strokes my face with the back of his knuckles and I stupidly lean into his touch, my eyes fill with tears. "Why Kitten, why him?"

"He owns me Cam, I have no choice. My heart belongs to him."

"Not all of it, I have a piece, all be it a very small piece, but I know; I just know if you gave me a chance…"

I shake my head. "No, no Cam, it's too late for us, you would've had to have met me when I was ten to have ever stood a chance."

"I don't believe you Kitten; don't have a baby with him. Please, wait a while, think about it, think about what you really want. Who you really want. If he owns you so completely then why did you let me fuck you just a couple of weeks ago. All this time and the instant we are together it's there, its back."

His words and the guilt that I feel cause me actual physical pain, like an ice cold blade has been stabbed into my chest, dragged down to my belly and twisted around and around a few times and it's no less than I deserve.

"I want you Kitten, no one has ever wanted anything more than I want you. Please, give me a chance, choose me, let yourself love me enough, let me show you how good it can be. I'll never hurt you; I'll never make you doubt me, not for a second." A sob escapes me and fat tears plop from my lashes onto my cheeks, he wipes them away with his thumbs.

"I bought this house for you."

"*What*?"

"That night, when we argued in the restaurant, when I behaved like a prick, I had put an offer in on this place, I knew you would love it. It was close to your parents and it had stables and you'd told me how you wanted to start horse riding again, that you hadn't had time to get out to your Mum's and ride and I saw the house, the location, the stables and knew you'd love it." I shake my head in complete disbelief at what he's telling me.

"I was all over the place that night," he continues, "I was in negotiations to buy this place and I had a business deal falling apart in Amsterdam. Someone else was bidding on this and it looked like I was going to have to leave the country, that's why I was in such a bad mood." He swallows and I watch his adams apple bob up and down as his eyes dart over my face.

"But on the Saturday morning, the other party pulled out so the deal was done, this place was mine. That's why I flew home from Amsterdam early, that's why I came straight to the club. I wanted to tell you about the house, I wanted to ask you to move in with me." I can't believe what I'm hearing, I shake my head continuously, my tears flow, continuously and I hold my hand over my mouth, as I sob.

"I can't do this, I can't do this Cam. I don't want to hear this, please, please, I'm begging you, leave me alone, just leave me to love my Husband in the way he deserves."

He kisses each of my eyes. "I can't Kitten, it's killing me, I won't chase you, but every chance I get, every time I see you, I will remind you of how it could, how it should be."

He presses his forehead against mine.

"Buy the house kitten, live here and be happy." He turns and leaves the room and I walk on shaky legs to the nearest bathroom, I splash my face with cold water and stare at myself in the mirror for a long while. I hear my Mum call my name, so I flush the toilet, wash my hands and head toward my Mum's voice, wondering what the fuck I'm going to do now. I've already called Sean, and told him that I've found 'The One' and arranged for him to view the place with me tomorrow morning. Could we live here, would Cam really be happy that I lived here or would he hate it because it would be with Sean and not him?

My mother absolutely glares at me when she sees the state I'm in. I claim a headache to Vera and arrange to meet her back at the house tomorrow at ten and we leave. I'm shaking as I get behind the wheel of my Range Rover and see Cam standing in the front doorway, arms folded across his chest, once again, watching me leave him.

"Are you going to tell me what's going on Georgia?" I sob as I start along the driveway to the gates at the front of the property and I have to stop the car as I can't see to drive, my Mum just undoes her seatbelt, leans across and holds me while I cry, stroking my hair and shushing me gently, the way she hasn't had to do since the night Sean and I broke up. When I'm able to, I speak.

"Oh Mum, I've done something terrible, so, so terrible, I'm so ashamed of myself, I love Sean, with all my heart, you know I do, you know right?"

"Yes babe, of course, of course."

"Then why do I have these feelings for Cam? Why does he affect me the way that he does? Why did I let him fuck me against his office door just three weeks ago? Why, why did I do that?"

She's my Mum, I want her to have all the answers, I want her to tell me it will all be okay, that I'm not a bad person.

"Oh Georgia... you silly, silly girl, what were you thinking? Bloody hell child"

We swap places and she drives me back to her place, she pours us a glass of wine each and I tell her about what happened between me and Cam that night, then I tell her what he just told me about the house and then I drop the bombshell about not being on the pill and not using protection with Cam.

"Have you done a pregnancy test?" I shake my head.

"I did one before I went out that night and it was negative, I haven't done one yet as I didn't think it would show up and I didn't want to give myself false hope that everything would be okay and any way, I had sex with Sean, later that same night."

I start to cry again.

"When's your period due?" she asks.

"In two days."

"Well best to wait then but if it doesn't come in the next three days, do a test and we'll go from there."

I smile at her. “We?”

“You’re my baby girl George; I’ll stand by you no matter what. We all do stupid things at some time in our life darling, believe me, you’re not the first woman to be in this predicament and you most definitely won’t be the last.”

CHAPTER 24

I don't tell Sean that Cam owns the home that we are walking through, if I tell him, he will want to know how I know and I'll have to either tell him about seeing Cam here yesterday or I'll have to come up with another lie and I don't want to tell him any more lies. At least that's how I justify not telling him in my twisted, two timing, and cheating brain. Sean absolutely loves the place. I have asked Vera to let us walk through on our own; I also called her yesterday afternoon and asked her to say nothing about the owner of the house or our running into him yesterday. The hint that it could lose her a big fat commission is enough to garner her silence and we are left alone to wander through. We stand looking at the pool, hand in hand.

"What are your thoughts Georgia? I love it, it feels like home already." I don't know what to say, could I live here, should I even be considering this?

"I don't know Sean; I felt like that yesterday, I'm not so sure today though."

"Why, what's changed?" About a million different things. What if I'm pregnant? What if it's Cam's baby? I'd be bringing up his child, with another man, in a home that he planned to live in with me, everything about this is all so fucked up and wrong and it's all my fault, I'm a monster. I suddenly become aware of a dull ache in the bottom of my belly.

"Georgia, what don't you like today that you did yesterday?"

"I don't know, I'm not sure, I don't feel very well." My head swims slightly, I feel so trapped by my own wrong doings that I feel on the verge of an anxiety attack.

"I need the toilet." I head toward the toilet in the pool room and Sean follows me, we never close the door when we use the bathroom so I leave it open now as Sean talks about getting planning permission for a recording studio on the grounds. I pull up my skirt, pull down my knickers and see that they are full of blood. I've got my period, and I burst into tears. Sean gets completely the wrong idea about why I'm crying, which just goes to worsen my guilt and makes me cry harder.

“Gia, baby, please don’t cry, it’s only September, we said six months remember? Next year, that’s when we’ll be pregnant, next year, baby please, don’t cry, I hate seeing you cry.” He’s kneeling in front of me, as I sit on the toilet, in the home of the man that hasn’t made me pregnant and I don’t know if they’re tears of joy, regret, guilt or sadness.

“I love this house G, let’s put in an offer, and let’s buy this fucker!” He’s so happy and excited, that I just blow my nose and nod yes.

***

The next few months go by in a blur, we completed on the sale of the house on the first of December but have no plans to move in until next year. I want a new kitchen and bathrooms, the place needs painting and I want new carpets in all of the bedrooms and we’re still waiting on planning permission for Sean’s studio.

We have a massive family Christmas at my Mum’s and leave all of the grandchildren with my parents on the day before New Year’s Eve and fly out with the band to New York, where they’ll be playing at a special concert in Time Square.

I’ve felt strangely off the last few days, I’ve skipped my December period and I’m hoping beyond hope that I’m pregnant, in fact, I know that I am. I know my own body, but I decide to buy myself a pregnancy test just to be sure before I pass up an opportunity to consume vast amounts of alcohol during the New Year celebrations. I take the test as soon as we get to the hotel and it’s positive. I can hardly contain myself, luckily we had to drop the boys off en route for some interviews and I’m actually sitting watching my Husband live on the television as the two blue lines appear on the stick I just weed on and as I watch him, I hatch a plan.

New York in December is freezing, we have dinner with all of the band members later that night and I get away with saying that I’m saving myself for the next night when I turn down any drinks. We have an early night, and then spend New Year’s Eve daytime, lazing at the hotel and doing some shopping. When we head back, I get a manicure, a pedicure, and have my hair and makeup done in our room. Courtesy of the television station airing the show, the boys will play a two hour long set starting at eleven thirty, get the crowd warmed up and then count the New Year in and rock them through the first few hours of the year two thousand. We arrive around nine and are interviewed by various TV stations and shows about what the new millennium means for us and we give up more than usual by admitting that we are moving into a new home and looking to start a family. I wait for the boys to start their set before I talk to the shows director and tell him what I want to do. He's over the moon and gets the announcer on the TV broadcast to repeat to the viewers to stay tuned for a very important announcement regarding Carnage. I don't tell Ash, I don't tell Jim and at five to twelve when I walk on stage in between songs and stand next to my Husband, everyone seems a little confused but Sean just goes with it.

"Hey baby," he says to me but into his mic. "This is my beautiful Wife New York City, just look at her, ain't she just fuckin' gorgeous!"

The crowd goes wild and my cheeks burn despite the cold, I wrap my arms around his neck, and I kiss him like my life depends on it, making the roar from the crowd deafening. Then hand him the stick with the two little blue lines on, saying into his ear, "Happy New Year baby, we're pregnant".

He looks at the stick, registers the words I've just told him, and I watch as his mouth drops open. I nod at him. There's a camera crew right in our face but we don't even see it, we just have eyes for each other. Sean bursts into tears and kisses me so softly. The people at home have obviously been told what's going on, but the crowd in front of us have no idea what's happening. Sean moves the cameraman out of the way pulls me into his side and sobs into his mic.

"My Wife, my beautiful Gia, has just made me the happiest man alive, she's told me people that… " He pauses and I don't know if it's for effect or so that he can regain his composure. "SHE'S FUCKING PREGNANT!" he roars. The crowd roars, Jimmie, Ash and Lennon are all on the stage with us and the rest of the boys from the band, we all kiss, cry and hug and count our way down to the year 2000 and it will forever be one of the happiest moments in my life.

***

We celebrate back at the hotel into the early hours; I head off to bed around five, leaving Sean and the rest of the boys and a few other people I don't even know, to party. I'm woken at around eight am by someone banging on the door of the suite, as I look through the spy hole, I see that it's Milo and Dave, carrying Sean between them. I open the door and look at the state my Husband has got himself in, he is, quite literally, legless; he grins at me. "Gia, baaaby," he tries to sing to me. "I'm sooo fappy, huck, huckin, fuck." He looks up at me and laughs. "You know what I mean."

"Park him on the bed." I stand aside so the boys can fit through. They take him through the lounge area and into the bedroom, laying him face down on the bed. The boys are both puffing and sit down for a few seconds.

"Are we gonna make the flight?" I ask them.

"Fuck knows," they both say together, they high five at their unity and I smile.

"You two want a coffee, some food?"

"Na, we're good thanks George, we're all coffeed out. You might wanna try and get some down his Gregory in a coupla hours. I can't see them getting us another flight out of here on New Year's Day, private jet or not, so if we don't get on this one, I reckon we'll be stuck here for a few more days."

I feel absolutely exhausted now and just want to get my head down before I work on getting my Husband sober. "What's the latest we can be at the airport?"

"About four but Marley's in an even worse state than him and Lens not much better." I shake my head.

"We even had to carry Ash to bed." Dave laughs.

"Well it's gonna be a quiet flight home." Dave nods his head.

"That's not a bad thing. You alright George, you look a bit pasty?"

I don't actually feel too good but I don't know what sort of not good it is that I'm feeling, I've never been pregnant, perhaps this is normal. "I'm okay thanks Dave; just need some sleep I think."

"Well don't you go trying to lift him, just call me if you need anything and try and get your head down for a bit." I'm touched at his concern, I thank them for returning my husband to me and tell them to go and get some sleep.

The boys leave and I pull off Sean's chucks and undo his jeans, but I can't get them down so I just curl up on the bed next to him and manage to get another four hours sleep. I wake up to the sound of Sean throwing up down the toilet. Well at least he woke up and didn't do it over the side of the bed as he has done before, more than once. I get up and go and make us a coffee. I'm starving so I call room service and order us a couple of fried egg sandwiches, always the perfect hangover cure, fresh orange juice and some real coffee. Sean actually manages to eat his and half of mine. I'm still not feeling so good and don't fancy being stuck on an eight hour flight with a funny tummy.

"You need to eat more G, I'm finally gonna get to fatten you up," he smiles at me as he speaks; he hasn't stopped smiling since I gave him the news about the baby.

"Not hungry right now, got a bit of a funny tummy."

"You okay to fly?"

"Yeah, I'm fine; just don't wanna be stuck in the toilet the whole flight, that's all."

As it turns out, I'm barely allowed to breathe on the flight, let alone get up and use the bathroom. Sean makes me lay back on one of the lazy boy style chairs, puts a blanket over me and tells me to sleep. Everyone else is extremely hung over and very quiet, the cabin lights are dimmed and everyone seems to go off to sleep, although I do hear the bathroom doors opening and closing and people throwing up and I really do not envy them their hangovers, although, I can't help thinking that despite the fact that I didn't touch a drop of alcohol, I still feel rough, my belly seems to have settled down but I have a dull ache in my side and I'm feeling a bit clammy.

Sean is snoring beside me, Ash and Marley are in the seats facing me, and Jimmie and Len across the aisle, Milo and Dave are in the front section with Billy and Tom and their wives. I press the call button and our stewardess Sara appears at my side as if by magic. Sean had told her as we got on the plane that I was pregnant and she kneels down next to me now with a look of concern on her face. We've travelled with Sara looking after us a few times and I've always liked her, unlike some of the girls, she had never openly flirted with Sean or the other boys so I had never had cause to want to punch her.

"You okay Mrs McCarthy, you look a bit pale?"

"Please call me Georgia, yeah I'm okay I think, just a bit tired, didn't get to bed until five, we did a bit of celebrating."

She smiled. "Yeah, I saw the New Year's show and the way you told Mr… Sean, the news about the baby, I think the whole world must have watched that clip by now. I have to say, it even made my Husband cry, I was a blubbering mess, as I'm sure most people watching were."

I actually get teary as she speaks. "You and Sean will make great parents. You lot are probably one of the most down to earth bands I travel with, some of them can be complete arseholes."

Yep, I think, we've met a lot of them in our time. "So, what can I get you Georgia, how about a nice cup of tea and a biscuit?"

"Sounds perfect, strong, no sugar, thank you."

By the time we are getting into the back of the limo, I'm feeling really unwell, the pain in my side is worse, much worse. I feel cold but sweaty. It's seven in the morning, London time and I just want my bed.

"You okay George?" Jimmie asks. I decide not to lie anymore, something's not right and I think I might need to go to the hospital or at least see a doctor.

"I actually don't feel so good."

The smile Sean has been wearing for the last thirty six hours vanishes from his face. "Baby, what's wrong?" He puts the back of his hand against my forehead. "Shit G, you feel really clammy."

Jimmie feels my head and agrees and as soon as the car starts to pull away I feel sick, we pull over and I throw up at the side of the road, my head is swimming and I feel really dizzy, we get back in the car and Sean pulls me into his lap. Marley has told the driver to head to the nearest hospital, Milo is in the front with him and gives him directions, luckily we had landed at City Airport so he knew the area.

Any woman that's ever had a period will tell you that one of their biggest fears is leakage and in the ten minutes it had taken us to get from the airport to Newham General Hospital, I knew that I was bleeding, enough for it to have leaked through my underwear to my jeans and I just knew that I was losing my baby.

The limo pulled up outside accident and emergency and Milo jumped out, telling Sean to pass me out to him, but Sean wouldn't let me go and instead struggled out of the car while still holding me. Len had run inside and grabbed a wheelchair, but Sean wouldn't set me down in it. Marley had run ahead and was shouting for help and I was soon being whisked through to a bed behind a curtain, where Sean still held me, sitting down with me in his lap, pulled into his chest. I was shaking violently and could feel the beads of sweat forming on my top lip and as they trickled down my spine. I think I started to lose consciousness at that stage, I could feel Sean's arms around me, I could hear him and others call my name, but I just couldn't get back to them.

I don't know if it's seconds, minutes, hours or days when I next try to open my eyes and I'm not sure how long it is that I try, before sleep pulls me under again. Then suddenly, I'm wide awake, alert and aware that I'm in a hospital room. I gaze around; I have fluids dripping through a cannula in my left hand. Sean is in a chair next to my bed, he has my right hand in both of his and his head resting on our joint hands, my mouth is dry and my throat is sore, I have a belly ache, very similar to period pain. I lay still and stay silent for a few seconds and wonder what could have happened to me. I know that my baby's gone, I just know and I start to sob at the thought. Sean is going to be devastated, he was so happy. I try to swallow down my sobs so that I don't wake him, but fail, he lifts his head and his eyes come up to meet mine, he's out of his chair and on the bed holding me in a second.

"I'm so sorry," I sob and gulp in air as I speak.

"No, no, no, Gia baby, no, it's not your fault."

"What happened, what went wrong?" I ask him, we are lying side by side on my hospital bed, looking right at each other. Sean wipes his nose, then he covers his mouth, trying to hide a sob, he moves it away and blows out a breath slowly.

"It was an ectopic pregnancy." His face crumbles, while he shakes his head and sobs. "I nearly lost you G. It had ruptured, and you were bleeding internally. You went into shock, I thought you was gonna die." His shoulders shake as his sobs wrack through his body. I try to comfort him, but he just keeps sobbing and shaking his head. "I stayed in the hotel bar getting pissed and all the time you was bleeding internally, you could have died up in that hotel room, all on your own. I was so hung over on the flight; I didn't even notice how sick you were. It was Sara the stewardess that said you hadn't been feeling well. I let you down G, I fucking let you down, I'm so, so sorry."

I was numb, I had no idea what to say to him, so we just held each other and cried for a long while, eventually Sean went back to sleep, while I laid quietly and thought about what this meant. Could I still have children? What did they do when they operated? What did they take away? The door opened and a nurse walked in, I raised my fingers to my lips, asking her to keep quiet.

"Good to see you're awake Georgia, how are you feeling?" I shrugged and my eyes filled with tears.

"Will I still be able to have babies? Can I still get pregnant?" I asked her as she took my temperature and checked my blood pressure, I hated that she ignored my question and just carried on with what she was doing. She went down to the end of my bed and read through my notes.

"The doctor will be in to see you shortly Georgia, he will talk things through with you and your Husband." She gives a little nod, and then tilts her head to the side. "You were very lucky, you needed four units of blood during your surgery, if you hadn't have got here when you did, things could have been much worse. Now, try and get some sleep, I'll be back with the doctor very soon."

I looked right into her bright blue eyes and said, "I just lost my fucking baby, how does that make me lucky?" Again, she ignored me and left the room, I laid my head back on my pillow and cried. I cried for my dead baby, I cried for Sean and his lost chance at fatherhood and I cried because of the guilt I felt. This was my fault; this was my punishment, punishment for cheating on Sean, punishment for being a lying, cheating, adulterous, whore of a Wife.

I was allowed home after two days, but I was to stay off my feet and do as little as possible for the next few weeks and I wasn't to drive for the next month, for all of these reasons and the fact that I just didn't want to be alone with Sean, I went and stayed at my parents. Sean was busy in the studio and would come and stay with me every couple of nights, he was coping in his own way, music, writing and laying down tracks for the new album were getting him through, whereas I just laid on my Mum's sofa and then went and laid in my own bed; visitors came and went and I assured everyone that I was doing fine.

I had, it turns out, been very lucky, my fallopian tube had ruptured on my left hand side and I had bled internally for a while, my tube and ovaries on that side had to be removed but there was no reason that I couldn't get pregnant again. There was a slim risk of another ectopic but I would be monitored closely as soon as I was to get pregnant, which we were told would be safe to do in about three months, if, we felt emotionally and physically ready.

I knew that everyone was watching me, waiting to see how I handled things, if I would withdraw the way I did after Sean and I split up, so I decided to behave in the exact opposite way that my Husband and family expected and embarked upon what I can only describe as a manic episode. As soon as I could drive, I went straight over to the new house and looked over the renovations. I worked with the interior design firm we had hired in choosing paint and fabrics, and I shopped for new furniture. We would need a lot to fill that big empty house and I bought two horses and hired a stable girl, Jess, to look after them and I did all of this alone. I didn't consult Sean, and I didn't ask for his input. On the nights that he came and stayed with me at my Mum's, I virtually ignored him, feigned tiredness and went to bed early, pretending to be asleep when he joined me. I couldn't sleep so I would sneak out of the house and drive over to our house and ride before Sean was awake and I wouldn't return until well after I knew he would be gone.

I loved and missed him so much but I needed to go through this alone, I needed to grieve and learn to accept my guilt for what happened to my baby.

After six weeks Sean asked me when I was going to move back home, I told him I wasn't; I wanted to be near the new house and the horses. I didn't eat, I rarely slept and I couldn't sit still for longer than a few minutes. I didn't want a chance to think, I didn't want a chance to feel, I just needed to keep busy. For everyone else, alarm bells started ringing, for me, I was just getting by the best I could. Sean let it go for another two weeks, then early one Saturday morning he turned up at my Mum's and told me to pack my bags, we were going home and then we were going on holiday.

"I can't, I need to look after the horses."

"I've spoken to Jess, she can manage the horses, pack your bags Gia, you're coming home with me." I sat down on the bed in my old bedroom, he comes and sits next to me and takes my hand in his.

"I miss you baby, I want you home, I have a few things to finish up in the studio Monday then we are going away, just you and me, a week, two weeks, a month, I don't fucking care, I'm done sitting back and watching you trying to run away from everything."

"I'm not running away."

"Then what are you doing Georgia? I come over here to sleep, to be near you and you don't touch me, you won't let me touch you, I'm not talking about sex, I just want to hold you, I want to be held."

I sit in silence, I have nothing to say, I'm numb, it's the only way I know how to handle things, I'm so scared that if I let go, it will all be too much, if I let the pain out, it will overwhelm me, and I will drown in it.

“Georgia, you don’t eat, you don’t sleep, you don’t even cry, everyone is worried about you.”

“I’m dealing with it the best I can,” I say quietly, without looking at him.

“Well good for you, I’m glad you’re all right then. What about me? Have you even given me a second thought in all of this?” He stands up and goes over to the window and stands with his back to me and I’m unsure whether he expects an answer.

“I miss you G, I come home to that empty house and I can smell you, but you’re not there so I come here to be with you and you’re not here either, I’m lost and I’m lonely without you. I want my Wife back, I want my best friend back, I want us to get through this together.” I want to go to him, I want to hold him and breathe him in but that would bring me comfort and I don’t deserve comforting, losing our baby was my punishment for what I did with Cam and I will never forgive myself.

“I don’t know what’s worse?” Sean’s voice suddenly interrupts my thoughts. “In the hospital when you started to go into shock and I saw you convulsing on that bed, I was terrified, they took you away, they wheeled you off and I wasn’t allowed to come with you, I didn’t want to let you go, I was so scared I would never see you alive again, I thought I had lost you.” He turns around and looks at me. “But this, how you’re behaving now, shutting me out, it’s just as fucking painful G, it hurts just as much.”

I stare blankly ahead, not daring to meet his gaze, because I know I’ll have to go to him, hold him, let him hold me, allow him to make me better.

“It was my baby too,” he suddenly roars. “I lost my fucking baby too and while all that was going on, I thought I was losing you, you lost your baby, our baby but I thought I was losing so much more, you’re my life G, my world, my fucking reason for existing.”

I finally force myself to look at him and my damn breaks, the anguish in his voice, in his face, his eyes, it breaks me. Once again, I had been selfish, I had lost our baby and it was a terrible thing but he had to stand by and watch as I was rushed into surgery too. He thought he might lose me, as well as the baby, the thought of him going through all of that, alone, broke me and I started to sob.

Sean comes over to the bed and kneels in front of me. “Hold me Georgia, please just hold me?” He was as broken as I was and I needed him so much, just like he needed me. We climbed back on the bed and just held each other, both of us crying quietly, like we had done on the bed in the hospital.

“You and me G, just Sean and Georgia, it always comes back to this, to us, as long as there’s an ‘us’, we can get through anything, okay?”

I look up into his beautiful brown eyes, which are dull and sad and full of tears. “I’m so sorry, I love you and I’m sorry.”

He kisses my tears away and says, “Don’t be sorry babe, just love me, that’s all I want, just love me and let me love and take care of you, let me do my job.”

His lips brush mine gently and for the first time in almost two months, desire stirs in me. Sean rolls me over onto my back and looks down at me. “I’ve missed you so much. There’s too many clothes between us G; I need to feel your skin on mine.”

I’m not sure if he’s asking permission, but I nod anyway. He pulls off his t-shirt as I undo his jeans; he pulls them down, along with his boxers as I pull off the vest I was wearing. Sean pulls down my pyjama bottoms, it’s all rushed and we are panting, then suddenly we are naked and completely still; he lays between my legs, his erection digging into my pubic bone and lower belly, our hands are at the side of my head on the mattress, our fingers laced together, his eyes are all over my face and I ache for him to be inside me. “I love you Georgia, never leave me again.”

I shake my head slightly. “Never, I love you,” I whisper.

He presses his forehead to mine. “I need to be inside you, is that okay?”

“Of course it is I want you inside me.” And I do, I want him right where he needs to be, I want his world to be perfect.

He slides inside me. "Fuck I've missed you; I'd almost forgotten how perfectly we fit together, how perfect you are."

I want to cry again, I'm most definitely not perfect but right now, I will be perfect for him.

We make love gently, tenderly, Sean strokes into me slowly and when I moan and he feels my muscles start to clench he whispers, "Together baby, together."

We stare into each other's eyes as we both come, I sob as I come down from my high and he smiles, his lazy lopsided boy I fell in love with smile and sings, "Georgia Rae, when we made love you used to cry… You said… " He waits for me to finish 'our' song.

"I love you like the stars above, I'll love you till I die." We smile and cry at the same time.

"There'll be more babies G, we'll never forget this one, never, we'll just have to make sure that we give all the others the extra love we couldn't show this baby."

God I love him, I love him so much, he holds me while I cry some more and we make love again, before I pack my bags, thank my parents and drive back to Hampstead. We decide on the way to just take a week away and while we are gone, we'll get the removal company in and move straight into the new house. 'La Macas' as we have christened it, a play on both our surnames.

We book a week away in the Dominican Republic, enjoying ourselves, chilling out and reconnecting so much, that we stay another week and move straight into our new home as soon as we arrive back in England and settle into our new lives in the Essex countryside.

Sean is home a lot; the album is finished and will be released at the end of April. The boys have decided they don't need to do a massive world tour to promote it; they are big enough now that it's not necessary. In fact pre-orders have already guaranteed it will go platinum in the first week. Interviews and TV appearances will have to be carried out though and the boys will partake in a whirlwind tour of the UK, America and Europe during the last week of April and the first two weeks of May. As much as I will miss Sean, I won't be going to Europe or America with him, it's too soon, too painful and we'll only attract press attention. The press have been pretty good since news of our loss broke, we have received untold amounts of letters, cards and good wishes from around the world and I spend a lot of time reading through them while Sean is away. Many of the letters are from women who have gone through an ectopic pregnancy and have gone on to have more children with no problems at all. I reply to all of these messages, thanking the women for taking their time to reassure me that all will be fine for us in the future. I have no doubt about this anyway, no doubt at all.

CHAPTER 25

Sean's flight lands at noon on Sunday May the 14th and I go with Milo to the airport to collect him, I'm so excited that I wait out on the tarmac as the plane lands and I'm bouncing on my toes as I wait for the doors to open, he doesn't know I'm coming and I can't wait to see his face. It's a warm sunny day and Len blinks a few times as he steps out of the doors, he looks at me and frowns but I hold my finger to my lips telling him to shush, he nods and carries on walking down the steps of the plane. I hide behind Milo in case any of the other boys say anything and spoil the surprise, I just want Sean to know how much I love him, he loves small gestures and I know he's hated leaving me. He's been so unbelievably attentive since we lost Baby M, as we now call our 'not meant to be' baby; he's looked after me so well and I just hope that as soon as we get home, I'm going to be able to give him some good news.

He appears at the top of the steps and my heart skips a beat and then trebles its speed, I wonder if it will always do that around him? I step out from behind Milo and he sees me instantly, I start to move toward him and almost stumble as his face lights up, he runs down the aircraft stairs, not caring who he pushes out of the way, namely Marley, who's seen me and thinks he's funny by deliberately getting in Sean's way. In the end, he jumps over the side of the airplane steps and runs toward me. He slows down as he gets near me and swings me around.

He has the biggest smile as he says, "I've missed ya Georgia Rae, show us your tits."

I pull up my t-shirt and flash him my red lace bra. "Fuck babe, I've missed ya, let's get a room somewhere." I laugh and shake my head.

"No, I wanna get home."

He reaches for my hand and starts pulling me toward the car. "Well let's go then."

We chat about his trip as Milo drives us home and because it's Sunday and the traffic is light we are home within the hour and head straight for our bedroom as soon we are through the front door. I have a pregnancy test stick waiting and ready to be used, in fact I have two and Sean looks totally confused as I pull him into the bathroom. "Georgia… Nooo, fuck first, shower later, I need to be inside you," he whines.

"Sit down." I gesture to the edge of the bath, I'm busting for a wee and need to do this soon before I wet myself. I hold the plastic stick in front of his face and his eyes widen, he doesn't say a word while I wee on it, wipe and wash my hands, then sit on the edge of the bath next to him as we wait and stare at the little piece of plastic that might possibly be about to change our lives.

Two lines appear.

Pregnant.

Sean looks from the stick to me and back to the stick again.

"G," he whispers.

"I knew, I mean, I didn't know, I guessed before you went away but I didn't want to worry you."

"Pregnant, you're really pregnant?"

"Yes, I'm really pregnant."

"We need to see a doctor."

"We are and I've made an appointment for tomorrow at eleven."

"Who with?" I look at him and chuckle.

"Does it matter, if I was to tell you his name, would it make any difference?"

"Yes, I only want you to see Richard Curtis." What. The. Fuck?

"How do you know who Richard Curtis is?" He looks exactly like the thirteen year old boy I fell in love with when he smiles at me.

"Because I did some research and he's the best around and I want you and the baby to see the best." I'm actually amazed,

Richard Curtis is exactly who I have an appointment to see tomorrow.

"But I only just told you I was pregnant."

"Yeah… but I knew you would be pregnant again sometime and I wanted to make sure that you and the baby were all set to be looked after by the best." His eyebrows are pulled in together; he's worried that he's said something wrong.

"Baby, it's fine, you don't need to explain, I'm, I'm just…" I start crying, I really am the luckiest woman in existence. "I couldn't love you any more than I do right now."

He looks over my face and reaches out and strokes his thumb over my cheek and across my lips, he raises his eyebrows and smiles as he whispers, "We're having a baby Mrs McCarthy."

I grin stupidly, because I just can't help myself. "We are Mr McCarthy."

"Let's fuck."

"Sounds like a plan."

* * *

By midday Monday, my pregnancy had been confirmed and I was laying on my back waiting for an ultrasound to be carried out. I feel sick with nerves. Sean and I have not discussed the possibility of anything being wrong, it couldn't happen again, surely? I have just missed my second period and from all the research I have done, I should be feeling the effects if this is another ectopic pregnancy, but I feel well, really well in fact; thinking back now, I didn't feel right from the very beginning with Baby M but this time, apart from feeling a little sick in the mornings, I feel great.

I notice that the ultrasound machine they have wheeled in is the trans-vaginal kind, the same as they used on me when I was in the hospital before.

"Is this one of them ones they put inside ya?" Sean asks as he sits in a chair next to the bed holding my hand. I nod.

"You okay with that?" he asks while I shrug my shoulders.

“It’s what needs to be done, are you okay with it?” He shakes his head.

“Not really, I hate the thought of another bloke, knowing what you’ve got going on down there.” I can’t help but smile, Sean McCarthy, Rock God, lead singer of Carnage, his face and body have graced the covers of so many magazines, often with near naked women draped around him and he doesn’t like the idea of a doctor examining his pregnant Wife.

“It’s his job Sean, all in a day’s work, my Mildred is just like any other woman’s as far as he’s concerned.” Now Sean smiles.

“No way G, your Mildred is fucking special, it’s small and neat and tight and perfect and it’s fucking mine and he better remember that.” I shake my head and sigh.

“Sean, the man’s in his fifties, he’s not interested in my Mildred and stop saying sexy things, or I’ll get all turned on.”

“You better fucking not.”

The door opens and Professor Curtis walks in, with his curly grey hair and bright yellow bow tie, any desire I might have been feeling evaporates and the nerves kick back in. I have a sheet over me from the waist down and thankfully nothing on show. We both watch at first, as the doctor slides a condom on the wand and then noisily squirts lube over it. I suddenly want to giggle and my eyes swing across to Sean’s as he makes a small sound, his lips are pursed together as he tries to contain a laugh, I narrow my eyes on him.

“Okay, let’s find out when this little one is likely to make an appearance, relax now Georgia and just let your knees fall apart.” I suddenly want to cry, I’m absolutely terrified that we are about to have all our dreams ripped away again. Sean squeezes my hand tight and I look right at him, there’s not a trace of a smile on either of our faces, we don’t look at the doctor or the nurse, we don’t look at the screen or around the room, we just look at each other.

“I love you G, so fucking much,” Sean whispers to me and a tear rolls down the side of my face and lands in my ear, there’s a whooshing noise, then the room is filled with the sound of our baby’s heartbeat, loud and strong and I let out a sob.

"There you go, right… there." We both turn to look at the screen, where there appears to be a whole load of nothing going on, apart from a tiny pulsating pea, thrumming away.

Our eyes are back on each other's and we both cry and laugh at the same time.

"Perfect," the doctor says and after calling out some measurements to the nurse, tells us that our baby is due on New Year's Eve, the same day as I told Sean that he was going to be a Daddy before. We're reassured everything is as it should be and that I'm about eight weeks pregnant. I'm given another appointment for four weeks' time but told to call if I have any concerns at all. Sean and I practically skip along Harley Street and back to our car.

"I'm starving," I complain as we jump in.

"Thought you might be, good job I've booked us a table for lunch."

"Really, where?"

"An Italian place in Knightsbridge your Mum recommended, I told her we were coming in to town for a meeting and I wanted to take you somewhere nice for lunch because I'd been away and wanted to spoil you." I grin at him. We'd decided not tell anyone about the baby for another couple of weeks, after such a public loss of our last pregnancy, we want to keep this one as low key as possible until we are in the 'safe' zone at around four months.

"I love you," I look across at him and say while he drives.

"You better," he replies as he reaches for my hand and kisses it.

There's valet parking at the restaurant and my door is opened for me before Sean gets the chance to get around the car, as I go to step out, I hear him say to the valet, "I've got it mate, you just park the car." He throws him his keys, and his eyes meet mine as I go to step onto the footplate of the Range Rover, he takes hold of both my hands while I step down and he kisses me gently on the mouth, and then leads me into the restaurant. As we enter the reception area, we walk straight into Cam and a stunningly beautiful red head on their way out. Sean must spot him just as I do as his grip around my hand tightens, Cam stops dead in his tracks and I can feel his eyes remain on me as I move mine away to look at Sean. Cam speaks first.

"Sean, Georgia, how are you?"

Sean stops walking and let's go of my hand and shakes Cam's. "Good mate, very good."

Sean looks across to me, I smile and nod toward Cam but I can't look him in the eye, not with Sean and the red head looking at me so I just smile and repeat that we are good.

"How are your parents Georgia?"

"They're good too, thanks." I briefly meet Cam's gaze, then move it across to the red head.

"Tamara, this is Sean and Georgia McCarthy. Sean, as I'm sure you know is the front man for Carnage. Georgia's father is an old business friend of mine and the pair of them happened to buy my house out in Essex last year."

Fuck.

"You what?" Sean gives a nervous laugh as he speaks, Cam's eyes flash to mine, just for an instant as he realises what he's just done, too late now.

"Well, yeah, sorry, did you not know, that's my old place you bought, hope its erm… hope it's working out for you there?" Sean's nodding as he listens to Cam.

"Yeah, yeah, we love it, couldn't be happier. Anyway, nice to see ya mate, gotta go, tables booked and we're running late." I smile as best I can at Cam and the red head and then follow Sean and the Maître d to our table as it starts to dawn on me that this is the same restaurant that Cam brought me to a long, long time ago.

As soon as we are seated and Sean has ordered a double bourbon and coke, his eyes are on me and I know that I'm in trouble, that's the problem with lies and half-truths, they always come back to bite you on the arse. Sean's legal team had dealt with the purchase of the house, he may have signed some of the documentation, but he never mentioned anything so I didn't either.

"Did you know? And don't even think about lying to me." I nod my head and swallow.

"You fucking knew and you let *us* buy it, you let *us* move into your ex's old home. Why, why the fuck would you do that? Why the fuck didn't you tell me?" The waiter brings our drinks. Sean drinks his straight down and orders another.

"I didn't know." I start. "Not at first, I looked around and loved it and then I called you and arranged for you to come and view it and then that's when I found out, after I'd already called you and told you that I loved it."

"So why the fuck didn't you tell me then?" I shrug… because I'm a lying, deceitful, cheating, whore.

"You loved the place so much the next day when you saw it; I thought it would put you off."

"He's your fucking ex G, of course it would fucking put me off, would you like me to move you into Haley's house without you knowing?" I throw my sparkling water in his face, get up and head for the door.

"Georgia, get the fuck back here." The restaurant falls silent.

"Fuck you," I call out back to him over my shoulder as I make my way outside.

Cam is just putting the red-head into a taxi, I stand and watch as the valet pulls up in a large black sports car of some kind, I have no idea what it is but he gets out and hands Cam the keys. I turn to the other valet and ask him to get me a cab. I assume while I wait, Sean will appear, then Cam's at my side.

"Kitten," he sighs out my name, the way he always does. "I'm so sorry, did I cause a fight?"

I give a little laugh. "Its fine Cam, just go."

His eyes look into mine, through mine, into me.

"Are you sure, do you need a lift?"

"Cam, please, just go." He nods but doesn't move. I stare past him for a few seconds then finally allow my eyes to meet his again. "Please Cam, for me, just go."

He nods and leaves this time.

I change my mind about getting a taxi and decide that if Sean is going to stay and get drunk, then I might as well take the car home, by the time its brought around and I'm in the driver's seat, Sean walks out of the restaurant and jumps into the passenger side, he doesn't look at me and we drive home in complete silence. Once we get back to the house he heads off to the study and I can hear him going through our filling cabinet, I leave it five minutes and then go to see what he's doing, there are papers everywhere. Sean is leaning over the open drawer, drinking straight from a bottle of Wild Turkey, his eyes come up and meet mine and he looks at me with complete contempt.

"What are you doing?" I ask him.

"Looking for the paperwork on this place, is his name on it, if it is then why didn't I spot it?'

"His name was on it, I thought you would notice then, that you would mention it and I would just tell you, but you didn't so I just stayed quiet and it was wrong and I'm sorry. I couldn't be sorrier." And it was the truth, we should never have bought this place without Sean knowing who the previous owner was, keeping quiet was now causing more problems than speaking up would have and had now spoilt what should have been an absolutely perfect day, and I had no one else to blame but myself.

"Do you have any idea how much of a cunt you made me feel earlier, in front of him, Cameron fucking King, your big time gangster ex-boyfriend?" I shake my head.

"I'm sorry, I should've told you, I didn't realise it was so important to you."

"Don't lie G, this is me you're talking to, you knew exactly how important that little piece of information would be to me, that's why you didn't say anything, that's why you kept quiet." I can't meet his gaze, he's right, I knew Sean wouldn't want to live here knowing it was Cam's, I never for a minute thought that he would.

"But what I don't get Georgia, what I don't understand is, if you knew it was his house, if you knew, then why the fuck would you still want to live here? Why would you want to move into your ex-lovers home?" He takes a swig from the bottle and sneers at me. "Hmm, tell me G, did you want to feel close to him, is he even your ex or have you still been seeing him all these years, sneaking around behind my back?"

"Fuck you, now you're just being ridiculous."

"Am I, then explain to me, fucking explain to me G, why the fuck would you want to live here?" he shouts and throws the bottle of drink at the wall, it smashes and glass flies everywhere, I shake my head at him and turn and leave. "That's it, fuck off G, walk away and go and rock in a corner somewhere, shut it all out and make pretend it's not happening. Ain't that what you do best? Shall I ring Mummy and Daddy to come and pick their little princess up coz the big bad rock star is swearing and smashing the place up?"

I keep walking, I feel exhausted, worn down by the weight of the guilt that I carry for doing what I did last year. Seeing Cam today, the panic I felt when he revealed he was the previous owner of our home, just went to prove to me, how much I love Sean, why I did what I did last year, I will never understand and the thought that Sean is hurting because of me cuts me in half. I felt nothing today when I saw Cam with another woman, whatever confusion about the feelings I thought I had for him have gone. Losing my baby was a massive wake up call, I love Sean beyond measure, my life is and always will be with Sean and I am terrified in that moment that I may have completely fucked everything up.

CHAPTER 26

It's dark when I wake up, my mobile is ringing and I badly need a wee. I sit up on the bed and see that Sean is sitting in the armchair that we have in our room, the lamp is on at the side of the bed and I can see that he's just sitting there, staring at me, his index finger and thumb are cupping his jaw, his elbow is resting on the arm of the chair, his left ankle resting on his right knee. I stand on unsteady legs and go into our bathroom, the bathroom we sat in just yesterday so happily, so united in our love, so hopeful for the new life we have created. I feel sick to my stomach, it's my fuck up and all I can hope is that Sean will forgive me. I go to the toilet, wash my hands and head back into the bedroom.

"Come here," he orders. I go to where he's sitting and stand in front of him.

"Is there anything going on between you and Cameron King?" My pulse throbs so hard I can feel it in my neck.

"I love you, I'm with you, and I will always be with you."

"That's not what I asked Gia."

"No Sean, there is nothing going on between me and Cameron King, I love you. I didn't say anything about the house because we both loved it, it felt right, if I had something going on with Cam, do you really think I would move us into his old home? Do you really think that I'm that kind of a person?"

Without saying anything, he pulls me toward him. I sit on my knees in the chair, straddling his lap; he looks up into my face. "I'm sorry about what I said about Haley, I shouldn't have said that."

I instantly fill with tears, I shake my head. "I'm sorry for all of it, it's my fault, I shouldn't have kept it from you, I should have told you the truth, given you the choice, we should have discussed it."

"Don't cry I hate it when you cry." He pulls my face down to his and kisses me softly on the mouth, my hands go to his hair and I kiss him back harder as I grind my hips into his crutch, he holds onto my arse as I wrap my legs around him and he walks us over to the bed, where he lays me down and undresses me. When I'm completely naked, he takes all of his own clothes off, then pushes each of my feet up onto the edge of the bed, opening me wide to him, he kneels down between my legs and kisses me, from the inside of my knee all the way up to the inside of my thigh. He runs his nose down from my clit to my opening, then using the fingers on both his hands, he spreads my lips wide open and laps all the way back up to my clit.

"You taste delicious G, there's nothing better than the smell and taste of you when you're turned on." He leans over and grabs a pillow and puts it behind me.

"Put your elbows on it, I want you to watch me; I want to see your face when you come." I do as he says and watch as he looks down between my spread legs. "You have the most beautiful cunt Georgia and its mine, all fucking mine."

He pushes his thumb down onto my clit and circles it, he slides his middle and index fingers inside me and curls them slightly, then he slides is ring and little finger into my arse, I arch my back and force myself down onto him harder, not losing eye contact with him at any time. "Fuck me, fuck my fingers, I want to feel you come all over my hand," he says between gritted teeth. He tilts his head down and flicks his tongue over my clit a few times, then stands, his fingers still inside me, he strokes himself, his eyes still on mine and I find the sight so erotic, I come, bucking and clenching all over his hand as he spurts all over my belly.

We have a nice long bath together later and both repeat how sorry we are, we talk about the baby and how as soon as this one is born that we'll go straight in for another, our plan had always been to be young parents but we'd been enjoying our life together so much, we just kept putting it off but now the time was right and neither of us could wait.

The house phone and our mobiles had been ringing while we were making love and bathing, they had rung so many times now that I'd started to worry, so I climbed out and went and retrieved both of our phones. We both had untold missed calls, the last being from Lennon so I called him first. I pulled the belt of my towelling bath robe tighter as a shiver ran through me, something was up, I just knew it.

"For fucks sake George, where have you been? Is Maca with you? Why haven't you been answering any of your phones?"

"We were busy, whatever's wrong?" I head back into the bathroom and sit on the edge of the bath that Sean is still lying in and admire my Husband's chest and his tattoo with my initial. I reach out and trace the G with my finger nail and I smile when Sean shudders at my touch.

"What the fuck happened today?" Shit, did someone see us at the obstetricians?

"What, nothing, why?"

"Were you at Decadenza in Knightsbridge today?"

"Yeah, why?"

"Well according to the news, you and Sean bumped into Cameron King, and Sean wasn't happy because, according to the news, you had an affair with him last year, remember the pictures in the Sunday papers?"

I nod and lock eyes with Sean, who is currently sucking on the finger that I was tracing his tattoo with. I sigh. "Yes, I remember."

"Well the story being run in tomorrow's papers and which the record label has been fielding questions about all afternoon goes like this… You had an affair with Cam last year because Sean is gay and you wanted a baby. Cam got you pregnant, you lost the baby so now you are back seeing Cam to try and get pregnant again and you and Sean run into him at Decadenza today. Sean is pissed off, you argue, you throw a drink in his face then storm off. While you're outside, Cam declares his undying love for you, then jumps in his car and drives off, Sean comes out after him and now you two are getting divorced."

I can't help the simile that spreads over my face. "And you believe that do you Len?"

"It's not what I believe that matters George, it's what they're gonna print, you're gonna have the press all over your arse now. Oh and there are pictures, I don't know how but there are pictures of you and Sean walking into the restaurant and of you and Cam talking outside."

Shit, I never told Sean that I spoke to Cam outside. "George?"

"Yes, I heard you."

"Are you and Sean all good, I mean, there's nothing to all of this is there?"

"Of course not Len, we went to lunch, we bumped into Cam and his date. Sean and I argued about something completely random and yes, I did throw a glass of water in his face, but it was nothing. We're fine, in fact we've spent the whole evening having make up sex, that's why we haven't answered our phones. Tell that to the fucking press."

"What the fuck George, what's going on?" Sean has sat up in the bath and is asking me now.

I try to sound as nonchalant as possible. "Someone's gone to the press about us arguing in the restaurant today, they've put two and two together and come up with twenty seven," I reply.

"And what about the rest George, what about what Cam said to you outside?" Len asks. I'm going to have to just face this so I look right at Sean as I speak.

"Cam was waiting for his car to be brought around when I stormed outside, he asked if I was okay and if I needed a lift. That's all; there was nothing else to it."

"As long as you're sure."

"I'm positive Len."

"Good, I love you little sister Georgia, now put Maca on."

"I love you too big brother Len." I pass the phone to Sean, who hasn't taken his eyes from mine and didn't flinch as I confessed to talking to Cam outside the restaurant.

“Len,” is all that Sean says into the phone, he reaches across with his free hand and holds mine, brushing his thumb over my knuckles.

“It was a stupid argument over nothing, I said something I shouldn’t have and you know what your sister’s tempers like, she threw her glass of water over me.” Sean’s eyes are looking over my face as he speaks; he’s quiet for a moment as he listens to whatever it is Len is saying.

“Len, this stays between us just us right now, Georgia will tell Jim in her own time, but she’s pregnant and we really don’t need this shit, make it go away.” He’s quiet again as he listens to my brother. My heart swells with how much I love my Husband, despite the story being basically complete bollocks, his first thought is for me and our baby and I just love him so much.

“Early days mate, just eight weeks and thanks.” He gestures toward me and asks silently if I’m okay, I nod but leave him to talk as I go downstairs and pour him a drink, good job there’s more than one bottle of Wild Turkey in the house; otherwise he’d be licking the office walls to get a drop. By the time I get back upstairs with a bottle and a glass, he’s out of the bath and standing with a towel wrapped around his hips, leaning in the doorway between our bedroom and bathroom and staring down at our bed.

“I’m sorry that I didn’t tell you that I spoke to Cam outside the restaurant, I didn’t even think about it until Len mentioned it.”

He shakes his head and without looking at me he says, “I already knew, I watched you.”

“You what?”

“I watched you, I followed you straight out and I watched you. I watched him come over to you, I watched you shake your head at him.” His eyes finally come up and meet mine.

“Why, why did you watch?” He shrugs his shoulders and his jaw trembles slightly as he speaks.

“I wanted you to choose me, I wanted you to send him away and choose me so I stayed back and watched and waited to see what you would do, I was terrified that you would leave with him.”

I put the glass and bottle down on the chest of drawers. "What, no, no Sean, never, why would you think that?"

"Because there's something there G, you told me once that you thought that you loved him." He shrugs his shoulders as he looks at me. "I think that I know you better than you know yourself, I know that you love him, I knew it that night when he turned up at Ashley's party, when we first got back together. I knew it as soon as I saw you look at him and I knew it when I looked at that picture of you and him in the papers last year, there were more than the one I showed you, there were hundreds and I looked at all of them."

I'm standing right in front of him now and he reaches out and strokes my cheek with the back of my hand. "And I knew it was true when you couldn't make eye contact with him yesterday, you love him G, it's just as simple as that. So I stood back, I waited inside the foyer of the restaurant and I let you choose and I just hoped and prayed that it would be me you chose or at least that you wouldn't choose to go home with him."

"I left him for you, why would I choose him, I love you Sean, I'm in love with you, there's no one else, there never was, it's still only ever you." I reach out and touch the tattoo at the base of his neck that's made up of the words of the song that he wrote for me, the words that we both included in our wedding vows. He takes my hand and kisses my wedding ring.

"I know I watched you tell him to leave, but I saw how much it hurt you to do it." I let out a sob, I hate that he doubts my love for him; it's like a physical blow.

"No, no, it didn't hurt because it was a hard choice. I just didn't want to hurt him, he's only ever been good to me Sean. Despite his reputation, Cam's a good bloke and I asked him to just go away and leave me alone, I didn't want him, I don't want him."

He pulls me toward him. "I wouldn't survive G, if you left me, you might as well kill me because I wouldn't survive."

He kisses my hair and my head and my temples and eyes, my nose and my cheeks, along my jaw and then my mouth, he sucks my bottom lip into his mouth, then his whole mouth is over mine, his hand is in my hair. I kiss him back with even more passion and pull the towel from his hips, his cock is already hard and I begin to stroke him, I rub my thumb over the tip and can feel that it's already wet. He undoes the belt on my robe and slides his hands inside and cups my left breast in his hand, I kiss his neck and his chest and slide down his body and kneel in front of him. I gently brush my fingertips over his arse cheeks and down the back of the inside of his thighs, as I look up at him, he brushes my hair from off of my face I take him in my hand first and then guide him into my mouth, swirling my tongue over his tip, pushing my tongue into the slit at the end, he closes his eyes for a few seconds, then continues to keep looking into my eyes.

"That is one of the most beautiful sights I've ever seen, you Georgia, are so fucking beautiful and I love you so much." I take him into my mouth as far as I can and squeeze his balls in my hand, they're hard and tight, I stroke my fingers along the seam underneath to the crack of his arse and press two fingers onto but not into the hole at the back.

"Fuck," he hisses between clenched teeth. He bends his knees slightly, almost pushing himself down onto me, I lift my fingers of my other hand up to his mouth and he sucks on them, making them wet, we've never done anything like this before and I have no idea what I'm doing but I'm going to try this. I move my hand back between his legs and retrace my strokes along the seam under his balls until I get to the hole again, but this time I don't stop, I slide my fingers straight inside him, his knees buckle slightly.

"Ah fuck G, fuck." I push in further and he pushes down onto me harder, he takes his cock in one hand and holds onto the back of my head with the other and he wanks himself into my mouth. I push my fingers in as far as I can and he comes, almost instantly, in my mouth, over my chin and over my tits as he calls out, "Georgia, fuck baby, fuck!"

I look up at him, his cum dripping from my mouth and chin. "Fuck baby, I take that back, you looking up at me like that, with my spunk all over you is now most definitely the most beautiful thing I've ever seen."

He drops to his knees and cleans me up with his tongue and I almost convulse with pleasure at the thought of what he's doing, he then turns me around and fucks me on the floor doggy style and makes me come loud and hard as he presses his fingers of one hand onto my clit and pushes two from his other hand into my arse, all whilst still pounding into me from behind.

CHAPTER 27

The next few days are insane, the stories printed about us are beyond ridiculous and we have to get extra security at the house to stop the press intrusion. Luckily we issue a trespass warning to all of them and they don't venture further than the gates but trying to get in and out of the property is beyond impossible. In the end, Sean calls all of my family over on the Saturday, we announce our pregnancy, which makes both of my parents cry, but Sean tells my Mum and Dad how worried he is at what all of the stress is doing to the baby. I'm actually not that stressed, the stories are laughable and I know that Sean and I are solid, we are closer right now than we've ever been in our lives and I've never been happier or more in love. If only the press would fuck off and leave us alone. Sean's main concern is that I'm going to get hurt in the scramble to take our photographs. We've issued a statement and invited one journalist and a photographer into our home to give an interview and answer questions on the rumours and to take a couple of photos of us together, but the interest still hasn't died down. Cam has even made a statement, categorically denying all the allegations.

Then while my family are all at our place on Saturday, Len receives a call from the band's offices telling him that Haley has crawled out of the wood work and is touting a story around the Sunday tabloids that she's happy to confirm that Sean is gay and has in fact been in a long term relationship with Marley. Len is onto the lawyers straight away; last year when I had my little run in with her, Sean's lawyers agreed to pay for her nose to be reconstructed, as apparently I had broken it, in several places and the deal she got meant that she was never allowed to sell a story or talk about us to the press again. The rest of the evening is spent with Len making arrangements for a lawsuit to be filed against her and any newspaper that prints the story. I'm not laughing any more, not now that she's involved, I want to run away and hide and as if reading my mind my Dad says, "Maca, why don't you go to our place in Portugal for a coupla weeks, stay out the way till this all blows over."

Sean is biting down on his bottom lip as he looks across at me. "Is it safe for you to fly?"

I shrug my shoulders. “I can call the doctors tomorrow and find out, but I’m pretty sure it’ll be fine, it’s not like it’s a long flight.”

“You two have a photo shoot Monday don’t forget,” Len looks from me to Sean as he speaks. “I don’t think it would be a good idea to cancel, go and do the shoot, show a united front and then disappear for a couple of weeks, I can deal with whatever else you have booked.”

“Portugal it is then.” Sean smiles across to where I’m sitting in the sunshine, it’s a beautiful day, my family are all here, I’m pregnant with a healthy baby and I love my Husband beyond measure. All of our dreams, everything that Sean and I hoped would happen in our lives, have been far exceeded. Carnage have become more successful than any of us could ever have thought possible, from the four boys in a band, practising in the summer house of our old back garden, they are now known across the world and have had hits right across the planet and we are all basically living the dream and I’m not going to let Whorely and her shit once again spoil my life.

Rather than run the gauntlet of the press at our gates, my family all stay over Saturday night and I love every second of having our home filled with the sound of laughing and talking, kids shouting and screaming, they have put the pool to good use and even the sounds of the splashes as they jump in and out make me smile. By Saturday evening, everyone is in the pool apart from my two youngest nieces who are passed out and sleeping soundly in their baby buggies, right where we can see them. My Mum is in the kitchen with Sam, Bailey’s partner; cooking God knows what to feed us all, we would normally call out for a takeaway of some kind but it’s just too much hassle with the twenty or so photographers parked at our gates.

I climb out of the pool and watch Sean with Ziggy on his shoulders, who’s throwing a Frisbee to his brother Jimmy, who’s on Lennon’s shoulders and his cousin Joe, who’s on Marley’s shoulders. Connie, Annie and Paige are using my Dad and Bailey as a spring board and diving into the water. As I watch, I suddenly see the resemblance between me and Paige that my family are always telling me is there. She’s tall for her age and skinny, she has Len’s dark skin and hair but with the most amazing blue eyes. When I was younger, I always thought my eyes looked odd against my olive skin and chestnut hair but on Paige, they look stunning, my hand instinctively goes to my belly as I wonder what I'm carrying inside me. After what happened with my last pregnancy, I just want a healthy baby and I'm pretty sure Sean feels the same way. I look up as I hear Paige shriek as she is thrown in the air by my Dad and is caught by Bailey, he and Sam have a little boy called Freddie who's just a couple of months old and in his baby capsule in the kitchen with my Mum and Sam.

As I watch the kids all play, it strikes me that Sean and I weren't much older than my nieces and nephews when we met, were we really so young? Just children and yet I knew, we both knew, at eleven and thirteen, our eyes met that very first time and we both felt something that neither of us had any understanding of. How many people on this planet find that? How many ever have that connection with another person, ever? Let alone go on to marry, have a family together and live the life that we have. Okay, things have been rough at times, a four year separation; my stupid, stupid mistake with Cam; and the loss of our baby were tough times, but on the whole, we have been so lucky. We've survived everything that's been thrown at us and still love each other in a way that most people will never comprehend, even our families still laugh with the way that we are with each other, how intense our feelings have remained and as if to prove a point, I look up and toward Sean, because I just know that his eyes are on me.

He has a bemused look on his face as he strides through the water, Ziggy still on his back and I can't help but grin at him. "What you thinking about G, you okay?"

Before I can answer Ziggy shouts down at me. "I wanna get down Auntie George, I'm hungry."

Sean swings him off of his shoulders and I grab a towel from behind me and wrap him in it as Sean passes him to me, we walk over to a sun lounger and both tickle and dry Ziggy at the same time as he screams and kicks with laughter. "No, no Maca," he can barely speak, he's so puffed out from the fight he's putting up. "Make him stop Auntie G, make him stop."

He wraps his arms around my neck and clings to me, his cheek pressed against mine, Sean stops and stares at us both. "You're going to be such a great Mum Georgia."

Our eyes both fill with tears. "Have you got a baby in your belly Auntie G, must be really little coz your belly's not big like Sam's was when Freddie was in there." We both laugh as we explain that our baby is only tiny and has a lot of growing to do before Ziggy can see him just after Christmas and it suddenly strikes me, that Sean and I have both called our baby a 'him'. Ziggy escapes us and goes in search of food and as we watch him run away, we both call out to him to walk and not run.

Sean turns to me and says, "Dya think it's a boy?" I nod, because I do, don't ask me how but somehow, in the last few minutes, I've become 100% sure, that we're having a boy.

"Me too," Sean almost whispers. "And I cannot fucking wait to meet him."

We smile at each other, his hand on my belly, oblivious to all of the noise going on around us; we lean into each other and kiss, very gently, our lips barely brushing. "I love you so much Georgia Rae, our son is so lucky to have you for a Mum and I'm so lucky to have you as my Wife."

Before I can reply, my Mum and Ziggy shout at us all to come and get some food so I just smile at him and let him lead me out to the patio where a banquet has been prepared from the contents of my fridge and freezer. We eat, drink and celebrate our pregnancy in noisy Layton style, the kids are put to bed and the adults stay up till the early hours of Sunday, talking, laughing, reminiscing and sharing stories of our lives as we were growing up. I go to bed happy and content, appreciating my fantastic family but not realising that it's the very last time that we will all be together, that our dynamics will be changed, shattered irreparably before the year is out.

CHAPTER 28

Our photo shoot is done on Monday morning and by Monday evening we've been taken by helicopter from our home, to a private jet waiting for us at City Airport in London, then on to Faro Airport in Portugal, from there we were picked up by a town car and Sean drives us to my parents villa, in Albufeira. We spend an entire week doing very little except sleep, swim, eat and have lots and lots of sex, which still isn't enough to sate my pregnant, hormonally charged libido. Sean is overjoyed with the fact that I can't get enough of him, he may be one of the biggest stars on the planet, but we've known each other for almost twenty years and have had about fifteen years of sexual experiences together so even for us, things sometimes get a little normal, everyday. Just because you're rich and famous, doesn't mean that your sex life is always super exciting every time. We're no different to any other couple that have been together for a lot of years, but right now, despite the years together, things are hotter than ever and being alone at my parent's place and away from the worries of what the papers and magazines might be saying about us, things are definitely on fire.

Just over a week after we arrive, we are up and taking a walk along the beach at seven in the morning, it's June and the sun is getting stronger every day that we are here so we've been waking early, making beautiful wake up love, taking a quick shower and then having a walk on the beach before heading back for breakfast and more lovemaking.

Today is a little cloudier and I shiver as a wave from the Atlantic Ocean washes over my feet. Sean puts his arm around me and pulls me into his side as we walk; I wrap my arm around the back of his waist and grin up at him.

"What?" he asks.

"Will ya be my boyfriend Maca?" He smiles my favourite cheeky smile, the one that I have known for so long, my smile, the one he has smiled at me with for over half of our lives.

"Hmm that depends Georgia Rae."

"On what?" I stop walking and fold my arms across my chest. I'm wearing a t-shirt with the Carnage logo on it, a red heart shaped iris, with a black pupil, crying blood red tears that are collecting underneath in a pool. Sean, Lennon and Marley came up with the design one wet and rainy afternoon in our summerhouse and it was almost as well-known an image across the world now as the golden arched M of MacDonald's. I'd worn this t-shirt as it was Sean's and loose on me, my boobs were getting bigger every day and I needed to leave the top button on my denim shorts undone the last few days as they were also getting too tight.

I looked at Sean with raised eyebrows, waiting for an answer to my question. I started to tap my foot. "I'll be your boyfriend G but only if you show me your tits."

I laughed at him, looked up and down the deserted beach to make sure no one was watching and lifted my t-shirt, I wasn't wearing a bra so he got to see them in all their naked glory and I just loved the look on his face as he took them in. "Fuck Georgia, they're getting bigger every day, our boys gonna be one well fed baby."

He pulls me toward him and tilts his head down and sucks on my right nipple, he drops down to his knees and kisses my belly as he holds onto my hips. "Now listen here little man, your mother has a great pair of tits and I know that's all you'll see when you look at them is food, but you will still need to share. I'll make sure that they're all yours at meal times, but the rest of the time, those girls are mine, you got me?"

He nods his head, as if he's actually heard a reply. "Good."

I push his long dark hair from his face and look down into his brown eyes with their little flecks of gold.

"What are you doing?'

"I'm just having a little father son convo with my boy."

"Well can you please not discuss my boobs with him, talk to him about music, football or someone else's boobs, not mine." His grin gets bigger.

"Well son, it's like this, your auntie Sam has a massive rack and she used to get them out for a living but uncle Bails put a stop to all that."

"Sean!" I shrieked. "You cannot tell our child things like that and why are you looking at Sam's rack anyway?"

He laughs as he stands up, catching me around my waist and lifting my feet off the sand; I wrap my legs around his hips. "I'm just joking, Sam's tits are fake and horrible, and yours are real and perfect."

We look into each other's eyes for a few long moments and despite our lovemaking just an hour or so ago, I can feel my insides coil and tighten with desire for him.

"I love you," I whisper.

"I love you more, let's get back and get naked baby, I've got a massive hard on again." I slide down his body until my feet touch the sand. We walk back along the beach to the villa, stopping at a little bakery along the way to buy fresh bread.

Later that afternoon as I lay in the shade reading a book. Sean's mobile rings, he's lying on a lounger next to me but he's in the full glare of the sun, which finally broke through the clouds a couple of hours ago. We have only been taking calls from our family since we've been here and Sean mouths, "Len," to me as he answers with, "Alright mate, what's up?"

The smile almost instantly vanishes from his face. "What?" He stands and takes my hand, pulling me up and with him as he walks inside. "For fuck's sake, yeah, that was this morning."

His eyes look over me; I'm wearing bikini bottoms and nothing else. "Can we threaten them with anything?" He rakes his hand through his hair as I watch and assume this is another press related issue. "Yeah, yeah, I understand." He walks over to the patio doors and pulls them shut and closes the blinds. "Well if they know we're here, we might as well come home." He looks back at me again. "No, we can be ready in a coupla hours, see what you can do and let me know." I don't wait to hear the rest, I head to our bedroom and start packing, we didn't bring much, we already have a supply of clothes and our favourite toiletries here left over from previous visits. As I throw stuff into my Louis Vuitton luggage I can feel Sean's eyes on me, he wraps his arms around me from behind and kisses my neck, just below my ear, sending goose pimples down my body.

"Will you always do that when I kiss you there dya think?" I turn my head and smile at him.

"As long as my heart is beating, I will react to you." He grinds his hips into my arse.

"You've made me hard," he says into my ear and my nipples feel like they are going to explode.

"And you've made me wet, but stop avoiding the issue, what's wrong, why are we going?"

He sighs and pulls me down into his lap as he sits on the bed. "Someone took photos of us on the beach this morning"

"What, how, that beach was deserted?"

"I don't know, those lenses they use can zoom in from miles away, they could've been anywhere." Well if one photographer has taken shots of us, that means there will be plenty more turning up trying to get the same thing. I'm glad we're going home.

"Oh well, it's been a nice unexpected break and at least they didn't get pictures of us fighting this time." I smile and kiss his nose as I speak.

"No, they got pictures of me sucking your tits and kissing your belly instead."

"Oh, fuck."

"Yeah, oh fuck, Len said you can't see your tits in the pictures but that's not the point and now the pregnancy stories are doing the rounds because of me kissing your belly." I smile at him.

"Well at least they know you love me and not Marley now." He laughs and raises his eyebrows.

"Yeah, I s'pose." He's quiet for a few seconds as he traces random patterns over my bare back.

"I'm sorry G, its fucking ridiculous. Why can't they fuck off and pick on someone else? Why can't the Beckhams be a bit more interesting so they leave us alone?"

"Don't say that, I wouldn't wish this shit on anyone."

"I'm getting worried now, how will they be when the baby comes, I feel like going back to Australia, leaving all of this bollocks behind, I'm over it G, I'm really fucking over it."

"Sean, it will be someone else's turn in a couple of weeks, I know they are being a pain in the arse right now, but you can't let them make you walk away from everything. You can't give up your music or the band; you would hate it and eventually hate me and our baby for being the cause."

"Don't talk shit, I'd do anything for you and the baby, I want you safe G, I want you and the baby safe and I will do anything, give up the band if that's what it's gonna take."

"We'll take on extra security and see how we go, let's not make any decisions until after the baby's here, I love you, stop worrying."

* * *

The photographs of us on the beach actually do us a massive favour, they're really quite beautiful and show nothing but a couple in love and enjoying each other, they put paid to the ridiculous rumours about Sean's sexuality. They show Whorely up for the complete liar that she is and have hopefully convinced the press of what a complete bullshit artist she is and they will now actually leave us alone and move on, looking for their next victim.

The Monday after we arrive home, we are back at Richard Curtis's office for my twelve week ultrasound and we have been told that as long as the baby is lying in the right position, we might be able to find out the sex.

Sean has a tight clammy grip of my hand as the room fills with the now familiar whoosh of our baby's heartbeat, all of my other checks were fine, my blood pressure is perfect, nothing unusual was detected in my urine sample and my bloods have all come back fine. Despite this, we are both as nervous as hell as we look from each other to the screen. It's amazing the difference a few weeks make, we can now clearly see the baby's spine and arms and legs, the doctor calls out information to the nurse and she types everything into the computer, I stare, amazed that all of this is going on inside of my belly and as yet I haven't felt a thing.

"Look at his arms move about G, dya reckon he's gonna be a drummer?" I smile at Sean.

"Shit I hope not, listening to you practise guitar in the early days was hard enough, let alone listening to an aspiring drummer."

"Cheers babe and there was me thinking that one of the reasons you loved me back then was because of my amazing guitar skills."

"No, I loved you because I couldn't not, I loved you because it was what I was put on this earth to do." I look away from the screen and back to Sean, his eyes are full to the brim with tears, he brings my hand to his lips and kisses my palm gently, I realise the room is silent, Richard Curtis and his nurse Moira are both staring at us.

"Well," Professor Curtis breaks the silence. "Your baby has decided to cooperate, we don't usually tell parents the sex until the sixteen week scan because we can't really be sure until then but looking at these images, I'm pretty confident that you have a son on the way, congratulations." I burst into tears.

"A son G, we're having a boy." I nod and smile through my tears. "Thank you, thank you so much," Sean says through his own tears.

The doctor and nurse leave us alone for five minutes while we pull ourselves together, eventually returning to tell us that everything is perfect. We make an appointment to return in four weeks and head home to share our news with our family. Sean actually doesn't wait until we get home, he's on the phone to Marley as soon as we are out of the building, then Lennon, then he insists we call into my parents on the way home, where him and my Dad share almost the entire contents of an eighteen year old bottle of Laphroaig whiskey and from where I end up driving us home and putting a very drunk, but ecstatically happy Sean to bed.

CHAPTER 29

Thanks to the hot and steamy photo shoot we did before leaving for Portugal and the pictures taken of us on the beach, the press left us alone for the rest of summer.

Over the years, Sean and I had done a few shoots together, but that was by far the raunchiest, the photographer had me wearing not a lot and draped all over Sean on a motorbike, wrapped around him in bed and various other poses where we looked as though we were having sex with our clothes on. They were all very tasteful and I must admit, the whole thing got us pretty turned on, to the point where the helicopter taking us to the airport cost Sean an extra thousand pounds as we were late getting ready after the unplanned sex we had, twice, once we got home. Best grand he ever spent in my book.

On my birthday in late September, the boys played at a charity polo game, it was a beautifully warm and sunny Sunday and I chose to wear a long flowing cheesecloth dress that we had bought from a retro stall at Camden market a few weeks before, it was cream and very seventies in style and showed off my growing baby bump beautifully. I teamed it with a big floppy orange hat and a pair of espadrilles and was thrilled with the look.

Dave picked me up with Ash and Jimmie already in the car, the boys had left earlier to sound check, I get kisses, cuddles and birthday wishes from all of them and for some reason I have butterflies in my stomach today and no idea why.

When we arrived we were shown through to the VIP area where we were offered champagne, I obviously declined and asked for water, we were there about fifteen minutes before I spotted Marley appearing from behind the stage and head over to us. Tom and Billy appeared next followed by my Husband. I watched him, waiting for him to spot me; my heart was racing in my chest. He looked stunning and quite literally stole my breath away.

“Fuck me, he’s hot,” I laughed as Ash whispered in my ear, stating exactly what I was thinking. He was wearing a pair of leather jeans and a v necked t-shirt that wasn’t quite long enough and showed off just enough belly and the start of that V thing he had going on that drove me absolutely insane for him.

"Put your tongue away G, you get to go home and tap that for dinner later."

I smiled as Sean stopped, spoke and shook hands with various people.

"I taped that for breakfast and I want it again for lunch." We had spent the morning having birthday wake up sex, followed by birthday shower sex, my libido hadn't waned a bit during my pregnancy and my belly wasn't big enough to get in the way yet so we were enjoying every inch of each other as often as possible before the baby arrived.

"Maca for breakfast has gotta be better than a Macbreakfast any morning." I smiled at Ash, my dirty minded sister in law, some people might be offended at someone else perving over their Husband but I knew how much she loved my brother, despite her comments about Sean. "Yep," I said to her. "A MacGasm is definitely the way to start the day; in fact, I can't get out of bed until I've had multiple MacGasms." Ash spat champagne everywhere as we both shrieked with laughter, causing the best of British society to turn and look at us.

Sean was talking to a footballer I recognised and I watched as the footballer's Wife/girlfriend/date twirled her hair around her finger as she looked my Husband over like she wanted to lick him from top to toe and stop for a while somewhere around his middle. As if he suddenly sensed my eyes on him, he looked up and met my gaze, his head tilted back as he looked me up and down and I knew that he wanted me just as much as I wanted him. He licked his top lip as he replied to something the footballer's companion, whore, slut, whatever, said, but didn't take his eyes off me. He held out his hand and gestured slightly with his head for me to join him and kept his eyes on mine as I walked toward him. I took his hand as I reached him and he pulled me in, kissing me full on the mouth.

"You look stunning Wife," he said into my ear.

"You look totally fuckable. What are you trying to do to my blood pressure Husband?"

The footballer laughed, his thing didn't.

"Tony, this is my Wife Georgia." I put my hand out and shook his.

"Sorry darling, what was your name?" Sean continued and I couldn't have loved him more.

"Melinda but everyone calls me Mel," she squeaked. I smiled sweetly but didn't offer my hand.

"Melinda, my Wife Georgia McCarthy." I nod and smile some more and almost combust as Sean rubs his hand over my bum through my dress, I turn my head to his and smile.

"What time you on?" I ask him.

"In about an hour, how you feeling?"

"I feel fine." He nods at me as he rubs his hand over my belly and leaves it to rest there.

"Congratulations on the baby, do you know what you're having?" Footballer Tony asks. We do but it's not public knowledge and we both say no together and laugh.

We politely say our goodbyes and make our way over to the rest of the band. I give my brother, Tom and Billy a cuddle and every one wishes me a happy birthday and comments on my bump. Sean spends the next half hour with his hand protectively over my belly as people come over and talk and congratulate us and I can't believe how much our son responds to his Daddy's voice and every time I feel a little kick, Sean looks at me with the most heart breaking smile on his face but he doesn't say a word, it's just between us, communication between us and our son.

We had first felt him move when Sean had got back from America, I thought that I'd felt a few flutterings during the week Sean was away but as soon as he started talking in the car on the way back from the airport where I had gone to pick him up with Milo, I'd felt a definite kick and had grabbed Sean's hand and placed it on my belly.

"Say something let him know you're home, he's missed you."

Sean's eyes had filled with tears as he said, "Hello little man, hope you've been a good boy for your Mum while I've been gone?"

The rapid movements actually made me feel quite sick but I said nothing, loving the sensation and the look of absolute pure joy and love on Sean's face. Since then we'd spent endless hours lying on the floor or the bed at home, Sean, singing or talking to my belly as our little boy kicked and squirmed inside me. We knew he had to stay there until he was cooked and ready to be born but we were beside ourselves with excitement and couldn't wait till we could finally meet him.

Len appeared as if by magic, my handsome, organised, big brother and manger of Carnage.

"Ten minutes," he lets the boys know, he kisses Jim, then Ash and then turns to me. "Look at my baby sister, happy birthday, you look stunning George, pregnancy definitely suits you, can't believe how much that belly's grown in a couple of weeks." He kisses my cheek.

"Don't she look fucking gorgeous, Len." I blush furiously as I feel like the eyes of the whole place are on me. Sean kisses my cheek. "Sorry baby, didn't mean to embarrass ya, I'm just so proud of my beautiful Wife and the fact that the little person inside your belly was put there by me."

I don't respond at first, I can't, I know that I will cry if I speak, I swallow down my sobs as I whisper to him, "I love you so much Sean, so much."

He smiles down at me. "I know you do, but I still love you more."

"Never." I smile and shake my head.

"Right people, time please." Len claps his hands.

Sean kisses me. "Stand where Milo tells ya, I want to be able to see ya, don't leave his side."

I smile and shake my head. "Go, I'll be fine."

There's about two thousand people at the event and many of them are now crowded around the stage waiting to watch Carnage perform. Len has gone with the boys and Jimmie and Ash grab each of my hands and lead us out of the marquee to where Milo is waiting for us with two more security staff from the event, they lead us through the crowd to the front of the stage, where there is a small sectioned off area, there are a couple of people already there but I don't know them.

"Right there George." Milo points to a spot that's been sprayed on the grass in bright yellow.

"What?" I'm confused.

"You need to stand right there divvy," Ash says and moves me towards the spot by my shoulders.

"'Scuse us love," she says to the lady in pearls standing next to the yellow marking. "But this spots taken."

The three of us burst into laughter, even Milo laughs at Ashley's joke, he then proceeds to make everyone other than us three girls move out of the sectioned off area.

"Why do I have to stand here, I don't understand?" I ask anyone that wants to listen.

"Sean's orders, he's worked out where he can see you best from the stage so he insisted the organisers let him have this area marked and sectioned off with extra security so that he knows your safe."

"You're fucking kidding me?" I ask in disbelief. Milo shakes his big head.

"Nope, boys got it bad George, he was worried that you would get pushed about and he wanted you to be able to watch from out here and not the wings, your safety is his priority at all times right now, you have precious cargo on board remember?" My hands instantly find their way to my belly; my son has stopped doing acrobatics for now and is resting quietly. I turn back toward the stage as I hear a guitar twang a few times, the boys are having their guitars adjusted by the roadies and sound crew in the wings, then suddenly they're on stage and the crowd goes wild, well as wild as posh people get over a band.

Sean looks right at me and winks and despite the years, my knickers still melt at the sight of him on stage. "Good afternoon Surrey, thank you for joining us on this beautiful day and donating to a very worthy cause, now let's get you all loosened up."

The band crashes out 'Wrong' and 'Come for me' two of their earlier hits, they then play stuff from their latest album, then take a few minutes to grab a drink, as they come back to the stage, I notice Sean has swapped to his acoustic guitar and a stool has been set up for him to sit on. He sort of sits and sort of stands against it, one foot resting behind him, he doesn't say a word as he looks out over the crowd and they begin to quiet.

"I nearly turned this gig down today people." There are boo's from the crowd and people calling various things out. "Don't get me wrong, I wanted to donate, contribute in some way to this very worthy cause." The charity was to help young drug addicts start a new life once they had been through rehabilitation and gotten themselves clean and one that the band had played benefits for on a number of occasions. "The problem was you see, the date, today is a very special day for me, today is the day that the woman I love, the woman that owns me, mind, body, heart and soul was born. Today is my Wife's birthday."

Oh God, I swear, I will kill him later. There are cheers and whoops from the crowd and I just know that everyone is looking. I don't take my eyes from Sean; he winks at me and shrugs. I look around and smile and wave, my cheeks feeling like that are about to ignite, I tilt my head slightly so that the wide brim of my big floppy hat covers my face. "So you see people, you all need to thank my Wife because when I told her about today, she told me that I couldn't turn the offer down, she said, 'There will be other birthdays, we can celebrate later, the charity is more important'." He looks across the crowd as they cheer some more and then he looks back at me. "So, what you lot need to do is wish my Wife a Happy Birthday as a show of thanks for letting me be here today."

Sean then proceeds to lead the band and the crowd in a rendition of Happy Birthday Dear Georgia. I inwardly groaned but smiled and said thank you continuously, when it was finally over, Sean said "Happy Birthday Georgia, this is for you".

Marley started playing softly, then Billy joined in as Tommy came in quietly on his drums, then Sean began to sing, in that beautiful soft raspy voice of his.

"Our eyes they met and we were done; no one else felt the effect,

No one else knew from that moment, we would always be one.

Now after loving you for all of these years,

Sharing some heartbreak and some tears.

I no longer know where I begin or where you end.

You're my lover, my life, my Wife and best friend

And I don't know where you begin or where I end.

Our life, our love, the bond that we share.

It means nothing; it's pointless if you're not there.

They broke us once, they kept us apart

But we fought and we found a way back into each other's hearts.

And just look at us now, stronger than ever and soon we'll be three.

We've made someone new, a mixed up bundle of love

Made from a little bit of you and a little bit of me

You're my lover, my life, my Wife and best friend

And I just don't know where I begin or where you end.

You're my lover, my life, my Wife and best friend.

Now with that little bit of you and me that grows in your belly.

The story of us, will never end"

I'm stunned into silence for a few moments, along with the rest of the crowd, Ash and Jim both have their arms around me as I watch Sean climb down off the stage, climb the barrier and walk toward me, hands reach out and pat his back but his eyes don't leave mine and suddenly he's there, right in front of me.

"I love ya Georgia Rae, Happy Birthday." I wrapped my arms around his neck as he wrapped his arms around my waist, pulled me as close as we could get and kissed me with everything he had, our baby kicking his belly through my belly all the while.

CHAPTER 30

On a freezing cold December afternoon, we left Richard Curtis's office to drive to the Nursery shop along the high street near where I used to live; I'd gone there because I knew they produced custom made baby equipment. I hadn't told Sean and I couldn't wait for him to see our baby boys pushchair that I'd had especially made.

The shop had called this morning to say that my order was ready and as I had an appointment in Harley Street this afternoon, I told them that we would call in on our way home.

Milo was driving us, it had snowed the night before and despite it only being two in the afternoon, it was already getting dark and the ground was starting to freeze over again.

My check up with the Professor had gone well, the baby and I are in excellent health and I was now thirty six weeks pregnant and as healthy as a horse.

By the time we got through the Friday afternoon London traffic, it was four o'clock when we reached the shop. Milo dropped us off and then went in search of a parking spot as there were none directly outside the shop.

Sean loved the pram, it was custom made in the bands logo shade of red, with a black trim and had 'My Daddy Rocks' embroidered on the front, it looked more like a sports car than a pram and I could see by the look on Sean's face that he couldn't wait to push our son around in it.

"Do you like it? You don't think it's a bit much for a little baby?" He threw his arm over my shoulder as we headed out of the store.

"Babe, it's perfect, I love it and anyway, nothings too much for our kid." We had spent half the time in the shop having our photo taken and Sean signing autographs, but we didn't mind, Sean pulled me in closer as we stepped out of the shop, it was dark and snowing again.

"Hold on to me G, that ground is icy, where the fuck is Milo?"

We looked up and down the street but couldn't see the Range Rover. Sean pulled out his phone. "Where are you man? It's fucking freezing out here and slippery as fuck."

He looked up and down the street again. "No mate, still no spaces." He looked at me. "No, it's too slippery, pull round and double park; we'll just walk out and meet ya."

He put the phone back in his pocket and wrapped his arms around me. "He's had to park miles away but don't worry, I'll keep you warm." I snuggled in as I watched an elderly couple climb into an old style Mercedes behind us and I smiled as the man held the door open for his Wife. He must've been about a hundred and judging by the way he shuffled around his car, he probably felt it in this cold weather too. I watched as he seemed to take forever to start the car up as he spoke to his Wife, he looked in his rear view mirror but instead of reversing into the road, the car shot forward. I think I screamed Sean's name, the roar from the engine was so loud, his eyes were on mine as we both flew through the air, the car following us, we spun sideways and I landed hard on my side. Sean was still beside me, and the car came to a stop next to him. That's what I thought was happening, but I wasn't sure, I wasn't sure if any of this was even real.

Everything was very quiet for a few seconds, I looked at Sean, his face was level with mine, his eyes were wide, and he gave me a small smile. "I love you Georgia Rae, show us your tits," he whispered, then he closed his eyes, his beautiful brown eyes, with their flecks of gold.

CHAPTER 31

Beau Francis McCarthy was delivered at 6.08 pm on Friday the first of December 2000; he never took a breath and was instantly declared stillborn. My uterus had ruptured either from the force of the impact of the car or from the force of landing on the cold concrete, nobody could tell me for sure, my baby was delivered and an emergency hysterectomy had to be performed to stop the bleeding.

Beau was brought to me to hold at 8:30 pm that night when I came around from my surgery, my whole family were around my bed, but I asked them all to leave. Marley refused and he stood and watched as I bathed and dressed my perfect little boy in the coming home outfit that was packed in my hospital bag, which was already in the car and had travelled everywhere we did these past few weeks, thanks to my very organised Husband.

Beau had a mop of curly brown hair and looked exactly like his Daddy.

I wrapped him in the blue fleece blanket that Milo and his Wife had bought for us, it had guitars on it and Sean had asked where it had come from and ordered a half dozen more.

I sat on my bed with my brother as he held my son, his nephew and sobbed while we waited for the nurse to come and fetch me.

At 9:45 pm I was wheeled in a wheel chair up to intensive care and allowed to introduce Sean to our son. Lennon and Bailey helped lift me onto his bed, where I curled into his side, his arm around me and our little boy.

Sean's life support was switched off at 11.28 pm, and he died peacefully at 11.43pm on that same night, with me and our son in his arms, surrounded by all of my family and his parents.

We buried them together two weeks later, when I was eventually 'recovered' enough to attend the funeral.

My only regret was that I wasn't already dead and going in the ground with them, my life was over now anyway, so it was only a matter of time before I joined them.

I wanted to be numb, and I wanted not to feel but I was in agony. Once the funeral was over I knew exactly what had to be done.

I stayed alive purely to say my goodbyes and to see my Husband and Child buried but as it turns out, I really don't remember anything about the day, I don't remember much of anything about the past few weeks. All I know is the pain, the massive aching hole inside me and the pain that comes from it, but now the funeral onceover, I knew I could put a stop to it.

When I was at school, a very over enthusiastic religious and social education teacher told my class that suicide was wrong and that God would not allow any one that chose to take their own life into heaven. Heaven is exactly where I knew Sean and Beau were so I had to wait until after I'd said goodbye to them forever at their funeral before I could do what needed to be done.

I laid in the dark on the bed in my old bedroom at my parents' house, the combination of Valium and sleeping tablets finally pulling me down into blackness I so desperately sought. I wasn't scared, I was impatient, I wanted the black nothingness so badly, I wanted the pain to be gone so desperately that I just gave myself over to it, without any kind of a fight I let it take me.

EPILOGUE

My eyes fluttered as I felt Sean kiss across my shoulder, along the curve of my neck, up my throat and along my jaw to my ear.

"Wake up Gia, it's time to go baby." I sighed and reached out until my hand found his hair, and I ran my fingers through it.

"No, I'm so tired, I want to stay here, let's just stay in bed." I hear him chuckle.

"We can't G, you need to go, it's time to open your eyes and go." I try, I really try, but my eyes are just so heavy I can't open them. He kisses me again and I breathe him in.

"I love you," I whisper.

"I love you more Georgia Rae, but it's time for you to go." I shake my head.

"Gia, I'll be with you baby, always, every single day, I'm not asking you now, I'm telling you, open your fucking eyes."

"Alright I will, just not yet, in a minute."

"Now G, open you're fucking eyes right now."

So I did and in an instant he was gone, the room was too bright and it took ages for me to be able to open them fully.

My Dad was sitting at the end of a two seater sofa, my Mum was lying with her head in his lap, they were both sleeping, Marley was in a chair right next to me, his head on the bed and my hand in his.

And then the pain punched right through me and my breath caught. Why, why was I here? I didn't want to be here breathing and feeling I didn't want to be alive.

***

I lay on the on the warm and worn leather sofa and stared up at the ceiling, my hand was inside my pyjama shorts, tracing over the very feint indentations on my lower belly, they're barely noticeable now. Most women probably can't wait for their bodies to bounce back into their pre-baby shape and for their stretch marks to fade but the very few that I have, I want to remain with me forever, the very fine silver lines and the scar from my surgery are the only physical reminders of what I had and what I lost.

I let out a loud sob and let the tears roll down my face and into my ears. I pull my knees up to my chest and wrap my arms around myself, squeezing myself tight, holding on, it doesn't ease the pain, it doesn't stop the ache and doesn't do anything to fill the massive gaping hole that's been punched through my heart, through my life, through my existence. But for a few short seconds it stops the sensation that I continuously have of falling but only for a few short seconds and then its back, I rock from side to side, just to give me something else to focus on. The tears that have collected in my ears escape and run all the way around to the back of my neck. I sob louder, my throat aches, my chest aches, but it hurts more to hold it in and the counsellors, the shrinks and every other expert that I've been made to sit and listen to for these last three months have all agreed on one thing at least, it's good to cry, it's better to let it out than to keep it in. Personally, it makes no difference to me either way, it all still hurts just as much and they're still gone, my Husband and my baby, our little boy, my handsome, vibrant, clever Husband and our beautiful baby boy, gone, snuffed out, in just a few seconds of complete and utter carnage. Carnage, how ironic is that? That it's the perfect word to describe the circumstances of their deaths three whole months ago.

Three months, I can't believe it's been three months, I don't really remember December. In January my family had me committed to a private mental health facility after my second suicide attempt, they kept me there for almost three weeks, I don't know what they thought it would achieve, other than stopping me from once again taking my own life, but what did they think I was going to do once I was out? I wasn't insane, I wasn't mentally unstable, well no more than the next woman that's just had her Husband and Child killed in front of her. I just didn't want to live, I don't want to live but I convinced those that needed convincing that I wouldn't attempt to take my own life again and they let me out into the care of my family and I had every intention of ending it all as soon as I got the opportunity… and then Jimmie came to see me and she brought all of the kids with her, my nieces and nephews.

I was sitting on my Mum's sofa when she came in, she carried Harley in her arms, Jimmy, Paige and Ziggy trailed in behind. I knew as soon as I looked at her that she was pissed off. Ziggy overtook her and threw himself into my lap; he'd just turned six and was the absolute image of my brothers. I held him close and breathed him in, it hurt and it healed me a little all at the same time. Just like my brothers, he'd taken to calling me Porge after learning the Georgie Porgie nursery rhyme.

"Auntie Porge, we've missed you so much." He almost strangles me as he wraps his little arms around my neck so tightly.

"I missed you too Zig, I've missed you all."

"But not that much George?" I looked up at her from the sofa, my Mum stood from where she'd been sitting in the armchair, my dad, Len and Marley all walked into the room.

"Not in front of the children please Jamie," my Mum said to her.

"Erm, yes, actually Bern, I think the children need to hear this. I think that George needs to tell the children why they aren't important enough to her? Why they mean so little to her, that she doesn't want to hang around and see them grow up?"

Lennon walks over and takes Harley out of Jimmie's arms, Marley walks over and takes Ziggy from my lap. My eyes don't leave Jimmies. My bottom lip trembles as I try to swallow down the lump in my throat, my tears escape freely, with no effort from me, down my cheeks.

"Why don't we count George? Why does it not matter to you what you are putting us all through?" She swipes tears away with the back of her hand.

"Sean was like a son to your Mum and Dad, he was like a brother to me, Ash and the boys, he was a favourite uncle to all of your nieces and nephews and we love him, we didn't get the chance to get to know Beau, but we already loved him regardless, his cousins love him, his aunts and uncles love him and his Grandma and Pops love him and we all lost him and we all lost Sean and it hurts." She sobs as she speaks and can barely get her words out. "It hurts so fucking much George, we are hurting for our loss and we are hurting for your loss, which we can all only try and imagine but let me tell you now, what you are doing, by keep trying to top yourself, it's so selfish. You've watched us all suffer George; you've seen what everyone has been through these past couple of months. Marley is barely hanging on, Len is in bits and all you want to do is add to that. Where does it end a George? Where does it stop, you kill yourself, then what?" She looks around the room at my parents and brothers, there's silence, except for the sound of sobbing and it's my Dad that's sobbing the loudest and that hurts what's left of my heart so much.

"You kill yourself, how does that leave your Mum and Dad feeling? How does that leave your brothers feeling? How do you think it will leave me, Ash and Sam feeling and what about your nieces and nephews, my babies, Ashley and Sam's babies, when they grow up and realise what you did, how do we explain to them? Can you imagine the issues that could leave them with, have you, for one single second, thought about anyone other than yourself?"

She kneels down in front of me and looks down into my lap at first, she draws in a breath as she tries to compose herself, I don't bother, I just let the tears and the sobs and the other awful, inhuman noises that I'm making, come at will. "We need you George, getting *you* through this, is what will get *us* through this. Sean would be so fucking angry with you George, so fucking pissed off." She lifts my hands out of my lap and holds them in both of hers. "No one, no one ever should have to go through what you have, but you need to look at the bigger picture, you need to consider the consequences of your actions. Can you die, knowing that Marley will probably be right behind you, that you will be leaving Ash without the love of her life, that you will be leaving Joe, Con and Annie without their Daddy, after losing their uncle, auntie and baby cousin, you are quite happy going to your grave, knowing that you are probably taking their Daddy with you, are you?" I let out another loud sob. "Are you George, fucking answer me?"

I shake my head. "No," I whisper. "No I'm not."

She wraps her arms around me. "Then this shit stops now, we will love and mourn for Sean and Beau for the rest of our lives, we'll never forget them and we *will* help each other deal with their loss the best we can but we will *not*, none of us, add to the untold grief, this family is already suffering. Are we understood?" I nod my head slowly and take in a few breaths. "I love you George and I don't want to lose you. You need to go and live your life and you need to live it large, you need to live it for Sean and for Beau too and you need to make every day count."

If I thought listening to Jimmies words was hard, it was nothing compared to Ashley's silence, she arrived at my Mum's later that same afternoon. I was leaning against the worktop in the kitchen, watching my Mum make a cup of tea, Marley was sitting on a bar stool talking to us both about how well Joe was doing at football, when Ash walked in, the kids were with her but they'd all gone straight to the playroom. She ignored Marley as he said hello and strode purposefully toward me, then smacked me hard around the face as soon as I was in reach.

"*Ash*," Marley shouted at her, she held up her finger for him to shush, she looked back at me. "That's the last time George, the last fucking time you put us through this shit. Your Husband would be so ashamed, so fucking ashamed of you right now." She then pulled me in for a cuddle and told me how much she loved me.

That all happened three weeks ago, three weeks in which I'd been alive, but dead, I didn't die, I didn't try and die, but I was dead anyway, death without dying is the worst kind of death.

The door to the soundproof studio at my parents' house swung open and Marley walked in. "Up ya get George; I've got something out here for ya to see."

I wipe my tears on my sleeve and stand from the old Chesterfield where I've been spending most of my days and follow my brother outside. There on the drive is Hilda, I turn and look at Marls. "Where did you get her from, have you been to my house?"

Marley hooks his hand over my shoulder and kisses my head. "I did, hope you don't mind, I thought you might like to take her out for a drive?"

For the first time since December, I feel something other than pain in my chest, it's like a tiny, tiny flicker of warmth and I look up at my brother and smile. "I don't want to drive her out on the roads Marls but I'll drive her around out here."

“Yeah?” He grins down at me.

“Yeah.” I grin back.

“Well it’s a fuckin’ start I s’pose.”

And it was, more than he could ever know, in that moment I realise, it was a start, a very, very small start but a start nonetheless, the tinniest of steps forwards, the very first time this year that I have actually wanted to do something. It wasn’t much of a something, but by getting in that car and driving, my mind would have to focus on something other than my Husband, my Son and my own death and as I stand with my brother’s arm around me, staring at my beloved Hilda, I suddenly feel the merest glimmer of hope, hope that I might just get through my empty, painful, black hole of a life.

CARNAGE PLAY LIST

The Jam, Liza Radley

The Jam, Start

The Jam, English Rose

Queen, Crazy Little Thing Called Love

Dire Straits, Romeo & Juliet

Gloria Estefan, Don't Wanna Lose You

Alexander O'Neal, Fake

Soul 11 Soul, Back To Life

I owe so many thank yous with regard to this book, firstly to my family for once again putting up with unwashed clothes and an unwashed Mum and Wife as well as lots of uncooked dinners and un-mopped floors, they are slowly but surely realising that 'Feral' is the way things are in our home whenever I'm writing but they love and support me regardless and I love them beyond measure for it.

Kaylene, I really cannot thank you enough only you and I know exactly what you did and I'm eternally grateful!

To my Beta readers, I thank you for your time and your honesty.

To my SC ladies, Vix, Kaz, Tash, Nic, Chell and even Wendy who couldn't bring herself to read Carnage unless I could assure her of an HEA, which sadly with this book I couldn't, I thank you all regardless, for your love, support, unprintable conversations, your humour and just for always being there, despite the miles, I love ya lots, like Jelly Tots.

To my Twitter Pimps, Ally, Peita, Mags, Sara, Nellie, OfficeLady, Gi Gi, Susie and everyone else that has tweeted, retweeted and recommended my books, I thank you.

To Rachael from DCT Promotions and Rebecca @ www.thefinalwrap.com for my amazing cover, I thank you all for your patience.

If you are new to my work, you can find my other books Saviour and Resolution @ amazon.com and amazon.co.uk

You can find me on Twitter @Lesley__Jones

On facebook @ https://www.facebook.com/saviour.lesleyjones or just search for

Lesley Jones Author

On Goodreads @ https://www.goodreads.com/author/list/7061349.Lesley_Jones

Lesley was born and raised in a small working class town in Essex, just outside of East London. She's married with three sons and in 2006 they all moved to the other side of the world, settling on the beautiful Mornington Peninsula, about fifty kilometres outside of Melbourne Australia.

Lesley is currently 'a stay at home mum', but in the past she has worked at 'good old Mark & Spencer' for thirteen years and as a teacher's assistant.

As well as writing, Lesley loves to read and has been known to get through four or five books a week, when she's not writing that is. Her other interests are watching her boys play football… the round ball version. She's happy to admit to being an addict of social media and owes a lot to her Face book and Twitter family in promoting her book. Lesley is also rather partial to a glass or bottle of wine, a nicely chilled Marlborough Sav Blanc being her favourite.

Being a born and raised Essex girl, she will happily admit to be being a big fan of spray tans, Shellac and is regularly, waxed, tinted and sculpted, although she doesn't own a pair of white stilettos…

If you are affected by any of the issues covered in this book and need to talk, please contact :

Lifeline Australia 131114

The Samaritans UK 08457 90 90 90

The Samaritans USA 1(800) 273-TALK

Printed in Great Britain
by Amazon.co.uk, Ltd.,
Marston Gate.